Editing by Jodi Christensen and The Crimson Wordsmith
Cover Design by Dawn Burdett
Internal Formatting by Ben Thomas
Internal Images by Chryselle Webb

BLACK HARE PRESS is a small, independent publisher based in Melbourne, Australia.

Founded in 2018, our aim has always been to champion emerging authors from all around the globe and offer opportunities for them to participate in speculative fiction and horror short story anthologies.

Connect: linktr.ee/blackharepress

MEMORIES DON'T LIE

Pauline Yates

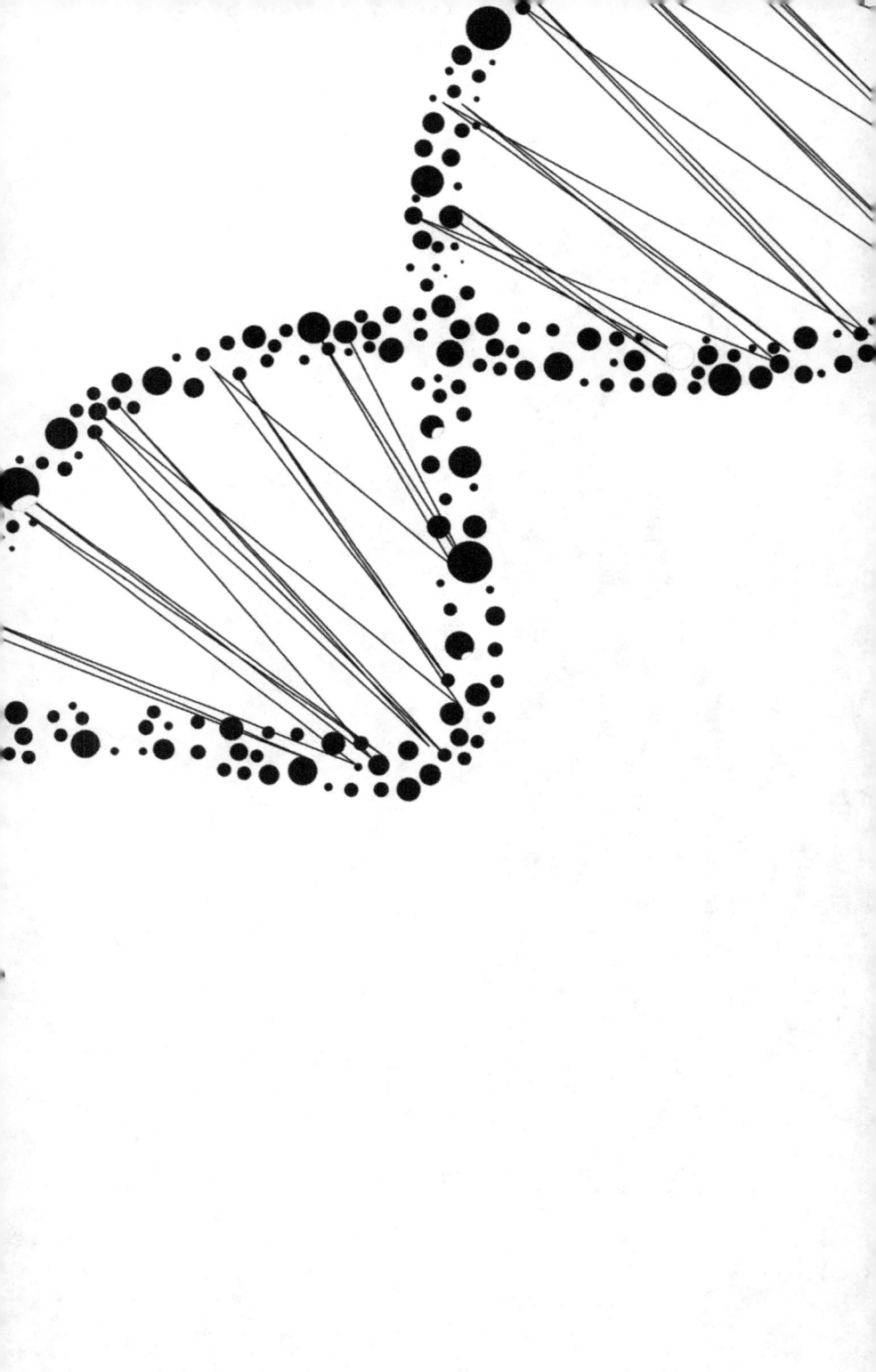

To Mum,
who never knew

And Dad,
who would be proud

Pauline Yates, March 2023

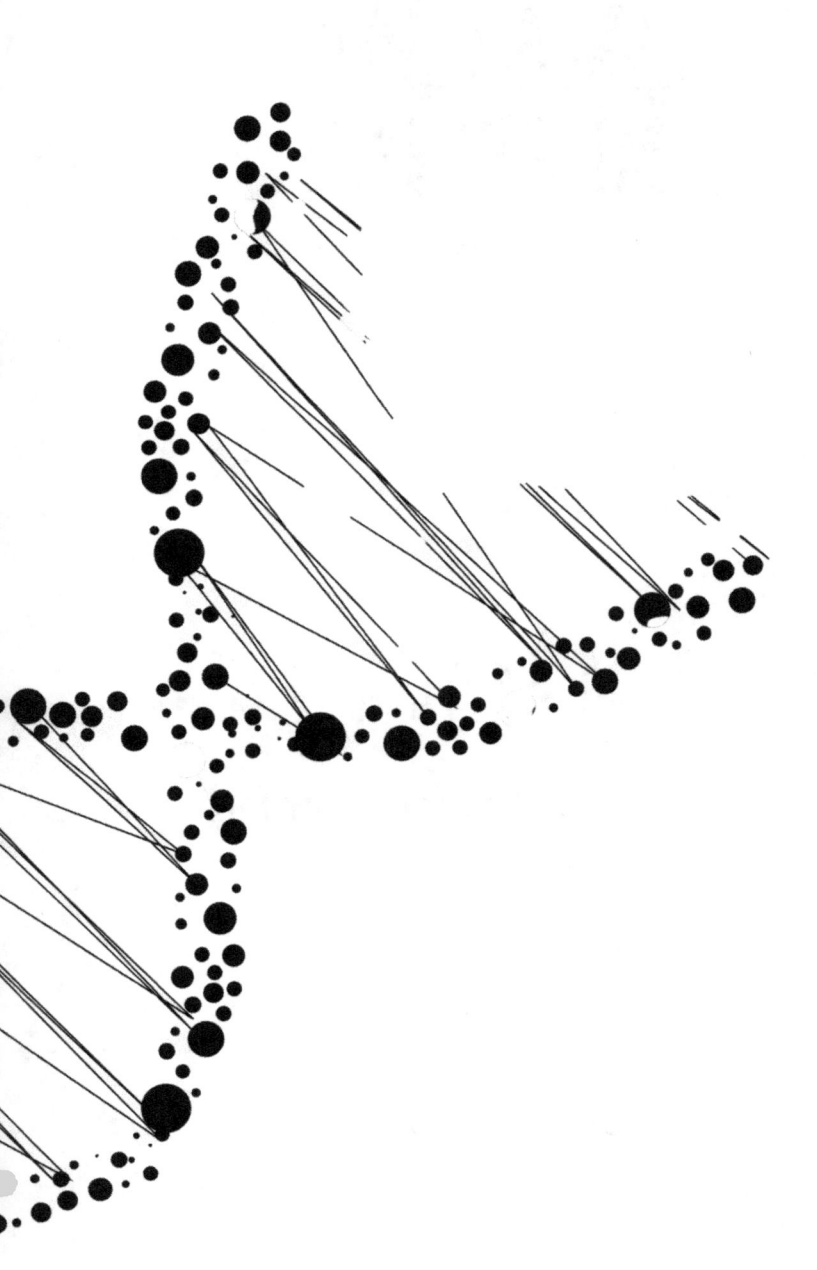

CONTENTS

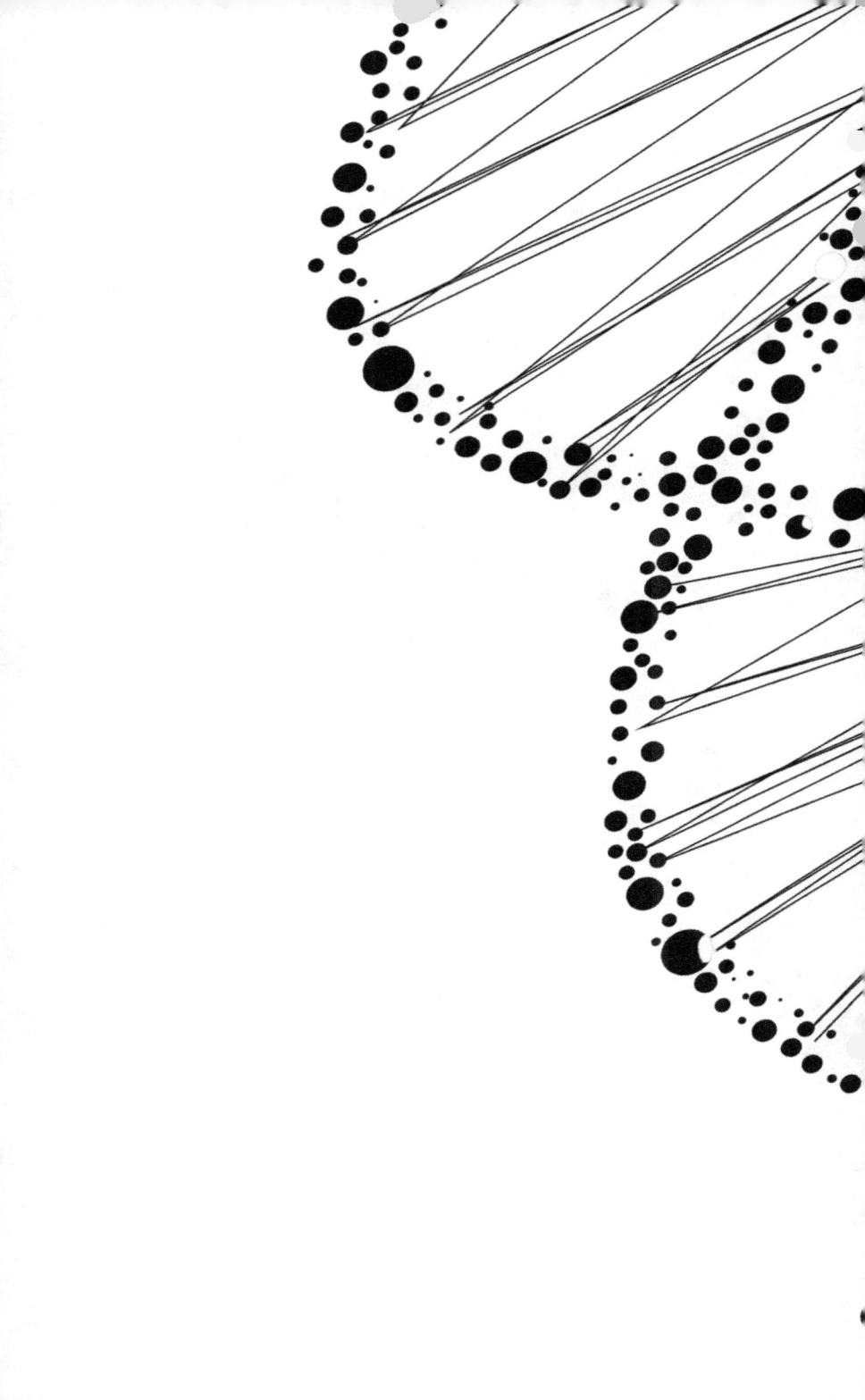

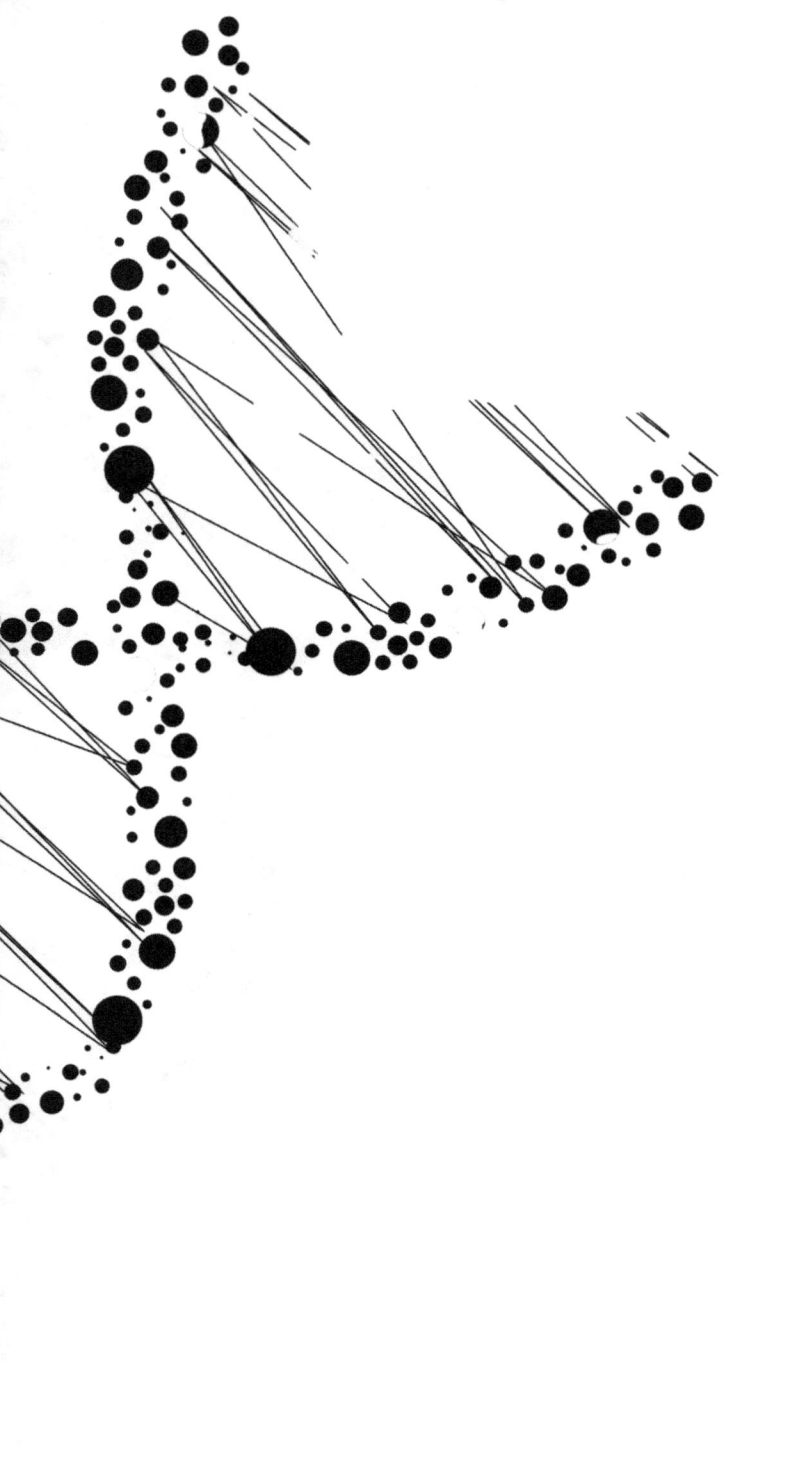

"Traits acquired during one's lifetime—muscles built up in the gym, for example—cannot be passed on to the next generation. Now with technology, as it happens, we might indeed be able to transfer some of our acquired traits on to our selected offspring by genetic engineering."

—Nick Bostrom, *The Guardian*, 09/05/2006

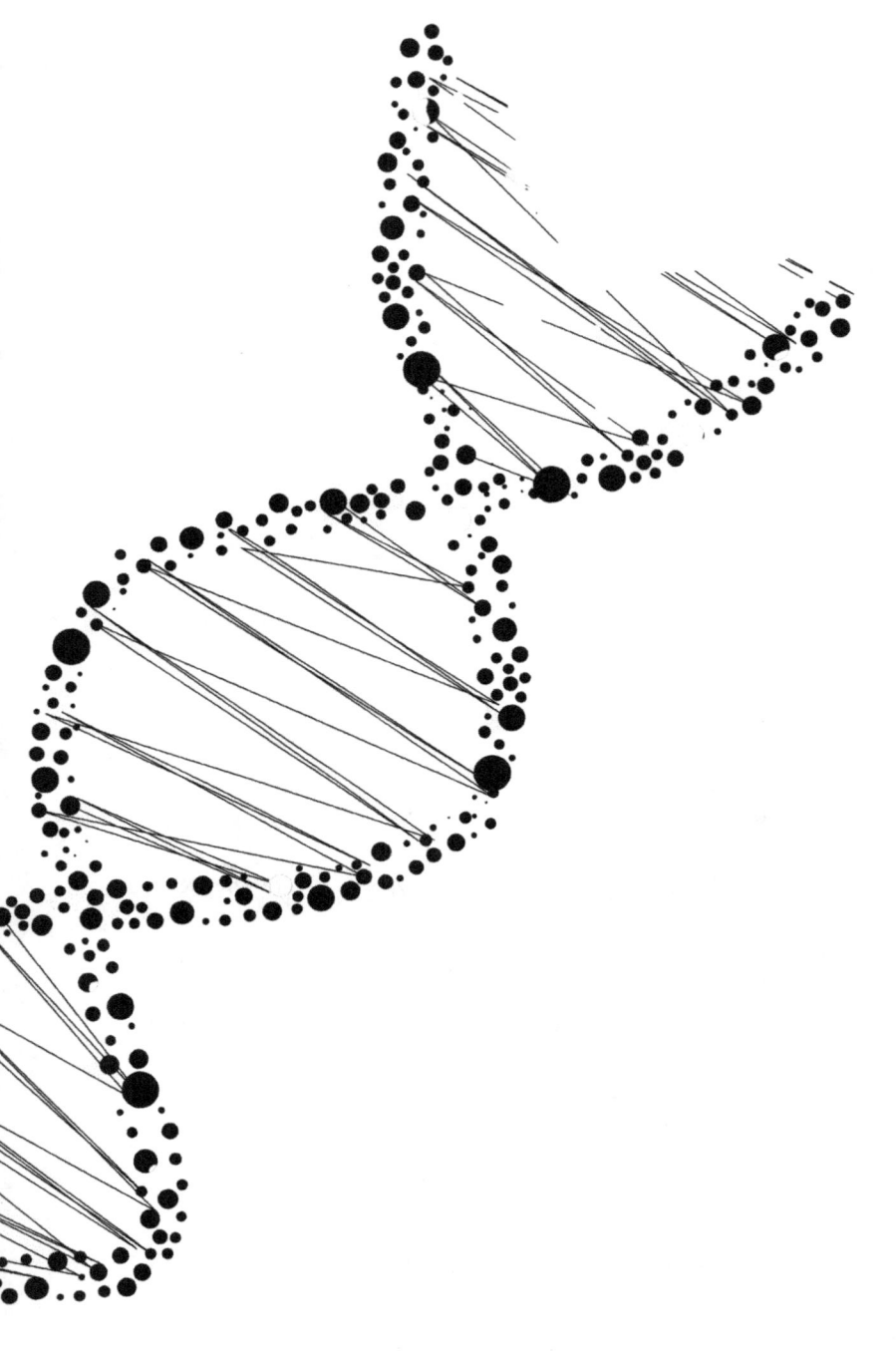

CHAPTER I

Don't let him find her.

M Y DEAD MOTHER'S DESPERATE PLEA takes my thoughts hostage, shattering my composure and threatening the freedom I long for. Why am I remembering this when nothing's happened in the last thirteen years? All my focus needs to be on passing my final sharpshooting assessment. The cryptic recollection should be the last thing on my mind.

Irritated at the intrusion, I block out her voice and pace around my barracks room as if running the course. A win will earn me the Tactical Skills Program's top graduate title, and I'm determined to claim it. It's the only way to show Marrick Daniels I'd be perfect for his C.S.R. team.

His crime-fighting unit is the best and his vacant position unprecedented. I'll never get another chance. But the memory continues to haunt me.

Damn my mother. Civilian Safety Response soldiers are supposed to have nerves of steel. We could assist local law enforcement in anything from hostage situations to firearm offenses to bomb threats. I'm a day away from graduating, and my nerves have shot through the roof. How can I expect to fight crime if I can't arrest my anxiety?

Frustrated, I give the memory attention it doesn't deserve so I can bury it with my mother. It was the last thing she said to my uncle before the door closed, shutting her out of my life forever. She didn't mention who or why. I assume she referred to my unknown father, although what he'd want is beyond me. He hasn't shown his face in my seventeen years of existence. I'd be lying if I said not having a father doesn't bother me, but after losing my mother, any resemblance to a normal life stopped.

Instead of Sarah, I became known as the orphaned niece of Lieutenant John Wilson, which meant no friends, private tutors, and around-the-clock security. The only places I frequented outside the house were my uncle's office, here at Red Bluff Military Base, a measly twenty-minute drive from our neighborhood, or a private indoor shooting range on the outskirts of Redding with my minders. I couldn't even shop for personal supplies without an escort.

I never complained, never questioned, but now I'm older, my patience with my uncle's control over my life has worn thin.

He's the only family I have, but there's an uncomfortable distance between us, like I'm an unwanted houseguest. I'm certain it's why he insisted I sign up for this program. Once I graduate and get placed on a team, I'll move out of home permanently.

I jump at a rap on the door. It will be my trainer, Staff Sergeant Darius Kingsley, but he's arrived too early to collect me. Growing angrier by the second at how frazzled my nerves are, I yank the door open, only to be knocked aside by Darius, who barges in. Whatever's happened won't be good.

"What's wrong?" I mask my churning emotions with indifference, but Darius pulls off his sunglasses and frowns—he knows me too well.

"They brought forward your start time," he says. "Nixon's out with a fractured hand. Boyd's in the hospital wing after ingesting a banned substance. Gaucini's on course. Let's go." Motioning for me to follow, he jams his sunglasses back on and strides from the room.

I'm glad he spared me a lecture about emotional flare-ups during finals week, but rising anger displaces my anxiety. Intimidation tactics between cadets are normal at any stage of the training program, but Gaucini has done more than make idle threats. He deliberately stomped on

Nixon's hand during their combative assessment yesterday, then started a rumor about Boyd using performance drugs to boost his stamina—an unfounded allegation; Boyd's as clean as me.

Catching up to Darius, I jump down the stairs with him. "Did Gaucini slip something to Boyd?"

"If he did, we'll never prove it," Darius says, taking the path around the northern end of my barracks, the quickest route to the outdoor range.

I grit my teeth—Gaucini is another distraction I don't need.

"We should've reported his threat to me."

Darius grimaces. "I did. You, of all people, should know how it works in this program."

"Get tough or get out? There'll be no one left to graduate if Gaucini has his way."

"I don't like it either, but better to discover a weakness here at Red Bluff than on the streets in Sacramento. Nixon and Boyd knew Gaucini would do his damnedest to take them out of contention, but overconfidence made them complacent. As for Gaucini"— Darius clenches his jaw—"if he claims the top graduate title, I'll hand in my resignation."

"That can never happen, so I'll make sure it doesn't."

Darius resigning would be Red Bluff's loss. He's old enough to be my father but is as tough as they come. I've never told him, but I want to be as skilled as him, so I'll be ready for whoever wants to find me should they ever show their face.

I trust that I am. Darius trains his cadets like elite athletes and his method of incorporating resistance, plyometric, and continuous training over Red Bluff's variety of terrain has produced multiple top graduates, including Marrick. My pulse quickens thinking about him. He won't accept anyone less than the best, even if we share the same trainer. Trying to join his team might be like trying to punch through a brick wall.

I walk on, but Darius grabs my arm and pulls me to a stop.

"Do better than your best. No holding back. Not today. And watch out for Gaucini. This isn't over yet." He lowers his glasses, looks me straight in the eye for emphasis, before continuing along the path.

I smile. Do my best? No holding back? Gladly.

Throughout my training, Darius had me hide my skills to mislead the other cadets. Our ruse protected me against attacks from Gaucini—until yesterday's combative assessment. I won every round, annihilating my opponents with maneuvers that could have put them in the hospital wing with Nixon.

Darius raged, saying I painted a target on my back, proven right when Gaucini cornered me in the gym and threatened to break my shooting hand. Secretly, I don't care. For the past six months, I've done what Darius asked:

kept my points low and stayed out of the spotlight. What he doesn't know is when my adrenaline starts pumping, it wakes something predatory inside me, making it difficult to ignore a challenge. On multiple occasions, I had to sneak into the gym late at night for an extra workout just to wind down.

Adding to my frustration, I've found the program easy, despite Red Bluff claiming it's one of the toughest courses in the military. It's like I've done every aspect of their training before. I have, in theory, because of my uncle's C.S.R. supervisory role. I know the program and understand team expectations. Darius says I'm a natural, and that C.S.R. is what I was born for. I hope I prove him right today.

I catch up to Darius at the end of the path and we stride past the engineering sheds—refurbished aircraft hangars from Red Bluff's days as an air defense command station. They run alongside the airstrip, now training fields, ending at a mesh fence surrounding the outdoor range. The sheds are usually a hive of activity, but the sharpshooting rounds are prime-time entertainment for Red Bluff personnel, and everyone is at the range.

When we reach the entrance, Darius approaches the M.P. on gate duty. "Is Gaucini on course?"

"Yes, Sir," the M.P. says. "Seven targets in."

Darius continues through the gates, quickening his pace. I jog to keep up. The soldiers milling around inside stare at me. Usually, I'm the unremarkable cadet destined to ruin Darius's track record of producing top graduates. Not now, after my spectacular combative performance. This new attention stirs up my nerves again. With Boyd and Nixon out, the spotlight will be on me—another pressure I hadn't expected.

Darius lifts a rope separating the spectators from the course. We duck under it together and stride across the sun-baked field to the armament bench near the start of the sharpshooting course. A cliff forms a natural wall around the target practice area and the granite radiates late-summer heat. Bullet marks pepper the cliff face, some of them mine; Darius had me shoot wide on purpose during group sessions. I won't shoot wide today.

I pull my half-gloves from the leg pocket of my pants and jam the soft leather deep into the grooves between my fingers, smoothing the creases over my knuckles. A whiff of gun smoke in the breeze settles me; I'm in familiar territory now and my confidence restores. This assessment is also a chance to show my uncle I can look after myself. He'll have to relax his security measures after I graduate, anyway. He won't be responsible for me once I turn eighteen and I'm only three months shy of that. If he remembers my birthday, that is. We've never celebrated it.

"Is my uncle here?" I've rarely seen him since relocating to base.

Darius shakes his head. "He has a video feed of the

assessment directed to his office."

Would it kill my uncle to come and watch? I glance at the cameras around the range, hoping to convey my disappointment at his failure to show the family support I ache for. Instead, I see two of Marrick's team members, Red Bluff's Kelly Olsen, and Lakeport Military Training Academy transfer, Magelon Caruso. They stand near the large screen televising the sharpshooting rounds for the spectators.

I don't see Marrick, or Reece Matthews, the team's logistical analyst, another transfer from Lakeport. Reece never comes to base—I don't know why—but Marrick goes everywhere with his team. He'll be here somewhere.

On the armament bench, an M1911 pistol lies among the selection of guns. Marrick scored forty out of forty targets using this model. He's also the only person in T.S.P. history to achieve a perfect score on a Sergeant Hayes' course. If I match Marrick's achievement, he'll have to notice me.

Eager to start, I turn my attention to Darius. "Any advice?"

He pulls off his sunglasses. "This course is designed to fail you. You'll only get one shot at this, so make every target count. Use your speed. Trust your instincts. Find your zone and stay there until the last buzzer sounds."

Speed and instinct are my best skills, but the only time I've tested them is during my private training sessions with Darius. What if I didn't hone them enough to get me through this course?

Hayes approaches, clipboard in hand. "Wilson, Sarah. You're up next."

Darius claps his hand on my shoulder. "Remember, one bullet per target." Replacing his sunglasses, he strides back across the field.

One bullet per target is half the challenge. If I miss and shoot twice, I could fail by running short of bullets. An uncomfortable fluttering starts in my stomach, but I don't know why I'm worried. I'm at my peak and ready to tackle this course. Darius will have made sure of that.

It's my mother's memory. It lingers in the back of my mind, niggling for attention. Why today?

Determined to block it out, I collect my gear from Hayes—a SIG Sauer P226, my preferred weapon, the allocated number of magazines, safety vest, helmet, and gun belt. As I load the SIG and slot the extra magazines into my belt pouches, the buzzer sounds, ending Gaucini's round.

The video screen faces away from me, but the murmur from the crowd suggests Gaucini's score isn't high. I search for Darius. He stands next to Kelly and holds up three fingers, then two to show Gaucini scored thirty-two out of forty targets.

With my accuracy, I'll easily beat him. But while a score of thirty-three will win me the assessment and the top graduate title, it won't impress Marrick.

Gaucini strides from the course, a scowl etched into his square face, sweat pouring from his thick black hair. Seeing me, he smirks and heads in my direction. A smart cadet would move closer to Hayes, who barks target reset instructions to the ground crew through his radio, but I stay put, anger flaring at Gaucini's attack on Nixon.

Gaucini bangs his shoulder against mine, then dumps his gun on the armament bench and strips off his belt and vest.

"I'm surprised to see you here, Wilson," he says. "Word around base is you were hiding in your barracks. Afraid of the competition?"

His cocky attitude is as annoying as his intimidation tactics. "There's no competition with Nixon and Boyd out."

"None left that I can see, either." He looks across the field at Darius. "Don't blame yourself. You showed potential yesterday, but Kingsley's training methods are outdated. Time he retired, if you ask me."

If we weren't near an instructor, I'd shove my fist down Gaucini's throat for his dig at Darius. "Nobody's asking you, so why don't you put your popgun away and watch how it's done from the playpen."

"Funny, Wilson. What say you and I meet afterward? I'll help pick your bullets out of the cliff. They'll make great souvenirs. You can share them with Boyd and Nixon."

His taunt at my aim is easy to ignore, but Boyd and Nixon deserve a better keepsake than a spent bullet. Raising my SIG, I tap my finger on the trigger. Giving Gaucini a lesson in speed and accuracy, the second part of the sharpshooting challenge, would be an ideal gift.

Darius appears in my peripheral and drives his voice into my head with a pointed stare—*Focus, Wilson. Don't waste energy on Gaucini. To beat him, beat the course.*

I turn away, determined to wipe the smile off Gaucini's face with a winning round.

He leers at me. "Funny how you moved into the lead. Weren't you in tenth place at the start of assessment week? I'd say bring your best to beat me, but I guess your uncle has that covered."

His comment strikes a nerve. What if other people think my current position is because of my uncle? Hating the inference, I raise my SIG again, all while glaring a hole through his head.

Gaucini's expression darkens. "Watch it out there, Wilson. You know how this course is. Accidents happen all the time. Not everything's recorded."

Is he planning something worse than a broken hand? Only the target zones are televised, not the areas in between. Tired of his tactics, my temper snaps. "Then you better make sure you don't stand in any of the black zones, or I might accidentally mistake you for a target."

Gaucini grins. "Did you just threaten me, Wilson?"

He speaks loudly enough for Hayes to hear, who lowers his radio and crosses to us.

"You've had your chance, Gaucini," he says, stepping between us. "Get your butt off my course." He turns to me. "I don't care who your uncle is. I won't tolerate threats of any kind. First and final warning, Wilson. Take your position. You start in three minutes."

I jerk my SIG down, furious with myself for falling for Gaucini's baiting. To cop a warning right before my round is bad—one more step out of line, intentional or otherwise, will see me booted from the program. But learning Hayes thinks I believe I'm above reprimand because of my uncle is gut-wrenching. How many other instructors share his view?

Fuming, I walk to the start of the course. With so little time to regain focus, I hold Darius' voice in my head. It's not enough. We're trained to fight our enemies, but they're not all on the streets. One is here, at Red Bluff, and it sits like a chip on my shoulder.

The only way I'll remove it is to match Marrick's score with an unforgettable performance to prove beyond a doubt my skills result from hard training, not favoritism.

Otherwise, I'll always be the privileged niece of a lieutenant.

CHAPTER 2

R ESET COMPLETE. THE COURSE IS clear. Wilson, one minute." Hayes' booming voice silences the crowd.

I step into the first firing point, a spray-painted white circle marked with a large number one. Forty consecutively numbered circles identify my shooting zone for each target. They lie ahead in a purpose-built course simulating streets in a high-level crime area near Sacramento.

I can't see all the circles but remember their locations from the map issued with our start time. The firing points are in front of timber buildings that mimic shop fronts, at the bottom of stairwells leading to upper doorways, or next to cars salvaged from a scrap metal yard to represent traffic. Mannequins dressed as civilians, complete with distracting multi-colored hats and scarves, add reality to the streets. Hit a civilian and I fail.

I'm confident I won't, but the privileged tag plays on my mind. Needing help to focus, I glance at Darius. Marrick stands next to him.

Does Marrick consider me privileged? He knows I'm related to his boss. We met once, an awkward introduction in my uncle's office before I started training. Awkward on my part because while Marrick's warm smile as he shook my hand felt like a welcome into his private circle, his former team member, Joanna Johansson, made a cutting remark about how my Red Bluff uniform would fit better once I'd earned it.

The perception of privilege would have escalated when my uncle overruled Red Bluff's requirement for all recruits to complete an eight-week basic training course. I went straight into the Tactical Skills Program, the youngest cadet on record.

If Marrick views me this way, I'd reconsider joining his team. I want people around me who value me for who I am and what I can do, not who I'm related to. But if I don't concentrate, I'll be lucky to finish the course, let alone impress Marrick with a perfect score.

His calm demeanor reaches me across the field and settles my anxiety. How he does it, I don't know, but coupled with remarkable tactical skills, it's no wonder he's rated the best leader. I've seen him in action. Civilians under threat respond positively to his directives and his ability to defuse panic is incredible.

He should add emotional influence to his resume: T.S.P. top graduate at eighteen; leader for three consecutive years, including best-rated team since the military took over C.S.R. training from local law enforcement thirty years ago. His crime-fighting unit is the best I could ever hope to be on, so why shouldn't I attempt to punch through the brick wall surrounding them?

Because I'd take Joanna's position, that's why. And like my mother's memory, her belittling remark continues to haunt me. My uncle would also be my supervisor. How would it look if he insisted on providing extra security for me? Marrick wouldn't want to be monitored around the clock. Damn my mother. Why didn't she say who's after me? And why hasn't my uncle hunted them down? He has an army at his disposal, and Red Bluff's best on call twenty-four-seven. Marrick's team can find anyone.

"Sixty seconds, Wilson," Hayes barks.

I need to focus. I'll deal with my uncle's inaction after this assessment. Forty targets. Top graduate title. Marrick.

Our eyes meet and he doesn't look away. Darius talks to him, nods at me multiple times, but Marrick's attention is solely on me. My concern about Joanna's remark and my uncle's interference could be unfounded. Marrick watches me like I'm exactly who he wants.

"Ten seconds, Wilson."

I snap all focus back to the course. The first firing zone is outside a shop. In the foreground, two mannequins sit at a round white plastic table. Glare from the tabletop is a sharp reminder that climatic conditions, including haze, rain, and fog, will not always act in our favor. Crimes occur regardless of the weather. To break the glare, I shift to the outer edge of the circle. Vision restored, I relax. With God in the detail and a gun in my hand, the targets don't stand a chance.

Confidence growing, I imagine the backdrop to be a bustling café. My breathing slows. The spectator's chatter fades. The trigger warms beneath my finger. There's nothing, no one. Just me, and my gun, and—

The blare of the start buzzer splits the silence. The target, a flat wooden disk the size of a small dinner plate, pops out from the far side of the wall. I fire, splintering the timber with a perfect first shot. Now to reach the next firing point before the target pops up, the second part of the challenge.

Racing to firing point two, I face an open window in a brick wall. Movement in the lower corner of the window catches my eye. I fire again, shattering the disk. The third firing point is farther along the street, at the bottom of a stairwell. I'm halfway there when the target pops out from a doorway at the top of the stairs. Skidding into the circle, I aim high and fire. The bullet chips the edge of the disk.

My near-miss explains Darius's warning—the speed required is faster than I've practiced. Determined not to fall victim to a course designed to fail me, I sprint to the fourth firing point. The target pops up from behind a car on the opposite side of the street the second I step into the circle.

I shoot—a clean strike—then run around the corner to the next firing point. Obstacles block my path: rubbish bins; a crowd of mannequins representing panicked civilians; another parked car. I leap onto the hood and slide across, landing like a cat on the other side. One stride and I'm back at full speed.

A shiver of exhilaration burns like wildfire up my spine. This is the real me: sharp reflexes, switched on, agile and fast. I'm faster than the other cadets and now everyone at Red Bluff knows it. Cheers from the spectator's mute the sound of my gunfire as I take out target after target. I'm delivering a textbook sharpshooting display, one that will dispel any doubt about my abilities, wipe the chip from my shoulder, and crush the wall around Marrick's team into dust.

As I run from circle to circle, the predatory feeling I get returns. I don't know what it is, but it sharpens my senses and makes me more aware of my surroundings than I ever felt during my practice rounds. The course is no longer a simulation. I imagine real streets, with live civilians to protect and dangerous criminals to hunt down. No movement escapes notice. No target goes undetected. I weave around obstacles as easily as running in a straight line. I reach every firing point ahead of time, despite oil spills and burning rubbish placed to slow me.

The final firing point is in the middle of a street between two double-storey brick buildings. One of them is makeshift, constructed for the course. The other adjoins the spectator arena, with an adjacent fence covered in bulletproof glass. The upper level is used for storage, the lower level by the course reset crew. Out of bounds to spectators, soldiers cram into the area alongside the building to watch me blast the last target.

The roaring crowd would make focusing difficult had I not been deep in my zone. I register faces, hear my name, but nothing distracts me. When I reach the firing circle, I use precious seconds to study the makeshift building. A dozen tall windows stretch the length of the wall on both levels. Some are open, some closed. The reset crew did a great job erasing all evidence of shots from previous cadets. The windowpanes are intact. No broken glass litters the ground. Will this target be my undoing? I have to find the target to shoot it. It could appear anywhere.

One window at the end isn't open as wide as the others. The narrow gap would test my accuracy if a target popped up there. I double-check the lower-level windows. All are closed and curtained, and they reflect the building behind me. I spot the camera mounted on the wall to record my shot, and a person on the second level holding a rifle.

I'll keep her safe. You have my word.

My uncle's reply to my mother refreshes the memory, freezing my heart. Outside of my uncle's personal security, there's nowhere safer than Red Bluff. Am I overreacting? A soldier could have sneaked inside to get a better view of the course. There are multiple entries on the far side of the building, easy in, easy out. I scrutinize the reflection. It's blurry, but the soldier looks familiar. Square face. Thick black hair.

Watch out for Gaucini.

Darius's warning refreshes Gaucini's threat about accidents on the course. It's him. I'm sure of it. The end of his rifle rests on the window ledge, aimed right at me.

The target pops up in the narrow gap, as I suspected. I ignore it and keep my eye on Gaucini's reflection. Did the sun shift, causing the reflection to darken, or did he adjust his aim? It's hard to tell. He'd have time to shoot and escape the building undetected. In the chaos, he'd mingle with the crowd and appear shocked at the shooting of a niece of a lieutenant. I'm the only one who sees him. Everyone else is looking at me. The target beckons, demanding my last bullet, but what's the good of finishing with a perfect score if I'm dead?

Pivoting, I aim at Gaucini and pull the trigger. The bullet passes within millimeters of the window frame. Gaucini jerks and falls from sight. If he were a target, it would be the shot of the day.

Ignoring the silence that descends on the crowd, I run to the building. Did I kill Gaucini? Or is he slithering from the room like the snake he is? A door opens and I run into Sergeant Walsh, chief of the reset crew.

"Sniper, top floor," I shout, pushing past him.

I take the nearest stairwell to the second floor and kick open the third door along the corridor, keeping my SIG outstretched, though I'm out of bullets. Gaucini lies on the floor, still gripping the rifle. I walk closer, then stop with a sinking feeling like I swallowed a lead weight.

It's not Gaucini. It's a mannequin holding a walking stick. The room is full of similar dummies, dark mops of hair atop square, plastic faces. Tables and chairs are stacked along the walls with bags of clothing stashed beneath. It's a storage room for the props used on the course.

Outside, the buzzer sounds, signaling the end of my round. Sergeant Walsh steps around me, holding a gun outstretched. He looks at the mannequin, glances at me, then shoves the gun in his belt holster. Nothing needs to be said. It's written in the bullet hole through the mannequin's head.

Hayes will record my last shot as shooting into the crowd—it's an instant fail. I won't graduate. With one shot, I killed my career.

CHAPTER 3

WALSH RADIOS FOR SERGEANT HAYES. He strides into the building like a bulldog straining on a leash and escorts me to the start of the course.

If you survive a walk of shame, you'll survive anything.

I don't remember who said that, but I take no comfort from the intrusive thought. I walk past Red Bluff soldiers and wish myself invisible. Whispered chatter creates a throbbing hum like a swarm of hornets ready to attack. I can't see what's on the screen, but everyone would have seen me turn and shoot. They won't know what I shot, but word will spread fast. I'll be the laughingstock of Red Bluff.

When we arrive at the armament bench, Darius ducks under the safety ropes and strides toward us. Marrick, Kelly, and Magelon stare at me, their expressions indecipherable. I catch Marrick's gaze but look away. Stupidity is all he saw today.

Hayes stops me with an arm across my chest. "Get your butt back to the barracks and stay there until called."

"Yes, sir." I don't know if he heard me. My chest is so tight I can barely breathe, let alone talk. I can't even see which direction to walk. All I see is the bullet hole through the mannequin's head.

Darius arrives and helps me strip off the vest and belt, then takes my elbow and steers me across the range. When we reach the entrance gates, Gaucini pushes past a group of soldiers and laughs.

"Nice job, Wilson. Say hi to Boyd and Nixon for me."

I clench my fists so hard my nails dig into my skin. Gaucini is a threat. To me. To the other cadets. I step toward him, intent on showing his smart mouth the whites of my knuckles, but Marrick arrives and stands between us.

"Keep walking," he says. "Don't give him another win."

"Is this your minder, Wilson?" Gaucini asks. "Did your uncle organize that, too?"

Crack.

A fist comes out of nowhere, connecting with Gaucini's face. He spins and falls flat on his back, blood gushing out of his nose. Magelon steps forward and stands over him, but Kelly ducks around her, pulls Gaucini off the ground by the scruff of his shirt, and holds him upright.

"Be thankful she used her fist and not her knife," he says with a cheery grin.

Magelon winks at me. "I was tempted."

"Enough," Darius says. "Wilson, move."

He pushes me to the entrance gates, then takes my arm again and drags me past the engineering sheds. I glance over my shoulder and look for Marrick, but soldiers can sniff a fight a mile away and multiple beige uniforms conceal him from view. It doesn't matter. I've got Darius to contend with now.

When we reach my room, he shoves me inside and slams the door behind him.

"What the hell happened?" he asks.

I can't think how to explain, except the obvious. "I shot the wrong target."

He yanks off his sunglasses. "Bullshit. You had the target in sight, and you didn't take the shot."

I press my fingers against my temples. "I screwed up, okay. Gaucini insinuated he'd cause an accident on the course. A reflection in the window looked like him holding a rifle. I figured a perfect score wouldn't do me any good dead, so…" Lowering my hands, I sigh and stare at the wall. "I let Gaucini get to me and handed him the win. That's it."

Darius's face darkens to a furious shade of red. "Gaucini menaced you again? When?"

"Before I started. He baited me, and I fell for it. And I copped a first and final warning from Hayes."

Darius glowers. "What for?"

"For threatening to shoot Gaucini."

"You wouldn't have wasted a bullet." Darius wipes his hand across his mouth, as he does when he says something he shouldn't. "What did you hit if it wasn't Gaucini?"

"A mannequin." I shake my head. "It stood against a window in the room used to store props."

"Sounds like a detail Hayes overlooked, especially around that last target. I wouldn't worry about it."

I stare at him. "Not worry about a shot to the head? What if it had been Gaucini? Or a soldier from the reset crew? I wouldn't be standing here. I'd be under M.P. guard charged with murder, and they'd claim intent because of my threat to Gaucini."

"Hayes should award you extra points for detecting an unseen danger."

"Swing it any way you want, but it will be recorded as shooting into the crowd. That's an automatic fail. I won't graduate."

"The hell you won't. You were in a pressure cooker of an assessment. The course is designed to test your ability to locate and neutralize a felon at speed. You hit a misleading target, sure, but no one is dead. One word from your uncle—"

"I will *not* allow my uncle to cover for me."

"Who said it's a cover?"

"Don't you get it? Everyone already thinks I'm the privileged niece of a lieutenant. Even Hayes suggested as much. If my uncle steps in to save me, how will that look to the other cadets? What about Boyd and Nixon, who saves them? You know the drill. Get tough or get out. Gaucini was my tough, and I didn't handle it. I'm a liability. No team will take me."

"One will. Caruso punching Gaucini speaks volumes about how privileged they think you are."

My mouth drops open. "Wait. Marrick's team?"

"They're here to pick you up. You were to leave right after the graduation ceremony tomorrow. Your uncle has already lodged the paperwork."

"Without asking me? What if I don't want to join Marrick's team?"

"Why wouldn't you? You won't find a better team anywhere."

"That's not the point. Don't I get any say in my future? Why do I always have to do what my uncle says?"

"He's got your best interest at heart. Trust me."

"Trust you? You don't know what it's like to live with him. He tells me nothing and decides everything. I don't care what he wants. I'll quit altogether if he forces me to join a team without my consent."

Darius throws up his hands. "Being with Daniels is the best career move you'll ever make."

"A move you obviously knew about. Why didn't you tell me?"

"Because I didn't want you slacking off knowing you were already on a team." He rubs his mouth again, then sighs. "My job is to get you to peak fitness and oversee your training, so when you leave here, you're equipped with physical and tactical skills to keep you safe. I know you think everyone's making career decisions for you, but what you need—and you don't realize this yet—is people around you who can continue what I started. I sure as hell can't teach you everything in a simulated environment, no matter how good Red Bluff's infrastructure is. Daniels can offer the real street instruction I can't, and there's no one I'd rather see you with during the next stage of your career. You won't have to deal with your uncle. You'll take all your instructions from Daniels."

I cross my arms, so infuriated with him I want to scream. "If I do as you say and join Marrick's team, what happens when I screw up again?"

"Why do you think you will?"

"Because..." Because my mother's warning still plays on my mind and it's making me jump at shadows. How can I concentrate on the job if I'm looking over my shoulder for someone who might not even be there? But that's my worry, not Darius's. "It doesn't matter."

"If it matters to you, it matters to me. What's going on?"

"Nothing." I walk to the window and stare outside.

Darius follows and rests his hand on arm. "We've been training together for a long time, Sarah. I know when something's bugging you. You're...like a daughter to me. I want to help."

I turn and glare at him. "I don't need a father."

He removes his hand.

I look away, tears pricking my eyes. What I'd give to have a father, a mother, a family. Given the choice, I'd take Darius as my father any day. Confide in him. Tell him what my mother said and explain how her cryptic warning is ruining my life. But I can't. Darius says he has my best interests at heart, but he conceals information from me, too. How can he ask me to trust him when he won't reciprocate?

When I don't respond, Darius sighs.

"All right," he says. "But let me leave you with this. Your natural talent shone through today. I'd hate to see you waste it. You haven't experienced that level of intensity because I've held you back. There's always one standout cadet in a group. Daniels stood out in his. You in yours."

"Marrick didn't shoot a mannequin, did he?"

"He would have made the same decision. It's not about points when you're on the streets. It's about detecting and removing threats. Pull yourself together. You won't

fail, and I'll challenge anybody who suggests otherwise."
He raises his hand to clap my shoulder like he always does,
but then he walks to the door without touching me.

The tension I caused weighs heavily on my heart. I
turn to make amends, but Darius isn't looking back.
"Where are you going?"

"To talk to Hayes. Stay here until I get back. Do not
open that door for anyone." He leaves the room, banging
the door closed behind him.

I sit on my bunk and lean my head in my hands.
Could I have destroyed our relationship any better? Wiping
my eyes, I return to the window and look toward the
outdoor range in the distance. It won't matter what Darius
says to Hayes. After Hayes's comment about my uncle, he
won't let me graduate.

Do I care? I stretch my arms. After six months of
intensive training under Red Bluff's blistering sun, tanned
skin shimmers over hard muscles and calluses toughen my
hands. I erred shooting the mannequin, but all my shots
throughout the sharpshooting round were exceptional,
including that one. My combative skills are second to none.
I don't need a top graduate title to confirm I've gained
enough skills to protect myself. I don't need my uncle's
protection, either. As for the position on Marrick's team—
I can't believe I'm going to walk away from the first good
thing in my life.

With a heavy heart, I strip out of my uniform, change

into casual clothes, and pack my personal belongings into a black knapsack. I'm quitting. It's my only option and the sooner I leave, the easier it will be on everyone. I'll confront my uncle on the way out and insist he tells me who I'm in danger from. Then I'll do what he should have done years ago. Find them and end the uncertainty.

Slinging the knapsack over my shoulder, I yank the door open. A woman stands outside wearing a white baseball cap and large round sunglasses.

She smiles. "Hello, Sarah."

I stare at her, shocked. "Joanna? You're supposed to be—"

She raises a gun and shoots a dart into my neck.

A starburst of pain explodes in my head. I swipe at the dart and knock it out, but my vision blurs and my limbs grow heavy. Knees buckling, I slump against the door and slide to the floor. Joanna crouches beside me and presses her fingers to my pulse point. I try to speak, move, do anything, but the drug from the dart holds me incapacitated.

Two men appear behind Joanna. They wear Red Bluff uniforms, but I don't recognize them.

"Are you sure about this?" the shorter man asks. "She's too well known."

"I'm sure," Joanna says, smoothing my hair away from my eyes. "She's exactly who I want."

Escape is impossible. I can't lift my arms or move my legs. I fight to keep my eyes open, but the drug pulls me into darkness and my thoughts muddle. I must be mistaken. It can't be Joanna.

Joanna's dead.

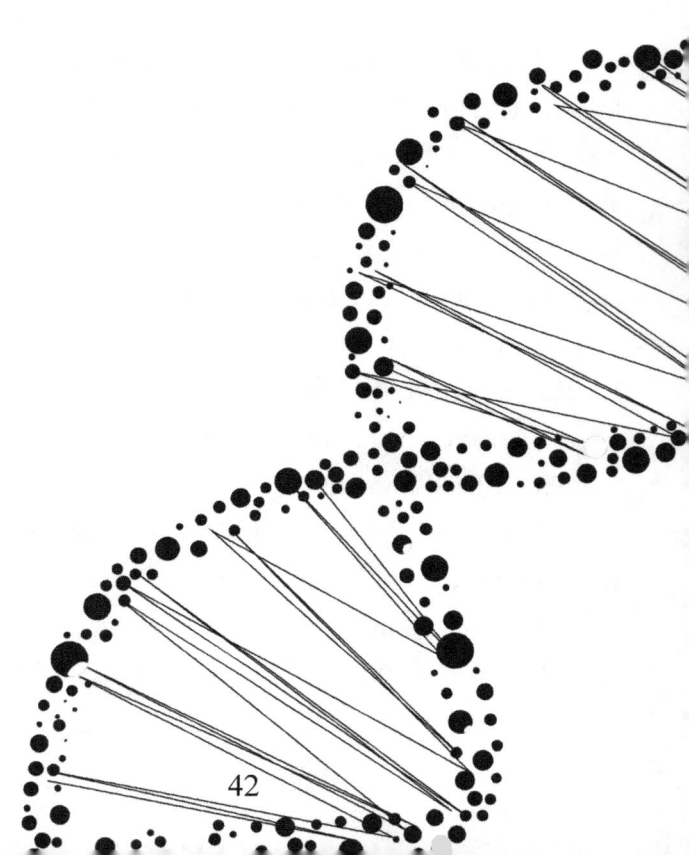

CHAPTER 4

A CIRCLE OF BRIGHT, WHITE light shines in my eyes. I try to lift my head, but a strap across my brow holds me down. I close my eyes, but the glow lingers, two white circles behind my lids. I raise my arms; straps cut into my wrists. Twist my body; I'm immobilized by a waist band. My heart bangs in my chest.

Where am I? Why am I restrained?

A shadow blocks the light. Someone pushes my head to the side and rakes my hair away from my neck. "This will prove him wrong. Together, we'll be more than perfect."

It's definitely Joanna. Her voice has the same derisive purr I heard that day we met in my uncle's office. How is she alive? Perfect together in what? I arch my back, desperate to break free, but she presses something metallic against the base of my skull and I'm flattened by a punch like screwdriver is driven into my head.

I scream, but my mouth is clogged like it's full of cotton balls and no sound passes my lips. A tingling sensation in my head causes a wave of dizziness and black spots appear in the bright light. I jerk my arm at a needle prick near my elbow, but a hot heaviness spreads and I lose all feeling in my body. The light fades. The shadow expands. Darkness wraps around me. Then I float through a tunnel filled with iridescent golden orbs suspended like morning dew caught in a spider's web.

Am I dreaming? Hallucinating? The restraints have vanished. I can move my arms, my legs, but I'm weightless. There's nothing solid beneath my feet. No air brushes my face. I'm not hot or cold—there's no temperature in this place. It's just me, the tunnel, and the orbs.

Are the orbs an afterimage from staring at the bright light? I close my eyes to chase them away, but when I look again, the orbs remain, clearer than ever. A face appears in one—Darius. Another orb shows Marrick, his hand outstretched, his brown eyes piercing mine. Raising my hand, I touch the orb. It's not solid, not anything, but my fingers sink into Marrick's image and my skin takes on the orb's golden hue.

Lowering my hand, I gaze at the next orb. It shows Magelon winking at me after she punched Gaucini. I focus on Magelon's face and try to comprehend what I'm seeing. The orb expands and shows Kelly holding Gaucini by his shirt.

Now I understand. These orbs show my memories, like an external recollection, separated from me yet connected by the tunnel. Am I viewing the inner workings of my mind? How is that possible? What did Joanna inject into me?

Another orb appears with a repulsive greenish-hue. It shows my face, mouth open, eyes wide from shock. A dart hits my neck and I fall to the floor. A hand smoothes back my hair—

She's exactly who I want.

Joanna's voice reverberates through me as though I'd spoken. But this isn't my memory. I'm looking at myself through Joanna's eyes, imagining how she talks in my head. It makes no sense. If this tunnel depicts a passage through my mind, how am I seeing Joanna's memories?

More green orbs appear. One shows an unfamiliar man's face. Black hair peppered with gray. Black glasses. Thin pale lips on a down-turned mouth—

Your help is no longer needed, Joanna. She's perfect as she is.

This isn't my memory either, but the man is chillingly familiar. How can I know his voice when I don't know who he is? Where have I heard him before? And why do I think I should fear him?

He appears in the next green orb, his face jubilant—

Finding her changes everything. The trial will go ahead, and it will succeed.

I recoil. Could this be the man my mother wanted me hidden from? Who is he? And what trial?

Another green orb pushes through and expands in front of me, the most repulsive yet. A different man glares at me through a mesh-imbedded glass viewing pane. His head is shaved, and his eyes look like they've been injected with black ink. His lips twitch, then his bitter tone stabs my mind—

Jack Arquet was nothing. I will unleash hell.

Jack Arquet. I know this name. From where? I stare past the man, hoping the scene will expand to show where he is, but a golden orb reappears. It blends with the green orb and the black-eyed man's face is replaced by a different man. Brown cropped hair. Clean-shaven, with hazel eyes similar to mine—

Trust me, Jack. This will change everything.

My mother's voice fills my mind. This isn't my memory. Or Joanna's. It's my mother's, and she speaks to Jack, the hazel-eyed man. Why is it captured in a golden orb, not green like Joanna's? Is it because my mother is connected to me? And the black-eyed man is connected to Joanna? Two types of orbs: gold, and green. The gold orbs hold my memories and bring security and a sense of self. The green orbs don't. They're alien to me.

I gaze around the tunnel. My gold orbs outnumber the green, but they clash and fight for my attention. Some of the golden orbs hold unfamiliar faces, but I'm drawn to them as if they belong to me. Is that why the name Arquet is familiar? Will I find the answer within a memory?

I reach out to touch another golden orb. It shows a man wearing a soldier's uniform. He stands with his arms outstretched like a human crucifix. Blood trickles down his right cheek from a gash beneath his eye. His expression is menacing, matching his smirk.

You gonna kill an unarmed man, Jack?

It's not you I'm killing.

Jack's response couples with a view of his gun rising to eye level. A shot rings out, causing the orb to ripple. The man drops to the floor with a bullet hole through his head. The scene expands to show one, two, three more bodies, all in uniform, all bleeding from similar bullet wounds. Then Jack turns the gun on himself and fires.

The orb explodes, splattering me in a golden light that absorbs all color. Everything turns white. No memory orbs. No tunnel. I fall, down, down, dragged by a heaviness that rises through my feet and up my body. Pins and needles stab my arms, my face—

I jolt awake. The weightless sensation lifts. Feeling returns. No longer restrained or lying down, I'm standing, shivering in cold air. My experience in the tunnel fades like a daydream fizzles out, and all I hear is my panicked breathing and a silence so loud it rings in my ears.

I stand in a new brightness—an all-white room with no windows, no obvious door. My clothes are different. I'm dressed in a white short-sleeved shirt, white pants, no shoes. Remembering the punch to the back of my head, I prod the base of my skull and touch a tender spot, but no broken skin. I inspect the inside of my elbow. A purple bruise marks an injection site. What drug does that? And the orbs? The tunnel? Were they real?

I check the rest of my body, but aside from a welt around my left wrist, find no other injuries. My mind is clear, with no lingering orbs or black tunnel. I'm not restrained, but the room holds me captive. There must be a door. Where is it?

Walking to a wall, I press the smooth surface and push up, down, sideways. It doesn't move. I slide my fingers along the wall, find the corner, then push the next wall. Still nothing. There are no joins anywhere, only smooth surfaces. There has to be a way in. I'm just not seeing it.

I search the room again with meticulous care from corner to corner. All the white strains my eyes. I close them but imagine multiple gold orbs crowding out green orbs that grow smaller and fade into the black walls of the tunnel.

Opening my eyes, I stare at my fingers. Are the orbs as real as me, or am I still affected by drugs?

A door slides open in the wall in front of me. The man I saw in Joanna's first memory orb stands in the doorway wearing a white laboratory coat. He's flanked by the two men I saw at my barracks. Ignoring them, I stare at the man with growing dread. The black-rimmed glasses perched on his nose jog a name: Doctor Flannigan. His name dredges up the memory of the last conversation my mother had with my uncle in vivid detail—

Don't let him find her. He can never learn the truth. Promise me. Promise me you'll do everything in your power to conceal her identity.

Flannigan won't find her. I'll keep her safe. You have my word.

I back away, my uncle's voice ringing in my ears. This man is Doctor Flannigan, the man my mother wanted to hide me from.

Flannigan steps inside the room. The two men follow. Both wear white clothes. The short man carries a baton. The tall man holds a weapon similar to a cattle prod, but it has a short handle imprinted with the word *Stinger*. I assume it delivers an electric shock, like a Taser, but I'm not keen to find out. The two metal prongs on the end look lethal.

"How are you feeling today?" Flannigan asks.

He talks with a detached tone like I'm a specimen to study, not a human to engage with. But there's something else. He's tense and peers at me as though searching for irregularities. I recall the other memories I saw in the tunnel. I'm perfect, he said, and he didn't need Joanna anymore. Is he looking for what she did to prove him wrong?

"Where's Joanna?" I ask. "What did she do to me?"

The anxiety drains from his face, so whatever he feared mustn't have happened.

He smiles. "Joanna? No one of that name is here."

"She brought me here. Where am I?"

"You've nothing to fear. You're in safe hands now." He talks pleasantly, but there's no warmth in his smile. "Introductions. Do you know who I am?"

"You're Doctor Flannigan." His name is poison.

"Yes," Flannigan says with his infuriating smile. "And your name is?"

"Jo—" I clamp my mouth shut. Why would I say my name is Joanna? It must have been accidental because I was thinking about her. I start to say Sarah, but again, I'm struck by a powerful urge to say Joanna. Her name rises from the depths of my mind in a horrid greenish hue, as though it were spat from one of those green orbs.

I silently repeat my name over and over. It takes all my concentration. I can't get Joanna out of my mind.

The tall man with the Stinger steps forward and stands beside Flannigan. If I don't give a name, will he strike me? Not wanting to find out, I imagine looking at myself in a mirror as I say my name again. It works. Joanna fades from my mind, but a gold orb dances across my vision, showing a memory of my mother.

I'm looking up at her, my head no higher than her knees. Another orb appears, but it blends with the first and skews the memory. Now, I'm looking at a younger version of Flannigan. His hair is all black, he wears similar glasses, but his face is minus the age spots on his cheeks now.

I look forward to working with you, Doctor Flannigan.

My mother's voice spills from the orb, causing tears to well in my eyes; I haven't heard her for thirteen years. There's no mistaking her, even though she sounds younger. But this is her memory. She must have worked for Flannigan before I was born. If she knows him, she might know what to say. She's desperate to keep me away from him. Why else would I recall her so clearly?

"My name—" I let the memory dictate my words. "Is Katherine."

Flannigan jerks as though stung by the Stinger. "Katherine?" His hand slides to a cylindrical bulge in his pocket that looks suspiciously like a syringe. "Interesting. Tell me about yourself."

Tell him what? My mother is a stranger to me and no more memories surface. I need to switch this around, so I ask the questions, not let him direct the conversation.

But it's hard to think straight.

My mother's memory fades and now when I look at Flannigan, all I can think about is Joanna and her furious responses to him. I get an uncomfortable feeling Flannigan did something to her, which is why she isn't here.

Flannigan slips his hand into the syringe pocket and steps closer to me. "What are you thinking about right at this moment?"

"I'm confused," I say, stalling.

"Confusion is normal." Flannigan's eyes narrow. "As you should know, Katherine."

He knows I'm lying. I should tell the truth and deal with whatever happens, but now Sarah Wilson sounds odd, like it's not my name.

I squeeze my eyes shut. I'm losing myself in this. I need to think about something relating to me. My uncle? His overprotective presence is never far from my mind. He also never let me set foot out of the house without a bodyguard.

So why hasn't he rescued me?

He can't know where I am, which means it's up to me to get out. I have the skills. I wouldn't have been within reach of the top graduate title if I didn't.

Thinking about my uncle refreshes the memory of meeting Joanna in his office. As I recall it, the green orbs belonging to Joanna grow brighter and she's stuck in my head again like a bad tune. I imagine soldiers staring at her as she walks by. Unlike me, she carried an aura of superiority that demanded attention. She didn't need a minder like Darius, but—

You'll only get one shot at this, so make every target count.

Darius. He's always been there for me, and he doesn't fail me now. The memory of us standing together before my sharpshooting round drives Joanna from my mind. Drawing confidence from him, I open my eyes and assess my predicament. Flannigan doesn't want me dead, only subdued. He has a syringe; his men have a Stinger and batons. I'm fast, faster than anyone. Stronger, too. I have the combative skills to take down three opponents. I'm not in training now; there's no need to hold back.

"I remember something." I shift my weight to the balls of my feet. "But I'm not sure. Could you clarify?"

Flannigan's shoulders relax. "Of course. What do you remember?"

"My name is Sarah Wilson."

I leap at the man holding the Stinger and drive my shoulder into his chest. Caught off guard, he stumbles, but grapples with the Stinger, trying to shoot. I knock his arm up, then slam my fist against his jaw. Eyes fluttering, he falls, his head hitting the floor with a crack.

Something hard strikes my back. Sucking in my breath, I twist and grab the baton, yanking it from the short man's grasp. Swinging wide, I smack it against the man's face. He drops to his knees, blood spurting from his nose.

Flannigan runs from the room. I give chase, reaching the door as it closes. Diving through the gap, I catch

Flannigan's arm, push him against the outside wall and clamp my other hand around his throat. The door slides shut, trapping the two men inside.

Flannigan doesn't resist me. "There's nowhere to go. You need me, Miss Arquet. Without me, you'll fall to the same fate as your mother."

There's that name again, Arquet. Why does he call me that? And what does he mean about my mother? She got sick and died, that's all I know. Is Flannigan insinuating something else?

I dig my fingers into his neck. "What did you do to my mother?"

"It's not what I did to her," he says, choking. "It's what she did to herself."

Infuriated by his cryptic answer, I bring my face close to his, determined to extract a sensible response. Instead, the memory of Jack shooting the unarmed man appears in my mind, filling me with cold-blooded, murderous intent. I spread my fingers. I've never snapped a man's neck before, but I know the maneuver. It's all in the twist.

Flannigan's expression changes. There's a hungry look in his eyes; he expected me to react this way, and it pleases him. It jolts me back to my senses. How I'm feeling is similar to when I wanted to attack Gaucini after my sharpshooting round; he's a threat to everyone. So is Flannigan, but he makes my blood boil with triple the heat. Is it because I recalled Jack killing those soldiers? I'm not

Jack. I trained to be resilient, but I'm not a murderer.

Regaining control, I relax my grip. If I kill Flannigan, I'll lose my chance of learning about my mother and finding Joanna. I should follow protocol and have him arrested for holding me against my will. My uncle will make sure that happens. But I need to get out of here to alert him.

Flannigan slips his hand into the pocket and grabs the syringe. Clutching his wrist, I plunge the needle into Flannigan's thigh and jam my thumb against the plunger.

He grimaces.

"Perfectly executed, Miss Arquet. Your mother would be proud." His eyes roll and he slumps to the floor.

Resisting the urge to kick him in the ribs, I crouch and search his clothes. Beneath his coat is a keycard clipped to his belt. Pulling it off, I jump to my feet and look for a way out.

There's a door on the other side of the room, beyond a table with webbing restraints dangling from the sides. A bright light hangs from the ceiling. Recalling Joanna's shadow passing through the light, I shiver. She put me on that table and held me captive with restraints and drugs. Syringes and a silver gun-like instrument lie on a bench along the wall. I touch the back of my neck. Did the silver instrument cause the punch to my head?

Sickened to think about what Joanna did to me, I hurry past the table. I can't waste this chance to escape.

Reaching the door, I stare at the glass viewing pane. It's the same as the one I saw in Joanna's memory. Are there more rooms like this? The black-eyed man might be in one. Joanna might be in another. Is that why she isn't here?

Hunt it down and kill it.

I stiffen. Why did I think that?

Hands shaking, I pass Flannigan's keycard over a crystalline panel. A short beep quickens my heartbeat, then the door slides open, and I face the last person I expected to see.

CHAPTER 5

"DARIUS?"

I'm so shocked to see him, I can't move. He conceals his identity with a blue security guard uniform, but he aims a gun at my face. Unsure if he's involved with Flannigan, I back away.

Darius lowers the gun. "It's okay. Where's Flannigan?"

I sigh with relief.

"Over there." I point past the table, the weight of my last interaction with Darius falling from my shoulders. "I drugged him."

Darius glances across the room then flicks his head, motioning me behind him. I run out and he swipes a keycard over the lock. The door slides closed, revealing

Procedure Room 1 printed in bold black letters.

The horror of my experience returns. "What is this place?"

"Never mind. Let's get you out of here."

I grab his arm. "Joanna. She's alive. She drugged me and brought me here."

Darius frowns. "Joanna's dead."

"She's not. She's here."

He glances at my white clothes. "You must have confused her with someone else. Let's go."

He doesn't believe me. I don't blame him. It's a ludicrous suggestion. Even Flannigan said confusion was normal. But I recognized Joanna at my barracks, and I wasn't under the influence of drugs then.

Darius pulls me along a corridor, giving me no chance to argue. We pass similar doors, each with key-swipe locks. The walls are gray—a relief to my eyes after staring at white—but the dim lighting and silence send chills up my spine. Flannigan and the two men can't be the only people here. Darius got his uniform from somewhere.

He glances at me. "Are you hurt?"

"No." The adrenaline pumping through my body must numb the bruise from the baton strike because I can't feel it. But my mind...

"Darius, Joanna did something—"

"Forget about Joanna," he says. "Do exactly as I say. I'll get you out."

Wishing I had a gun instead of a keycard, I follow him along the corridor. He tilts his head, listening. I listen, too. It's quiet. Any noise we make will stand out.

Signs on the doors draw my attention: *OBR6*, *OBR5*, *OBR4*. I pause at a door marked *OBR3*. The mesh viewing pane is the same as the pane in the memory of the black-eyed man. I step closer—

I'll unleash hell.

I stop, recalling a similar situation. I've peered through the glass insert before. Not recently. This moment happened a long time ago. Who experienced it? My mother? I get the odd feeling I'm looking through her eyes again. She must have worked here with Flannigan.

Heart pounding, I step closer, wanting to look in, wanting to run. Hunt it down and kill it? Not the black-eyed man. Something else. Something that shouldn't exist.

Darius tugs my arm. "Move."

I can't. Feverish aggression overtakes me, worse than what Jack's memories made me feel. Whatever 'it' is, I need to destroy it.

Darius drags me to the stairs at the end of the corridor and pulls me around to face him.

"Are you with me?"

His sharp tone snaps my mind clear. Aggression simmering, I look back at the doors, the walls; this place is familiar. Did I come here with my mother as a toddler?

Darius pinches my arm. "Sarah?"

I jerk at his touch. Am I still under the influence of drugs, hallucinating or suffering paranoia? If that's the explanation, there is no 'it'. I should focus on what's real. Darius is real. He'll get me out.

I need to get out.

I look Darius in the eye, so he knows he has my full attention. "I'm with you."

He squeezes my arm, then hurries up the stairs. When we reach the top, he stops at a steel door, grasps the knob, and turns it. The lock releases with a loud click and makes my heart leap into my mouth.

Darius cracks open the door, checks both ways, then steps through. I follow, holding my hand against the door so it closes softly behind us. There's no doorknob on this side, just a lock and a sign: *Restricted Area. Do Not Proceed Without Authorization.*

Blue night lights illuminate a corridor. A brighter light spills from a room farther along. Voices travel to us—a muffled conversation. Security guards?

"This way," Darius whispers.

He nudges me to the left, then strides ahead. We pass doors numbered *C10*, *C11*, *C12*—all closed. The next has a sign: *Low Bio-Hazard Area. No Admittance Without Authorization.* On the wall nearby is an arrow with *Dock C* above it. We follow the arrow's direction.

Nothing about this area jogs any memories. I search for a sign, a logo, something to provide a clue about where

I am, but the walls are blank.

The corridor turns left, then right, then left again. My heart leaps into my mouth as a woman steps from a doorway ahead. She takes in my white clothes and her lips pull tight.

"Hurry," she says to Darius.

I know her. Her voice. Her face. How, I'm not sure. She's tall and thin, her wispy gray hair tied in a bun. I imagine her younger with brown hair. And her name.

Pushing past Darius, I touch her shoulder. "Vera?"

She walks faster, ignoring me.

I stride alongside her. "How do I know you?"

"You shouldn't," she says.

Reaching a door at the end, she stops and turns to Darius. "Where's Flannigan?"

"He wasn't the problem I thought he'd be."

"I'm not surprised," Vera says.

"Don't read anything into it. Sarah knows what she's doing."

"You don't understand." She looks at my white shirt again and frowns. "She's vulnerable. It's crucial she gets to familiar surroundings." She shakes her head. "What was Flannigan thinking?"

Why am I vulnerable? "Please. It wasn't Flannigan. Joanna brought me here—"

Darius scowls. "Sarah—"

"She did," I plead to Vera. "Joanna Johansson. She's

taller than me, with blonde hair. Do you know her?"

"Johansson died six months ago," Darius says, his voice low, placating.

I glare at him. "She's not dead."

Vera rests her hand on my arm. "Confusion is to be expected. Doing as I say will help. Your uncle will explain."

Vera and Darius wear matching sympathetic expressions. What do they know about the drugs and the white room? Even if I'm wrong about Joanna being alive, why did I recall her memories?

"I'm not surprised Flannigan found her," Vera continues. "She looks so much like her mother."

Another surprise. "How do you know my mother?"

Darius steps between us. "We need to go."

Vera pulls a keycard from her pocket, swipes the lock and opens the door. An icy breeze slaps my face, making me shiver.

"Put this on." Vera takes off her cardigan and hands it to me. "You'll need it for more than the cold."

Our hands touch and her gaze holds mine. I get the impression she wants to tell me something, but she nudges me after Darius and closes the door.

"Stay close," Darius says.

Putting on the cardigan, I tuck Flannigan's keycard into the pocket and follow Darius along the side of the building. My white shirt is covered, but not my pants.

Conscious of my visibility, I stay between Darius and the wall. When we reach the corner, Darius pulls a flashlight from his belt. Aiming it into the darkness, he clicks it on and off twice.

No flash of light returns. Darius tucks the torch into his belt pouch and touches my arm.

"We're going to run straight. Don't stop, no matter what happens. Go."

We jump forward and race across a tarred road to an open field. Dry grass crunches beneath my feet. A tree looms from the darkness, its leaves shimmering in the half-moon light. The broad trunk provides cover. Beyond it, the outline of a forest cuts a jagged black line through the night sky.

We're halfway to the tree when headlights from a vehicle throw our shadows across the ground.

Darius pushes his hand against my back. "Keep going. Don't stop."

I sprint to the tree and dive behind the trunk, but pull up short when I hit a fence. It's higher than my head with coiled razor wire along the top. Dense forest continues on the other side, but I can't get over. Nor under, or around. I push the mesh. If Darius sent me in this direction, he must have cut the wire. But where?

A figure dressed in black appears on the other side of the fence. I jump back.

"Sarah. It's me. We're here to help." Marrick leans

against the fence and opens a slice in the wire. "Through here. Quickly."

Magelon slinks from the shadows behind him, also dressed in black, a balaclava hiding her white, spiky hair. She aims her Beretta through the fence.

"What's he's doing?" she whispers.

I look over my shoulder. Darius is still in the field, gun outstretched. The vehicle speeds toward him.

"Get her out of here!" he yells.

He shoots, blowing a headlight.

The vehicle veers, then circles around Darius and skids to a stop.

Darius shoots again, shattering the windscreen.

The driver, a security guard, jumps out and returns fire.

Darius unloads a round of bullets. The guard ducks for cover. Then Darius runs to the left, drawing attention away from us.

"Come on, come on," Magelon says, aiming her Beretta at the guard.

I grip the mesh and follow Darius's dark outline. He's out of the guard's range and has time to circle back to us. But then he lights up like a beacon as another vehicle speeds from the far end of the building, a spotlight blazing from its roof.

Darius continues across the field, but the driver cuts him off. Brakes squeal. Three people jump out—soldiers dressed in combat attire. They surround Darius, rifles raised.

I clench my hands, waiting for the handcuffs to appear. Instead, one soldier pins Darius's hands behind his back and another pummels his fists into Darius's stomach.

Darius doubles over, his grunt carrying on the wind. The soldier punches him again, then again, and again. The third soldier joins in, forcing Darius upright with a sledging knee kick to the groin. Darius collapses onto the ground.

"No!" My shout draws the spotlight toward us. Not caring if I'm seen, I run back to the field, murder on my mind. I'm at the tree when Marrick catches me around the waist with his arm, jerking me to a stop.

"Don't," he says. "If they catch you, they'll kill him."

"They're killing him now!"

Breaking his grip, I run into the field. The security guard from the first vehicle shouts. The spotlight shifts, blinding me. I avert my eyes, but gold circles similar to the gold orbs in the memory tunnel dance across my vision.

Startled, I veer to the left and crash into Marrick. He grips me around the waist so hard it forces the breath from my lungs. Swinging me behind him, he raises his gun and blows out the spotlight, then fires at the security guard, making him dive for cover. Magelon appears on our right and shoots at the soldiers holding Darius. They run behind the vehicle, dragging Darius with them.

"Go, go, go," Magelon says.

Marrick pulls me back to the fence. Securing me against his chest, he rolls us through the slit in the wire, then grips my arm and pulls me into the forest. I'm glad he holds me. I can't see where I'm going. The gold orb still dances in my vision, and I recall a similar situation with someone yelling, *abort, abort, abort.*

CHAPTER 6

T HE MEMORY EXPANDS, SUCKING ME into a vision where the forest melts away and I'm running between brick pillars in an underground parking lot. On my right, I imagine a soldier wearing riot gear and carrying a rifle. He holds up three fingers and points across the lot.

I shake my head and repeat, *Abort!*

She's vulnerable.

Vera's voice jolts me out of the memory. The car park vanishes. The trees return. I'm running beside Marrick, who helps me through the forest. I look for Magelon on my right, thinking she's the other person I saw. No one is there.

Shaken, I stumble. Marrick grabs my arm, keeping me upright. I concentrate on the ground, following a blue beam shining from Marrick's vest. The circle of light illuminates our path, but it refreshes my experience in the memory tunnel.

Am I still affected by the drugs Joanna gave me? The parking lot, the brick pillars, and the other soldier, were as real as me. But the voice yelling abort belonged to a man. Who's in my head? Jack Arquet?

"This way," Marrick says, pulling me to the left.

We run through rocks glowing milky white in the moonlight. The surrounding vegetation is various shades of black and grays. He changes direction again, heads along the top of a gully, and stops at a large tree.

"Climb down here," he says. "Use the roots to help."

The tree's roots reach down the side of the gully to a shallow creek at the bottom. The forest continues on the other side. The gully is a threshold to safety, but every step forward takes us farther from Darius.

"What about Darius?" I ask.

Magelon appears out of nowhere and skids to a stop next to us, breathing hard.

"Where is he?" Marrick asks.

"Don't know," she says. "The vehicle wasn't there when I got back. We need to move. It won't take the soldiers long to realize I lured them in the wrong direction."

I scan the forest. No movement. No sound. "We have to go back."

"You're the priority, not him," Magelon says.

Marrick glances at me. He appears to consider returning. But his expression hardens. "We keep going."

His call is a gut punch. I can't leave Darius. He didn't leave me. But what can I do? No gun, no shoes. And a head full of random memories that confuse reality. Vulnerable.

Marrick nudges me down the bank. Tears pricking my eyes, I climb down. Did my uncle prioritize my safety? He must have if he sent Marrick to rescue me. But why involve Darius? He hasn't been on active duty for fifteen years. It doesn't make sense.

At the creek, I jump across the rocks to the bank on the other side. As I climb up, a hand reaches for me.

"Take hold."

It's Kelly, with a jovial edge to his tone as though we're casually strolling through the forest. I'd heard that about him, how he jokes with criminals while snapping on the handcuffs. At least he doesn't beat them to near-death like the soldiers did to Darius.

Grabbing his hand, I jam my feet against the bank to help climb, but Kelly hauls me over the top in one swing and drops me beside him.

"Not much to you is there," he says, releasing my hand.

No one is much of anything compared to him. Built like a heavyweight boxer, his shoulder span is twice the width of Marrick's. A thick curly beard adds weight to his bull neck and his ember-red hair, tied back, gives him a menacing appearance like a medieval Viking warrior.

Marrick leaps up the bank, followed by Magelon. She turns and aims her gun back across the gully.

"We've got two on our tail," she says. "Keep going."

A beam of light on the other side of the gully illuminates the tree we used to climb down. Two soldiers appear. They shine their torches along the creek.

"Go," Marrick says, crowding me forward.

Kelly clamps his hand on my shoulder and motions for me to follow. I hurry after him, determined to return with the entire Red Bluff army. I don't know why my uncle hasn't sent them already.

The terrain changes—a steep decline through forest so dark, it swallows Kelly's vest light. I keep my eyes on his back to avoid running into a tree. Then the slope flattens, and an overgrown track stretches out in front of us. Kelly breaks into a jog. I follow, conscious of Marrick close behind me. Caught between them is an awkward reminder that Marrick wanted me on his team. Is that why he's here? Or is he just following orders?

Further along, the moonlight reflects off the side mirror of an older style four-door, hard-top Jeep Wrangler. Parked to one side of the track, its brown panels blend into the vegetation. On closer inspection, I question the Jeep's reliability. There are more dents in the doors than a tin can in a shooting alley.

"She's not *Betsy*, but she has it where it counts,"

Kelly says, seeing me scrutinize the Jeep. He opens the back passenger door. "Get in."

Wondering what type of vehicle is called Betsy, I climb in, scooting over to make room for Marrick, who follows me in. My pants catch on the ripped seat fabric, and the roof lining sags on my head. I hope the Jeep's interior doesn't reflect what's under the hood.

Kelly squeezes behind the wheel and turns on the ignition. He drives forward and stops in the middle of the track.

Magelon yanks open the passenger door and jumps in.

"Go, go," she says.

Kelly slams the Jeep into gear and guns the engine. The Jeep rockets ahead, throwing me back in my seat. Marrick raises his pistol and looks out his window.

"How many?"

"Still two. They've crossed the gully." Magelon glances at the speedometer. "Can you make this heap of junk move faster? If they get an ID on this vehicle, we're screwed."

I swivel around and peer out the back window. "What if they follow by car?"

"There's no vehicular access across the gully," Marrick says. "And they don't have the numbers in their security detail to give chase. If they call for backup, the closest response team is an hour away. Then they'll have to find us. Reece will keep us updated once we hit the highway."

"Backup?" I stare at Marrick, confused. "What military base is this?"

"It's not a base. It's Bio-Tech, a quarantine facility attached to the military's biosecurity division. We're not sure where the soldiers on patrol come from. We didn't have time to find out." He frowns. "I thought you knew about this place?"

"I don't even know where we are." My hands twist around each other. Has Joanna messed with my mind so much I've forgotten something crucial? Or does Marrick expect me to know everything because I'm related to his boss?

"Why don't we call for backup?" I ask.

"We can't," Marrick says. "Your uncle's directives. This isn't an authorized assignment."

I stare at him. "Why not? I was abducted."

"It's not that simple. Your uncle insisted—"

A thud against the underside of the Jeep makes the vehicle shudder and tip to the right. I'm thrown against the door, then forward when the Jeep bounces over the rocky ground. Marrick slings his arm across me, pushing me back against the seat. Magelon curses and presses her hand against the roof.

"Buckle up," Kelly says, changing gears. "We're in for a rough ride."

I fumble for my seatbelt and click it closed at the same time Marrick secures his. Grabbing the handgrip above my head, I peer through the windscreen. The track is an obstacle course of deep ruts, fallen rocks, and sections so narrow the Jeep barely fits between the trees. Then the vegetation thins, and we drive along the top of a ridge. The ground on my side of the Jeep drops away. Above the treetops, an orange line cuts the horizon—dawn. We're driving north, but from where?

"Brace yourselves," Kelly says. "We're going down."

The hood of the Jeep tips at an alarming angle. With only the headlights and the faint morning light, it's hard to gauge the length of this section of track, if we're on a track.

The ground levels out, then after another heart-stopping descent, Kelly spins the steering wheel and drives left along a graded road through trees less dense. The headlights shine on a pipe gate blocking the road. It's held closed by a lock and chain.

Kelly stops the Jeep, allowing Magelon to jump out and open the gate. When she's back in the car, Kelly plants his foot on the accelerator, making the tires spin. Ahead, the road arcs through the trees. We pass a weathered timber sign: *Stanislaus National Forest*. I don't recognize the name.

"Where are we?"

"Once we hit the highway, we're about twenty

minutes west of Dardanelle," Marrick says.

I can't get my bearings. I'm not familiar with Dardanelle, either. "Where is Bio-Tech from here?"

"Near Bridgeport," Marrick says. "We used the fire access tracks through the lower slopes of the Sierra to reach Bio-Tech's northern boundary."

"Bridgeport?" I can place the town on a map but being on the opposite side of the Sierra Nevada mountain range makes me a long way from home. "How did you know where to find me?"

"It wasn't easy," Magelon says over her shoulder. "Everyone assumed you did a runner after your sharpshooting round, so we searched for you in all the wrong places."

"What? Why would I run?" My face grows hot. I did plan to leave but never considered it would make me look like a sulky military brat.

"It looked like you ran," Marrick says. "We found your uniform but no personal belongings, and you weren't on base. When you didn't arrive at your home in Anderson, Darius suspected foul play. He got Reece to track every car that left the base after your sharpshooting round. Reece tracked a white van to Bio-Tech. Darius was adamant that's where you were taken."

"Based on what? I could've been in any vehicle."

"Darius knew Flannigan worked there."

"How does he know Flannigan?" Has Darius been to

74

Bio-Tech before? It would explain how he knew his way around.

"He didn't say," Marrick says. "He only said you have information about Flannigan's research into performance-enhancement drugs. He didn't give specifics and wasn't even sure if you'd remember."

Memory issues have plagued me since Joanna drugged me. Did she hope the drugs would force me to remember something? It didn't work. All she did was mess up my mind.

"Why would Darius think I'd remember anything about Flannigan's research? What is Bio-Tech, anyway? It didn't look like a place that researched performance."

"You'd know more than us," Magelon says. "Your mother worked there."

How did she know? I wasn't aware myself until an hour ago. I can't even confirm it. All I have are a bunch of weird memories that might not even be real.

"This doesn't make sense. What if I was a random target? A woman and two men jumped me with a dart gun. One man said I'm too well known. It sounded like it would be a problem."

"They got that right," Kelly growls from the front seat.

"What did they look like?" Marrick asks.

"The men were ordinary. One tall, one short. They wore Red Bluff uniforms, but I didn't recognize them from base. Turns out they work for Flannigan. The woman…" I hope they don't say I'm confused, too. "I swear it was Joanna, but with shorter hair. She concealed her identity with a cap and round sunglasses. She said I was exactly who she wanted. I don't know what she meant."

When no one says anything, I regret mentioning Joanna. I should have thought this through. Telling Marrick's team Joanna is alive could be like stabbing them with coffin nails.

Magelon twists around and glares at me. "Joanna's dead. We don't need the reminder. Anyway, she wouldn't want anyone, let alone you."

"It sounds like whoever abducted you did a good job concealing their identity," Marrick says, his voice hard.

Magelon glowers and slumps back in her seat. Kelly glances at her, then flexes his fingers on the steering wheel and stares through the windscreen.

God, I'm an idiot. They must still be grieving their team member. Why do I continue to insist she's alive when I'm not one hundred percent sure?

"What we are certain about," Marrick continues, not looking at me, "is your mother's connection to Flannigan. You weren't random."

"Then Flannigan must have made a mistake," I say, relieved he changed the subject. "He called me Miss Arquet. Do any of you know who that is?"

"Arquet?" Kelly frowns.

Marrick gives me a sharp look and sits up straighter in his seat. "You're sure?"

"Someone we should know about?" Magelon asks.

"Jack Arquet, former Red Bluff C.S.R. team leader," Kelly says. "Shot his entire team. Murder/suicide. Goes back, what, twenty years?"

Murder/suicide? I witnessed that through the memory, which proves it wasn't a hallucination. Is everything else I saw real, too?

"Nineteen," Marrick says.

"Yeah?" Magelon says. "Never heard about that."

"You wouldn't have," Kelly says. "Arquet doesn't exist according to the military. All records about him and his team were erased."

"How do you know about it?" Magelon asks.

"Rusty knew someone who knew someone involved in the cleanup," Kelly says. "A quip for soldiers who cracked under pressure began after that. 'Lost it like Arquet'. Officials stamped it out by slapping a breach of discipline action on anyone caught saying it. Rusty told us about it back when we were cadets, right?" He looks at Marrick in the rearview mirror.

"Yeah." Marrick stares out the window, pensive.

"Who's Rusty?" His name bounces around my mind like I should know it, but I don't.

"My older brother," Kelly says. "Civilian now. Works as a mechanic on the west coast."

"If Arquet cracked, how did he make team leader?" Magelon asks. "He must have given some sign during training he couldn't cope with pressure."

"Nope. Arquet had impeccable records." Kelly shrugs.

My uncle has security clearance. He'd know about the Arquet incident. Surely he would have warned me about the effects of job pressure if a Red Bluff leader murdered his team members. Unless—

Nineteen years ago. Never mentioned like he doesn't exist. I sink back against my seat and hug Vera's cardigan around me. If the memories I saw in the tunnel were real, my mother knew Jack Arquet. She spoke to him. A gold orb held that memory, which means it's connected to me. Is it possible? Is Jack Arquet my father?

The hairs on my arms stand on end. It would explain my exceptional skills. Jack made team leader and I would have inherited his abilities. But he lost it; killed his team in cold blood—like I wanted to snap Flannigan's neck.

I stiffen. "Take me home. Now."

"You can't go there," Marrick says. "It's the first place Flannigan will look for you."

"Then let me call my uncle."

"Can't do that either. We can't risk giving away our location."

Being caught is the least of my worries. If Marrick won't help me contact my uncle, I'll find another way. I need to know if I'm the daughter of a murderer and whether what happened to him is what's happening to me now.

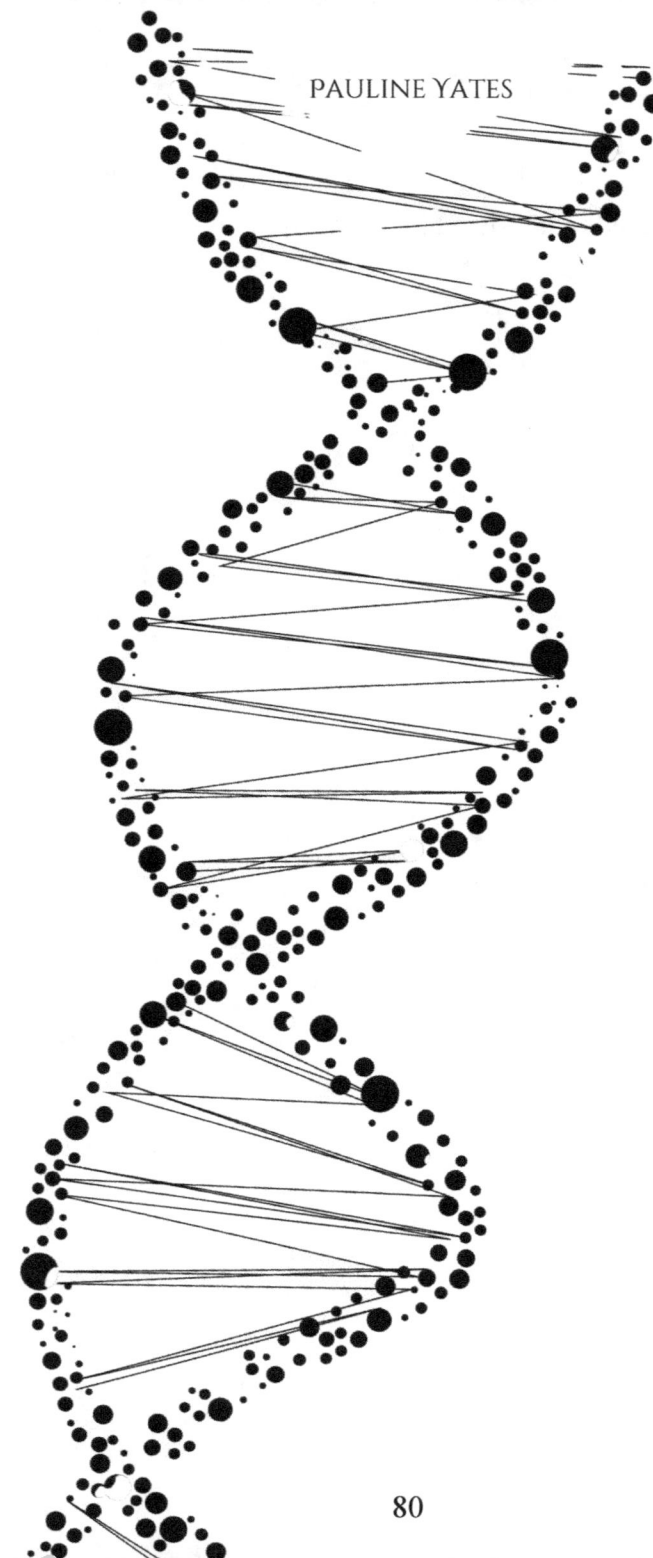

PAULINE YATES

CHAPTER 7

SARAH WILSON? OR SARAH ARQUET? I repeat both names in my mind. Sarah Arquet sounds familiar, like it's a missing piece of me I didn't know I'd lost. But the daughter of a murderer? It won't sink in.

When we hit the highway, Kelly drives west over the Sierra Mountain range. The Jeep purrs with fine-tuned precision, dispelling my doubt about its mechanical reliability, but I can't relax. The urgency to get home and question my uncle builds inside me.

Marrick taps a message into a com-link, a text-only communication device the size of a pager. If he's concerned about my connection to Jack Arquet, he doesn't show it. Perhaps I'm overreacting. If I'm inherently dangerous, my uncle wouldn't have insisted I sign up for the Tactical Skills Program. He knows how hostile cadets get when competing for points. Look at Gaucini. Unless my uncle doesn't know who my father is? My mother might not have told him.

I drum my fingers on my leg and try to remember if my mother ever mentioned Jack Arquet. Nothing comes to mind, not even in a random memory orb. If she severed their connection, it makes sense I'd have her maiden name, Wilson.

"Update from Reece," Magelon says, holding up a second com-link. "We're clear so far."

"Where's the closest military base to Bio-Tech?" I ask.

"Hawthorne Base, east of Bridgeport," Marrick says. "They have a crack general response team on standby, but we can't rule out a request for C.S.R. assistance from Riverbank Base to scout the highways on the western side of the Sierra."

"Riverbank won't waste time driving the roads," Magelon says. "They'll use a chopper for an air-search and set up a roadblock to perform vehicle checks."

"What if we can't get through before they set up roadblocks?" Discovering the truth about my father's identity might be the least of my worries.

Magelon looks at me in the rear vision mirror. "We cuff you and take credit for your capture."

I stiffen. Is she serious?

"Ignore her," Kelly says. "Our exit's coming up."

I sink lower in my seat and scan the passing traffic. Military vehicles are easy to spot, but C.S.R. teams are allowed to use private vehicles to travel between assignments. That makes every car we pass a potential threat.

Marrick tapping another message draws my attention.

"Can we be traced?" I ask.

"Only if we reply using the same com-link," Marrick says. "This one is to send messages. Magelon's com-link is to receive. Reece has two at his end. Because we don't complete the loop by sending a message back to its source, communication is undetectable."

"I didn't know you could use them that way."

The corner of Marrick's mouth curls up. "I didn't either. Reece is the brains on the tech side of things."

I resume scanning the traffic. I'm glad Marrick's here. If anyone can sort out this mess, it will be him. But he shouldn't dismiss the risk his team takes. If we're stopped, he'll have to say they arrested me, or they'll face arrest themselves. It makes being taken to my uncle even more urgent.

"Here's water if you need it," Marrick says, handing me a plastic bottle.

"Thanks." A metallic taste lingers in my mouth, and I'm thirsty after running through the forest.

I take the bottle, but Marrick grabs my wrist and turns it toward him.

"How did you do this?" He rubs his thumb over the welt.

His concern tugs at my heart, but I pull my hand away. "It's nothing." I don't want to talk about what happened. I might slip up and mention Joanna again, and I much prefer Marrick's current empathy to his earlier harshness.

Joanna: I wish I could stop thinking about her.

Magelon looks over her shoulder. "Is Jack Arquet the reason there's a blank space after your father's name on your military file?"

I stare at her. "You know about that?"

"We pulled your file," Marrick says.

Of course he did. He would've checked me out before deciding if he wanted me on his team. "I suppose you wish you'd picked someone else's file."

Marrick frowns. "Not at all."

He can't still want me. Not after the fool I made of myself in my sharpshooting round. It won't matter, anyway. I haven't graduated.

"I'd have done the same," Magelon says. "You won't get far on any base dragging that family baggage around."

She assumes Jack Arquet is my father. That's logical. I assume the same. But she insinuates I concealed my father's identity on purpose. I don't know how to respond.

Admitting I know nothing about my father doesn't hurt as much as it did with my mother, but I'm not comfortable talking about it. Magelon stops pressing for details, but Marrick and Kelly's silence suggests they jump to the same conclusion.

Irritated at having my family history examined, I open the water bottle and take a long drink. The water washes the metallic taste off my tongue, but I wonder if I'm drugging myself again. Wishing I could rinse my mouth with a high-pressure hose, I recap the bottle and rest it on the seat. And notice Marrick studying me.

He looks at the welt on my wrist, my filthy white clothes, the scratches on my bare feet. What must he think, seeing me in this state? I'm supposed to know how to protect myself, not be an easy abduction victim.

Uncomfortable at his scrutiny, I tug the cardigan's sleeve over my wrist and sit up straight. "Where are we going?"

"Kelly has a property near Grass Valley," Marrick says. "You'll be safe there."

I don't need safe. I need answers. "When we get there, can I call my uncle?"

"Not yet. We'll minimize contact in case his calls are being monitored. We can't risk jeopardizing the cover story he's using to explain your disappearance. Until we're instructed otherwise, our orders are to stay low and keep you out of sight."

I gather my hair together and tug it over my shoulder. "Why did my uncle lie about what happened to me?"

"He didn't want to alert Flannigan that he knew you'd been abducted," Marrick says. "He feared Flannigan would shift you before we got there. To make it look legit, he issued a statement saying your current whereabouts are unknown, then sent a C.S.R. team to search for you."

I take no comfort from imaging my uncle barking orders through his cell phone. This whole scenario is off. "How long have I been missing?"

"Four days."

My face grows cold. The penalty for three days' absence without leave is immediate discharge, one month's jail time, and a lifetime ban on reenlistment. And not graduating from Tactical Skills, or a similar program at another base, I can never join his team. Even if this mess with Flannigan is sorted out, I'd have to repeat a course. I couldn't do it, not after revealing my level of skill. With the competitive nature of any graduate program, I'd be dead before the end of the first week.

I stare out the window, a hard lump forming in my throat from the gravity of my situation. As we get closer to Red Bluff's jurisdiction, which extends from Redding to Sacramento and east to the foothills of the Sierra, another problem arises.

"How is my uncle explaining your absence?"

"He logged us as attending a team training exercise

near San Jose," Marrick says. "We're unavailable for a few weeks."

"Weeks? I need to talk to him now. I need to ask him about Flannigan"—I lower my voice—"and how I'm connected to Jack Arquet."

"It might not be the connection you think," Marrick says quietly.

Why is he so supportive? He can't still want me on his team. It's impossible, anyway, unless he thinks my uncle will intervene and dismiss my *AWOL* charge.

I'll never agree to that. I'd be the privileged niece forever. I swivel on the seat, intent on letting Marrick know I won't rely on my uncle to get me out of sticky situations but sitting close to him like this is strangely familiar. I know him. Not as this team's leader. It's more personal, like I've known him for years and we're more than casual acquaintances. Much more.

Uncomfortable, I turn away and pluck at the sleeve of my cardigan. I'm grateful for his help, that's all. Anything else is ridiculous. We've only met once, that day in my uncle's office. Sure, his warm smile, and the way his gaze held mine, sticks in my memory, but so does Joanna's unsavory remark about earning my uniform.

I won't deny I followed his career, but who doesn't? Anyone wanting to join C.S.R. aspires to be like Marrick. But outside of that, I wouldn't mind having someone to confide in because nothing makes sense. If I can't trust

Marrick, then who?

Summoning the courage to open up, I run my fingers over the welt on my wrist. "The restraints used to stop me escaping did this. And the drugs fed to me caused what I thought were hallucinations, but now I'm not sure because it all feels so real." Remembering my experience in the white room, I draw in a shaky breath. "Flannigan said something about a trial, and because he'd found me, it would succeed. What could he mean?"

"Did he mention performance enhancement drugs?" Marrick asks.

"No. The drugs didn't affect my body, that I'm aware." I touch the side of my neck, and almost mention how Joanna jabbed something at my head, but I can't say her name again. It's probably another hallucination, anyway. I don't feel anything.

It's enough about me, anyway. "What did Flannigan want to know?"

"I hoped you could tell us, but as it's obvious you can't..." He smoothes his long fringe away from his eyes and sighs. "The trial you mentioned fits with what we know."

"What trial?"

"Someone's approached military officials about using drugs to boost soldier performance. We haven't had time to find out who or what, but Flannigan's presenting his research in three weeks. If officials vote in favor of,

Flannigan's drug will be approved for use on all active-duty soldiers."

This makes even less sense. "Why is the military going down a drug path? Everyone knows any performance drugs are damaging to health."

"Because of the current statistics. Call outs to high-level incidents have increased three-fold in the last two years. On a good day, we'll get two hours of downtime between assignments—"

In the front, Magelon scoffs. "If that."

"On a bad day," Marrick continues, unfazed by her interruption, "we may not sleep for over thirty hours. We train to handle extreme situations, but the human body has limits."

"So does the military budget," Kelly says. "Otherwise we'd be wearing out the tread on a fancy armored vehicle instead of banging up our private cars."

I glance from one to the other. "What's money got to do with it?"

"Everything," Marrick says. "When the military took over C.S.R. from local law enforcement, they also took on an accumulated debt for training costs. Darius said officials have been trying to reduce the debt for years. Because of military budget cuts and reduced government funding, it's fallen upon individual bases to cut costs. It's why Red Bluff restricts the number of T.S.P. cadets to eighty per year. Those cadets are the most expensive to train. It should mean an extra sixteen teams, but given the high drop-out rate, we're lucky if we get half that number."

I think back to my group. We lost Nixon and Boyd because of Gaucini. "If instructors stopped the intimidation tactics, more cadets would graduate."

Marrick shrugs. "If a cadet can't handle the pressure during training, they won't handle it on the streets."

"Get tough or get out, right?" I shake my head, still angry I let Gaucini get under my skin. "I guess I failed that test."

"The error belonged to Hayes, not you. He should've triple-checked that last target so there was no confusion. Any one of us could have made the same mistake."

Kelly glances over his shoulder. "For what it's worth, it was a hell of shot."

I appreciate his support, but it doesn't make me feel any better. "If a drug is approved, how will it help lower costs?"

"I assume it means speeding up muscle development," Marrick says. "It would equate to a cut in training time, so less cost involved."

"No soldier would risk their health just so they can run faster."

Marrick sighs. "Don't bet on it. Just because drugs are banned doesn't mean they aren't used. There're always cadets who'll take something to improve their performance, especially around assessment week. On the job it's worse, particularly when fatigue sets in."

Darius was right—I do have a lot to learn about the job outside of Red Bluff's instruction. But I didn't expect it to be a crash course on illicit drug-use. "Do you think Boyd took drugs himself, and it wasn't Gaucini who slipped him something?"

Marrick grimaces. "I wouldn't put anything past Gaucini, but it wouldn't be the first time someone like Boyd, who appeared clean, resorted to desperate measures to win the top graduate title."

Magelon turns around in her seat. "What about you, Sarah? Would you take a drug to boost your performance?"

I stare at her, shocked. "Of course not."

Magelon flicks her gaze to Marrick then turns to face the front again. Is she questioning my improved performance during the assessments?

Heat floods my cheeks. "Darius had me hold back for a reason. You wouldn't know that, not being from Red Bluff." I stop, surprised at myself. It's a catty, not my usual form.

"Just checking," Magelon says. "Don't take everything so seriously."

Kelly catches my eye in the rear vision mirror and gives me a wink. "Ignore her. Performance enhancement drugs don't work that fast. And you'd never fool Darius. He can spot a drug cheat a mile away."

"As Red Bluff's leading trainer, does he get to vote?"

I ask.

"No," Marrick says. "But he's been vocal with his concerns. Not that it's done any good. The military's always looking at innovative technology to improve soldier performance. His methods are proven, but some consider them outdated."

"They should get Darius to set individual schedules, not upgrade from him."

"I agree," Marrick says. "But money talks louder than words, and if Flannigan's developed a drug that boosts physical abilities and shortens training time by months with no ill-health effects, how do you think the officials will vote?"

I lean my head against the back of the seat and stare at the roof. "I don't understand. If Flannigan already has a drug, why does he need me?"

"The drug he's trialing is based on your mother's research," Marrick says. "Darius said you have information he needs to complete it."

I jerk my head down. "My mother's been dead for thirteen years. What would I know about her research?"

"I don't know, but Darius thinks it's the same drug Flannigan trialed years ago, without success. There's nothing more I can tell you at this stage. We were focused on getting you out. Reece is searching for more information, but he hasn't found anything yet."

"When did Flannigan run the trial?"

"Twenty years ago, give or take."

I wipe my hands over my face. How can I help with research conducted before my birth? Flannigan might think I know something, but Joanna abducted me. What am I missing? How is she connected?

I clench my fingers together, thinking hard. The question I should be asking is how is it she's alive? It's crazy to think it, but did she fake her death so she could help Flannigan? Do they need another test subject because there's something wrong with the black-eyed man, something that would cause the trial to fail? That man said he'd unleash hell, and that Jack Arquet was nothing compared to him.

I jolt as a piece of the puzzle unravels. Jack Arquet's records were erased twenty years ago. Did Flannigan use him as a test subject in the earlier trials?

"Could performance drugs cause someone to commit murder?" I ask.

Marrick's eyes bore into mine as though he reads my mind. "You think Arquet was a test subject?"

Kelly lets out a low whistle. "That makes things interesting."

"Darius would've told us if Flannigan's drug caused soldiers to kill each other," Magelon says.

"Unless he didn't know," Marrick says. "We'll run it by Reece, see what he can find out. If Jack Arquet murdered his team because of Flannigan's drugs, any soldier who takes it could behave the same way. That places us all at risk, whether we've taken it or not."

"We should tell my uncle," I say. "He has security clearance and could access classified information about the previous drug trial."

"Reece can, too," Marrick says. "If there are files anywhere, he'll find them."

Magelon glares at Marrick. "No way. We don't know what we're dealing with here."

Marrick raises an eyebrow. "It wouldn't be the first time he's searched for something he shouldn't."

Magelon scowls and turns away.

"Stop worrying," Kelly says. "Reece knows what he's doing."

"Like hell, I won't worry," Magelon snaps. "And you should, too. Both of you."

Her response is a huge backflip for someone who jibed me for being too serious. Why the concern for Reece? He sounds more than capable. If he has security clearance, accessing classified files shouldn't pose a problem. But if he doesn't? If he's caught snooping, he'll face criminal charges.

Going to my uncle is the safer choice. But after lying to me for thirteen years, can I trust he'll tell the truth? He's an expert at deflection. If I want answers, Reece is my best chance. I can also ease Magelon's worry, so we don't waste time arguing about security protocols.

"What if I help Reece? Something we find might help me remember what I'm supposed to know. If we get caught, I'll take the rap. I'll say I used my uncle's clearance codes."

"You'd do that?" Marrick gives me an incredulous look, as if I'm the last person he expected to break the law.

"Why not? I'm already in trouble if everyone thinks I'm *AWOL*. Why not add cyber-crime to the charges?"

Marrick glances at Magelon. She huffs, still not looking happy, but then nods.

"Okay," Marrick says. "You and Reece can work on it as soon as we get home."

Home. That word hurts. Having a home means belonging somewhere, but I've never belonged anywhere. And I'll never get the chance if we're caught digging through sensitive files. But I'm not the only one involved.

I'm prepared to take the rap, but Marrick and his team still risk being charged as accomplices. Darius could face trespass charges. Even my uncle's credentials are on the line by sending out a fake search party. It makes sense everyone is willing to risk their career to stop a drug being used that will cause soldiers to commit murder.

The problem is Joanna, or whoever it was. In her memories, Flannigan said the trial would succeed now I've been found. Did he plan to make me the new test subject? If so, is the drug that caused Jack to murder his team already in me?

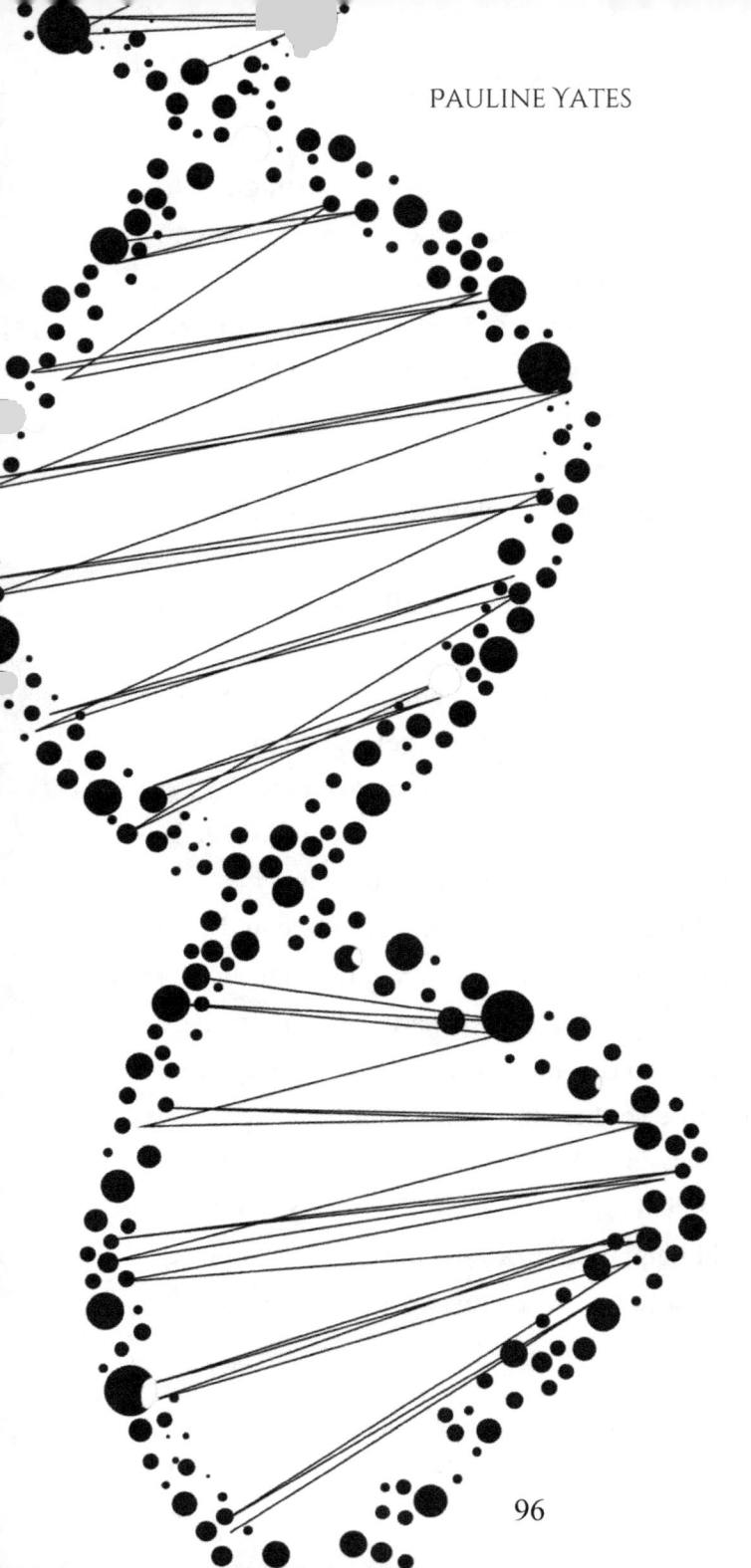

CHAPTER 8

A FIELD OF TALL GRASS running the length of a long, lonely road marks the front of Kelly's property. Beyond a locked gate, a crystal-clear creek flows over the dirt driveway. I can't see the house for the trees. There aren't any neighboring houses, either.

We passed a sign that said South Yuba State Park, but I don't know exactly where we are because I spent much of the drive searching the sky for choppers and worrying about my displays of aggression since escaping Bio-Tech. I wanted to snap Flannigan's neck, kill the soldiers who beat up Darius, hunt down and kill something. Given the circumstances, my retaliation could be forgiven. Who doesn't get angry when threatened, like the incident with Gaucini? But my volatile reactions at Bio-Tech were definitely more sinister.

Kelly stops the Jeep at the gate. While Marrick gets out and opens it, I study the surrounding landscape. A ridge rises beyond the trees, heavily timbered with rocky outcrops. It forms a barrier that isolates us from the outside world. Yet, something about this place puts me on edge.

"Are you sure we're safe here?" I ask Marrick when he gets back in the car.

"You can't get any safer," he says. "It's the only property on this road and is surrounded on three sides by the state forest. It's also not listed as our place of residency between assignments. We like our privacy."

Given the attention his team receives, I don't blame him for having a secret retreat. But my unease increases as Kelly drives through the crossing. The water swooshes against the bottom of the Jeep. On the other side, the track rises on an embankment, then veers left and dips again. The creek reappears on our right. The trees thin, and Kelly's house appears in front of us.

A rustic timber construction, it blends with the surrounding forest. At one end, steps lead up to a wide veranda that spans the front. The handrails sag, vines creep up the posts, and the roof iron is rusty in patches. Though rundown, it has the homely feel I ache for, but something's off.

I know this place.

I know the front screen door squeaks when it rains. A

hallway runs through the center to renovated bedrooms at the back. Out back is a shed used for parking vehicles and storing equipment. A grass clearing leads to the same creek we drove through.

I also know I've never been here before.

Kelly parks the Jeep near the steps. Magelon jumps out before he turns off the ignition. Leaving her door ajar, she runs up the stairs and strides along the veranda. A man with a mop of wavy black hair and wearing a black T-shirt emerges from inside. Reece, I assume. He looks at our car, but Magelon pushes him back inside.

Marrick gets out of the Jeep, jumps up the stairs two at a time, and follows her in.

I stay in my seat. Marrick and Magelon's abrupt departure unsettles me, but it's nothing compared to the jitters the house gives me. My recollection is vivid, as though I've lived here before. Impossible. Apart from Red Bluff and the occasional trip to Sacramento with my uncle, I've never left my hometown of Anderson.

"Come on," Kelly says, turning off the engine. "No sense sitting here when there's a fridge full of food. Are you hungry?"

"No." I get out of the Jeep, food the last thing on my mind. There must be a logical explanation for how I know this house. Did I visit here with my mother? "How long have you owned this property?"

"Been in the family for generations," Kelly says,

heaving himself out of the Jeep. "No one had much use for it after Gramps passed away, so me and my brother took it on. Makes for a great rest stop. Better here than at Red Bluff. Get no peace there. Nothing fancy, but we've got everything we need. Do you fish?"

"No." Growing more alarmed, I look around. Why is it so familiar?

Kelly frowns at my clothes. "I'll find you something else to wear. And a jacket. That thing you're wearing won't cut it. It'll cool down plenty when night falls."

The mention of cold weather makes me hanker for *my* jacket. And my clothes. Joanna took everything, even my bag from my room. No wonder everyone thought I took off. Angry, with myself more than at her, I swipe over the stains on the front of my white shirt. Dirt will wash out, but the pants are ripped in places. Worse than losing my clothes is not having boots. I dread to see the state of my feet beneath the dried mud. I collected scratches during the run through the forest, but I've no idea how bad they are.

"I'll shift some stuff out of the back room and make you up a bed," Kelly says, motioning me toward the stairs. "Mind the renovations at the rear of the house. It's functional, but not finished. The bathroom's at the end of the hallway. You can clean up in there. Got everything you might need. Just make yourself at home."

"Thanks." I appreciate his generosity but settling in is pointless. As soon as I get answers, I'm going home.

The familiarity lessens as I ascend the stairs. Am I mistaken about knowing this house? I look in at the kitchen as we pass the window, but nothing about the cupboards above a long bench, the sawn-cut timber table in the center, or the refrigerator against the far wall stirs any vague recollection of having been here before. I slowly relax. At least I'm in a house and not a cell.

Marrick's voice drifts from somewhere inside. I don't catch what he says, but the sharp edge in Magelon's muffled reply is unmistakable. When we reach the front door, the talking stops.

Marrick returns down the hallway. "Come in and meet Reece."

"I'll fix us some grub." Kelly ruffles my hair with his huge hand—still making light of the situation—then disappears into the kitchen. A pot clanks, then a whiff of gas drifts outside.

Feeling like I've lost my wingman, I step inside and pull the screen door closed behind me to see if it squeaks. It doesn't, but it hasn't rained, either.

I follow Marrick along the hallway, glancing in at Kelly as we pass. Seeing the table again, I recall someone saying it was crafted from a felled tree. A door opposite the kitchen opens to Kelly's bedroom, though how I know it's his is odd because there's nothing to suggest that. The next door, on the right, is closed. I guess it's another bedroom, with a view of the creek. I also imagine two single beds and a large wooden blanket box with a lock.

Creepy uneasiness returns. I could draw some of these details from observations. The creek curves around the house. Kelly owns the property, so it makes sense he'd have the main bedroom at the front. But the locked blanket box? The comment about the kitchen table? Those details are too specific to be drawn from assumptions.

Marrick stops at a doorway opposite the second bedroom. He gives me a reassuring smile. "In here. Reece won't bite."

I'm glad Marrick thinks I'm nervous about meeting Reece. Explaining how I know this house is impossible. Tugging Vera's cardigan around me, I enter the room. Reece sits at a desk with his back to me, typing on a laptop.

He's the only team member I haven't met. Anything I know about him comes from my uncle, or rumor—he's a computer geek, according to Red Bluff gossip. I recall my uncle's grumblings about how a transfer with low training points ended up on Marrick's team. Eager to form an opinion of Reece that isn't filtered through my uncle's view, I cross the room and stand behind him—

Déjà vu: I've done this before, walked across the room and stood behind him. Even the layout adds to the feeling I've been here before. Previously a small living space, it's now Reece's computer hub. A gray blanket covers the window above a long, narrow desk. A three-tier bookshelf stands against the left wall. Cardboard boxes filled with an assortment of knickknacks sit on the bottom shelf. The middle shelf is home to three stacks of fishing magazines. Photos in frames adorn the top shelf. A bearded man, holding up a large fish by its gills, grins at me from a black-and-white photo. The man's likeness to Kelly is strong. Gramps?

Heart hammering, I glance around hoping to find something that's not familiar. On the desk to Reece's left, a cell phone and two com-links sit within hand reach. A modem and printer take up the space on his right. Scattered documents cover the desktop. On the floor beneath, an assortment of electronic devices and cables spill from an open box. It's all exactly how I imagine Reece's workspace to look.

Magelon perches on the arm of a faded, floral green couch in the right-hand corner of the room. Her hand rests on the Beretta in her holster, but the way she frowns at me triggers a tingle in my head like a shot from the Stinger.

Raising my hand, I prod my temple. The tingling sensation stops as quickly as it started, but now Magelon is surrounded by a green hue that reminds me of the green orbs in the memory tunnel. Reece is tinged green, too, but he looks different—his hair is shorter than it was a second ago. His shirt is also blue, not black. He types a series of letters and numbers into a prompt box, pauses, and looks over his shoulder—

I'd rather you didn't mention this to anyone. It's not

103

something I want on my CV.

His voice is in my head. I must be hallucinating because this isn't now, and I'm not me. I'm reliving a memory. Not mine. Joanna's—beyond Reece, his computer screen reflects her face.

She appears as I remember her from my uncle's office. High cheekbones. Styled blonde hair. Clear complexion like she stepped off the front cover of a modeling magazine. Her raised eyebrows jog another thought: Reece is not an average computer geek.

He's a cyber hacker—the type of hacker the military employs because they can't keep them out. No wonder Marrick said he has security clearance. It also explains why Magelon's worried about him accessing sensitive data. If Reece gets caught, he'll face more jail time than any of us.

But there's something else, something no one outside this team knows. He's Magelon's—

"Brother?" The green hue fades, the memory dissolves, and time untwists. Marrick leans against the desk, looking at me expectantly. Reece stands in front of me, holding out his hand. Caught up in the recollection, I didn't notice him get up to greet me.

"The runty one," Reece corrects, eyeing me warily. "How did you know?"

They're twins? I hastily shake his hand to cover my time lapse then glance between them. They look nothing alike. I can't explain how I guessed they're related. But I can deflect. "I thought twins looked the same?"

"Non-identical," Marrick says.

"We didn't know we had a twin until after our mum died a few years ago," Reece says. "Our parents split when we were born. Mum took me. Dad took Mags."

"Quit with the family history lesson," Magelon says. "And don't call me Mags. You make me sound like hired help."

"Sorry, sis," he says, grinning.

Everything about this picture is wrong. Reece looks nothing like a typical C.S.R. team member. If Kelly, with his muscular frame, represents the higher end of the C.S.R. scale, Reece, with his wiry body and lack of muscle tone, represents the lower end. It explains my uncle's grumblings. Reece would never have passed the physical component of any tactical skills program.

Unlike Magelon. Her nature runs hot and cold, but I'm glad I didn't face her during training. Her taut muscles give her sun-tanned skin a vibrant, power-packed sheen. Physically, Reece and Magelon are poles apart, but...

Both transfers from Lakeport. Both placed on Red Bluff's best team. Coincidence? Or did Reece hack his way into Marrick's unit so they could stay together?

Marrick catches my eye as though he reads my mind but appears unperturbed I might have guessed Reece's secret. Is it because I'm prepared to break rules to get the information we need? I look away but can't help feeling like I passed a test.

Reece returns to his seat and opens a Team Tracker page showing the location of all C.S.R. teams on duty.

"You got through just in time," he says. "Flannigan requested assistance from Hawthorne, as we expected. They sent backup to Bio-Tech and set up vehicle check points at Coleville, Dardanelle, and Bridgeport. Riverbank received a request from Hawthorne for air support an hour ago. They sent a chopper. It's sweeping the fire access tracks near the northern entrance of the forest. There's been no request to extend the search triangle at this stage. Flannigan must think you're still in the area."

"What information did he give Hawthorn?" Marrick asks.

"Not enough to keep them longer than twenty-four hours. An unidentified group attempting to break into Bio-Tech is all that came through the dispatch. Plus that two security guards were injured."

My hopes for Darius lift. "Does that mean Darius got away?"

"Not sure," Reece says. "If he did, he'd have contacted us by now."

"What's Flannigan playing at?" Magelon asks. "Why call for help if he doesn't release Sarah's description?"

"To conceal her identity," Marrick says. "I bet he's hoping for a team to stumble across a suspicious vehicle with multiple occupants. When they find nothing, they'll call off the search. Who Flannigan sends after is our worry."

"To where?" Magelon asks. "He'll raise questions if he stakes out Sarah's house at Anderson. That's our jurisdiction."

"He might keep his people off the grid," Marrick says. "Have you found out where Flannigan's drawing those soldiers from yet?"

Reece shakes his head. "If they stay incognito, they won't show on the Team Tracker. I've searched everything I can think of, but nothing links Bio-Tech to any military base. There's no mention of a drug trial or the vote, either. I'll keep at it, but it'll take time."

Mysterious military connections operating off grid refresh my worry for Darius. "Now I'm here, can you go back and look for Darius? What if he escaped and is stranded in the forest?"

"We can't do anything while the search for us is underway," Marrick says.

But he'll return, that much is clear. Hope for Darius lifts. If anyone can find him, it'll be Marrick.

"What about Arquet?" Magelon says. "How do we find out about him when his files are erased?"

"Haven't I taught you anything? We don't need his military file to find him." Reece opens another page on the screen. "I'll run a general search. Aside from his name, what else do you know about him?"

107

"Sarah?" Marrick asks. "Did your mother mention Jack?"

"If she did, I don't remember."

"What about your uncle?" Reece asks.

I shake my head.

Reece frowns. "Other family members? Grandparents?"

I cross my arms. "No."

Magelon shoots me a contemptuous look. "There must be someone in your family who knows him?"

I keep my eyes on the computer screen. "I don't have a family."

Everyone falls silent. I wish I'd kept my mouth shut. I hate this. Hate revealing personal details that are nobody else's business.

"He'll turn up," Reece says, typing again. "Did Flannigan say anything else, even if it made no sense?"

"Nothing about Jack Arquet," I say. "He mentioned my mother, though. He said she died because of what she did to herself." My breath catches in my throat. Revealing this is like pulling off a scab and finding something nasty underneath.

"How did she die?" Marrick asks.

"She didn't recover from an illness. That's all I know."

"Symptoms?" Reece asks.

I shrug. "Tired, I suppose?"

"That's helpful," Magelon says, rolling her eyes.

"It does help. Sarah's mother could have been involved in the production of performance enhancement drugs," Reece says, excitement rising in his voice. "What did she do? What were her qualifications?"

"I don't know that, either."

I've never felt so useless. All these questions I can't answer. Is that my uncle's fault for not telling me, or mine for not asking?

"Come eat," Kelly hollers from the kitchen.

"Keep looking," Marrick says to Reece. He turns to Magelon. "Show Sarah where she can clean up. And find her something else to wear."

"What am I? A dress shop?" When Marrick frowns, she rolls her eyes and huffs. "Fine. Sarah, come with me."

I follow her from the room but have no interest in food and fresh clothing. All this talk about my mother dredges up the memory of the last time I saw her. I imagine my uncle's solid oak front door swinging closed, blocking her from view. The dim light in his hallway closes around me, filling me with a crushing sense of abandonment.

My mother shattered my belief she'd always be there for me, and I haven't been able to piece that back together. Now, when I need her most, I can't remember anything about her. Why can I recall Joanna's memories but not my mother's?

Was it because I blocked her out the moment that

door closed? I punished her by forgetting her. That's why I never asked about her, why I pretend, like my uncle, she doesn't exist.

A tear wells in my eye. The truth hurts, but there's no time for self-pity. I need information about my mother and her research. It must be in my head, in my memories, because in the memory tunnel, I recalled things I didn't know about her. Joanna messed up my mind, but she also did me a favor. If I can find those gold orbs, I might recall the information we need. I just hope dabbling in something I don't understand doesn't make me lose it like Arquet.

CHAPTER 9

MAGELON STORMS INTO HER ROOM and returns with a faded black tank top, gray leggings, and a pair of threadbare sneakers smelling like mice nested in them.

Handing me the items, she points along the hallway.

"Bathroom's that way."

I don't need directions. The renovations are how I imagine them, too. What used to be an open back veranda is now closed in. The room to my right is used for storage. It's full of furniture covered in sheets, cardboard boxes, and carpentry tools. Around the corner are two new bedrooms, one for Marrick, the other, Joanna's. Her presence is strong in that area, and my neck prickles as if I expect her to step out of her room.

Uncomfortable, I look at the other renovations. The space between the bathroom and bedrooms ends at a door that's nailed shut. I know without seeing there's a set of unfinished steps on the other side. Opposite the bathroom, a rectangular piece of plywood covers a cut out in the wall, a future window. The view will look out to the creek beyond the grass clearing.

Clutching the clothes to my chest, I hurry to the bathroom. I shouldn't know any of this and that I do creeps me out. Once inside the newly-tiled bathroom and out of Magelon's view, pent-up emotions spill over. Dropping the clothes onto the floor, I go to the sink and splash cold water over my face, then lean on my hands, head down.

What am I doing? I should find concrete evidence Joanna's alive, not worry why this house is familiar. I didn't imagine her reflection on Reece's computer screen. Or guess Reece and Magelon are siblings. Joanna's memories gave me that information. I need to figure out how that's possible.

Standing straight, I wipe back my hair and look at the mirror above the sink. My face is pale, and my eyes are strained, but I'm not tired. I'm wired like a ball of energy inside me is a snap from exploding. Vera said it's crucial I return to familiar surroundings, but though not at home, my reflection has a calming effect and I feel more...more me. It also helps untangle my thoughts. If I have Joanna's memories, it makes sense I know this house. She would have spent time here and I'm seeing what she saw.

It doesn't mean she's alive, though. I believe she is, but without proof, I won't convince anyone else.

"There's another explanation," I say to my reflection. "Joanna could be on my mind because, had I joined this team, I would have taken her place."

Confronting the truth is sobering. I already knew I'd replace Joanna, but have I been unconsciously comparing myself to her all this time? She was Marrick's second-in-command. How would I fill her shoes? I'm nowhere near as skilled as her.

The mirror reflects my widening eyes. Why think that? I've had moments of self-doubt, but nothing like this. I did the training. My skills are exceptional. Why wouldn't I measure up?

I scowl at myself. "Be honest. You're a good fit for this team. And Darius was right about not having to worry about my uncle interfering. Marrick's following my uncle's directives, but he runs his team his way. Look around you. You'd have a life here."

I won't have any life if I keep conjuring random memories. For all I know, I'm still affected by drugs and hallucinating. Food would help. A savory aroma drifts beneath the bathroom door and my stomach growls. Eager to eat and shake off the effects of the drugs, I take off Vera's cardigan and strip out of the white shirt.

Standing in my underwear—at least some clothes are

mine—I tend to my injuries. I wash my feet in the shower, first, and find multiple scratches. They're not deep, but the water runs a muddy-red down the drain from where they bled. Returning to the sink, I splash water over the welt on my wrist, then inspect my arm. A purple bruise surrounds multiple needle marks. No wonder I'm hallucinating. Joanna must have pumped drugs into me every day. The only other injury is a red splotch spreading over the side of my hip from the baton strike. It doesn't hurt, but it's going to leave a wicked bruise.

There's a Magelon thump on the door. "Did you die in there?" she calls.

"You wish," I mutter. "Coming."

I get dressed, pull on the sneakers, then rake my hair straight and flick it off my shoulders. I tie Vera's cardigan around my waist and roll the white shirt and pants into a bundle. Going to the door, I yank it open. Magelon stands in front of me, fist raised to bang. Lowering her hand, she looks at my arm.

"What did Flannigan do? Use you as a pincushion? I've seen drug addicts with less track marks."

I give her a smug smile. "Takes one to know one."

She glowers. My face grows hot, melting my smile. Why accuse her of using drugs when her record is as clean as mine? Embarrassed, I hold out the bundle of clothes. "What shall I do with these?"

She snatches it from my hands. "Burn them."

She strides back through the house, making the floor vibrate from her thumping steps. I follow, but glance in at Reece as we pass the computer room. He sits at the desk, eyes fixed on the laptop screen. I'd like to sit with him and search for information about Flannigan's previous drug trial, but I should eat before another unsavory comment jumps from my mouth. I've irritated Magelon too many times today. I don't know why I keep doing that.

In the kitchen, Marrick and Kelly sit at the table, scraping food from their plates. Magelon dumps the bundle on the floor, then sits beside Marrick.

Kelly pulls out the chair next to him and prods my plate with his fork.

"There's plenty more if you need it."

I sit on the offered chair. The meal is simple—fried eggs on toast, a slice of grilled tomato and sprigs of parsley scattered over the top. I cut the corner off a piece of toast and—

"I found him," Reece calls.

Dropping the knife and fork, I jump up, knocking back my chair. Kelly grabs it before it hits the floor, but I don't wait to apologize. Chairs scrape, but I'm the first to reach Reece. I stand behind him and stare at his screen.

"I can't find Arquet's military files," Reece says as the others crowd around us. "But I found this."

He nods at a photo on the screen, a newspaper article. A boy dressed in a school uniform shakes hands with a man wearing a jacket emblazoned with a fire and rescue logo. I don't recognize either of them.

"That's Jack Arquet, aged fifteen," Reece says, pointing to the boy. "The other man is Captain James Grant, Fire and Rescue. He presented Arquet with a bravery award for rescuing a family of three from a submerged vehicle after it crashed into a river in Arquet's hometown."

"What kind of kid hero goes on to murder his team?" Kelly asks.

"There's more." Reece scrolls down the page. "His parents, Margaret and Collin Arquet, along with his older sister Katherine, attended the ceremony." He types on the keyboard and brings up a photo from a senior school yearbook.

"Katherine Arquet. Your mother."

It's my face.

I grip the back of Reece's chair. Now I understand what Vera meant when she said Flannigan found me because I looked like my mother. Of similar age, we look identical, right down to our long brown hair.

"If that's Sarah's mother," Magelon says, "that makes Jack, Sarah's uncle."

I shake my head. "This can't be possible."

Because if Jack Arquet is my uncle, who's John Wilson? A family friend? My father? He's twenty years older than my mother, but why else would I share his surname? Unless he's not my father, and only pretends to be my uncle to protect me from Flannigan. If that's true, how dangerous is the information I know that warrants giving me a new identity and cutting me off from everyone?

Don't let him learn the truth; conceal her identity: that's what my mother said to John Wilson. She also told Jack *this* would change everything, whatever she meant by that. What did my mother do to Jack? To herself? Is that what Flannigan wants to know?

Marrick rests his hand on my shoulder. "Sarah?"

I shrug him off. I need to untangle the facts, but my thoughts are spiraling. My mother's research; Flannigan's trials; Jack possibly a test subject. Jack's death. My mother's death. All records erased. I'm the next living relative, and Flannigan wants what I know. Is it what I know, or who I am?

"She's not looking good," Kelly says.

"Sarah, talk to me," Marrick urges.

I don't want to talk. I need to figure this out. I press my fingers to my temples and think about what Flannigan said. He asked for my name but wanted me to say it, not for him to reveal it. Why? Even if I said Sarah Arquet, what would it prove? And how would that answer explain Joanna's involvement? The memories I saw about Jack Arquet are related to me, not her, but trying to find the connection to Joanna leaves me more confused than ever. I need more information. There's only one person who can give it to me.

I glance at the cell phone on the desk. "I'm calling my uncle."

"Not from here," Magelon says.

"Then take me somewhere I can. I'll drive the Jeep myself if I have to."

I lean over and grab the phone. As I close my hand around it, my head tingles again, then a rhythmic pulse starts like birds pecking at the inside of my skull. I stare at the phone, wondering what caused the odd sensation when a soft beep echoes from under Reece's desk.

"Stop!" Reece says, jumping up from his chair.

Alarmed, I drop the phone. It clatters against the com-links. Reece reaches into a box and pulls out a small electronic device. I recognize it—a wireless signal detector. He fiddles with a dial, then holds it in front of me. Nothing happens.

"Pick up the phone again," he says.

I do as he asks, growing more alarmed by the second. The signal detector beeps and a green light flashes on. The pulsing strobe makes my head ache.

"She's bugged," Reece says. "The phone's boosting the signal."

"Are you sure?" Marrick asks, stepping to my side.

"Great." Magelon steps around Marrick and starts patting me down. "She'll lead a team straight to us."

She bumps my elbows, wanting me to raise my arms so she can search my body for a concealed tracker. I comply. If Magelon finds something, this home visit is over. Flannigan could be on his way here right now.

"What's this?" Magelon asks, fishing Flannigan's keycard out of the cardigan's right pocket.

I forgot I had it. "I stole it from Flannigan."

Reece takes the key card and the phone from my hand. He runs the signal detector over them, then waves it around me. The signal detector stays mute.

"It picked up something," Reece says, frowning. "Hold the phone again."

He hands me the phone. As soon as I touch it, the ache in my head returns. Reece fiddles with dials, but as I wait for him to offer an explanation, images flash through my mind, places I've never been to, faces I don't recognize. Terrified of falling into the memory tunnel, I toss the phone onto the desk and squeeze my eyes shut, willing my mind to clear. The ache stops. The images fade. Opening my eyes, I look up to see everyone staring at me.

"It's not a tracker," Reece says.

"How can you tell?" Kelly asks.

"I set this to the I.S.M. band. It's a non-communication band used in microwaves, remote controls and," he glances at Marrick, "medical implants."

Marrick's eyes darken. "Have you checked yourself for unexplained injuries?"

The punch to the head; the silver instrument. Panic rising at dismissing the incident as a hallucination, I touch the back of my neck. "Here."

"You didn't think to mention it?" Magelon snaps.

"I didn't have time to write a list," I retort, angry my oversight could draw Flannigan right to me.

Marrick raises his hand to mine. "Show me."

I guide his fingers to the tender spot at the base of my skull. Marrick pushes my hand aside and parts my hair.

"Feel this," he says. "It's pink, like it's been laser sealed." He takes my finger and presses it against a smooth patch of skin the size of a coin.

"Looks like an entry point to me," Magelon says, peering over Marrick's shoulder. She slides a knife from her belt. "One way to find out what's in there."

"What are you, a brain surgeon?" Kelly says, stepping between us.

"Nobody's cutting anything," Marrick says. "Would military tracking equipment detect her whereabouts?"

"As long she doesn't hold a phone or something else electronic that would act as a signal booster, unlikely," Reece says.

"This is crazy," Magelon says. "What if we're dealing with new technology? I don't know about you guys, but until we know for sure, the safest place for Sarah is back with her uncle."

"No," Marrick says. "We're not going anywhere until we hear from Darius."

"What if we don't?" Magelon asks.

I tune out their arguing and run my fingers over the coin-size bare patch. I must have missed it when I checked the area earlier. Easy to do, with my thick hair. But finding this changes things. Not only do I have other people's memories, I have an unknown medical implant in my head. I don't know what we're dealing with. Neither does Marrick or Reece. The only safe option is for me to leave. I won't put this team at risk. Marrick doesn't appear to want to make that call. But I can.

Pushing past Kelly, I stride from the room. When I reach the screen door, I kick it open with such force, my foot almost rips the mesh. I'm halfway along the veranda, intent on taking the Jeep and driving home, when Marrick runs out of the house.

"Sarah, wait." He grabs my arm and pulls me to a stop.

I yank from his grip. "Magelon's right. I'm not safe here. And you're not safe hiding me. I need to go home and talk to my uncle." Referring to him as my uncle makes bile rise in my throat, but I've called him that for too long to suddenly change.

"If Flannigan catches you, you'll never know the truth," Marrick says. "Let us do our job. We can protect you."

"What if you can't? What if this is new technology, or has something to do with the drugs Flannigan's developing? We've already established they might be why

Jack Arquet murdered his team. What if he had a similar implant and this"—I stab my finger at my head—"causes me to behave like him?"

Marrick's expression hardens. "You're not Jack Arquet."

"I'm not Sarah Wilson, either. I'm Sarah Arquet, but she's a stranger to me."

Marrick clamps his hand on my shoulder. "I know you need answers. But give Reece a chance to find what we need to know."

"What if he can't?"

"He hasn't failed us yet."

I turn and lean on the railing. The sun shines over the veranda, but I'm shadowed by a darkness that comes from within me. Lies and deception trace back to before my birth and cloud everything I know. John Wilson could be my father. My real uncle, Jack, is a murderer. My mother is more a stranger than ever. I don't even know who I am. Add in Joanna, the hallucinations, the strange memories and now an unknown medical implant in my head, I'm not only a danger to myself, but to anyone I come in contact with.

I turn away to hide my distress. "I don't know what to do."

Marrick places his hand on my shoulder and turns me back to face him. "Then stay with us until you do."

He's not going to let me go. Resolve to help me burns

in his eyes. I'm so afraid of being let down again, but I don't think Marrick would do that to me. It's not him. The problem is me. It's come down to trust, and right now, I have to trust somebody, and Marrick's my only certainty.

Resigning to my only option, I let out a long breath. "Okay. I'll stay. But only until we learn more."

Marrick sighs, too, but I hope he keeps his guard up and doesn't place too much trust in me. I'd hate him to discover I'm exactly like Jack Arquet.

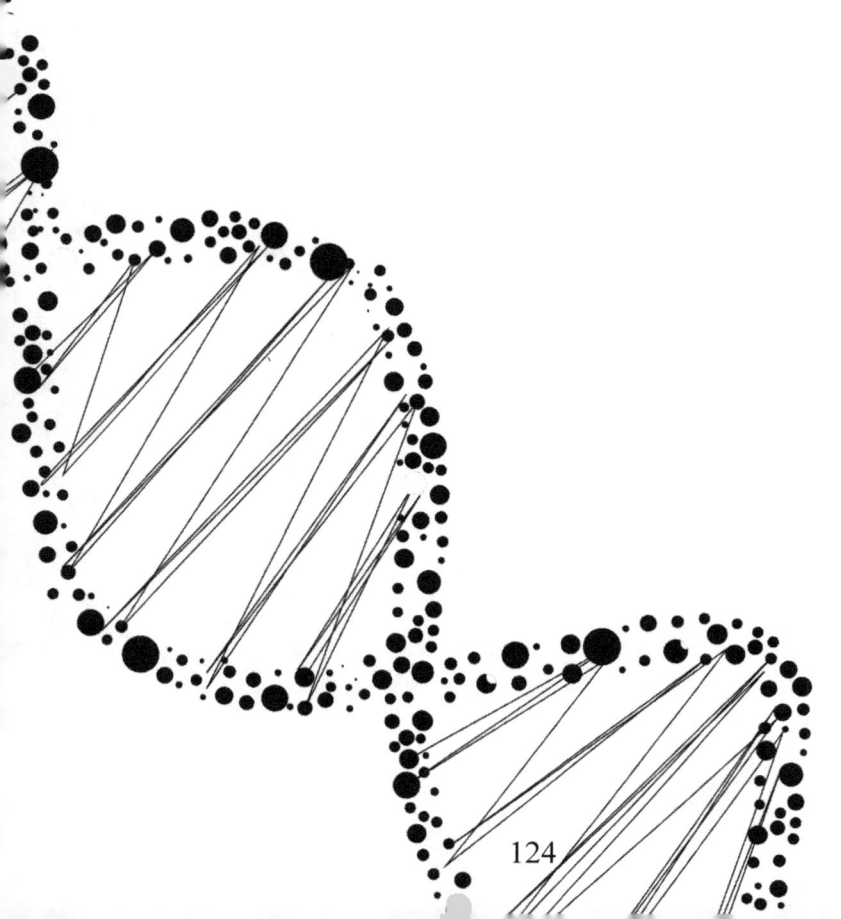

CHAPTER 10

MARRICK AND I RETURN INSIDE, but an argument between Magelon and Reece drifts from the computer room. When Magelon hisses my name, I doubt anything I do will earn her trust.

Kelly meets us in the hallway. "Twin spat. You'll get used to it. Come outside and help me unload the Jeep."

Relieved for an excuse to avoid Magelon, I head back to the veranda. Marrick continues down the hall.

"Don't let Magelon bother you," Kelly says, catching up to me. "She's just antsy because she thinks Reece doesn't take things as seriously as he should."

"It's okay. She's every right to feel that way."

I jump down the stairs, worry about the implant, and my sketchy past, weighing heavy on my mind. Kelly continues to the Jeep, but needing a moment alone, I walk around the side of the house.

The shed, the grass clearing, and the large tree near the creek add another layer of uneasiness. Everything is exactly as I imagine. There's a hole in the wall where the new window will go. A pile of timber for a new set of steps is stacked beneath the house to protect it from rain. An iron water tank sits between the house and a wooden three-bay shed. The roof is more rust than iron and I recall Kelly saying he needs to replace it before the next storm season. Timber double doors on the first bay sag on their hinges. The second bay has double doors, too, held closed by a lock and chain. A single door gives access to the third bay. I imagine a rusted key stuck in the lock.

I rub my neck. Is the implant to blame for these clear recollections?

Kelly parks the Jeep in front of the shed, and I cross the clearing to join him. Water runs through a drainpipe beneath the house. Someone takes a shower. Magelon, hopefully. She needs to cool off.

Kelly gets out of the Jeep and meets me at the back of the car. Lifting the rear hatch, he pulls out a green canvas bag and hands it to me. Metal clinks inside, suggesting tools. He picks up a similar bag and slings it over his shoulder.

"I'll give you a tour in case you need to find something in a hurry," he says.

I nod. Revealing I already know where everything is won't improve our relations.

Kelly slaps his hand on the hood. "Keys are always in the ignition. There's a drum of fuel behind the shed. The key to the front gate is in a notch at the bottom of the hinge-side of the post. You'll find it easily enough."

Going to the double doors, he lifts the wooden toggle and pulls open one side to reveal a parking space for the Jeep. Three trail bikes stand in the middle bay. A workbench fills the third bay, covered in tools and crates overflowing with ropes. Shelves line the walls, crammed with boxes, paint tins, tools and gardening equipment, tackle boxes, and bags of netting. Cobwebs claim a window in the middle bay. Above, three fishing rods hang from the rafters. Below it, more shelving, more boxes. In the far corner, a metal crate sits on the dirt floor.

The crate jogs a memory of Magelon arguing. Afraid of suffering another hallucination, I look away and focus on Kelly.

"There's a ton of stuff in here we don't use," Kelly says, taking the bag from me and shoving it into a space on a shelf. "Do you know how to ride a motorcycle?"

"I've got all my licenses." What is it about that crate?

"Good. You never know what vehicle you might need to borrow"—he makes quote marks with his fingers—"if a pursuit takes to the streets."

He talks like he's prepping me for an assignment. But

my gaze falls upon the metal crate again—

Did you get special clearance to take that from base, or is this Reece's doing?

Joanna's voice fills my mind as I recall her berating Magelon. Tensing, I prod my head. Joanna's memories are growing clearer. It must be the implant. I couldn't imagine her speaking this way if I tried.

Noticing my interest in the crate, Kelly goes to it and opens the lid to reveal plastic-wrapped blocks of C4, the blue putty-like substance used in explosives training at Red Bluff. It's no secret Magelon is an explosives expert. Is Joanna's memory clearer because I'm enhancing it with information I know?

"How did Magelon get permission to bring it here?" As soon as I ask, I know the answer. Reece forged the application papers. Did I assume that, knowing what Reece does, or did I draw that information from Joanna's memories?

"The way Magelon gets permission for anything." Grinning, he picks up a block and bounces it on his hand. "It's safe in its raw form. Just don't put a naked flame anywhere near this stuff. Can you believe Magelon wanted to store this in the house? Joanna went off her nut when she heard." He grimaces. "Had to agree. There are enough explosives in this crate to blow the roof sky high."

He's referring to the argument I imagined. If the implant is to blame, it's insidious how it fills my head with specific details. What technology could do that?

"Have to admit, it comes in handy when we're in a hurry," Kelly says, returning the block to the crate. "Magelon makes all our blasters. Big, small, whatever we need. Saves us having to race back to Red Bluff."

Needing a break from the war in my mind, I cross to the door and scan the clearing. A punching bag hangs from the tree. Behind the tree is the creek, behind it, the roadside field. The other direction is all forest.

Kelly comes to the doorway. Raising his hand, he draws a line in the air from the clearing to the top of the mountain. "From here up, the creek marks the property boundary. Beyond that, it's state forest right down to the Yuba River." He points north. "Got a cabin down yonder. Good fishing, if the season's right."

Odd. I can't imagine his cabin. Or the river. "Does everyone fish?"

"Nah. Fishing's my gig. Marrick comes sometimes. Reece, if I can get him off the computer. Magelon came once, but she tried shooting the fish and scared them away." He chuckles.

That sounds like Magelon. "What about Joanna?"

His smile fades. "Fishing didn't interest her."

Is that why I can't picture the cabin? It doesn't sound like Joanna's ever been there. Why, when everyone else has at one time or another?

"I've never fished," I say, curious about Joanna's

relationship with her team members. "Could you take me sometime?"

"You betcha," Kelly says, his eyes brightening. "Fair warning, though. Threading worms onto a hook is a turnoff for some people."

"Like Joanna?"

"Yeah. She didn't like the smell of fish, either."

Doesn't like fish. Argued with Magelon. Disapproved of Reece. For team members who've been together for three years, it sounds like a lot of things annoyed her.

Confused, I walk across the clearing to the punching bag. Raising my fist, I tap my knuckles against the weathered leather. The rope creaks as the bag swings.

Kelly joins me and pats the bag. "She's seen some time hanging here."

"Did you box before you enlisted?"

"Could've been a heavyweight champion." He puffs out his chest and rolls his shoulders back. "I decided my skills were better used elsewhere." He punches the bag, grinning like a kid playing with his favorite toy. "Did Darius teach you how to throw a decent punch?"

"In my combative sessions. But we focused more on grappling and clinch drills, disarming weapons, finishing techniques, things like that."

"Heard you were pretty good in the finishing department. Rare for a cadet to win every round during assessment week. Still, it won't hurt to have boxing skills up your sleeve. Give you some tips if you like."

"Yes, please." I punch the bag, remembering how I floored Gaucini in the assessment. I should've given him an uppercut to the jaw. It would have silenced his threat to break my arm.

"Let's see where you're at," Kelly says. "Give that bag a one, two."

I step to the bag but hesitate. Kelly's an expert, and his scrutiny makes me uneasy. What if he thinks less of me if I don't execute a perfect punch?

I catch the thought. It's the second time today I've questioned my abilities. I can't recall ever losing confidence in myself like this. Shaking it off, I reflect on what Darius taught me, then slam my fist into the bag. It feels good to hit something, to hear the familiar whack of my fist on leather. Raising my left hand, I strike the bag again, harder. The bag spins.

"Hold up," Kelly says, grabbing the bag. "You've got a ton of strength, but your technique's all wrong. Step aside. Watch and learn."

I move away, giving Kelly space. He adjusts his footing then drives his fist into the bag so fast the movement is a blur.

"Watch my body. Swivel your feet and hips, that's what generates your power. The strike is at the end of your hip to shoulder turn." He does another set of punches, then stops and holds out his arm. "Keep your wrist straight. Did Darius show you how to make a fist?"

"Yeah." I curl my fingers.

"Tighter. I don't want to see your fingernails. Lock that thumb down. It strengthens your wrist."

"We taped our wrists and hands for support during training."

"You won't have time to tape your hands if you corner a crim and they put up a fight. It's better to punch with the flat part of your palm to minimize injury, but sometimes you'll only get one hit, and you need to make it count. On the streets, your hands, feet, elbows, knees, even your head, are your weapons. Use all of them, or you'll lose. Can't have that."

"What about the combative skills we learned?"

"All necessary, but we deal with some real mongrels on the street. Three things. Never let your guard down. Always watch your back. And make your first punch count. Got it? Okay, let's see how you go."

Repositioning, I mimic how Kelly moved his body and throw another punch.

"Better." He grips the bag with both hands to stop it from swinging. "Again."

I punch with my left hand. The leather stings my knuckles. I switch back to my right and snap out two punches in a row.

"Now you've got it. Feet, hips, shoulder, fist. That's

your line for maximum power. Keep your wrist straight. Strike, retract. Strike, retract. Remember, you're protecting yourself as well as attacking. Keep those elbows locked to your sides. Don't let them flap around. You're not a bird. Eyes on the target"—he drums his fingers on the bag— "look anywhere else and you won't see your opponent's fist until it hits you in the face."

My jabs get harder, faster. Without gloves, my knuckles bleed, but I don't stop. Punching the bag vents my pent-up anxiety and sweeps away my self-doubt. Confidence restored, I pummel the bag with everything I've got.

Kelly's body jerks in time with my strikes. Darius did this—held the bag for me during training. I imagine him standing where Kelly stands, absorbing my strikes, delivering instructions. Another image floods my mind— Darius being gut-punched by the soldiers. Enraged, I slam my fist into the bag. The impact knocks Kelly off his feet. He falls against the tree.

"Hold it." Righting himself, he steps around the bag and gives me a curious look. "That was a hell of a punch."

I wipe my hair from my eyes. "Sorry. Worrying about Darius distracted me."

"Don't worry about Darius. He's smarter than all of us put together." He looks at my bleeding knuckles. "Good a time as any to call it quits."

I don't want to stop. Punching the bag releases more

than pent-up emotions. It's an opportunity to attack the uncertainty I face, the lies I've been told, the questions about who I am. However, during this workout, I didn't think about Joanna once. Likely because this punching drill is familiar to me, reinforcing what Vera meant about returning to familiar surroundings.

Kelly looks at something behind me. I glance over my shoulder. Magelon strides across the clearing. Her white tank top exposes multiple tattoos on her shoulders, intricate Celtic symbols including a small Trinity Knot on her upper left arm. Her hair is damp and slicked flat, confirming she's the one who showered. Pity she didn't scrub the scowl off her face.

She stops with arms akimbo and glares at Kelly. "Marrick wants Sarah."

"What's going on?" Kelly asks.

"Reece found more on Sarah's mother." Her icy tone suggests the shower didn't help her mood, either. "Take one guess what she studied in college."

"I'm not in the mood for guessing," Kelly says, the cheer in his voice gone. "Been too much of that already."

"Then come and see for yourself." Turning, she strides back across the clearing.

"What's Reece found now?" Kelly mutters.

"Aren't you bothered I'm related to Jack Arquet?" I ask.

"Nope. And you shouldn't let it bother you, either.

One bad egg doesn't make the rest rotten."

Relieved to have Kelly's confidence, I hurry ahead of him to the house. Hopefully, my mother's studies will clue me in to what Flannigan wants. When I reach the stairs, I'm blinded by a flash as though I walked face first into a yellow memory orb. My mother's voice fills my mind—

Results show a marked increase in speed, strength, and stamina, but the negative immune responses and heightened aggression in all test subjects are a concern.

Her research—

The viral vector we used in the DNA transduction process isn't inactive as we thought.

I know what she studied—

It's possible the vector reacted to the increase in adrenaline production and triggered the vector's natural defensive mechanism.

She holds a master's degree in virology.

Doctor Flannigan, I need more time. Proceeding with the field trial without understanding the effect the vector has on the host will risk those soldiers' lives.

Not 'those' soldiers. Her brother, Jack. And his team.

Horrified, I grip the handrail. This memory proves Jack was a test subject, but despite my mother's warning, Flannigan proceeded with the field trial; murder/suicide the result. If a viral vector caused Jack's out-of-character behavior, that must be what Jack meant when he said, *it's not you I'm killing.*

That much makes sense. But speed, strength, stamina? I'm stronger and faster than my fellow cadets—who else could knock Kelly off his feet? I'm unsure about my stamina; I've never been pushed, but I never get overly tired, either. I displayed heightened aggression when I pinned Flannigan against the wall. And despite my mother's efforts to prevent Flannigan from learning the truth, or discovering my identity, I'm perfect according to him and the trial will succeed.

My blood runs cold. There's only one reason why Flannigan would think that.

I'm genetically enhanced like Jack.

No, no, no. It's not possible. I'd know if my abilities weren't normal. Or would I? Darius had me hide my skills and I've never been given the opportunity to test my limits.

"Stop worrying," Kelly says, slapping his hand on my shoulder and nudging me up the steps. "Whatever Reece found can't be any worse than what we already know."

It is worse. I display everything my mother wanted to enhance. Flannigan didn't want my help to perfect her research. I am her research. I'm proof it works.

At another nudge from Kelly, I continue up the stairs. We found common ground, but he can't know about this. No one can. I'll be treated like a leper, a fraud, a cheat. Or worse. It's stupid to think I'll fit in with this team. I've never fit in anywhere and now I know why.

I hurry along the veranda, but I'm struck by a horrible

realization. The viral vector. My mother mentioned negative immune responses. Flannigan said I'd suffer her fate. If the vector killed my mother, will I die, too?

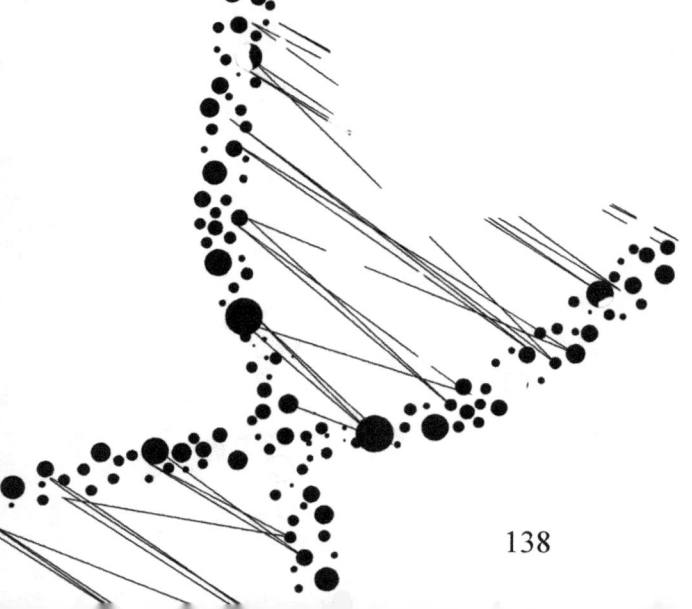

CHAPTER 11

I
T'S HARD TO CONCENTRATE ON what Reece reads from his computer when I'm plotting a return to Bio-Tech. That's where I should go for answers, where my mother conducted her research, and where hopefully, I'll jog more of her memories. I'll take one of the trail bikes. The key to the front gate is in the notch on the post. I just need Flannigan's keycard so I can get inside Bio-Tech undetected. I don't know where Reece put it, but it will be an easy steal. Once he's alone, I'll ask to see it, so Magelon doesn't see me swipe it.

I give Reece my full attention. I'm learning more from him about my mother than my uncle ever told me.

"Your mother held a degree in biotechnology," Reece says, reading from a document on the laptop, "and a

Master's degree in Virology. Bio-Tech was her first job. Doctor Michael Robert Flannigan, Bio-Tech's head geneticist, employed her as his research assistant."

I cross my arms to resist shoving Reece out of the chair so I can look up if there's anything other than increased speed and strength that proves I'm genetically enhanced. I could ask, but don't want to reveal my suspicion until I know more. The chance the vector will kill me is bad enough without also being labeled a freak. I already want to crawl out of my skin. Imagine how everyone else will react.

"What does a geneticist want with a virologist?" Kelly asks.

He stands too close for my comfort, considering I feel like a leper.

Marrick sits on a chair next to Reece. Magelon perches on her usual spot on the arm of the couch. She shoots Kelly a sardonic look.

"Why do you think? Flannigan's messing around with DNA."

"We don't know that," Marrick says.

He's dressed in a navy T-shirt and denim jeans. Water drips from his hair down his neck, suggesting a hasty exit from the shower. He frowned at my bloodied knuckles but said nothing else. After learning what my mother researched, does he question my performances at Red Bluff?

"What's DNA got to do with anything?" Kelly asks.

"Genetics and virology could mean Flannigan's conducting gene doping experiments," Reece says. "It would explain why I can't find anything about what he's doing. Gene doping is banned by the World Anti-Doping Agency. Genetic performance enhancement, even if conducted by the military, would fall under the same restrictions because viral vectors are used in the DNA transduction process and the implications for genetic manipulation are unknown. I need to do more research about how it works, but Bio-Tech's a bio-hazard quarantine facility, so it makes sense Flannigan's based there. But I still haven't found out where Flannigan's getting his soldiers from, or who, aside from Sarah's uncle, will view his trial prior to the vote."

"He gets to vote?" Of course, he would, as C.S.R. teams' supervisor. Surely, he wouldn't vote yes after what happened to Jack and my mother.

"Darius mentioned it," Marrick says. "He wasn't told who else. Keep looking."

Reece uploads a screen of encrypted data that makes no sense to me. I wish he'd look up gene therapy instead.

"This could take a while," he says. "I'm running out of options. Communications? Military grants? I might find something if I dig through their financial records."

"Start there," Marrick says. "Someone must be financing Flannigan."

141

"Over twenty years?" Magelon says. "That's a long time for the military to cough up money for nothing."

"Don't bet on it," Kelly says. "You know what research is like. It takes years to develop a drug that works. Drug trials happen all the time, but you rarely see the results. Empty promises, most of them, to keep the money rolling in."

"The military wouldn't waste money on bogus research," Magelon says. "Unless that's the reason they can't pay their bills."

"There wouldn't be a trial if it's bogus," Marrick says.

Magelon sighs. "Then who'd he test his drugs on? He must have done preliminary trials. Who else did he abduct?"

Kelly snorts. "Who says he abducted anyone? There are plenty of dumb nuts in the ranks who'd give their left leg at a shot to run faster."

That doesn't sound like Jack Arquet, but as team leader, he would've had to perform at his best around the clock. My mother told him it would change everything. He must have agreed to take part in the earlier trials to optimize his abilities. He'd trust my mother, being his sister. But Magelon's comment about health effects allows an opportunity to switch the topic to more pressing details.

"Does gene therapy affect health like performance enhancement drugs?" I ask.

"Worse," Reece says. "Aside from strokes and heart attacks, negative effects include immune reactions because changes are made at a cellular level. That's why there are regulations. Cell manipulation is permanent."

I dig my nails into my arms. Even if I negate the effects of the vector, I'm stuck being genetically enhanced. What do I do with that?

"What about soldier sick-leave?" Marrick asks. "Can you put together a list of anyone with serious health issues?"

"That's a lot of files to filter without a common denominator," Reece says. "And Flannigan could have used civilians."

"Darius would've told us if he experimented on people off the street," Kelly says. "If Flannigan used soldiers, well, you know how the rumor mill works. Someone would've talked."

"Unless they're dead like Arquet," Magelon says. "There's your common denominator. Or high training scores after initial poor progress."

Like me. Nobody knew about my level of skill until the final assessment week. I'm also not dead. I haven't had a sick day in my life. A part of me sighs with relief; I won't die from the vector. A bigger part sounds an alarm—what if there's another reason Flannigan wants me?

I notice Marrick studying me, his brow furrowed. Does he question my sudden improvement during assessment week? I fit Magelon's second common denominator. But he looks away and taps his fingers on his knee.

"We already push the limits of what our bodies can handle," he says. "How much more does Flannigan think we can improve?"

Is Flannigan trying to manipulate something aside from enhanced physical abilities? He insisted I say my name and appeared startled when I said Katherine. I also wanted to say Joanna and struggled to say my name. And Jack was in my head when I tried to help Darius. Why did I confuse my identity on so many occasions?

Is it the white room? When I stood in there with Flannigan, I imagined being my mother, then Joanna. Does the room do something that would explain all of this? All I can think of is that my mother worked for Flannigan. Joanna is in Bio-Tech. Vera knew my mother, and me. From when or where, I've no idea. Yet, I recognized her, and knew her name. We must have met before, perhaps when I was a child, unless I know her because my mother knows her—

The answer's coming to me. I just need to retrace details. Like when I imagined Jack yelling abort because of an impossible rescue. This house is also familiar because Joanna's been here, not me. In the tunnel, gold orbs held my memories. Green orbs held Joanna's. Vera said it was crucial I return to familiar surroundings. But I didn't. I came here. And since I've been here, I've recalled what Joanna saw, and talking about my mother dredged up conversations she had when alive. And with that, all the pieces fall into place. Why didn't I see this sooner?

"Is it possible to enhance memory?" The response is blank stares, so I try another way. "Like déjà vu. When you do something, but think you've done it before?"

Marrick's frown deepens, and Magelon shoots me an incredulous look.

But Reece's eyes light up.

"Not déjà vu, but there is something. Give me a minute." He opens a new tab and types "cellular memory" into the search engine. An article about it appears on the screen.

"A hypothesis suggests cells outside the brain can store memories." He swivels in his chair and looks at Marrick. "If Flannigan's conducting gene therapy experiments, the DNA he uses would, in theory, contain memories belonging to the host in the cellular structure."

If that's true, why didn't Flannigan put my DNA in someone else to get my mother's research? Joanna appeared to be a willing participant. Why not use her? Instead, she must have given me her DNA. What can I do that she can't?

"Like organ donation," Kelly says, stroking his beard, his expression thoughtful. "Don't recipients take on the traits of their donors?"

"It's similar in theory." Reece resumes typing. Another article, this time about body memory, uploads. "Experiments have only shown the possibility. There's no proof tissue can store recollections. Different thoughts and emotions are reflective of an immunosuppressant drug." He leans back in his chair and waves at the screen. "If Flannigan's transferring DNA, he'd use immune suppressant drugs. There's nothing in this."

It's not nothing. Joanna gave me drugs, but the details I'm recalling are too specific to be suggestive thoughts. She also said we'd be perfect together. Did she think our combined DNA would enhance my recall ability? Why didn't she take my DNA and put it in her?

I rub the back of my neck. Does my mother know that answer?

As soon as I think about her, my mother's voice echoes through my mind—

Destroy it all. If Flannigan finds out how she became immune to the vector, there's no telling what he'll create.

Does that include the child?

How dare you even suggest that?

If he finds her, he won't need your data. Given the right stimulus, she'll recall everything you know. If she resists, he'll force it out of her. You know he has the means. Think about what you're doing. She's more than what you envisioned, but she'll use whatever's in her arsenal to protect herself. It's too dangerous. Especially for her.

I'll hide her. I know someone who can help.

I jerk my hand away from my head. My mother's talking to Vera about me. Guilt about every horrid thought I directed toward my mother for abandoning me makes my hands shake. She protected me until she couldn't, then my uncle took over the role. What part Vera played in my life is uncertain, but she helped Darius get inside Bio-Tech. She's also right about one thing. If my mother and I didn't look so alike, Flannigan would never have known who I was. That's irrelevant now, because he doesn't want my mother's research. He wants me because I'm immune to the vector.

That must be why Joanna wanted to use me. Was she aware of my genetic enhancements and my capacity to recall other memories to enhance my skills? Or did she only discover that when Flannigan said I was perfect?"

Perfect? I'm a creation resulting from a radical cellular memory experiment. How will Darius feel knowing my accomplishments weren't because of his exceptional training methods? As gutted as me? Or—

He already knows.

He had me hide my skills. He knew Flannigan and knew about the earlier trials. Did he tell Marrick about me, or is that another thing he concealed?

I face Marrick. "Darius said you wanted me on your team. Was that your decision?"

"It was a team decision," Marrick says. "Darius

147

called us a month into your training, suggesting you'd be a good fit."

"With my scores at that point, I would've been lucky to graduate."

"He always gets his cadets to underperform, so they're not targeted until assessment week. He kept us updated with your progress in your private training sessions. Your uncle lodged the paperwork. You were to leave with us immediately following graduation."

My 'uncle', who controls every aspect of my life. Did he tell Darius what I am, or did Darius figure it out? He's no fool. But neither is Marrick. I'm afraid to ask, but I have to know.

"Did you suspect my skills weren't normal?"

Marrick frowns. "You did the work. You trained harder than anyone I know."

"Wait a minute." Magelon slides off the couch and prowls around looking me up and down. "How did we not see this?"

"See what?" Kelly asks.

"Ask her," Magelon says, razors sprouting on her tongue.

There's no escaping this interrogation. Everyone stares at me. I take a deep breath to hold back the hot tears that well in my eyes. "I know what Flannigan wants."

"You sure as hell do," Magelon says.

"Let her talk," Marrick says.

I twist my hands together. "It's not what I remember. It's because I'm"—I can't say it but can't avoid it—"I'm genetically enhanced."

"I knew something was off," Magelon says. "Placed with us, no one would suspect, would they? Not when she would've claimed the top graduate title. Her skills would have blended with ours."

"Darius would have told us," Kelly says.

Marrick stands. "Why didn't you tell us?"

His harsh tone crushes me. "I didn't know until now."

Magelon scoffs. "How could you not know?"

"For the same reasons you didn't." I can't look at Marrick. I should have said something the second I realized. Instead, I've betrayed his trust. And my uncle? He orchestrated the perfect setup. I'd be untouchable with Marrick's team. Yet, how convenient to have a vacant position on the top team that coincided with me graduating.

Joanna 'died' a month before I started training. A tragic accident, everyone believes. What if it wasn't an accident?

I cup my hands to my mouth. "He wouldn't."

"Who wouldn't?" Kelly asks.

I shake my head. How can I tell them my uncle might have had Joanna removed from their team to make room for me?

Magelon glares at me. "If there's something else you should tell us, I strongly suggest you spit it out."

I lower my hands. "If everything I've said is true, and my uncle wanted to make sure nobody found out what I am by hiding me with the best team, how can you be sure Joanna's death was an accident?"

Magelon looks at Marrick, her eyes blazing. Reece sits frozen in his seat. Marrick's fierce gaze reduces me to a quivering mute.

"You're saying he had her murdered?" Kelly asks. "That's a hell of an accusation."

"Is it?" Magelon says. "We just found out John Wilson isn't her uncle. What else did he lie about?"

Everything. I know that. But I refuse to believe he murdered Joanna. How can I when I know Joanna's alive? "He didn't kill her."

"How would you know?" Magelon snaps. "You didn't even know he's not your uncle." She looks at Marrick. "You know it's possible."

I glance from her to Marrick. "How?"

"Your uncle was at the hospital when Joanna went into surgery," Magelon says. "He called us an hour later and said she was dead. Blood clot or some bullshit." She runs her hands through her hair, making it stand up in sharp spikes. "Don't tell me that's not suspicious, not after everything we've learned."

"Joanna alive. She's at Bio-Tech." I raise my hand and touch my head. "She gave me the implant and the drugs, not Flannigan." I look at Marrick, willing him, of all of them, to believe me. "She must have given me her DNA, so I had access to her memories. It's how I know Reece is Magelon's brother, and that he's a cyber hacker. I know everything about this house. Please, I'm telling the truth. I don't know how she got to Bio-Tech, whether my uncle sent her, or Flannigan took her from the hospital. But she's there."

"We buried her," Magelon says through gritted teeth. "Did your uncle pretend that happened as well?"

"I don't know."

"Why not when you claim you have Joanna's memories?" She throws up her hands. "If John Wilson's involved with Flannigan, there's no guessing how he'll vote."

Marrick stalks across the room. He stops at the door then turns, stiff with fury.

"What's the status of those C.S.R. teams at Bio-Tech?"

Reece opens the Team Tracker. "Hawthorne's still there. Riverbank's on standby at the national park."

Kelly fixes his eyes on Marrick. "What are you thinking?"

"I'm going back. If I get there in time, I can enter Bio-Tech with the Hawthorne team. If Joanna's there, I'll find her."

"They'll pull out in a couple of hours if they find nothing," Reece says.

"Then figure out a way to make them stay until I get there. I'll take a bike."

"No way," Kelly says. "I'll drive. You can catch some shut eye on the way. You'll be no good to anyone if you're dead on your feet."

Magelon's fierce expression melts. "Marrick, no. Don't do this. If you find her, then what?"

He gives her the strangest look. "We unbury the past and fix it."

What does he mean? Nothing good from the glare Magelon hits me with. Pure hatred, like I've dug up something she preferred to leave in the ground. Whatever it is, I'm not hanging around to find out.

"I'm coming," I say as Marrick pockets a com-link.

"Stay here," he says, striding to the door.

I catch his arm as he passes. "I can help. I know Bio-Tech's layout. You don't. And Darius might be in there. I have to find him." He concealed everything about me. I want to know why. From him.

Marrick jerks his arm away. "I don't want you to come." He glances at Magelon. "Hold the fort."

Magelon scowls. "Great. Babysitting. My favorite job."

"Hawthorne will ask you to log in via the Team Tracker," Reece says. "I'll delete your details as soon as you're cleared so no one knows you're not where you're supposed to be."

If he means my uncle, who cares? He has more explaining to do than anyone. It's Marrick's response that crushes me. I'm a leper in his eyes as I feared, made worse because I have his former team member's DNA. No wonder he doesn't want me with him.

It's time to leave. I told Marrick I'd stay until we learned more, and we've learned enough—anything else I need is in my head. But where would I go? Bio-Tech's out. I want to help find Darius, but Marrick doesn't want my company. Home? Not yet. Not until I know more about my uncle's involvement with Flannigan.

So, I stay? I'm curious to know what Marrick needs to fix. The memories I've recalled already make me question Joanna's relationship with this team. Magelon acts like she'd rather Joanna stay dead, and they all grow somber whenever her name is mentioned. Also, Joanna went to Red Bluff. She could have alerted anyone she was alive. Why didn't she?

Is Joanna another Gaucini? I didn't trust him, and I don't trust her. But having her memories gives me an advantage. They'll allow me to separate the lies from the truth, even if they're from Joanna's perspective. If Marrick needs to fix something, he needs me. Because knowing Joanna as I'm beginning to, she'll lie through her teeth to hide her deceit.

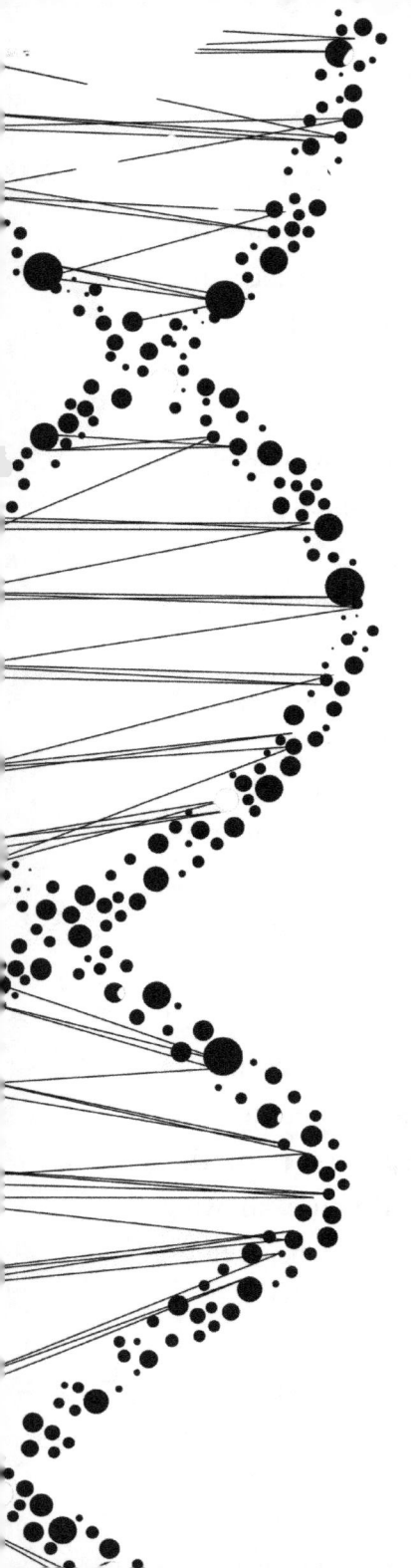

PAULINE YATES

CHAPTER 12

MAGELON'S IDEA OF HOLDING THE fort includes ordering me outside the house. Without Marrick and Kelly to buffer her hot temper, I have to comply. Night has fallen. Reece convinces her to give me a jacket—one of Kelly's by the size—and a blanket, but it's all the comfort she allows. She won't even let me use the bathroom.

Fine. It's not the first time I've roughed it. I've had plenty of practice in overnight drills at Red Bluff. I also have Vera's cardigan, but even with the jacket and the blanket wrapped around me, the chilly air bites into me. The veranda offers no protection; it's exposed to a stiff cold breeze that must blow from the Sierra.

Retreating to the shed, I choose a spot near the trail

bikes and lie down, but sleep remains elusive. I stare at the roof, listening to rustles in the scrub outside and scratching on the shelves.

I consider taking a bike and going after Marrick. Not knowing if he reached Bio-Tech in time to enter with the Hawthorne team keeps me awake. Damn Magelon. Reece will keep tabs on Marrick, but I've no way of talking to him.

For Marrick to search for Joanna, he must believe me. Flannigan also lied about her not being there. He called her by name in a memory. But if Joanna isn't at Bio-Tech, how will that make me look? A liar like my uncle as well as a freak?

Restless, I throw off the blanket and creep beneath the computer room on the other side of the water tank. I can't talk to Reece, but I can listen. I crouch below the window and hold my breath, hoping the leaves crunching under my feet didn't give me away.

I'm in luck. Reece's voice drifts through the walls.

"Now we see you, now we don't. Nothing to do but wait."

"Where are they?" Magelon asks.

"Marrick's just signed in with the Hawthorne team."

"Did you erase his sign-in details?"

"Yep. Any record he's there is gone."

A chair scrapes. "I'm crashing. Wake me in a few. I'll tag you."

"What about Sarah?" Reece asks.

"What about her?"

"Shouldn't we—"

"No."

The floor vibrates as Magelon leaves the room. Her bedroom door closes with a bang. Reece's sigh is followed by clicking. I picture him typing, searching for answers in his world. I sigh, too, wishing I could help him.

I return to the shed and curl into my blanket. Knowing Marrick is with Hawthorne offers some comfort. At least he's not alone. Will he find Darius and Joanna? I close my eyes. What will my world look like tomorrow?

When I wake, sunlight streams through the open shed doors. Kicking off the blanket, I get up and walk to the door. Outside, the sky is clear, but the muggy air hints of rain. Peeling off the jacket and cardigan, I return inside and hang them over a bike. When I pick up the blanket, I notice a food tray on the workbench.

The tray holds a packet of dried apples, hard biscuits, a lump of crusty home-baked bread, and a canteen. Reece, I suspect. He must have delivered it after Magelon went to sleep, though how I didn't hear him is a mystery. He's either good at sneaking, or I slept like a rock. After the events of yesterday, I suspect the latter.

Grabbing the canteen, I uncap the lid and sniff— water—then guzzle it down. Then I eat the apple and nibble at the bread but stop there. I don't know how long Marrick will take, and I could be outside for days. Reece won't be able to slip me food all the time.

I drape Vera's cardigan over the remaining food to hide it from Magelon, then creep around the side of the house and crouch beneath the window. If Marrick found Darius and Joanna, they could be on their way back.

No sound comes from the computer room, but a tap in the bathroom runs. Wishing I could bathe, I return to the shed, eat more bread, then, with nothing else to do, jog down to the creek.

Like everything else on Kelly's property, the creek is familiar. It winds around the back of the house, crystal clear water running through large flat boulders. Farther upstream is a dark section of water. Higher up, the rocks begin again, damp from sparkling waterfalls. The surrounding vegetation is heavy with dew.

Crouching on the bank, I scoop water into my hands and splash it over my face and wash my arms, not caring if my shirt gets wet. The water is cold but invigorating. A run would be good. I need to stretch my legs and it would help to settle my agitation from not knowing what's happening.

I follow a track alongside the creek. It's overgrown with ferns but well-marked. I speed up and imagine running this way another time. Joanna? I hate how her memories intrude. They're becoming more frequent. How long before I think like her, too?

I run faster, eager to reach unfamiliar territory where

my thoughts will be my own, but the track splits. Stopping, I study each direction. One track leads to a deep pool of water, impossible to cross unless I swim. The other leads into the forest. I follow it for a short distance, then pause to get my bearings.

I'm surrounded by a heavily timbered forest. Large boulders block my view of the creek, although splashing tells me it's there. I skirt around the boulders and run faster, confident the track follows the creek line. There are fewer trees in this area, more rock.

At another cluster of boulders, the track splits again.

The left track, washed out from rain, leads up a bank. I picture another track at the top, one direction leading to the ridge, the other down to the house. I won't go that way. That track must be familiar to Joanna, and I'm tired of thinking about her. I continue to the right.

My spirits lift. I don't know where it leads because this track isn't familiar to Joanna. Eager to clear her from my mind, I run at reckless speed. The creek appears on my right, more boulders than water, then the vegetation closes in, and I lose sight of it once more. The ground continues to rise, but the track turns to flat rocks. Vines and fronds snag my legs, but I push through and run faster. Being alone in unknown territory with no one telling me to slow down is exhilarating.

The terrain changes again, a steep incline between boulders higher than my head. The roar of a waterfall echoes from the other side. As I climb between the boulders, rock cliffs rise around me. I enter a gully. The track disappears, so I use the sound of running water as a guide. I clamber over another boulder and jump down onto a rock shelf. Stopping, I gaze about in awe.

The gully contains a series of rock pools, the water reflecting the blue sky peeking through trees. Rock walls on the far side form a barrier to the forest above. Rainbow-tinted mist rises from babbling waterfalls. The air trapped within the rock walls is heavy with moisture, adding to the mugginess. Ferns in multiple shades of green mark the gully's ascension to the ridgeline above me. Pips and chirrups from unseen wildlife echo from hidden crevices.

Stepping to the edge of the rock shelf, I breathe in deep, filling my lungs with moist air and soaking up the serenity. Right now, in this place, I'm me. No Joanna in my head, not my mother, no Jack. If I could imagine Heaven, this is it.

"Sightseeing?" Magelon asks.

And there's my Hell.

Magelon stands on the boulder above me. Sweat rolls down her neck. Her damp shirt clings to her chest. How she found me doesn't matter. Why she did, does.

"Is Marrick back?" I ask. "Is Darius with him? Did he find Joanna?"

Magelon scowls. "No. Don't know. And in your dreams."

I look away and stare at the rock pools. "Why are you here, then?"

"Believe me, I'd rather be anywhere else."

"Then go. I don't need company." My cheeks grow hot. Alone, I'm used to.

"I'm not here to keep you company. I'm here to escort you back to the house. What were you thinking, running off? Or is that a habit?"

Irritated by her reference to my disappearance from Red Bluff, I pick up a pebble and fling it across the gully. "I'm not your responsibility, no matter what Darius or my uncle say."

"Until Marrick gets back, you are."

I look up at her. "Does that include kicking me out of the house?"

She frowns. "Let's get one thing straight. I don't trust you. You're not who we thought you were. I don't know what's going on, but I won't let some two-bit rich kid with a family history of insanity hurt anyone in my team with crazy suggestions about Joanna being alive."

When she puts it like that, I don't blame her for kicking me out of the house. She makes another thing clear: I'll never shake the privileged tag. I'm also a medical misfit, with Joanna's, and Jack Arquet's murderous DNA mixed with mine. Who in their right mind would trust me?

"If that's what you all think, I'll go. I don't want to be here, either."

"At least we agree on something," Magelon says. "Unfortunately, you don't get to make that call."

"I never get to make a call," I say, bristling with anger. "Do you know what it's like to live with an uncle who decides everything about your life? Call me rich if you like but give me a rusty old shed to sleep in any day." Damn my uncle. Damn Darius. Why didn't either of them tell me who and what I am? No more. From now on, I'm calling the shots.

I climb up the boulder and push past Magelon. "I'm leaving. Don't come after me."

"Not a chance," she says, following me.

I stop and face her. "What will you do? Handcuff me?"

"If I have to." She smiles like a cat with its paw on a mouse's tail.

Something shifts, like a shadow passed over us and I'm seeing Magelon in a new light. She might think she's got the upper hand, but two can play at her game.

"To keep me from leaving?" I ask with a sugar sweet smile. "Or to protect your geeky, computer nerd brother?"

Magelon's eyes narrow. "What did you call him?"

"You heard me. That's why he hacked you both onto Marrick's team, isn't it? So you could stay together? Who else is going to look out for a weedy runt like him?"

Magelon clenches her fist. "Where'd you hear that?"

I share my best simpering smile. "Oh, Mags, you

discredit yourself by continuing with your delusion nobody outside this team will discover the truth."

Her fist flies at my mouth. I catch her wrist with whip-like speed and twist hard enough to break her arm. Gritting her teeth, she drops to the ground and angles her body so I can't—

Shock at what I said, and what I'm about to do, jerks me to my senses. Reece calls her Mags.

So does Joanna when she wants to be insulting.

Horrified, I release Magelon's wrist and step back, raising my hands to distance myself from the Joanna behavior I displayed. "That wasn't me, that wasn't me."

Magelon climbs to her feet and rubs her elbow. "What the hell are you talking about?"

"That wasn't me," I say again.

"No kidding. You sounded just like Joanna. She always said stuff like that."

I have Joanna's memories. I imagine her voice. Now I'm talking like her? "What exactly did Joanna say to you?"

"Why ask? You repeated her word for word. I suppose she told you about it."

"She didn't. I've never heard her say that. Trust me."

"Trust you?" Clutching her arm, she backs away. "Not in a million years. Don't come near me. Or Reece. Or Marrick or Kelly. I'm done with this bullshit."

She turns to leave, but I jump in front of her. "Please, it's Joanna's memories. They're affecting me more than I realize."

She shoulders past me. "I don't care."

"How else would I remember exactly what she said in a private conversation between you two?"

Magelon hesitates. "You're lying. She must have told you."

"She didn't. What if I'm right about the memory enhancement? Even if Joanna is dead, Flannigan could have got her DNA from the hospital. Think about it."

"I have. You're as crazy dangerous as your real uncle."

How do I prove I'm telling the truth? Then it comes to me. I've experienced it, Joanna's intense episodes of self-doubt.

"What if Joanna agreed to the trials? You heard Kelly. There's always someone who wishes they were stronger and faster and would do anything to achieve that. From what I've recalled of Joanna's memories, she didn't believe she was good enough."

"No. She didn't," Magelon whispers, staring though me. Then she frowns. "Joanna's dead and you're delusional. Go if you want. I'm not stopping you."

She runs back into the forest. I hesitate, unsure what to do. If I go, how will I know if I'm behaving like Joanna with no one around to tell me? As much as I hate Magelon's attitude, I need her to make sure I'm behaving like me.

CHAPTER 13

FOR THE SECOND TIME IN two days, I have a gun pointed at my head. I stand on one side of the screen door. Magelon stands on the other. Her scowl triggers a vision of me/Joanna smirking at her. With Magelon's finger hard on the trigger, I don't need a catty Joanna remark to slip out now.

To counter Joanna, I imagine the rock pools—my place, not hers. The vision fades, replaced with water running over rocks. Control over mind regained, I move away to give Magelon space.

"Weren't you leaving?" she asks.

"I want to help. Joanna mightn't be alive, but you can't deny I have her memories."

"We don't need help." She swings the inner wooden

door closed.

"Wait." I jump forward and press my hands against the screen. "You can't trust what my uncle says. You can't trust Darius, either." I cringe; I want to believe in him, though his non-disclosure about my genetic enhancements cuts me deep. "You don't even have to trust me. But if I have Joanna's memories, I'll know what happened to her. Memories don't lie."

Magelon's mouth curls like a snarling Doberman. "Then I suggest you remember something useful before I turn you into a memory I'll gladly forget."

"It doesn't work like that." I don't think. Lowering my hands, I look around for something familiar to Joanna to help draw out her memories, like when I saw the house for the first time. But I've already taken in everything around me and nothing new comes to mind. "Could I see her bedroom? Personal effects, if you still have them."

"Let you inside? Forget it." She slams the door. A bolt lock slides shut with a thud.

I retreat to the top step and sit with my head in my hands. I don't blame Magelon for not trusting me after nearly breaking her arm. I'm not even sure I trust myself. All I know is I think and talk like Joanna. Surely, I'd remember if she faked her death.

I prod the implant's insertion point. How does it work? It's in my head for a reason. If it aids memory recall, could I manipulate it by imagining Joanna's behavior?

Would a mechanical device know the difference between my memories and hers?

Closing my eyes, I picture Joanna being rushed to the hospital. What would I see? The inside of an ambulance? Paramedics? I sink deeper into Joanna's viewpoint, but then I see a ceiling, voices shouting around me. The ceiling whizzes by. I'm on a stretcher, being wheeled through a hospital. My stomach tightens, gripped by panic.

I press my hands against my temple. It's hard to separate Joanna's emotions from mine. Panic, yes, but there's more to her mood and it engulfs me: anger, frustration, and a gnawing unsettledness that feeds insecurity, similar to the self-doubt I suffered when at the punching bag with Kelly. Magelon agreed Joanna never thought she was good enough. That's significant.

I concentrate on expanding the images, but they fade, and my mind goes blank. Then I imagine Flannigan, standing with hands clasped, his mouth curved in that horrid, detached smile.

We can help each other, Miss Johansson. In return for your assistance, I'll personally guarantee any leadership position you desire.

If I agree, I want anonymity. No one must know what I've done.

That can be arranged.

I jerk out of the memory. Flannigan and Joanna made a deal. Her voice floods my mouth as though I'd spoken.

Did she agree to be Flannigan's test subject, and he took her from the hospital under the pretense of death?

I need more information, but I can't recall anything after their talk. There are too many gaps in these memories. I still don't know if my uncle's involved, or why Flannigan chose Joanna. I also don't know if Joanna desired a leadership position. Would Magelon know?

I hurry to the front screen, fling it open and pound on the inner door. "Magelon, let me in."

No answer. I thump harder.

Magelon opens the door. Again I face the wrong end of her Beretta.

"What?" she snaps.

I'm careful this time. Saying Joanna is alive will earn me a slammed door or a bullet. "Did Joanna ever request a transfer to lead another team?"

Magelon frowns. "She always bitched about wanting to lead. So what?"

"Could Reece find out if she lodged a transfer request?"

"How is that relevant?"

"What if Joanna hooked up with Flannigan because he promised her a leadership position? I recalled him saying he'd grant her that if she helped him."

"Even if she wanted to split, it still doesn't prove she's alive."

The proof is in my head, but I'm sure Magelon would

rather lodge a bullet in my brain than extract a memory from it.

Reece appears behind her, holding a document. "This might. Joanna's an organ donor. Remember the closed casket at her funeral? Organ donors don't end up in the morgue because doctors harvest organs and tissue immediately." He takes a deep breath. "Funerals still go ahead, but the casket is only for effect."

"Are you saying her coffin was empty?" Magelon asks.

"Most likely," Reece says.

Reece must believe me if he dredged up information about Joanna's funeral.

"Did you know she was an organ donor?" I ask.

"Of course not," Magelon says. "It's not something you discuss over the dinner table."

My uncle and I discussed organ donation prior to my start at Red Bluff. He drew my attention to an organ donor question on the induction form—*under no circumstances do you check that box.* I never wondered why until now.

"Organ donors who present at a hospital with life-threatening injuries must be noticed by somebody," I say. "What if that's how Flannigan got his test subjects? We were looking for a common denominator. Why not that?"

"It still doesn't prove Joanna's alive," Magelon says.

"She wouldn't have to be if Flannigan only needed her DNA," Reece says.

We're going around in circles. For every argument I present claiming Joanna is alive, there's opposing evidence proving she's dead. I wish Marrick were here. He's good at analyzing both sides and reaching a credible conclusion. Even Kelly would offer counter-arguments. At least Reece is taking what I say under consideration, but we're getting nowhere fast.

"I could search hospital transcripts," Reece says. "See if Flannigan's name appears on a sign-in list."

"Assuming he signed in," Magelon says. "With his connections, he could probably walk in and out of any hospital with no questions asked." She lowers the gun and sighs. "Marrick will want to know this. Where's the com-link?"

"Doubt you'll reach him," Reece says. "I've been trying all morning."

A worry knot tightens in my stomach. "When did you last hear from him?"

"When he signed in with the Hawthorne team," Reece says.

"And you're not worried?"

"Of course not," Magelon says. "He knows what he's doing." But there's hesitancy in her voice.

"It's not unusual," Reece says, fidgeting with the document. "He won't respond if it risks compromising our location."

"Kelly, too?" I ask with growing alarm. "What if

Flannigan caught them? Look at Joanna. A high-points graduate. Jack Arquet was a team leader. I would have claimed the top graduate title. And Marrick, he's the best there is. If Joanna's in Bio-Tech and saw him, what would stop her telling Flannigan another potential test subject walked through the door?"

Magelon's face turns whiter than her hair. "He's with Hawthorne. Flannigan won't risk detaining Marrick. He's too well known."

"I'm well known. It didn't stop Flannigan from detaining me. Reece also deleted Marrick's sign-in. There's no record he's there."

Reece pales. "I'll try him again."

He hurries back to the computer room. Magelon closes the door, locking me out. The house vibrates from Magelon running along the hallway.

I cross the veranda and lean on the railing. To think Marrick may fall victim to Flannigan fills me with dread. Darius, too. What if Flannigan uses him as a test subject? In his day, Darius was as good as Marrick. Time doesn't change DNA. Imagine the tactical information Flannigan could harvest given access to two sets of DNA from the best of the best.

"Please be okay," I whisper, gripping the rail.

I can't shake the fear they're not.

The door opens and Magelon walks out, a knapsack over her shoulder, her utility belt loaded with the Beretta, another gun, and multiple magazines. Warning me to keep my distance with a flash of her eyes, she strides along the veranda and jumps down the steps.

"What are you doing?" I ask.

She ignores me and runs around the side of the house. I consider following, but an engine revs and she returns riding a trail bike. She parks it at the bottom of the steps, secures the knapsack to the back of the seat, then bolts back to the shed and brings a second bike plus two helmets.

"Are you going to Bio-Tech?" I ask as she parks the bike.

She jumps up the steps and goes inside without answering. Using the floor vibration, I track her movement through the house: bedroom, computer room, back rooms, then along the hallway. When she enters the kitchen, I cross to the window.

"I'm coming, too."

"No way." She raids the cupboard for two canteens and fills them with water. "It'll be dangerous enough without worrying about you taking us out."

I sigh, frustrated I'm tainted by the actions of a man I've never met. "I'm not Jack Arquet. Anyway, you need me. I know where the holding cells are."

She shuts off the tap with a hard twist. "We'll manage."

Cradling the canteens, she leaves the kitchen, meeting Reece in the doorway.

"That storm's about to hit," he says, taking a canteen and shoving it into a backpack he carries.

"Rain won't kill us. Let's go."

Magelon keeps between me and Reece as they walk along the veranda. Rolling his eyes, he gives me a quirky grin. I don't know how I earned his trust, but I'll take it. But what am I supposed to do when they leave? I could follow. There's a third bike in the shed. Though, knowing Magelon, she'd shoot out the tires. I'd rather not, but the way to help is to stay.

"If you won't let me come, at least leave me a way to keep in contact with you," I say to Magelon as they jump down the stairs. "If something happens, I'll call my uncle." I don't want to do that either but won't have a choice if Flannigan detains everyone.

"Do what you want," Magelon says.

Reece intervenes. "It might not be a bad idea having someone on the outside. We don't know what we're walking into."

"We never know, and we've managed so far," Magelon snaps.

Reece pulls a com-link from his jacket pocket and tosses it to me. "Receive only. I'll only message if something happens. What you do after that is up to you." He looks at my head. "Keep it off your body in case you give off a signal."

"Okay."

Reece goes to the second bike. He wears a brave face, but I fear for him the most. He works behind the scenes, not on the front line. If those soldiers who beat up Darius got hold of Reece, he'd end up in a body bag.

Thunder rumbles overhead. I glance at the sky. Dark clouds roll in from the east. "You'll get soaked on the bikes."

"We'll pick up a hire car on the way." Reece glances at Magelon, then lowers his voice. "This storm precedes a cold front. Don't stay in the shed. You'll freeze."

"Let's go." Magelon puts on her helmet and climbs astride her bike.

Lightning flashes through the clouds, followed by another roll of thunder. The approaching storm hits the top of the ridge and releases a gray wall of water that pours down the slopes. The wind whips up, blowing my hair across my face. This storm is moving in fast.

"Damn it," Magelon says, glaring at the cloudburst. "Bring your bike back to the shed."

Revving her engine, she skids in a circle, spraying up dirt, and speeds to the shed. Reece slings the backpack over his shoulders and climbs onto his bike. He takes three goes to kick start it, then rides a wobbly line after her. I'm glad they're getting a hire car; he's not a competent rider.

The com-link vibrates in my hand: 'on our way back'.

Relief pours over me. It's a message from Marrick. Sprinting to the shed, I give the com-link to Magelon, who stands at the door scowling at the darkening sky. She reads the message. Reece looks over her shoulder and sighs, looking as relieved as I feel.

Further talk is impossible. The wall of rain hits the shed and the pounding on the roof is deafening. Thunder booms and static electricity make the hairs on my arm stand on end. Outside, day turns to night and the temperature drops to freezing.

Shivering, I watch the storm rage through the trees along the creek. In a brief interlude between the thunderclaps, another throbbing noise appears. It grows louder, a chopping echo like flat blades slapping the air.

The sound is unmistakable. Ignoring the rain, I step outside and search the sky. Two choppers swoop over the ridge, riding the storm directly to Kelly's house.

"Choppers!" I yell.

Magelon joins me in the rain. "Where?"

I point to the sky above the ridge. "Is it Marrick?"

She stares at the choppers. "That's not friendly. Move, move!"

I'm seized by dread. Not Marrick. Not friendly.

Flannigan.

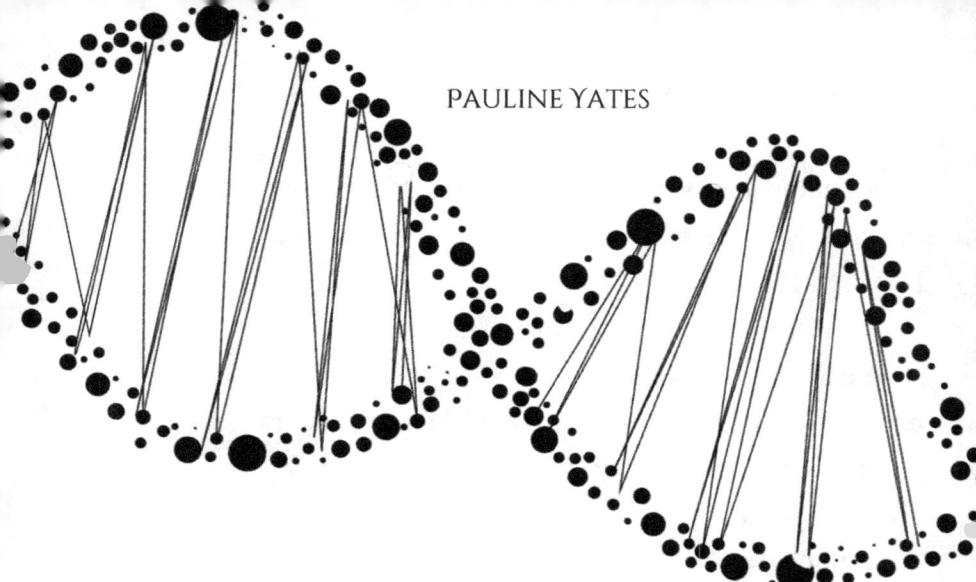

PAULINE YATES

CHAPTER 14

I DON'T WAIT FOR INSTRUCTIONS. Choppers mean soldiers were dispatched. Where from and on what grounds, we won't know until Reece can access the Team Tracker. There's no time to do that. We have less than a minute to get out.

Running to the third bike, I grab the jacket I'd draped over the handlebars, and a helmet, put them on, and slide onto the seat. Beside me, Reece sits behind Magelon. I'm glad he had the sense to ride double. We don't need a slow rider now.

"Take the track across from the house," Magelon says. "We'll go to Kelly's Hut."

"Follow the river south," Reece adds. "You'll see it."

They must mean Kelly's fishing cabin, but I can't ask

for more directions. One chopper flies low over the house, making the roof vibrate.

Magelon rides from the shed. Kick-starting my bike, I rev the engine and ride forward, keeping one eye on Reece while listening for the second chopper. Reece is perched precariously. With his legs hitched up to accommodate the bags strapped to the side of Magelon's bike, he risks falling. I can't help him. The pelting rain makes my seat slippery, and I throw all my weight against the wind to stop from toppling over.

The first chopper rises above the trees near the front entrance gate. Drop lines hang from the open side door. Whoever Flannigan sent is on the ground.

Magelon speeds toward the *ridgeline track* opposite the front of the house. Joanna's memories about the property layout will be useful if we get separated. But how did the chopper know to drop soldiers at the front gate? They block the only exit to the road.

The second chopper flies over our heads, in the direction we're riding. They'd only know the ridgeline track is another way out if they were told.

I twist the throttle, shooting my bike forward. I have to warn Magelon. If Joanna's helping Flannigan, she'd have seen Darius or Marrick. It would have taken her less than a second to link them with me. I should have thought of this earlier. Joanna knows how secluded this property is. If she's directing the soldiers, we're riding into a trap.

Magelon's too far ahead to catch her attention, and I don't know another way to go. The creek is an option, but it's too rough for a bike, and while Magelon and I would outrun soldiers, Reece wouldn't. Our best chance is to outrace the chopper and get past them before the second team drops to the ground.

A third option pops into my mind. Why not split? I have time to backtrack. Take the creek path and outrun Flannigan's teams on foot. It's me Flannigan wants, not them. Magelon doesn't want me around. Nor does Marrick. The way he spoke to me before he left made that clear.

I ease down on the throttle, but when I lose sight of Magelon and Reece, I jolt to my senses. Am I seriously considering the third option? I'd never run out on a team, which is what Magelon and Reece are, given our current situation. That way of thinking belongs to Joanna, not me. She abandoned her team the moment she agreed to help Flannigan.

I may not know my real identity, but I'm not Joanna. Twisting the throttle, I race after Magelon. Until we're out of this predicament, I'm not leaving her.

The track curves to the right. I glimpse the red taillight on Magelon's bike, blurry in the rain. Reece hunches behind her, but he's slipped to one side. Glancing up, I search for the chopper. The canopy's thick in this section and blocks my view of the sky. Could they drop in this area? Or are they farther along, waiting in ambush?

A flash of orange lights up the forest, and the ground in front of Magelon's bike explodes. Magelon swerves to avoid the blast, but the jerky change in direction throws Reece from his seat. He falls, dragging Magelon with him. They crash with the bike onto the ground.

I skid to a stop next to them. Magelon jumped clear, but Reece is pinned by the back wheel. Leaping off my bike, I yank off my helmet and lift the bike so Magelon can pull him out. Reece draws his leg up to his chest, a good sign it's not broken, but the lower part of his pants has a burn hole the size of my fist from the exhaust pipe.

Magelon hitches her hands beneath Reece's armpits. "Get up. Hold on to me."

Reece staggers to his feet. I take an arm to support him, but tense at a whizzing noise in the forest. A flash of lightning exposes drop lines through the trees.

"They're here," I say. "Twelve o'clock."

Magelon whips out her Beretta and aims toward the forest. "Take him."

Take him where? With both teams on the ground, we're surrounded. I need a fourth option, but I don't know this forest well enough.

What am I thinking? I don't know the forest, but Joanna does. I'd rather not tap into her memories again. I don't even know if I can. But it's the only way to save us.

Concentrating, I imagine Joanna in this section of the forest. What would she be doing? Running? Yes, I see myself/Joanna jogging along this track with Marrick. I/Joanna laughs at something he says, then veers right, taking a shortcut to the ridge.

A shortcut?

A soldier runs between the trees, jerking me out of the memory. Magelon shoots. Two more soldiers duck for cover.

"Go on foot," Magelon says, pointing to the edge of the track. "I'll cover you."

Reece limps in that direction, but he can't walk without help. Slinging my arm around his waist, I guide him to the shortcut I recalled. It's where Magelon indicated, a narrow track concealed by ferns and barely visible in the rain. It enters a heavily timbered area that will give us cover.

Reece hobbles alongside me as fast as he can, but we won't outrun the soldiers at this rate.

"Come on," I urge Reece, unable to keep the frustration out of my tone.

He pulls away. "You go. My ankle's twisted and I'm slowing us up." He takes off his helmet and drops it on the ground. In seconds, the rain flattens his hair and water runs down his face.

I hesitate. I want to leave him, want to save myself. But that's not me. Again, Joanna has corrupted my thoughts. I've got to stop thinking like her. She'd leave Reece in a second. I'm not doing that.

"You're doing fine." Forcing encouragement into my voice is hard. The Joanna in me wants to snap at him for being a liability, giving insight into their relationship. I can't think about that now. I need a fifth option.

I look through the trees. I can't see Magelon, but the gunfire continues. There's no return fire, though. The second team must be waiting for the first team to arrive. With both sides of the track covered, we'll be trapped. I have to get us out of here before that happens.

"This way," I whisper to Reece.

If the teams are converging on this area, the safest place is on the other side of the house. Reece's bike is in the shed. It's transport if we can get to it.

I guide Reece toward the house. The slippery ground and thick undergrowth must be murder on his leg, but he doesn't complain. I help him over a fallen log, then pause when a round of shots echoes through the forest. Magelon's bike revs, then the sound dies away as she continues along the ridgeline track to draw the soldiers away from us.

"Come on," I say, tugging Reece's arm.

"If she reaches the ridgeline, she'll be in the clear," Reece says.

"We'll meet her there." How? We can ride the bike along the creek track as far as the rock pools, but climbing higher from there will be impossible with Reece's injuries.

Out of options, I help Reece through the forest. He stumbles alongside me, his expression pinched from pain.

When the house comes into view, I pull Reece into the scrub and crouch. A soldier covers the entrance to the track.

Using hand signals, I point from me to the soldier and from Reece to the house. Reece's eyes widen and he looks unsure, but at least he understood what I meant.

I'm going to take out the soldier so Reece can make a run for it.

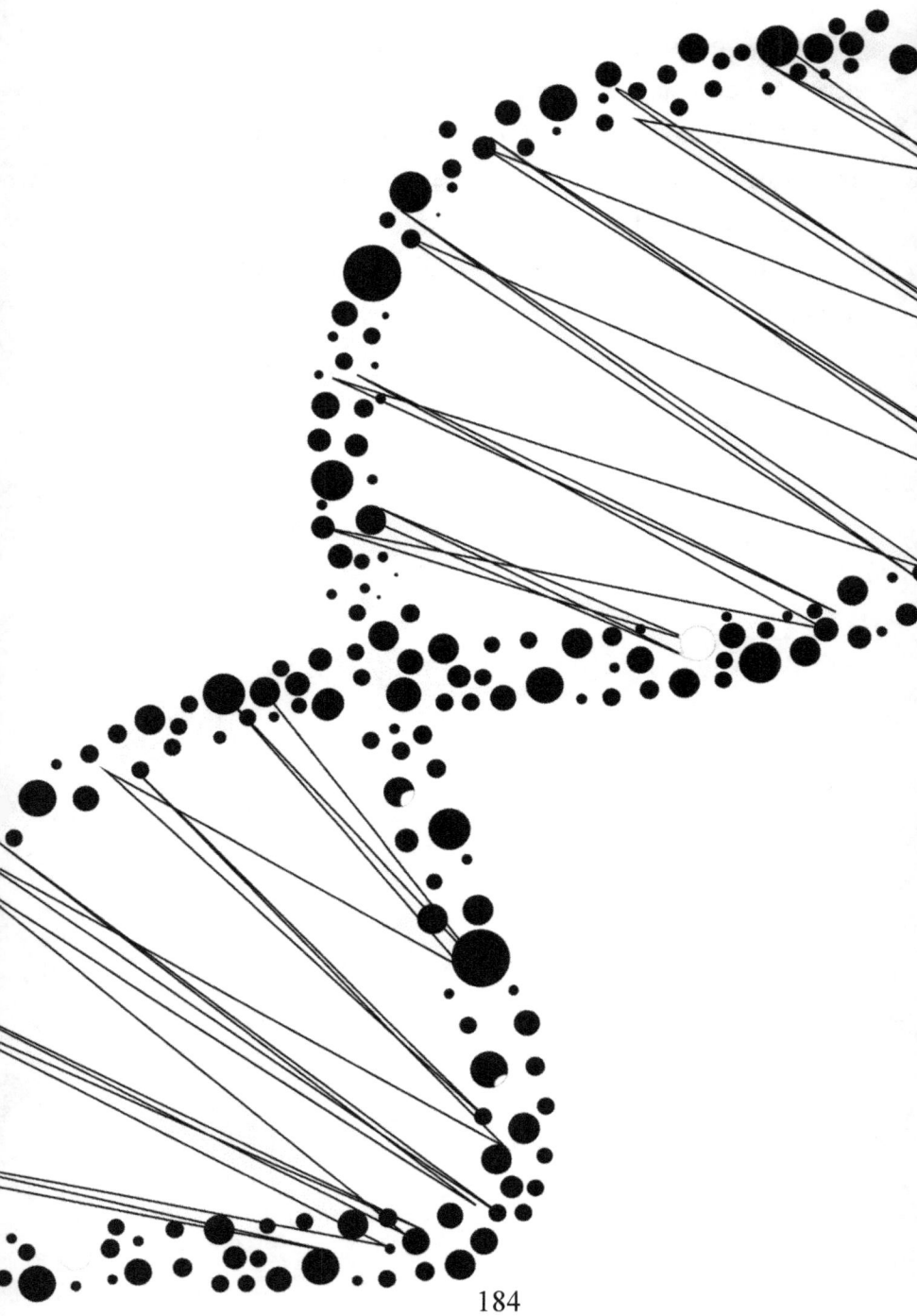

CHAPTER 15

I DON'T GIVE MY NEXT action much thought; instinct guides me. I'm not armed, but I have the element of surprise. Creeping through the undergrowth, using the trees as cover and aided by the rain muffling my movement, I sneak up on the soldier and jump him.

He sees me too late. He focused on the track, not his surroundings. What he lacks in skill, however, he makes up for in size. As tall and solid as Kelly, it's like hitting a brick wall. But driving my shoulder into his midriff and knocking him to the ground releases pent-up anger I haven't acknowledged—anger at my lost career, with Darius, my uncle, Flannigan, Joanna. And anger with myself for believing in people, for trusting them, when I shouldn't trust anyone but me.

My volley of blows smashes the soldier's nose and splits his lips. The rain turns crimson as it pours off his face. My second punch knocked him out, but I can't stop hitting him. I want him to hurt like I'm hurting—

"Sarah, Sarah," Reece says from another world behind me.

I pause, fist raised. Reece stands in the undergrowth, his eyes wild with fear.

"They're coming back," he whispers.

Feeling as I do, I want to take on both teams. Send Flannigan a message by making them all hurt. But my anger has got the better of me. Reece won't escape alone. He needs my protection.

Hands shaking, I take the soldier's rifle and handgun, then motion to Reece to make a run for the house. He darts from the trees, fear—of me or the soldiers—driving him forward in a jerky gait, his muddy backpack bouncing on his back. I skip backward, eyes trained on the forest. When I reach the house, I turn and run to Reece.

He waits by the water tank, next to an overflowing downpipe that dumps water around his feet. His face is white, and he shivers—from cold or shock, maybe both. I should reassure him and say he has nothing to fear from me, but I'm not sure I'd be telling the truth.

My anger won't abate. It boils inside me, demanding release. Is this the side effect of the vector, this rising fury, this murderous intent? How can I control something I know nothing about, something that might not be controllable?

I have to try. Reece needs me. Gritting my teeth, I give him the rifle. "Do you know how to use one of these?"

Reece nods, but he's apprehensive. "Mags showed me once."

Once? I hope she gave him an in-depth lesson. He won't get a second shot if his first one misses.

"Come on, we'll get the bike and take the creek track." I reach for Reece's arm to help him, but he flinches and steps away. I should have used my left hand, not the one red with blood.

Leading the way, I scoot around the water tank, keeping the handgun raised. A shout from the front of the house stiffens my spine. The first team has returned and found their beaten-up comrade. Running's no longer an option.

A tarpaulin lies folded on the ground behind the shed. I grab Reece's arm, whether he likes it or not.

"Hide under here." I push him down and spread the canvas over him. Reece clutches the rifle like it's his life support.

"What will you do?" he asks as I pull the fabric over his head.

I don't want him to know what I'm going to do. "Just trust me, okay?"

Creeping back to the front of the house, I peek around

the corner. Two soldiers run toward the house. One ascends the veranda. Another heads in my direction.

You'll only get one shot at this, so make every target count.

My last sharpshooting instruction from Darius makes tears well in my eyes. Why didn't he tell me what I am?

I shoot before the soldier sees me—one shot to the head, dead before he hits the ground. A queasy churning starts in my stomach. I killed him yet feel nothing, like my human side has shut down. I didn't even consider wounding him—we're supposed to be on the same side. All I saw was a threat that needed to be removed. Is that another side effect of the vector?

She'll use everything in her arsenal to protect herself.

I don't know what Vera meant, but I need to focus. It was the soldier or me, and there are still three more unaccounted for.

The screen door squeaks. My shot gave away my position but I'm already moving. Jumping into the scrub growing next to the house, I crouch and wait. The soldier from the house appears, rifle raised, eyes darting every which way. He kneels beside the dead soldier and checks for a pulse. Finding none, his expression hardens.

Standing, he continues around the house, rifle outstretched. Adrenaline burns through my muscles, turning them into over-tensioned springs. Part of me wants to jump the soldier, another part says to wait. The tingle in my head returns, and images flood my mind. Similar situations, what worked, what didn't. The implant might be responsible for jogging the multiple memories, but the information overload makes it hard to concentrate. Where am I in all this? Am I me, or Jack, or Joanna? I don't know, I don't know, I don't know.

Focus, Wilson.

Darius again. His voice has a calming effect. Hating him for deceiving me, grateful for his guidance, I take a deep breath and return my attention to the soldier.

I can't tell if he's C.S.R. He's in a team of five, but he could also be part of a general response unit. From where? Not Hawthorne, they're too far away. Not Red Bluff. I'd recognize them. Riverbank? They use choppers. But if Riverbank dispatched units, my uncle would know and intervene.

Unless something happened to him?

Multiple scenarios play out in my mind—my uncle detained for concealing my whereabouts or questioned about the location of Marrick's team. Called in to explain Darius's absence, perhaps. I even imagine him turning me in, though that thought unravels threads I've no time to explore. It's better to assume Flannigan sent these soldiers, off record, so no one knows they're here.

The soldier passes the water tank. When he reaches the lump of canvas, he stops and lifts the corner with the end of his rifle. I balance on the balls of my feet, ready to move. The soldier lifts the tarp higher, revealing Reece's boots.

I leap from the bushes and shoot. Struck in the neck, the soldier spins around, squeezing off a round of fire as he falls. Bullets hit the shed wall with ringing pings, rupturing the fuel drum near the end. Fuel spills from the holes and spreads in rainbow colors across the wet ground.

The rifle fire draws the other two soldiers. They appear at the creek end of the clearing. They don't see Reece—he has the sense to stay hidden. They see me, though, and the soldier I just killed.

I run toward them, arm outstretched, firing shots in succession. One soldier drops like a lead balloon. The other dives behind the shed.

I chase after him, but stop to check the downed soldier. He pants, eyes closed, chest rising rapidly, blood soaking his shoulder. Kicking his rifle out of his reach, I continue around the shed, gun outstretched. I can't see the other soldier. It's a cat-and-mouse game now. He's here, but where?

The whine from a motorbike echoes through the forest. Magelon. She must have heard the shots and realized where we are. Hoping she's not far, I resume the search for my elusive target.

Scuffles and banging against the back wall ring out. Fear for Reece rolling over me, I sprint to his aid, but skid to a stop. The soldier has his arm clinched around Reece's neck and presses a gun to the side of his head.

"Drop it or he's dead," the soldier says.

The soldier's hand explodes, splattering fleshy chunks across Reece's face. The gun drops into the mud at their feet. Another hole appears above the soldier's nose. He falls to the ground, his face a bloody mess, but it's only now I realize I've shot him twice.

Reece fell, too, and he scrambles backward, his cheek dripping with blood. My gun follows him, but a voice in my head—my voice—screams to lower the gun. It's Reece, he's not a threat, I need to protect him.

I relax my trigger finger—

Another shot rings out and my upper arm feels like it's been whipped by a hot metal rod. Dropping to my knees, the searing pain takes my senses hostage, separating me from myself. Here, but not here, I swing my gun around and shoot the other soldier I thought I'd taken out. He's propped on one elbow, looking like death, but alive enough to hold a handgun. My bullet finds its mark, permanently removing the threat.

It's raining inside my ears, a steady downpour that mutes all other sounds. Heat in my arm spreads through my body. Pain receptors hit overload. I suck in the pain, harness it, roll it into a ball and shove it to the back of my mind. Somebody shouts, *move, move, move*, their voice ricocheting through my head like a broken record, and I push from the ground, trembling from the chaos in my mind, in my body. Gripping my gun, I search for Reece.

He lies on the ground propped up by his backpack, his hands raised in futile defense. Rain smacks his face, but his eyes are wide with terror—he expects to die.

Flipping the gun around, I hold it out, then peel my voice from the ball of pain. "Take it and go. Take the creek track. Magelon's there. I heard a bike."

Reece hesitates, then scrambles to his feet, snatches the gun, and hobbles toward the creek, glancing at me multiple times. Pain leaks from the ball, making Reece swim in my vision. Gritting my teeth, I check at my arm. The sleeve of Kelly's jacket is soaked with blood but there's no time to wrap the bullet wound. The second team could arrive any second.

Going to the fallen soldier, I unclip his utility belt and snap it around my waist. The gun I shot from his hand is dead on the ground with the barrel blown out, but he has another gun in a holster on the belt. Pulling it out, I face the forest and listen for the sound of a motorbike. The forest is eerily quiet: the calm before the storm.

The back of my neck prickles. Something's coming, fast. It must be the second team. Will they abort when they see their dead comrades? Or would that incite a feverish hunt with murder on their mind instead of apprehending me alive?

I run for Reece's bike—it's our last chance to escape. Sliding onto the seat, I kick it into gear and ride from the shed. As I cross the clearing, I'm blinded by a spotlight.

A chopper hovers above the house. An order to stand down shouts through a megaphone. I skid in a circle, unsure which way to go. If I head to the creek, I'll lead the chopper to Reece. If I take the entrance track out, the locked front gate will hinder me. There's no time to stop and search for the key. Taking the ridgeline track is out, too. The second team will come from that direction. That leaves one option.

Raising my gun, I fire at the chopper, shot after shot after shot. The spotlight blows. The windscreen cracks. Then a bullet finds its mark. Pilot dead, the chopper dips and falls toward the shed.

Gunning the bike, I race from the crashing chopper. It hits the shed, and the rotors rip the roof apart. Sparks ignite the spilled fuel at the back of the shed, then the drum explodes. Fire spreads to the chopper with pops and crackles, then the ground rocks from another explosion.

In my haste to get clear, I nearly run down Reece. He stands at the start of the creek track, clutching his hair, eyes wide, mouthing something I can't hear. A third explosion creates a shock wave that bends the surrounding trees. The force hits my back, tossing me off the bike and blowing Reece off his feet.

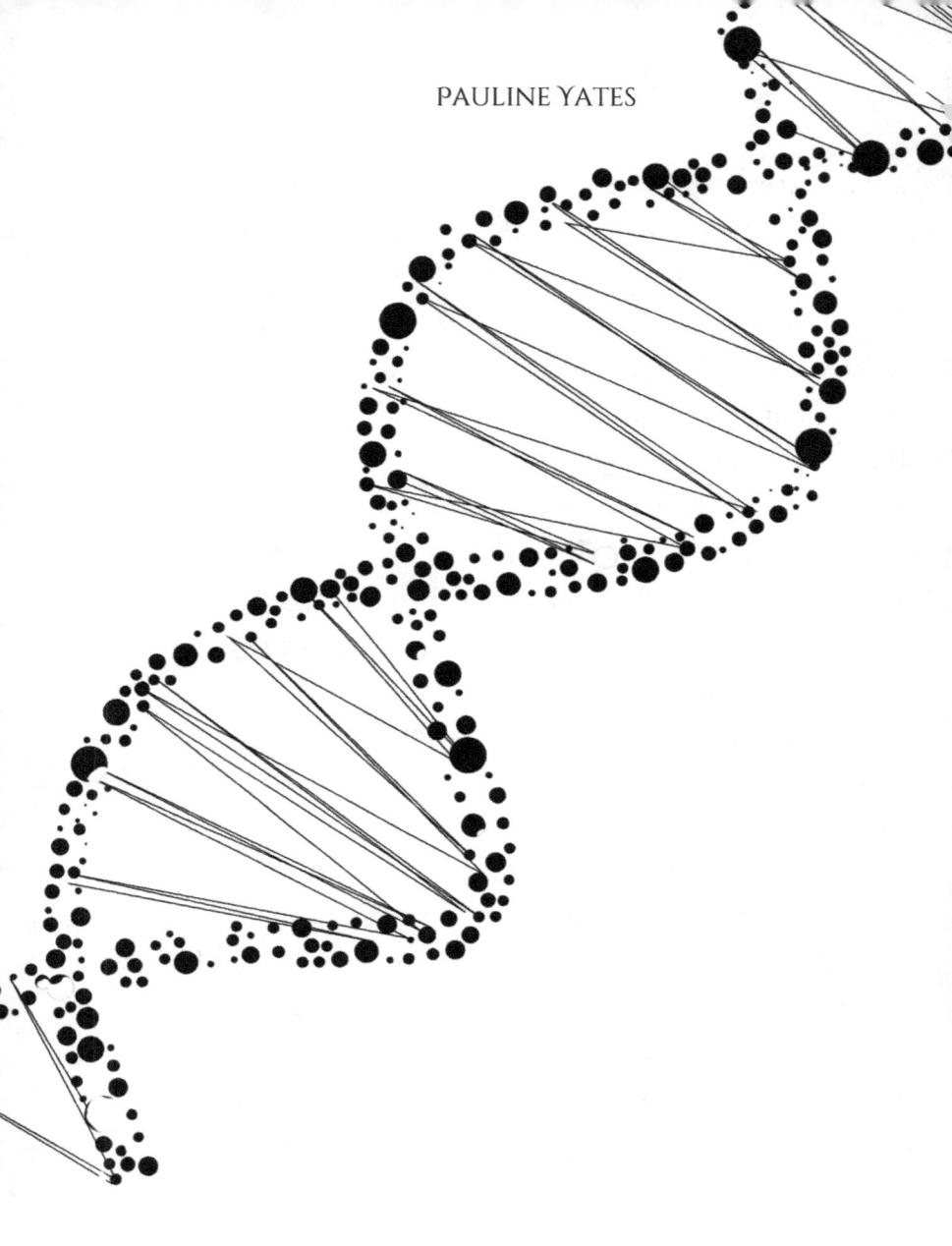

CHAPTER 16

KELLY RUFFLES MY HAIR LIKE a big brother teasing a younger sister. His infectious grin warms my heart. I've never experienced this type of knock-about family shenanigans. I like it. Want more. But Kelly's grin fades and his expression turns grim.

There's enough explosive in this crate to blow the roof sky high.

I jolt alert. Reece, not Kelly, shakes me conscious. He's frantic, mouthing something, but I can't hear him for the ringing in my ears. Lifting my head, I look at the plume of black smoke rising from the clearing. The shed's gone. The chopper's a twisted pile of burning metal. Flames consume the house, the smoke turning the rain black.

"Get up," Reece pleads, his voice breaking through.

I push to my knees and crawl to the trail bike on the ground nearby. Grabbing the handlebars, I stagger to my feet, then lift the bike and slide onto the seat. "Get on."

Reece climbs on behind me and clasps his hands around my waist, evidently all fear of me gone. Praying the bike still goes, I jam my foot down on the kick start. The engine splutters, then runs at a high rev. I ease back on the throttle. The inferno might smother the sound of the engine, but if the second team has arrived, they'll see us.

Twisting the throttle, I ride alongside the creek, then veer into the forest, slowing because the rocky ground makes Reece bounce. He tightens his grip and does his best to stay balanced, but we're one bad bump away from falling. When I reach the second split, I brake.

Left or right? Right will take us to rock pools, a dead end. Left is a stream of water pouring down from the forest above, too steep for the bike. We'll have to go on foot.

"That way," I say, pointing to the sodden slope. "You go. I'll ditch the bike."

Reece slides off the seat and starts upward, but he's slow, hampered by his injured leg. I ride the bike along the other track and dump it where the rocks start. Hopefully, if the second team follows, they'll find the bike and think we've continued in that direction. It might give us a head start. Might.

I run back and climb after Reece. He's halfway to the top but struggles in the mud, slipping every second step.

Plunging my hands through the streaming water, I grab rocks and roots to pull myself up. When I reach Reece, I shove my shoulder under his buttocks and lever him higher, then suck in a breath as my ball of pain unravels. Swapping to my uninjured arm, I push him again.

He squirms over the top and lies on his stomach, heaving for breath. Pulling myself up beside him, I turn my face to the rain and fill my mouth with water to wash away the mud and ash. I'm glad it's all I taste. The body count I left in my wake is high.

If we don't keep moving, we'll add our bodies to the list. The other chopper circles around the smoke, a searchlight sweeping the creek. If the second team gives chase, we don't have long to disappear.

Standing, I help Reece up. "We need to go. They'll find us if we stay here."

He shivers uncontrollably. Perhaps being hunted by the second team is the least of our worries. Soaked from the rain and chilled by the wind, hypothermia is a real threat.

"Where's Kelly's Hut from here?"

"Other side of the ridge," Reece says, his teeth chattering. "We'll never make it on foot. It's too far."

"Magelon's somewhere." I search the forest. See nothing but trees. We stand on the track leading to the ridge in one direction and to the house in the other. "Does this track loop around the ridge?"

"Yes." Shaking harder, he crosses his arms against

the cold and tucks his chin against his chest.

We can't wait for Magelon. Reece is freezing to death. I'm cold, too, but the adrenaline burning through me takes the edge off. "How far to the ridge?"

"I don't know," Reece says. "Four, five kilometers."

Five kilometers traversing unknown terrain in the dark during a storm. Do I tap into Joanna's memories to get more insight into the topography? What if I forget myself and leave Reece to perish? Joanna would—I've learned that about her from her memories. I'll have to chance it.

"Just give me a second to see what Joanna knows."

Reece frowns. "You...what?"

"Never mind." I'll explain later, if we survive.

Concentrating, I imagine the earlier memory of I/Joanna running with Marrick through the forest. This image is warm. Not from the sun shining through the trees. Marrick's smile generates the warmth. It's easy, carefree, not a smile he's shared since we escaped Bio-Tech. How old is this memory? Will it be useful, or a waste of time?

They run up the ridgeline track, our original escape route, racing each other to the top. Joanna's in the lead, but Marrick runs past her, claiming the win. He compliments Joanna's effort, and remarks about the difficulty of the terrain. I/Joanna forces a smile.

It's cold, her smile. I feel the edge in her emotions— angry because she lost and didn't perform to her expectations, and afraid Marrick will think less of her. It confirms the self-doubt about her abilities, her dissatisfaction with herself. She doesn't like coming second, wanted to beat Marrick, be better than him, better than everyone. That need gnaws at her mind, at my mind— she wants recognition and praise for her abilities. From who? I can't reach any further into her psyche, but there's something hidden deep. Whatever it is must be why she wanted to be team leader. There's no higher honor.

I sift through the memory and try to determine how long the track is and what ground conditions to expect. The top of the ridge is flat, with more rock than trees, but I can't recall anything about the terrain beyond that point. Joanna and Marrick must have returned to the house the same way.

"How do we get to Kelly's Hut from the ridge?" I ask.

"Fire access track," Reece says. "It runs down the other side."

"Has Joanna been along it?"

He shakes his head. "She didn't like fishing."

Do you have to do that here? The house will stink like fish for a month.

Joanna berating Kelly because he's scaling fish in the kitchen sink pops to mind. Her irritation flows through me, making me nearly snap at Reece. Exasperated at how her mood affects me, I blow raindrops from my lips with a huff.

"If we reach the ridge, could you find the fire access track?"

"In daylight, easy," Reece says.

Which is rapidly fading, but what choice do we have? "Let's keep moving. We'll find Magelon on the way."

I haven't heard the bike again. Magelon would've seen the fire. She could think we're dead. She won't hang around looking for us. She'll get word to Marrick and…

"Do you still have your com-link? Magelon has the receiver. We could send her a message."

Reece uncurls his arms, reaches into his pocket, and pulls out his com-link. He cups it in his hands, protecting it from the rain. "I'll tell them where we are. They can't respond, but at least they'll know we're here."

My spirits lift. "Tell them we're heading to the fire access track."

While Reece taps a message, I look around to get my bearings. Our destination is the ridge. The rain has eased, but fog rolls in, making vision impossible. Tree trunks are black pillars, the rocks dark lumps. The track is almost impossible to see, the lack of vegetation the only guide.

I pat along the belt I took from the soldier, identifying items that might be of use. Knife. Empty holster—I lost the gun when thrown from the bike. Flare. I can't use it so close to the house. Extra magazines. Useless, as I have no weapon.

"Do you still have your gun?"

"No," Reece says, pocketing the com-link and crossing his arms again. "I dropped it when I fell."

"What about your backpack? Is there anything in

there we could use?"

Reece slips off his pack and holds it out. "Only a change of clothes. Everything else is in Mags's bags."

"Doesn't matter." I continue patting the belt and find a torch. Perfect.

"Let's go," I say, pulling out the torch and switching it on and off—the bright beam boosts my hope. "How's your leg?"

"It's okay." He steps forward, but his twisted ankle can't support his weight and he almost falls.

The seriousness of our situation sinks in. We won't get anywhere if Reece can't walk. I could return for the bike, but I'd never lift it up the slope. The chopper still circles the creek so the second team could be down there. We can't wait and hope Magelon finds us. We'll freeze to death. It leaves an option that will save us or kill us.

Shrugging out of Kelly's soaked jacket, I sling it over Reece's shoulders. "Put this on."

Reece frowns. "Why? What about you?"

"Don't worry about me." The jacket is big enough to fit over the one Reece wears. The layers will act as insulation. Reece will insulate me. I turn my back to him. "Climb on."

"You can't carry me."

"Why not? If my mother's experiment made me stronger than Marrick and Kelly put together, you'll be like those backpacks I hauled during training. Get on. Leave your bag."

Reece hesitates, but when another blast of icy wind whips our faces, he tosses his pack into the scrub and grabs my shoulders. My ball of pain unrolls when he bumps my bullet wound, but I suck it back in and crouch to hoist him up, hitching my arms under his knees to carry him piggy-back style. When his weight settles against the small of my back, I switch on the torch and walk.

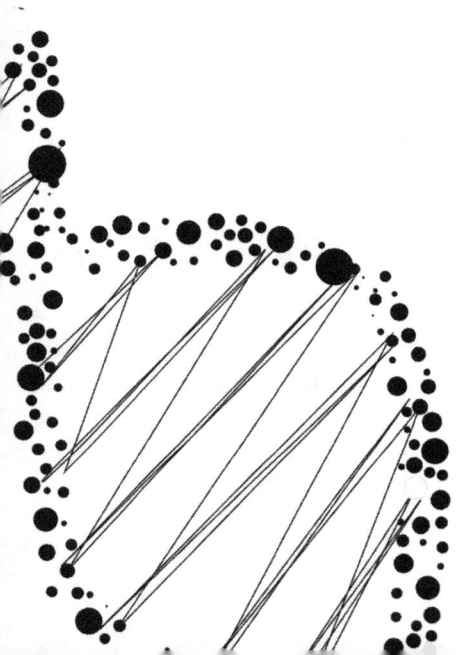

CHAPTER 17

IT'S A GAMBLE CARRYING REECE through the forest. I've never tested the limits of my strength because Darius held me back. The conditions are equally challenging. The track weaves between trees and rocks, and the overhanging undergrowth is so thick I lose the path multiple times. The terrain gets steeper, the despite its brightness, the torchlight only reaches a few feet in front of me, making it hard to prepare for what's ahead. With no hands to aid my balance, I'm relying on my core body strength to stay upright, which is exhausting.

I tread a jagged path upwards, eyes locked to the circle of light. Reece keeps still on my back, the only way he can help. I listen for Magelon's bike. I hope she wasn't caught, but I don't mention that. Better to imagine her waiting for us on the ridge.

The higher we climb, the sparser the trees, opening the canopy, revealing stars. The storm clouds disperse, blown away by chilly wind that numbs my face and arms. My elbows ache from holding Reece. My feet squelch in wet sneakers—with no socks, blisters are a new threat. I shorten my journey goals: climb over rocks, pause, scale a steep incline, pause, navigate through a stand of trees. Push on when it's clear.

The ground levels out. I stop to get my bearings.

Reece leans over my shoulder. "Are we on the ridge?"

"I think so." I shine the torch around. Flat ground stretches away from us. The slant of the trees indicates a sharp decline on the other side. But which way is the fire access track? "Do you recognize anything?"

"No. But we should go left. We're west of where we should be."

"A hacker and a compass? Any other skills I should know about?"

He doesn't respond, so I continue walking. After a while, he leans over my shoulder again.

"Can you really recall Joanna's memories?"

I'm glad he feels safe talking to me about Joanna. "It's the only thing that makes sense. You looked up cellular memory. What do you think?"

"I don't know. I'd have to research it more. It's

definitely uncanny how you recited what Joanna said word for word."

"Magelon told you? I suppose you think I'm a freak." Like Marrick does.

"If you are, then you're in good company, or so Joanna liked to tell me."

"She didn't like you, did she?"

Reece sighs. "She tolerated me. And only because of Marrick. I wasn't her ideal team member as far as physique goes."

"Let me guess. You weren't strong enough, fast enough, or tough enough. She's wrong. Look at everything else you do. The team wouldn't be half as good without you."

"Even if I've never graduated from a training program?"

"Especially then. Why did you become a hacker?"

"I grew up not knowing I had a twin. When I found out, I decided no one would ever lie to me again. I'm handy on a computer. One thing led to another, and here I am."

"Lost in a forest on a stormy night? Here is not a nice place."

"Better than dead. Or caught."

We still could be either, so I concentrate on keeping us alive. The top line of the ridge is more rock than vegetation, making it easy to walk, especially with the trees on the down slope acting as a guide.

I take a personal inventory. Reece weighs on my lower back. He's no burden, yet, but his legs around my hips aggravated the bruise from the baton strike and a dull ache spreads. The bullet wound stings, but I haven't moved my arm, so it's easily ignored. I'm not tired. A few hours must have passed, but with only my body to use as a time-keep, my guess could be wrong. I've never reached the point of exhaustion, so don't know what to look for.

Reece squirms, he must be stiff.

I stop to give him a break. "We'll rest here for a moment."

He slides off my back but sucks in a sharp breath and drops to a sitting position.

"Are you okay?" I ask, crouching beside him.

He grimaces. "I can't put my weight on my ankle."

I shine the torchlight over his leg and foot. I can't tell how bad his injuries are, but charred fabric sticks to the burned area. It needs cutting away, and the wound cleaned and dressed, but we can't do that here.

"It's bad, isn't it?" he says.

"I've seen worse." Standing, I stretch my back to hide my lie. We have to keep going. Get him to the hut where, hopefully, Kelly has a medical kit.

"Should we send another message?" If there's ever a need for a bike, it's now.

Reece pulls the com-link from his pocket, taps the screen, then shakes his head. "It's dead. Water got into it."

Great. With no way of sending a message, our predicament just got worse. I extend my hand. "Do you think you can climb back on?"

"Yep." He shoves the com-link into his pocket, then grabs my hand.

Pulling him upright, I crouch and hoist him onto my back.

He's stiff from the cold and has difficulty bending his legs around me. I'm uncomfortable, too. Letting Reece down exposed my back to the cold and when he presses against me, my wet shirt feels like a sheet of ice. I keep walking, but he's a dead weight. The temperature drops, too, the air so cold I could snap it.

I shine the torch ahead and search for the fire access track. Surely I would have seen it by now. Everything looks the same. Same rocks, same trees. There's nothing we can use for shelter either, to wait out the night and continue in daylight. We have to keep going.

I stop once more, but getting Reece off and on my back is a painful exercise for both of us. I resign to keep walking until we reach the top of the ridgeline track, the place I saw in Joanna's memory. It can't be much farther. I've been walking for hours. Has it been hours? I don't know. I've lost track of time, too.

A figure looms from the darkness. My heart leaps into my throat. "Marrick?"

"Marrick?" Reece mumbles. "Where?"

The figure doesn't move. My hope deflates. It's not Marrick. Not even a person. It's a pile of dumb rocks.

My spirits drop as low as the temperature. I didn't realize how much I relied on Marrick finding us. I don't know why when he can't reach us without a bike. I haven't given up on Magelon, but if she's around, we would have heard her. Instead, the forest is quiet, dampened by the rain. Even the wind has stopped. Mist drifts through the torchlight, the only moving thing other than us. I continue to walk, but for the first time in my life, I'm struggling.

Everything aches—my calf muscles, my thighs, my lower back. The inner soles of my sneakers eat holes in my feet. My arm throbs, a dull ache that matches a thump in my head. Not from the implant. There's nothing familiar around here to trigger it, if that's what happens. This headache is from thirst and fatigue, the first I've ever experienced. I want to sit, never move again, and that alarms me. Have I reached the limit of my strength?

If I have, then my mother's experiment to enhance stamina failed. But it will take more than fading strength to make me quit. Gritting my teeth, I give myself an order.

"Keep walking."

***

THE COLDEST PART OF THE night is just before dawn. I can't remember where I heard that. Is it an inherent knowing? It's definitely true. If I wasn't walking, forcing the blood to flow through my veins, I'd freeze. Reece must feel worse. He hasn't spoken for hours. That rings alarm bells. I walk faster.

***

THE STARS FADE. OR ARE the batteries in the torch running out? Or is it my eyes demanding I close them, fatigue weighing down my lids? I turn my head, feel Reece's slow breathing on my cheek. He's asleep. I hope. I wish I could sleep.

No. Keep walking.

***

I DREAM ABOUT MY MOTHER. She talks about *"suppressing symptoms of fatigue to trick the body."* Marrick appears in the dream, too, saying how *"we train to handle extreme situations, but the human body has limits."* Am I pushing those limits because the vector removes my body's natural safeguards? I wish Reece was awake. He knows more about this stuff than me. He might even know what compels me to keep walking. How long before I drop? Or will I keep moving even when, physically, I can't?

A warm breeze tickles my face. Forcing my eyes open, I watch a new light chase away shadows and brighten the surrounding trees. Sunrise.

I stop and turn my cheek to Reece. He hangs over my shoulder, still sleeping. His breath is warm, but shallow, so shallow, like he's afraid to expel a breath in case it's his last.

"Wake up," I say, dropping my shoulder to give him a nudge.

He stirs, his shifting weight nearly sinking me to the ground.

"Where are we?" he asks, his voice croaky.

Sunrise in the east means the river should be in front of us. The cluster of rocks must hide it from view; if it's on the other side. I might only see more forest.

"We must have missed the fire access track." My voice is as hoarse as Reece's. "But if the River is north, we should be able to see it from up here."

I step forward, but the brief stop cemented my muscles. Hitching him higher on my back, I sink my weight into my aching calves and clamber over and around the rocks.

The sky opens up, brilliant blue and cloudless. Below, a valley sleeps in the mountain's shadow, cut by a wide, shimmering river.

CHAPTER 18

THE NORTHERN SIDE OF THE ridge boasts a commanding view of the forest in every direction, but I'm too tired to give it the attention it deserves. I lean against a boulder for support while Reece slides from my back. He lands on his good leg, hops for balance, then sinks to the ground and stretches out his injured leg.

I crouch beside him. I can't see his ankle because of his boot, but I can check the burn. "Let me see."

Reece rolls his leg, so the side of his calf faces up. I peel back the charred fabric and stifle a gasp. The skin around the burn is an angry red, an early sign of infection. Using the knife from my belt, I cut away the material and make a hole in his pants. The burn mark weeps, and the blistered area is dotted with yellow specks. It's a mistake to stop. This needs medical attention fast.

"How far to Kelly's Hut?" I ask.

Reece looks at the river and frowns. "I'm not sure. If we've passed the fire access track, we should travel upstream." He shades his eyes with his hand and points upriver. "See that bend? The hut's there."

My stomach twists into a tight knot, not from hunger or thirst. The bend is the width of a ribbon, another half-day journey at least. I don't even know how we'll reach the river. The mountain is steeper on this side, with thicker vegetation. The upside is with daylight, we can see, but once we leave this ridge and lose sight of the river, we could easily get as lost as we were in the dark.

The alternative? There isn't one. "We'll rest a minute more, then keep going."

Reece leans back against the boulder. "Why don't I wait here? You'll be faster without me."

It's tempting. Without him, I could run to the hut. But I'd have to run back if no one's there. Without the com-link, I've no way of messaging anyone.

Reece must have read my mind because he pulls the com-link from his pocket and gives it a shake.

"Dead," he says, inspecting it from all angles. "They might have received the first message."

They might not have, too. I consider another option. Get Reece to the river. Leave him there while I travel to Kelly's Hut. Reece would have water. I could rig up a shelter. But I don't like the flush in his cheeks. He could be running a fever. I can't leave him.

I take a personal inventory again. I mustn't have reached my point of exhaustion—I would have collapsed if I had. My headache lingers, but a drink from the river would help. My feet are cause for concern. Unlacing the sneakers, I peel them off. Blisters cover my heels and toes, and the damp shoes wrinkled my skin. I stretch out my legs and dry my feet in the sun. Then I check my bullet wound.

A lump of congealed blood marks a four-inch gash across my arm. I raise my elbow and immediately wish I hadn't. The movement tears the wound open and blood trickles down my arm. Using the knife, I cut a strip of fabric from the lower seam of my shirt and fling it around the wound.

"Need help?" Reece asks.

"I got it." Using my chin to hold the fabric in place, I fiddle with the ends one-handed, then tie a knot and pull it tight with my teeth. Satisfied my makeshift bandage won't slip, I put on the sneakers. They're still damp, but I can't wait for them to dry.

Standing, I extend my hand. "Ready to go?"

"Yeah."

Shifting onto his good knee, he scrambles upright, using the boulder for support. I crouch so he can climb onto my back. Every muscle in my body screams in protest. Gritting my teeth, I hoist Reece higher and stand up. He bumps my bullet wound, and a peal of pain shoots through my shoulder. I suck in my breath and try to shove it back into the ball, but it rolls down my arm making me light-headed.

"Sorry," Reece says, shifting his hand. "I should've been more careful."

"I should've dodged." The dead soldiers, the destroyed chopper, Kelly's decimated house, refresh in my mind. Even if the teams were operating incognito, the military will want answers. "I made us all a target, didn't I?"

"Better a live target than a dead one," Reece says. "But don't worry, that's Flannigan's problem. He should have known what he created."

I'll unleash hell.

Not the black-eyed man. Me. I'm the creation, and I unleashed hell.

"We should go." The smarting sting in my arm is nothing compared to the agony caused by Reece's comment.

"Oh, hey, I didn't mean it to sound that way."

"Forget it." I blink back tears. I am a creation. Reece couldn't have described me better.

Picking a line through the trees, I start downhill. My feet slide on loose rocks. Branches tear at my hair and clothes. Leaves whip my arms, my face, as I push though the vegetation. Reece flinches numerous times so his leg must be copping an assault, too. He slumps against my back, but with his weight pushing me forward, every step becomes a battle not to stumble. The strain on my back and legs is unbearable.

Farther down, the trees thin and the ground isn't as steep. Walking is easier, but the sun is high over our heads by the time we reach the river. We stop for water. I let Reece down on the bank, and he lies on his side and scoops water into his mouth. I cup my hands but take small sips and only drink enough to quench my thirst. I don't want to cramp when we trek upstream.

After we've rested, I help Reece onto my back and continue walking, but the sandy loam alongside the river is murder on my legs. My feet sink in the soft soil and the toes of my sneakers catch on the grass, tripping me up. When I step into a puddle, the mud sucks the left sneaker off my foot. I kick off the other one. The ground is soft enough to walk barefoot. Zoning out, I watch dragonflies hovering above the river surface instead of looking where I'm going. It's like I'm on autopilot with no off switch.

A creation? I'm a walking nightmare.

Reece nudges my shoulder. "Sarah, look."

The river turns, a long, sweeping bend. Kelly's Hut is nestled among trees away from the riverbank. It's a good size cabin but is more run-down than Kelly's house. One window, a door. A chimney sticks out of the roof at an odd angle. A pile of split logs is covered in a tangle of fishing nets. Magelon's bike is parked beside the cabin. I'm too numb to express relief, but I quicken my pace.

"I don't see the Jeep," Reece says.

Did Marrick get Reece's message? He'd have seen the smoke. He and Kelly are smart enough to scope the property before entering. Has something happened? Joanna's never been to this cabin, but she'd know the general location. Did she send choppers here to search for us? What if Marrick, Kelly, and Magelon were caught while waiting for us?

I stop, unsure what to do. The cabin appears empty, but the soldiers could lie in wait. It's too late to run. I don't think I could, anyway.

The cabin door opens. Magelon steps out, followed by Marrick and Kelly. Reece and I sigh together, but our relief is short-lived. Magelon climbs astride the bike and revs the engine. Marrick and Kelly stride around the other side of the cabin. An engine starts; it's the Jeep, concealed from view.

My heart leaps into my throat. "They're leaving. Hey, Magelon!"

I shout as loud as my hoarse voice can manage, but we're too far away. Reece joins in, yelling at the top of his lungs, raising an arm, frantically waving to catch Magelon's attention. But she rides behind the cabin, oblivious to our presence.

"Leave me," Reece says. "Run. Run."

He pushes off my back and lands on the ground with a thud, but even with my enhanced speed, I'll never catch them. I need something to attract their attention. If I had a gun, I'd shoot into the air and hope one of them heard the shot. But I haven't got a—

The flare.

Pulling it from the belt, I crack the end and fling it into the air. The red smoke arcs over our heads. The Jeep's brake lights flash on. The wheels spin and Kelly drives toward the river. I bend forward and lean on my knees, choking up with relief.

The cabin door opens and Darius steps out. Tears spring in my eyes. I look beyond him, but when Joanna doesn't exit, all my relief sinks into my gut like a lump of lead. Is Joanna inside, or did Marrick fail to find her and she's preparing to strike again?

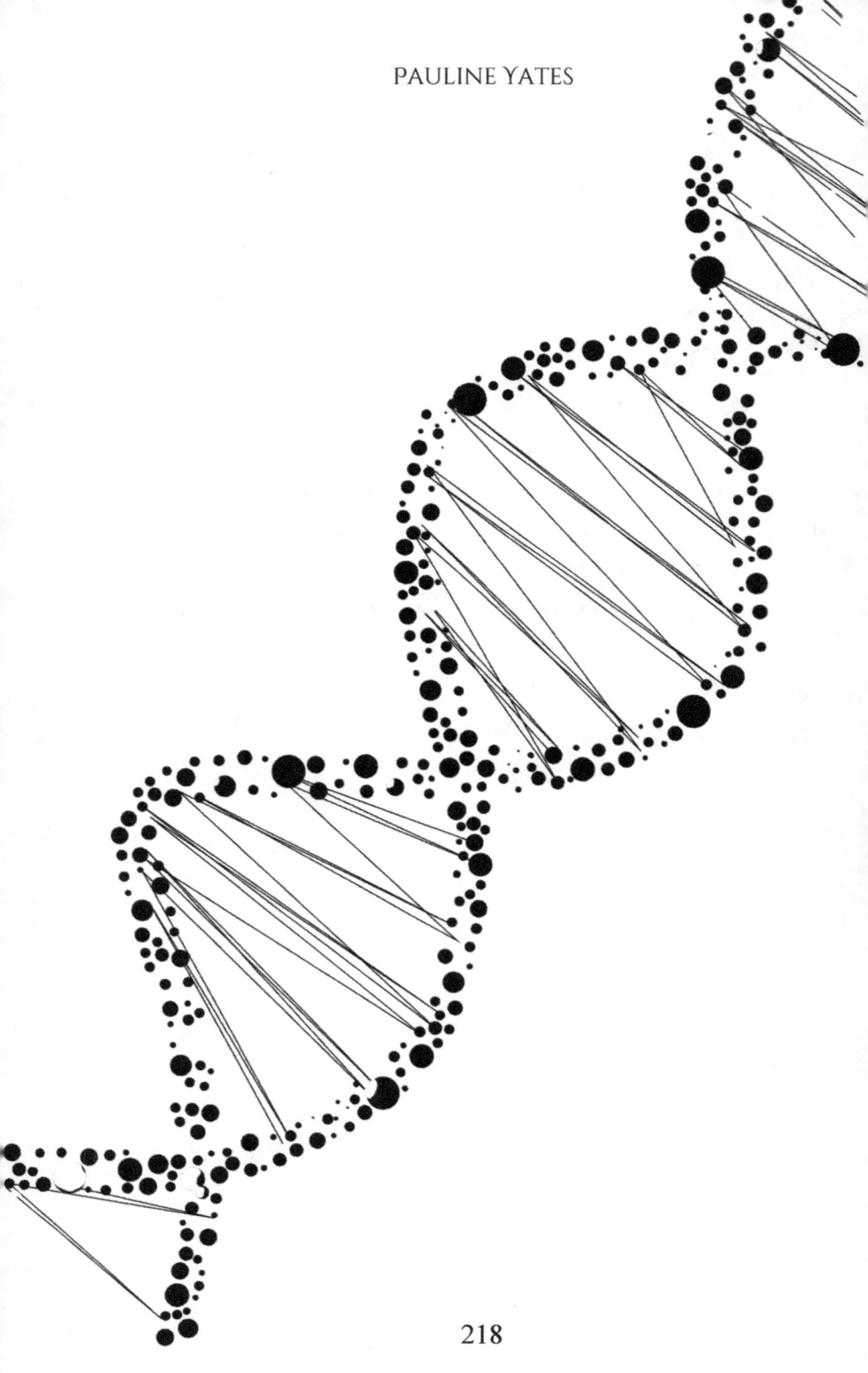

CHAPTER 19

KELLY STOPS THE JEEP IN front of us. Marrick's the first out. He runs to my aid and slings his arm around my waist, stopping me from collapsing. Kelly and Magelon help Reece, and they all talk over each other in their excitement. I can't share their euphoria.

"If the second team is still looking for us, they might know to come here." I don't mention Joanna's involvement because I don't know if Marrick will believe me and I'm too tired to argue.

"They're not looking," Marrick says. "They were busy with the clean-up, then left. Let's get you inside."

He scoops me off the ground and carries me to the cabin. If my feet weren't a muddy-blistered mess, I'd have refused his help. I don't want him, or anyone, to help me. All I've done is drag them into my living nightmare.

Kelly's Hut isn't big enough to allow much room between us. It's built for two people, not six. A square wooden table with four mismatched chairs takes up a third of the space. If the burn on Reece's leg wasn't serious, it'd be comical watching them scramble around each other to treat him. Or it's funny because I'm delirious from exhaustion.

"Watch his leg," Magelon snaps at Kelly when he dumps a medical kit close to Reece's injury.

Kelly ignores her and digs through the contents, passing swabs and ointment to Darius, who oversees Reece's first-aid.

I lie on the second camp bed, guarded by Marrick, or so it appears. Darius glances at me, and I lock eyes with him, delivering the questions I burn with. He knows it, too. He reverts to giving orders, his comfort zone.

"Blankets. For both of them," he says. "And get a brew on."

Kelly rummages through a storage box on the other side of the door. He pulls out two gray blankets, tosses one to Darius, the other to Marrick. Then he stomps to a gas burner set up on a crate in the other corner of the hut—a makeshift kitchen. A match strikes, a whiff of gas wafts through the room, a pot clangs, water glugs. Glass clinks, then peppermint replaces the smell of gas.

Marrick shakes out the blanket and drapes it over me. I hug it around me; I'm not cold but my body won't stop trembling. Drawing up my legs, I curl into the blanket and tuck my face into my arms. My heart races, my head hammers, and wondering where Joanna is spikes a surge of adrenaline that makes calming down impossible.

"See if she'll drink this," Kelly says.

"Sarah," Marrick says. "Sip this."

I peek at Marrick. He holds a mug containing Kelly's brew. The peppermint scent churns my stomach. I shake my head.

Darius comes to my side and presses his fingers against my neck. He must feel my racing pulse because he frowns. Do I tell him it's the compulsion to keep moving, even though I can't? Or does he already know that if he knows what I am?

"Darius, I need your help," Magelon says.

"Watch her pulse," Darius says to Marrick. "Keep her calm." He strides back to Magelon.

Marrick smoothes the hair from my face. "Try to relax."

"How can I, with Reece hollering?" I don't smile. Reece hasn't said a word since Kelly carried him from the river. I sit up, wanting to see him, but Marrick pushes me down.

"He's in good hands," Marrick says, tucking the blanket around me.

I close my eyes but see the burning house. "I'm sorry about Kelly's house."

"Don't be. You're alive. So is Reece. That's all that matters."

He rests his hand on my forehead. It's warm, like his warm smile in Joanna's memory. My heart bangs harder. I don't understand the change in his behavior. I didn't imagine the coldness in his eyes back at the house. I don't imagine the warmth in them now. Is it because Darius is here, and Marrick's orders were, and probably still are, to protect me? Or did Magelon tell him about the organ donor document, and Marrick is softening me up to get answers about Joanna?

Reece sucks in a sharp breath, making my eyes fly open. Darius dabs ointment on his wound. Magelon stands at the end of the bed, wrapping a bandage around Reece's injured ankle. With his boot off, it looks like it's swollen to twice its normal size.

Marrick touches the strip of cloth I tied around my bullet wound. I gasp as the ball of pain escapes its confines and rolls through my shoulder.

"What happened here?" Marrick asks.

I unleashed hell, that's what happened. "Took one for the team."

Marrick frowns and lifts the bandage. "Darius?"

"Yeah?"

"She's been hit."

"I've got this," Magelon says.

Darius comes over and unties the cloth, then prods the wound. I jerk away, using all my self-control not to punch him.

"There's no bullet, but it needs stitches. Kelly? What have you got?"

"Nothing she'll like." Kelly picks up a tackle box, opens the lid, and sifts through the contents.

"How's her pulse?" Darius asks.

Marrick presses his fingers against my neck and frowns. "Racing."

Kelly hands Darius a plastic jar containing needles and a spool of fine fishing line. "Best I've got."

"It'll do." He rests his hand against my cheek. "Think you can take it without pain relief?"

"Not bloody likely," Kelly says.

I can't meet his eyes. He must be furious about his house.

"I can take it." Darius will be quick. I've seen him in action with injured cadets at Red Bluff. After everything I've endured, I can tough this out.

Kelly mutters under his breath, then stomps across the room. He returns with another mug. "Get this into her first."

Marrick slides his arm under my shoulders and sits me up, then takes the mug from Kelly. "Drink this."

I sniff the liquid. My nose wrinkles—whiskey—my

uncle sneaks a nip on occasion. At Marrick's urging, I swallow a large gulp, blazing a fiery trail down my throat. I cough, then sway, lightheaded.

"Easy," Kelly says, snatching away the mug. "Knock your socks off, this stuff."

"Not wearing socks," I mumble.

"Hold her," Darius says.

"Lie down." Marrick pushes me down and places his arm over my chest.

Holding me down isn't necessary. Kelly's drink warms my stomach with a slow-burning fire, and I drift into a comfortable numbness. When the needle pricks my skin—

My ball of pain explodes, and I jerk against Marrick's arm. He pins me to the bed. I clench my teeth, so I don't scream obscenities at Darius, as he tugs the fishing line through my skin. How can a fine needle cause so much pain?

Magelon clamps onto my knees and fixes me with a steely gaze. "You can do this. Just think about being somewhere else."

I don't know what I've done to deserve her concern, but I'll take it. Somewhere else. Somewhere pain-free. The rock pools in the forest? The calm, the serenity. My heaven.

I imagine the waterfalls and wonder if the stream is a torrent after the storm. Water crashes over the rocks, washing my pain away—

***

I OPEN MY EYES. It's quiet. A gas lantern stands in the center of the table, the flame low. I raise my injured arm. It's bandaged. So are my feet. My headache's gone, but my tongue's furry from Kelly's drink.

Marrick's asleep on the floor below me. Magelon is curled into a blanket beneath Reece, who sleeps with his arm over his face. Kelly snores near the stove. Darius sits at the table.

Seeing me awake, he turns in his chair and leans on his knees, hands clasped.

"How are you feeling?"

"Okay, I suppose."

He nods at my arm. "Could've been worse."

Who cares about my arm? "Why didn't you tell me?"

He doesn't respond—just stares at me, his expression grim. Then he looks at his hands and picks at his fingernails. "Magelon told us about Joanna. That you have her memories."

"That doesn't answer my question." I prop myself up on one elbow. "Why didn't you tell me I'm genetically enhanced?"

He sighs. "For a lot of reasons. It wasn't supposed to go like this."

"Well, it has. And I've dragged this team into it. Why did you get them involved? They don't deserve this."

Darius shrugs. "They were your best chance of evading Flannigan. Still are, truth be told."

I lie down and stare at the roof, fuming that Darius expects them to stick by me after I destroyed Kelly's house. "Their cover's blown. The sooner I leave, the safer they'll be."

"Flannigan's research affects them, too. It affects everyone."

"And, what? You stop the trial by hiding me? Flannigan won't stop. If he can't find me, he'll find another test subject and the vote will proceed." I pause, afraid of the answer to my next question. "Why hasn't my uncle shut down Flannigan?"

Darius clenches his hands. "Too many officials want to see this research work. Lieutenant Wilson's influence only extends so far."

"When those officials see what I did to the teams Flannigan sent, they'll change their mind."

"If it's seen, you'll change some minds, but excite others."

"If it's seen? Let me guess. Those soldiers' deaths, the ones I killed, the destroyed chopper, will be erased from the records, like Jack Arquet?" I stare at the roof again, not needing Darius to confirm.

"Jack Arquet's a long time ago," Darius says. "Records get erased. Memories fade."

"No they don't." Furious, I sit up. "Flannigan's enhancing memory, isn't he?" I want, no, need Darius to admit he knows, so he'll stop dodging the truth.

"I don't know." Darius looks older than I've ever seen him.

"Why else would I have Joanna's memories? And not only hers. My mother's. Jack Arquet's. It's why Vera insisted I return to familiar surroundings. Similar situations trigger my recall, which adds to my skill set. Do you know what that means? No one would have to spend months training because they'd already know what to do."

Darius sighs. "If what you're experiencing is true, it's why Flannigan's continued to be financed. Genetically enhanced memory would change the face of the military."

"Where do you stand?"

"You should know that. Nothing good ever came from something not natural."

My anger fades. "You're right."

"Hey, that's not what I meant," Darius says, leaning back in his chair. "With you, it's different."

"Sure it is." I change the subject so I don't burst into tears knowing the one person I thought I could count on classes me as unnatural. "Marrick said he didn't find Joanna."

"No. I didn't see her either."

"Do you still think I imagined her?"

"Not after what Magelon told us. Knowing Joanna as I do, it makes sense she'd hook up with Flannigan to genetically improve what she couldn't attain naturally. Does that mean she's alive now?" He studies his fingers. "I don't know. I just don't know."

"She must be. How else would those teams know where to drop? She'll keep looking for me. She said I'm exactly who she wants, and she wants to prove Flannigan wrong. I need to know what that is."

"Let it go," Darius says. "Flannigan can't proceed without you, so that puts his drug trial in jeopardy. He's spent too long on this research to risk another knockback. The vote won't proceed without a trial, so let's make sure we don't give Flannigan what he needs." He sits up straight, ending the debate. "We'll talk more tomorrow. Get some rest."

I can't let it go. What Joanna wants is the missing piece to explain everything that's happened to me. Darius isn't interested in Joanna, but Marrick is. He wants to unbury the past and fix it.

Pulling up the blanket, I feign sleep until Darius looks away. When his chair scrapes, I peek at Marrick. He frowns in his sleep. Does he believe Joanna's alive even though he didn't see her? He might after listening to Magelon. If we share a common goal, it won't be hard to convince him to bust in and search for her again. He has the skills. I have the inside knowledge. Between us, Joanna won't see us coming.

CHAPTER 20

I WAKE TO REECE TALKING in hushed tones. He sits at the table with his bandaged leg stretched out to one side of his chair. Magelon sits on another chair next to him, Marrick and Darius opposite her. Kelly stands at the end of the table, drying a mug with a rag.

I close my eyes so no one knows I'm awake. If I'm going to approach Marrick about busting into Bio-Tech, I need to know how he feels about everything that's happened. And everyone else, too.

"She was so fast," Reece says. "The soldier didn't even have time to blink before he was dead. And I don't know how she shot the cylinder out of his gun so it wouldn't fire. It has to be the shot of the century."

"Jack Arquet could do that," Darius says, quietly.

Nobody responds, and Darius doesn't elaborate. It confirms what I said about already knowing how to do something, but also begs the question: when I killed those men, how much of my behavior came from Jack?

"Any idea what base those soldiers came from?" Marrick asks.

I wonder if he changed the topic because the chance I'll behave like Jack in other ways has increased exponentially.

"Most likely the same base he contracts his security detail from," Darius says. "I have a name. Crohn. He was one of the soldiers that grabbed me."

"Get me on a computer and I'll find him," Reece says.

"What about Joanna?" Magelon asks. "Did you find any evidence she's there?"

Marrick's chair squeaks. "No. But I was denied access to the lower level. At that point, I didn't want to make a fuss and risk Darius being detained longer." He pauses. "If Joanna agreed to work for Flannigan, as Sarah recalled, why would Lieutenant Wilson lie about her death?"

"Who said he lied?" Darius says. "Flannigan can amend hospital reports. I know you think Lieutenant Wilson set this up to make room for Sarah on your team, but that's not the case."

"So, is Joanna alive or isn't she?" Kelly asks.

"What do you think?" Magelon says. "Those teams knew exactly where to drop. They arrived at the right time, after Marrick entered Bio-Tech and secured Darius's release, and they had both exits covered. Don't tell me they took a good guess. They were told where to go. Outside of us, Joanna's the only other person who knows the layout of your property."

"Information Flannigan could've gained if he gave her memories to someone else," Darius says.

"You believe she's dead?" Magelon asks.

Darius sighs. "She's been with him for six months. Based on what I know of Flannigan's earlier research, no one leaves Bio-Tech alive."

"Well, I believe Sarah," Magelon says.

"Thought you didn't trust her?" Marrick says.

Magelon huffs. "I changed my mind. She said it was Joanna right from the start. Also, it would've taken someone with inside knowledge of Red Bluff's security to get in and out of base without being seen. That's Joanna all over."

I never thought Magelon would become an ally, not after the things I said.

"Why didn't you tell me she's genetically enhanced?" Marrick asks, so quiet I barely hear him.

"Would it have changed anything?" Darius asks. "Does it change anything now?"

Silence. I open my eyes but get caught by Marrick.

"No," he says, holding my gaze. "It changes nothing."

What does he mean? The answer is there, in his pensive gaze, but I can't decipher it.

"Should've guessed sooner," Kelly says, clenching his fist and studying his knuckles. "She damn near knocked me off my feet."

"I'm surprised no one guessed after her sharpshooting round," Magelon says.

"Flannigan can't know what she's capable of," Reece says. "Those soldiers at the house didn't stand a chance. Thought I was a goner, too, when she aimed her gun at me, but I wouldn't be sitting here if not for her."

"Are you afraid of her? Any of you?" Darius asks.

"She's not Jack Arquet," Marrick says, directing his attention back to his team. "If she was, she would've shot Reece, and we'd be having a different conversation right now."

"What about Lieutenant Wilson?" Magelon asks. "Is he her father?"

"No," Darius says. "He's no relation. Sarah's mother needed help, and he had the means."

"Who is then?"

"That answer's for Sarah, and for her to reveal if she wants to."

He ends it there by pushing back his chair, allowing me the opportunity to wake up.

I'm in an awkward position. Marrick knows I overheard them. I'm grateful for his support, but he didn't see me beat the other soldier to a pulp during the raid. I can't let myself lose it like that ever again, though how I do that, I don't yet know.

But first, I need to talk to Darius. I can't believe he knows who my father is. Kicking off the blanket, I swing my legs over the edge of the camp bed and sit up.

"Let's take a walk," Darius says, not looking me in the eye. He must have seen me awake, too.

Magelon scoffs. "You're joking, right?"

Getting up from her chair, she comes and sits next to me. "Only a lunatic would piggyback someone over a mountain during a storm. What the hell were you thinking?" She rolls her shoulders back. "For what it's worth, you can be this team's lunatic any day."

Reece grins. "That spot's taken."

It's a weird way to say thank you for helping Reece, and I'll take it, but I can't accept her offer. Any future with any team is over for me. All I want to do is find out what Joanna wants and stop Flannigan from proceeding with his drug trial so I can resume some resemblance of a life far away from everyone.

"How's your leg?" I ask, changing the subject.

"I've still got it," Reece says. "Unlike my clothes." He smoothes his hand down his pants. The bottom half is missing below the knee.

"Hey, Kelly," Magelon says. "Got any clothes in that box?" She smirks at Reece. "For Sarah, not you."

"Might have." Kelly rummages through the box and pulls out an old pair of track pants and a T-shirt. "They'll be too big for you," he says, bringing them over to me. "But better than what you're wearing."

"Thanks." I'm grateful for any clean clothes. Mine are filthy. But… "Kelly?"

"Yeah?"

"About your house."

He frowns. "Don't worry about it. Full of dry rot anyway." He glances at Reece. "A house can be replaced."

"Darius is waiting," Marrick says from the doorway.

He shares a ghost of his warm smile. If it's because he agrees with Magelon that I have a spot on their team, I'll hate to see that smile fade when we part ways.

***

AFTER CHANGING CLOTHES AND REMOVING the bandages from my feet, I join Darius by the river. He sits on a large log near the edge, staring at something in the distance. It might be the sun shining off the river's surface, but Darius looks old today. Daylight reveals bruising from the beating he took; a purple splotch on his jaw, another on his left arm. I can't see his stomach, but he must hurt—he hunches as if in pain.

Sitting on the log, I study my feet, wondering how to ask about my father. My toes are still wrinkled, and the blisters sting exposed to the air. My arm is sore, but the stitches don't pull. Darius did a neat job.

"You'll have a scar," he says. "Good place for a tattoo if you want to decorate it."

"Why would I do that?"

He shrugs. "That's what Magelon does."

I thought Magelon's multiple tattoos reflected her fierce personality. "What are her scars from?"

"Bullets, knives, blaster burns."

"Is that why she's so…intense?"

"She defines rebellious. If there was trouble on the streets, she was in it up to her neck. That changed when she learned she had a twin. You could say Reece saved her from herself. He wiped her juvenile criminal record so she could do something more constructive with her life."

"You know about Reece?"

He nods.

Good. Now I won't have to check my words regarding Reece's hacking abilities. "Does my uncle know?"

"If he does, he'll never admit it."

"Would he admit he's my father?"

Darius frowns. "Where'd you get that idea?"

"Is he?"

"No. I can attest to that."

"So, who is?"

He stares across the river again. "A man too scared to

let his daughter know he exists."

"You know him?"

"Oh, yeah, I know him. He swore not to say anything until you'd finished training and found your feet in a career. He didn't want to sidetrack you."

"Then he'll never get the chance because I'm out of career options." I look away to hide my tears.

"From where I'm sitting, one option looks good."

It's no secret he wants me on this team, but he must realize it's impossible. "What name would I use? Sarah Wilson? Or Sarah Arquet? Both have a history of shooting things they shouldn't."

"Don't you listen? No one thinks you'll behave like Arquet."

"How can they be sure?" Sighing, I stand and watch the current form rippling eddies, the churning water so like my emotions. "If I don't know what I'm capable of, how can I expect anyone else to?"

"You showed who you are when you carried Reece over the mountain."

"Any one of them would've done the same."

"Not Joanna."

I turn and face him. "What's with Joanna and this team? I'm recalling so many things she isn't happy with."

"Some might call her a spoiled brat, but…" He shakes his head. "She didn't suit this team. She's not a team player. You are." He sighs. "I'd like to think I know what you want. Tell me I'm wrong you'll find it with them."

He's got me there. Despite my memory issues, in the short time I've been with Marrick's team, I've touched on elements I want so badly it hurts. I want to belong somewhere. Have close connections, people I can rely on, confide in, people I can call friends. I'd find that with this team. They treat each other like family. I want that more than anything. But…

"I can't stay with them, even if I wanted to. There's too much I don't know. If I'm not behaving like Joanna, it's Jack, or I recall my mother's memories. I don't know who I am half the time. Then there's my mother's research and the implant in my head. I've always relied on my instincts, but after escaping the white room, I don't feel in control. What if, in the heat of a moment, I forget myself, like when I nearly shot Reece?"

"But you didn't shoot him. Do you think there's a reason for that?"

"I don't know." I look towards the cabin. Kelly and Marrick are outside, talking. Magelon sits on a stump nearby, twirling a knife between her fingers. They glance in my direction, but I look away. "I'd never live with myself if I hurt them. The sooner I'm out of their lives, the safer they'll be."

"I doubt safety is on their minds," Darius says, standing. "There are qualities in team members that have nothing to do with skill or ability. From a team perspective, you proved your allegiance when you saved Reece. They won't let you go easily." He pauses. "Marrick won't."

"It's not up to him."

"No, it's up to you. You can either make it work or spend the rest of your life running from the one thing you want."

He claps my shoulder, then walks back to the cabin. Crouching, I pick up a stone and fling it into the river. Trust Darius to know what I want better than I do. But how do I make things work?

"Would you mind company?" Marrick asks.

He stops beside me, picks up a stone, and rolls it around his fingers. I pick up another stone and hold it in my hand.

"How does Darius know what makes us tick?" I ask.

"That's what makes him so good," Marrick says.

I drop the stone at my feet. "What do you want?"

"What do I want?" He tosses his stone across the water. "I want to apologize for how I spoke to you at the house. I was angry, but not at you."

"You had every right to be angry." I hesitate. "You must think I'm a freak."

He looks at me, surprised. "No. I don't think that." He frowns. "Is that how you see yourself?"

I scuff the ground with my toes. "Yeah. I suppose."

"Don't."

"Don't what?"

"Don't think what's been done to you changes who you are."

I sigh. "How can you know who I am when I don't?"

He smiles, then picks up another stone and flings it across the river. "It's not hard to see."

Is it my imagination or does the day brighten like the wall of fog that sprung between us blows away in the breeze? This could work—us, being on this team. But not before I navigate another fog first.

"I want to return to Bio-Tech," I say. "Joanna's in there, I know it. I need to find out why she wants me. It wasn't for Flannigan. Joanna didn't know who I was until he saw me. It's something else. I need to know what."

"Then we'll make it happen," Marrick says.

I stare at him, surprised. "Just like that?"

"Yep. I want answers, too." He turns to face me. "There's another thing I want, but that's a decision for you to make."

Join his team. It's clear on his face. He fixes me with an intense gaze that says I'm exactly who he wants. And he'll fight to get it. I see that, too. And that decides it for me. If we stick together, we'll both get what we want.

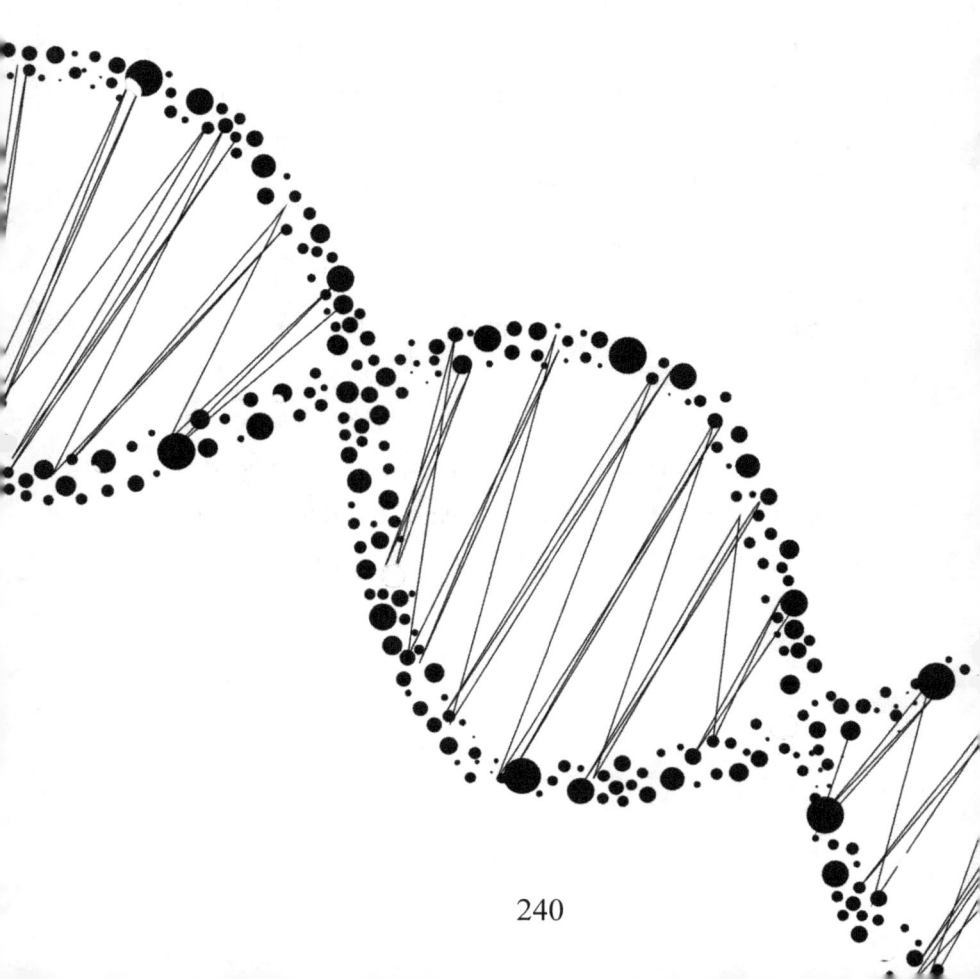

CHAPTER 21

M ARRICK PUTS OUR PLAN IN motion with incredible speed. In one conversation, everyone agrees the way forward is to find Joanna and ask how she's involved with Flannigan. Success will depend on whether she's willing to divulge information. We won't know until we get her out.

Darius agrees with the plan, providing I don't go anywhere near Bio-Tech. Understandable, as I'm the key to Flannigan's success. To put him at ease, I lie, saying only Marrick and Magelon will break in.

We relocate to a travel inn at Olivehurst, a town Kelly's familiar with. Marrick secures a two-bedroom unit at the far end of the complex. Kelly leaves for supplies, and by nightfall, we're all wearing new outfits and eating takeout burgers while Reece types on his laptop. Luckily, it was in one of the bags strapped to Magelon's bike.

"Anything on Team Tracker?" Darius asks.

"Nope," Reece says. "I've checked the local fire services and there's nothing about the fire, either. Either someone's good at covering their tracks or the storm extinguished the blaze before it was noticed."

The photo of Kelly's grandfather pops into my mind. If the storm put the fire out, would there be personal items, family heirlooms, left to salvage? No one mentions returning to the property. It wouldn't be safe, anyway, if Flannigan's soldiers continued to monitor it. Kelly puts on a brave face, saying it's only a house. It's much more than that. It's his home, his family's history. To lose it must be devastating.

I can empathize.

I help Marrick with preparations. We sit together on a two-seater couch next to a coffee table inventorying our possessions: Flannigan's keycard, the cell phone, the com-links—Reece pulled the damp com-link apart and says it should work again when dry. Marrick has his gear bag, and it contains two handguns, his gun belt with extra magazines, spare clothes. Magelon has her bag, too. In it, her gun belt, her Beretta, and multiple magazines.

Marrick writes a list for Kelly of the items we don't have—combat clothes for all of us suitable for our assault on Bio-Tech, a gun, and boots for me.

"You'll need another entry and exit point," Darius says. "You can't use the same fire access tracks as last time. Flannigan will tighten security in that area."

"What about Vera," Marrick asks. "Can she help again?"

"Not with this," Darius says. "We can't risk compromising her position. She's too important, and we might need her later."

He doesn't elaborate on why she's important, but I don't like his glance at me. I recalled she helped my mother, but in what capacity? Darius might know, but I'm hesitant to ask while everyone's around. Something about Vera feels personal, private, only for me.

Marrick places another sheet of paper in front of me and gives me the pen. "Can you draw the inside layout? I know the guard station level, but not the sub-levels."

"Sure." I take the pen and draw the lower corridor, marking the stairwell, the number of cells, and the door at the end. "I was in this cell," I say, marking it with a cross. "Between there and the stairwell were six other cells." I write corresponding numbers, but when I write three on the third cell, I stop, pen poised over the paper. The square on the paper refreshes the flight/fight response I experienced standing outside the door. Who's in there? The black-eyed man? Or Joanna?

Marrick places his hand over mine. "What's wrong?"

I tap the pen on the paper. "There's another man. I

think he's Flannigan's test subject. I'm not certain he's in there, but if he is, there's something wrong with him. He's…" Evil? "I don't know. Maybe he's already dead."

"Let's assume he's still there," Marrick says.

I look at Darius. "Did you see anyone else before you got me out, or when Flannigan detained you?"

Darius shakes his head. "They took me to the guard's station. Questioned me until Marrick showed up with the Hawthorne team. Once he negotiated my release to Hawthorne, we were escorted out."

"Would Vera know?"

"Possibly. Can't ask her, though."

The tingling sensation from the implant returns, the first time since the raid at the house. Would Darius know what it is? I consider asking, but don't want to jeopardize our plans if he insists I see a doctor. I already know how it works, anyway. There was nothing familiar at Kelly's Hut, but talking about Bio-Tech triggers it. Memories might surface with information we can use.

I draw a line down the center of the corridor like I'm retracing steps taken by…who? My mother? I imagine running to the door at the end. The memory becomes clearer: I/my mother pushes open the door, revealing a—

"There's a stairwell on the other side of the door." I make four strokes on the paper. "They lead to—"

An indoor gymnasium with state-of-the-art treadmills, bench presses, squat racks, dumbbells, and pull-up frames. And computers on benches, with cords running to each set of equipment.

"It's a performance testing area, a gymnasium, with computers and data recording instruments." I draw a circle and write G in it to mark the room.

"How do you know this?" Marrick asks.

"I remember it."

"You've been in there?" Magelon asks.

"Not me. My mother." I block them out, needing to concentrate. I/my mother is running again to a door on the other side. She pushes it open—I mark D for a door—and hurries into another room. "A maintenance room, gas bottles, air conditioning unit." I write M and circle it to mark the area.

Marrick places his hand over mine. "Sarah, stop."

I flick his hand away. "No, this is important." My mother's running scared. Why?

I/my mother stops and clutches her stomach. Then she runs to a door on the other side of the maintenance room. I scribble her path, turning the paper over when I reach the edge, desperate to keep up with my recollections so I miss nothing.

"The door exits at the rear," I say, drawing a line to mark the back of a building. "A mesh fence surrounds a power plant, it's not large." I sketch a square with crisscross lines. Beyond the power plant, the ground drops away. My mother climbs down, skidding in her soft-soled shoes.

"Give her more paper," Reece says, as the map I'm drawing reaches the edge of the page again. Marrick slides another sheet next to the first and I keep drawing a line, curving it as I follow my mother's path. But then she stops.

"There's a hole in the ground." It's as clear as if it's in front of me. I/my mother slides into it. Below the surface, the hole widens.

"It's a cave," I say, drawing an oval as she slides into darkness. She pulls a torch from a pocket and shines it about, revealing the cave system. But then I imagine a different tunnel, with rock walls supported by timber beams. The torchlight reminds me of the golden orbs. Is this a relapse and my recollections are a trick of my mind and there is no tunnel?

Large wooden double doors appear. One door hangs ajar. I/my mother pushes through the gap. The door scrapes her stomach—

"Oh." I bend forward. Or is it my mother bending forward? I'm so deep in the memory I can't separate myself from her. I imagine a squeezing, knee-buckling cramp ripping through my pelvis, but it's so real I drop the pen and clutch at my stomach.

Marrick grips my shoulder and urges me to stop, but I'm pulled into another memory: my mother again, kneeling in straw.

My mind goes blank. My mother, the pain, the cramping, gone. I hold my breath, anticipating something, then I recall pressure squeezing my chest. Gasping, I see my mother's face, through my eyes, not hers. She's dripping with sweat, her hair plastered to her neck, but she's smiling, crying, crooning.

Shocked, I sit up straight, realizing what I'm seeing. This is my first memory.

Marrick takes the pen. "What did you recall?"

"I remember being born."

***

I curl into the corner of the couch and hug my knees to my chest. If anything confirms I've had my memory enhanced, this is it. No normal person remembers their birth.

Recalling my birth leaves me physically and emotionally exhausted, but I've never felt happier. My mother loved me. I saw it in her eyes, her face, her tears. It must have killed her to abandon me.

Darius rubs his hand over his mouth, then retreats to the bedroom and closes the door. He mustn't have realized the extent of my memory recall and it's freaked him out. Kelly frowns, then goes to the kitchenette and fills a kettle. Marrick goes to help Kelly but stares out the window long after the kettle whistles.

Magelon snatches up the sheets of paper and gives them to Reece, who stares at me shell-shocked.

"Can you recreate this?" Magelon asks.

Reece looks at my hand-drawn map. "I don't know. I

could try matching it against satellite images and geographical sites."

Could he do that? Knowing Reece, probably.

Marrick returns, carrying two mugs, and sits next to me. He gives me one, then sips his, sitting quietly as though unsure what to say. It occurs to me I know nothing about his family, where he's from, brothers, sisters?

Hoping it's a comfortable topic that will ease the tension, I rest my mug on my knee.

"Do you have siblings?" I ask.

"Two brothers." He leans back against the couch. "Both older."

"What do they do?"

"Air force and navy. They made Captains a few years ago. When I joined the military, we joked we had the entire country covered." He smiles.

"Your parents?"

"Dad's Montana's chief fire warden. He lost his leg in a freak accident while clearing an emergency fire access track. He has a prosthetic leg now, but it doesn't stop him from running operations, or being first to the scene of a fire."

"Is that how you knew about the fire access tracks near Bio-Tech?"

"Yeah. Dad keeps records of track locations in every state, current and old. It wasn't hard to find what we needed."

"What about your mum?"

Marrick drains his tea, and his shoulders relax. "She breeds quarter horses. Can you ride?"

"No." But I imagine clutching leather reins, patting a hot neck, wiping lather, the white foamy sweat, on the leg of beige riding breeches. "Does Joanna ride?"

"Yeah," Marrick says, frowning. "I took the team home for a week when we first formed, a team bonding thing. She was capable. Why?"

"Just wondered." I sip my tea, irritated Joanna's memory replaced my birth memory. I wanted to hold on to it for as long as possible. Now all I can think about is sitting astride a sorrel gelding waiting for Marrick to open a gate from the back of a flighty dun-colored mare. The mare prances on her toes, but Marrick rubs the mare's neck, and she settles and stands still, ears pricked. Curious how the way he handled the mare reflects how he treats people.

My irritation with Joanna increases. By hooking up with Flannigan to be better than everyone else, she gave up the freedom to live a normal life and experience normal relationships. I've never had that. Probably never will.

"You won't believe this," Magelon says. "Come look."

Marrick stands and extends his hand. I clasp it without thinking. Holding his hand is as natural as breathing. He pulls me up, but I'm slow to let go. Or is he?

Reece swivels the laptop so we can see the screen.

"This is a satellite image of Bio-Tech." He zooms in, bringing up the power plant inside the mesh fence. "According to Sarah's map, the hole in the ground is over here. Now, look at this." He switches screens and brings up a land title transfer map. "South of Bio-Tech is an abandoned gold mine, and it shares a property boundary with Bio-Tech. The government reclaimed the mining camp area because Bio-Tech's a quarantine center. This is where Sarah's map gets interesting." He switches screens again and brings up a geographical map. "The mine shafts are still there. Two main shafts, with smaller shafts running between them. The line Sarah drew matches one of the main ones. It runs from the southern end of the mining camp to a natural cave system beneath Bio-Tech. The hole in the ground is an eroded washout that links to the cave." He looks up at Marrick. "If we can get into that shaft, we could get in and out of Bio-Tech and they'd never see us coming."

Marrick lets out a long breath. "Get as much information as you can about those mines." He looks at Magelon. "Get a list together for Kelly. We'll need extra gear."

"Yes!" Magelon punches the air, then mutters, "Ropes, harnesses, blasters."

Kelly stands behind Reece, eyes locked on the laptop. His grim expression is out of character for the Kelly I know. Does he see a chance to get retribution from the loss of his house? I hope he doesn't go down that dark path. It's not him, not in a million years.

"We'll need another vehicle," he says. "I'll wake the boss." He goes to Darius's room and thumps on the door.

Marrick rests his hand on my shoulder. "You ready for this?"

I nod. Seeing my map replicated as a real mine shaft is surreal, but the length of the shaft bothers me. It must run a couple of miles underground, at least. There's only one way my mother could have run that length while in labor. She must have been genetically enhanced, too.

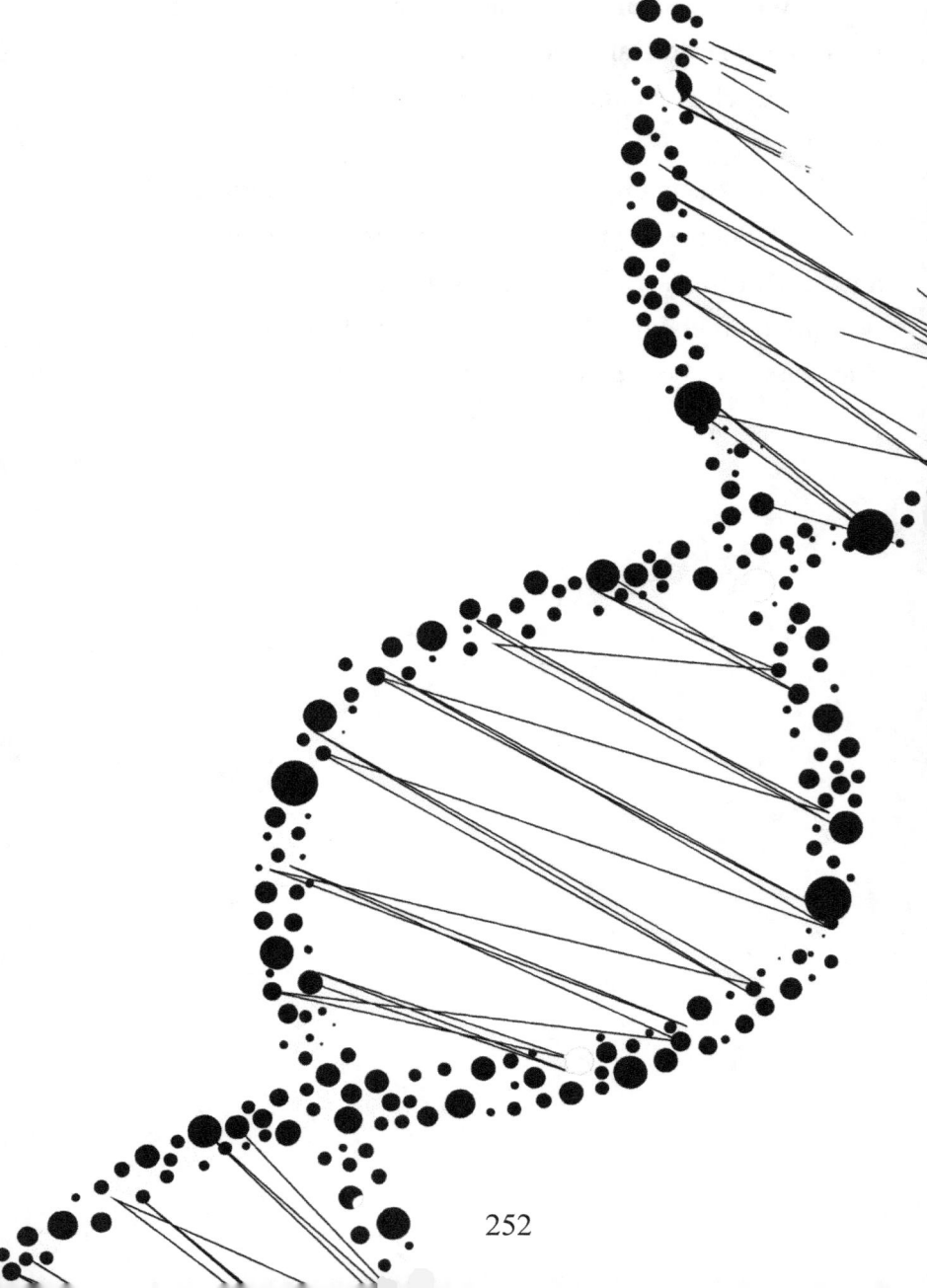

CHAPTER 22

M ARRICK INSISTS EVERYONE GET A good night's sleep before we leave for the gold mine. I share the main bedroom with Magelon. She must have decided I bring the fun factor—her type of fun— but it's like having a girl's pajama party. Her excited chatter makes sleep impossible.

"Marrick leads," she says from her side of the double bed. "We take all instructions from him. And this is important. If he says abort, we abort, no questions asked. Remember that. It could save your life."

She prattles on about the order of command should something happen to Marrick, and how she's next in charge. "But if I'm taken out, you're up, even though we should switch because you'd be better at leading than me."

I don't mention if I take the lead, it will mean she and Marrick are dead. I don't want to think about that. It would be cruel, finding a sense of normality with this team, only to have it snatched away.

That raises another consideration. I might find normality, but how does everyone else see me? Am I accepted because of who I am, or for what I can do?

Magelon drifts off, but wondering about Darius keeps me awake. When he emerged from his room after Kelly called him, he remained tight-lipped while Marrick outlined the plan. Marrick was careful not to include me. The only reason Darius allows us to do this is because I promised to stay on the sideline. Either Darius knows I lied, or something else is troubling him that has nothing to do with Bio-Tech.

I eventually sleep, but daylight comes too quickly. Then it's too hectic to worry about anything. Darius and Kelly leave for the west coast, to Kelly's brother's house, to get the equipment we need. Kelly organized a hire car for Darius; Kelly's size makes doubling on the bike impossible. After they leave, the rest of us pile into the Jeep and head east over the Sierra. Marrick drives. Magelon rides shotgun. I sit in the back seat with Reece.

"Did you check the Team Tracker before we left?" I ask, scanning every car on the highway. The open road is enemy territory.

"No unusual activity," Reece says. "Which is

unusual." He leans forward to get Marrick's attention. "Why hasn't Flannigan requested more teams to resume searching for Sarah?"

"Why do you think?" Magelon says. "He didn't know who he was dealing with and can't find the skills he needs to catch her." She sounds proud, which adds to my worry she only likes me for my abilities.

"Flannigan would need to issue a target profile and reason for apprehension to request more teams," Marrick says. "That he hasn't suggests he's keeping his search in-house, which makes him impossible to track."

"If Flannigan sends teams anywhere, it'll be to Red Bluff, or Sarah's uncle's house," Magelon says. "The last thing he'll expect is for us to return to Bio-Tech."

"Then let's hope that gives us the advantage," Marrick says.

Magelon has a point, but we shouldn't underestimate Joanna. She was with this team for three years. She'll know Reece has the capacity to watch Flannigan's movements.

"What about Joanna?" I ask. "Is there anywhere else you go if you want to stay out of sight?"

Marrick half turns toward me, but stays silent, deep in thought.

"She might think we'd go to Rusty's," he finally says. "Can you get a message to him so he can alert Kelly?"

"Consider it done," Reece says.

I sink into my seat and resume looking out the

window. It's a six-hour drive to the abandoned gold mine because we need to stop twice along the way for fuel, supplies, and minimalistic camping gear. Reece does the purchasing, being the least recognizable on surveillance cameras. At each stop, I hunch low in my seat, watching everywhere.

We reach Bridgeport around mid-day. As we drive through the town, Marrick points out the road leading to Bio-Tech. As I stare at it, a fleeting memory of driving along it pops into my mind: my mother's memory. I try to recall more, wondering if she lived nearby, but the memory of that third cell intrudes and my predatory feeling returns, putting me on edge. Who is in there? What do I need to hunt?

"Take the next right," Reece says, reading directions from his laptop.

Off the main highway, the landscape is flat, with dry, sparse vegetation and few trees. Reece guides Marrick along ungraded roads. Another sharp right turn, then the road straightens, and we drive through country so isolated, I doubt it's seen a vehicle for years. Abandoned farmhouses dot the landscape, surrounded by barren fields. Rusty wire hangs between termite-eaten posts.

The road surface abruptly changes to tarmac, and a fence similar to the perimeter fence at Bio-Tech appears in the distance: six feet high with coiled razor wire along the top. When we reach a gate, Marrick stops but keeps the Jeep idling. The gate is chained and padlocked. On the other side, solid timber beams mark the mine entrance. It's sealed shut by a double wooden door.

"Let's check it out," Marrick says.

He turns off the engine and we all get out. Magelon goes to the gate and shakes the chain.

"Need bolt cutters for this."

Other than ours, there are no tire marks, no footprints. Weeds push through cracks in the tarmac. According to Reece's maps, the second mine entrance is farther west of our position, but I can't see it. I look toward the mountain behind the mine entrance. Bio-Tech is somewhere up there.

"Warning. Restricted Area. It Is Unlawful To Enter Without Permission From The Installation Commander," Magelon says, reading a sign on the fence. "Internal Security Act, blah, blah, blah. Use Of Deadly Force Authorized. Excellent. We have permission to shoot." She kicks the mesh. "Says nothing about cutting a hole in the fence."

Marrick looks along the fence. "Kelly will bring cutters. Let's set up camp. Reece, where's Sarah's barn?"

"Back a bit, behind the last farmhouse," Reece says.

We're using my 'birth barn' as a base. How will it feel returning to the place that brought joy yet led to pain? I return to the Jeep but don't get in. I gaze across the fields to a red roof in the distance.

"You okay?" Marrick asks, stopping beside me.

"Yeah. It's just…weird."

He rests his hand on my back, then gets into the Jeep.

Sighing, I climb in next to Reece. Whatever I feel when I walk into the barn, I must ignore it. This is no time to be weakened by emotions attached to my past.

Marrick turns the Jeep around, veers off the road where Reece points, and drives along an overgrown track. The farmhouse looked intact from the road, but on closer inspection, it's returning to the earth. Surrounded by weeds, one side has collapsed under the weight of a fallen tree, the roof caved in. Smashed windows have jagged glass sticking out from the edge of the framework. The front door's missing. There's nothing to show it was somebody's home. The ghost of its history has long fled.

Marrick drives toward the barn in the distance. It's close to the perimeter fence, but I wonder how my mother climbed over. Did the fence exist back then? It's been seventeen years. A lot could have changed in the mine, too. It might be impassable, collapsed, like the farmhouse, rendering our plan to sneak into Bio-Tech useless.

The barn is in better condition than the house. The double doors sag on their hinges. A frayed rope hangs from an overhead pulley extending from a hatch in the loft. The gutters are rusted, sheets of roof iron lift. But the rest of the structure is solid, providing us with the perfect base. As Marrick rolls the Jeep to a stop, I prepare for the emotional assault when we go inside.

"Home sweet home," Magelon says.

We get out of the Jeep, Marrick checking all around. Magelon goes to the doors and pulls one side open. The hinges creak, loud in the quiet surroundings. Disturbed dust drifts out, carrying a musty smell from moldy hay. Magelon walks in, looks about, then crosses to a door on the other side and opens it. A rectangle stream of sunlight pours in, brightening the dim interior.

I'm not sure how I expect to feel, but no intense emotions wash over me. There's a sadness about the barn, like it conceded to being forgotten, a relic never to be revisited. A plow stands at one end. A harness, the leather dry and cracked, hangs over one of the wheel struts. Lengths of twisted twine dangle from nails on the wall, the loops filled with cobwebs.

Marrick walks to the center and turns in a circle, looking at the roof. A sheet of tin has rusted through, only a problem if it rains.

"Hey!" Magelon calls from outside. "Check this out."

We join her, except Reece, who pokes at bales of old hay stacked in the corner. Magelon stands at a concrete trough, pumping a metal handle. Water spurts out of a pipe, then changes to a steady stream.

"Who wants a bath?" she asks.

I scoop up a handful of water. It's lukewarm and brown. Magelon continues pumping until the water runs clear. "It smells fresh," she says. "There must be a stream around here somewhere. I'll boil it first, just in case."

"This will do," Marrick says. "Let's get the gear out of the Jeep."

We unload sleeping bags, torches, food, enough for one night. Kelly and Darius will arrive tomorrow with more supplies. I help Reece make a hay bale table for his laptop so he's ready to go when Kelly arrives with the requested satellite uplink. I cover the bales with hessian bags found near the plow, then search the barn floor for evidence of my birth.

What do I hope to find? Bloodstains? Discarded clothes? Seventeen years would have consumed organic material, but there might be an impression in the straw, footprints. I find nothing, a wiped scene. Erased, like me. Disheartened, I wander to the main door and stare across the paddock at the house.

Did someone live there when my mother arrived at the barn? We're in the middle of nowhere. She would've needed help to get herself and a newborn to her next destination. Being genetically enhanced, she could have walked, but which way and to where? No, she had help.

When it gets dark, we sit around the makeshift table to eat. I pick at my food and don't join in the conversation. A torch, its end stuck in the hay, provides light. Marrick backed the Jeep into the barn and closed all the doors, but the hole in the roof gives a view of the stars.

Magelon passes me a bottle of water Reece purchased

from the store. I'm glad we don't have to boil the creek water yet. Imagine falling ill out here, with no medical help for miles? I think about my mother again. What if she needed a doctor after giving birth?

I excuse myself, saying I want to wash up in the trough before retiring for the night. Once outside, though, I follow a track running between two fields until I reach the perimeter fence. Sitting, I stare at the mountain, hoping the proximity to Bio-Tech, or the mines, will jog the memories I need.

But nothing comes. No images, no faces, nothing about the barn. Access to my mother's memories would've ceased when I was born. The answers might be in my memories, but there's not enough familiarity about this barn to trigger them.

The crunch of dry grass beneath boots alerts me to Marrick's arrival. I should have known he'd come looking for me.

"You okay?" he asks.

"Yeah. Just thinking."

He sits next to me, lies back on his elbows, and looks up at the sky. "I forgot how many stars there are. It's like this at home. No city lights to block them out."

I look up at the glittering world above us. "I suppose you don't have time to relax when on the job."

"Not always, but downtime's important. It's why we went to Kelly's house when we could. It gave everyone a chance to reset."

I draw my knees up and clasp my arms around them. "You're a good leader, Marrick. Your team's lucky to have you."

I don't understand why Joanna turned her back on him. The answer's probably in my head, in her memories, but I don't want to ruin this moment by thinking about her. It's my chance to have a normal conversation without shooting someone or being chased.

"What about you? Do you fish, like Kelly?"

"Sometimes." He smiles. "I prefer rock climbing. Up the mountain behind Kelly's house is a series of rock pools. They run right up to the top of the ridge. It's a great place to practice."

"I've seen them." It's nice knowing Marrick likes the rock pools, but I hope Magelon didn't tell him that's where I nearly broke her arm.

"And you?" he asks. "What do you do in your free time?"

I welcome the diversion, but hobbies aren't something I want to discuss. I have none. "Does spending my day at an indoor shooting range count?"

"No." He smiles as though that amuses him, then lies back and closes his eyes, hands clasped behind his head.

When he doesn't speak again, I resume star gazing. This is nice, sitting with Marrick, with no pressure to keep the conversation going. I could stay here all night, if not for the dew.

"We should go back," I say, climbing to my feet. "I don't want to spend another night in damp clothes."

Marrick opens his eyes, looking in no hurry to leave, but when I extend my hand, he reaches up and grabs it, letting me pull him to his feet. This is even nicer, a normal, helpful gesture.

I squeeze his hand, drawing out this moment. "Thank you, for helping to rescue me. I don't know what would've happened if you hadn't."

He raises his hand and cups my cheek in an unexpected show of tenderness. "No. Thank you for rescuing me."

He gazes at me with a serious expression, like he's afraid of overstepping a boundary that might scare me off.

That makes my heart bang in my chest.

How did I not see this? It explains his answer to Darius when asked, *did it matter then, does it matter now?* Marrick doesn't want me to fill a vacant position, or because I'm genetically enhanced. He wants me, has always wanted me, for me.

I'm not immune to his warmth, or to the way he brings stability to my questionable and chaotic life, but am I afraid of crossing that boundary, too? My uncle's mantra is "personal and professional don't mix." Have I unconsciously adopted his view? I haven't forgotten my emotional flare when I sat with Marrick in the Jeep. Or been blind to his calming presence, or his protective guard. He crushed me when he didn't let me go to Bio-Tech with him. I assumed he considered me a freak and didn't want me around. That cut deep, but now I know why.

I've ignored the obvious, that we share a natural attraction. Easy to do after my restrictive upbringing. Getting involved with someone is so far off my radar, but is this what I'm looking for? More than a family or a sense of belonging. Even finding my place in the world. This thing: being with someone who likes me for who *I* am.

His gentle touch opens my heart, making it easy to press my lips to his. And when he kisses me back, it erases all uncertainty because being in his arms is so natural and right. He pulls me close, and our hearts pressed together ignites a slow-burning fire that promises I'll never be cold again. But in his kiss, in his soft caresses, I detect a hidden vulnerability.

And I wonder: what did he need rescuing from?

CHAPTER 23

MAGELON DERAILS MY PLAN TO quiz Marrick about his hidden emotions. She wakes me at dawn to run the fence line and find the second mine entrance. I suspect she wants to get me alone to ask what's going on between Marrick and me—she saw us holding hands when we returned to the barn. It must have driven her crazy all night wondering about the change in our relationship.

I hope searching for the mine will distract her because I'm not ready to share details. My lips are still warm from Marrick's kiss, and I want to hold the fire in my heart for as long as possible. He's helping Reece change his leg bandage when we leave but catches my eye and grins as though wishing me luck with Magelon. When it comes to her, I'll need all the luck I can get.

Magelon and I jog along a dirt road that runs between a barren field and the perimeter fence. We check for weak spots, but the fence is in pristine condition. The coiled razor wire glistens with dew, making the barbs appear extra sharp.

"There," Magelon says, stopping to point through the mesh to a wooden framework of timber beams in the distance. The door is sealed shut with a *No Admittance* sign tacked to the timber.

"Can we crawl under?" I search for gaps beneath the bottom rail but find none.

Magelon kicks the mesh, making it rattle. "Makes you wonder, doesn't it? Is the fence to keep people out, or to keep someone in?"

Like the black-eyed man? An uncomfortable prickling creeps up my arms and I think about that third cell again. I look along the fence. It runs straight and disappears into the scrub on the lower slopes of the mountainside.

I sigh. "We didn't come this far to be stopped by a fence."

I'm struck by a fleeting feeling of having done this before. Knowing how my episodes of déjà vu work, it wouldn't have been me, but could have been my mother. Did she search this fence line from the other side, trying to get out after escaping the mine? The fence must have existed if I'm recalling this. She got through, but how?

A patch of scrub grows against the fence farther along. The spindly trees are too low to help climb over, but they're strongly attached to the déjà vu. Curious, I jog toward them, hoping to remember something else.

The road ends at the bushes, and the ground drops away to a gully. The sides are steep and look like they've been machine dug.

Magelon stops beside me. "Is that the creek?"

"I don't think so. Look." I follow the gully with my finger. It extends under the fence and continues to a steep embankment west of the mine entrance. About twenty meters up is a hole in the rock.

"What's that?" I ask.

"Another tunnel?" Magelon says. "We'll ask Reece when we get back." She studies the gully. "Can't get under down there, either."

The fence bends with the gully, the bottom rail buried in dirt from runoff. Where it turns at the top, though, a blackened tree stump sticks out of the ground. The roots are sheared off where the ground's cut, but the soil is eroded around them, leaving gaps extending under the fence.

"Over here." I push through the scrub. When I reach the stump, I crouch and scrape away more dirt, making the gaps larger. It's easy digging. The soil is dry and friable and within minutes, there's enough room to squeeze through.

I roll back on my heels and appraise my effort. Even a pregnant woman would fit if they lay down. This might be how my mother got under. Or the tree could have been alive in her time, and she used overhanging branches to climb over the fence. However it happened, she got through. And so can we.

"We'll fit if we slide." I lie on my stomach and wriggle under the rail. Standing, I grin at Magelon from the other side of the fence.

She pushes through the scrub and copies me.

"Good idea bringing you along," she says, dusting dirt off her clothes.

So she doesn't want to ask me about Marrick. I'm relieved but also saddened. Marrick might want me for me, but Magelon clearly only likes the abilities I bring to the team. I try not to let it hurt me.

"Do you hear that?" Magelon asks.

"Hear what?"

"The quiet."

I listen, and see what she means, though until she drew my attention to it, I hadn't noticed. It's not quiet. It's total silence. Not a breath of air stirs. No birds. No insects. Nobody but us.

"Creepy," Magelon says. "Come on. Let's check out the mine."

The land between the fence and the entrance to the mine is flat and barren, putting me on edge. We're out in the open with no cover. Magelon pulls her Beretta from the holster and holds it low, her finger on the trigger. When we reach the mine entrance, she grabs a timber beam and shakes it. Nailed firm, it doesn't move.

"A job for Kelly," she says. "He'll bring the tools we need to open this."

She inspects the door hinges, then runs her hand over the timber beams. "Nothing else we can do until Kelly arrives." She cocks her head. "Listen."

A hollow whistle makes the hairs on my arm stand on end. "What is it?"

"The wind through the tunnel. Your mother must have had nerves of steel being in there alone."

A dull ache starts in my head, the implant, triggered by Magelon's comment. Rubbing my neck, I stare at the door of the mine, hoping to pry out the right memory. A familiar face surfaces—Vera. Of course. My mother wasn't alone. Vera helped her escape.

A wave of relief washes over me. This is how I recognized Vera and how she knew my mother. It's comforting to know Vera helped my mother give birth and supported her postpartum. It won't help us now, but it's another missing piece to my life puzzle, and finding it leaves me lighter than air. Happier than I've ever been, I hug my arms around myself.

"Is this how you're going to be now?" Magelon asks.

"What?"

"This." She gestures at me with her hands. "You're miles away. No guessing where. Or with who."

"Oh." Heat creeps into my cheeks. She thinks I'm daydreaming about Marrick. "No, I remembered something about my mother, that's all."

Magelon frowns. "Now I'm worried. Is everything all right between you two? A crush to his confidence is the last thing he needs."

Is this what Marrick meant about being rescued? I'd rather talk to Marrick, but Magelon might help me understand what I need to ask. "What do you mean? What happened?"

She sighs. "Between you and me, he was a mess after Joanna died. Blamed himself. Nearly quit. We were assisting police to apprehend a suspect after he shot three people in a botched armed robbery. We tracked him to a house. On the surface, it was an easy takedown."

I imagine a house; single story, brick, an overgrown yard filled with rusty cars and rubbish.

"Reece alerted us to possible multiple occupants," Magelon continues. "He was waiting on confirmation, but Joanna insisted we go in."

Joanna's voice filters into my mind.

We've got enough intel. We're going in. You and Magelon enter through the back. I've got the front.

Marrick replies—

Too risky. We don't know who else is in there. We should wait.

I cringe hearing Joanna again—

You're not the only one who knows how to make a call. Go.

Joanna's irritation with Marrick for questioning her judgment radiates through me. I imagine Marrick and Magelon glancing at each other, then they run around to the back of the house. Kelly's with Joanna, dressed in riot gear and holding a battering ram. Joanna signals him to break down the front door. He slams the battering ram against the door, busting it open. Joanna jumps past him, gun outstretched, but the second she steps through the door—

I jerk. The impact of a bullet hitting Joanna's hip feels real, as though I've been shot. Sucking in my breath, I clutch my hip, expecting to feel blood.

"Hey, hey, what's wrong?" Magelon asks.

I bend forward and close my eyes, breathing hard from the memory of excruciating pain. "Can you tell me something I won't remember?"

"You're seeing this?"

"Yeah. In detail." Joanna drops to the floor. A second person hides in the corner of the room. A man shouts. More shots. A child cries.

"There was a child?" I ask, squeezing back tears.

"Yeah. Sorry. I should've realized, you having Joanna's memories. God, that must suck." She wipes her hand over her head. "The suspect held his kid. Used him as a shield. The kid's mother, the one unaccounted for, hid in a corner near the front door. She shot Joanna. Everything

271

went to hell after that. Multiple shots were fired, from them and us. I took out the woman. Marrick took out the man. But the kid…"

"Got caught in the crossfire." The child's cries cut off, making me choke up.

"Yeah." Magelon shakes her head. "A kid dying on your watch is the hardest part of this job. It happens, but it didn't need to this time. Joanna should have waited. Instead—"

"She wanted the glory."

If there's ever a time I hate Joanna, it's now. Her thoughts and emotions as she jumped through the door make me sick to the stomach. She didn't once consider the safety of her team. All she thought about was the praise she'd receive when she walked out the hero. Because of that, she took a bullet and got a kid killed.

"No wonder she faked her death," I say. "She humiliated herself."

"She did more than that," Magelon says. "Marrick got hauled in to explain what happened, and he covered for her. Said she based her decision to proceed on the intel provided. And he's blamed himself ever since."

"Why did Marrick give her the lead?"

"Joanna hated being his second. Only the leader receives the accolades, even though any success is a team effort. Joanna wanted that recognition. It got worse the longer we worked together. She pushed Marrick to let her call the shots. Tried every trick in the book, too, if you know what I mean."

I don't, but want to hear more about Marrick. "What made him change his mind?"

"Joanna started dropping hints about transferring to another team. Said Marrick denied her opportunities to improve her leadership skills. Her guilt trips worked. Marrick thought he was being unfair. So, he gave her a shot. And she blew it." Magelon scuffs the ground, stirring up dust. "He lost more than a team member when Joanna died. He lost faith in himself."

"Is that why he said he wanted to unbury the past and fix it?"

"Yeah. Marrick took her accusations to heart. He questioned himself over and over about whether he should have given her more chances earlier. He eventually came round when he realized how much she played on his emotions. That's what stings him the most. He wants to know why she did that when he put everything of himself into safeguarding his team. Then there's her fake death. He wants an explanation about that, too, because that's the same as lying to him." She looks in the barn's direction. "You're good for him, Sarah. He's the Marrick he used to be when he's around you."

"What am I doing?"

"You're not pretentious, for a start."

"How can I be, when I don't even know my real

name?"

Magelon smiles. "I take it back, what I said about you not being the person we thought you were. I was wrong. You're exactly that person. You've just been screwed over by Joanna like the rest of us."

"How can you be sure? You barely know me."

"We've been watching you for months. If one thing comes out of the Tactical Skills Program, it's a person's true personality. I just hope..." She shakes her head.

"You hope I don't shoot you all?" I offer.

She fixes me with her steely gaze. "I'd take a bullet in the back from you any day before I'd see Joanna return to this team."

I never considered that possibility. Technically, Joanna's still their team member. Surely she wouldn't want to return, not after everything that's happened. She'd need Red Bluff's permission, but—

Transfer denied.

The words jump off the fleeting memory of a letter bearing Red Bluff's header. Joanna must have requested a transfer but got knocked back. I know why. Teams are expected to sort out their differences.

"Don't worry about it," Magelon says, as though reading my thoughts. "We don't want her back. What did you remember about your mother? It might be important."

"Um, Vera, she helped my mother when she birthed me in the barn." I can't think straight. What if Marrick is forced to take Joanna back? Where does that leave me?

"So that's how Vera's connected to all this," Magelon says, looking thoughtful.

"Darius never said?" I don't know why Joanna returning to the team bothers me. It's not like I can join the team.

"No. Anything about her is confidential," Magelon says. "For her safety, Darius said."

What if everything gets sorted out and I'm free to resume my career? I'd have to repeat a training program, but I could go to another base where nobody knows me. Reece hacked himself and Magelon onto Marrick's team. Why couldn't he hack Joanna off it?

"Sarah?"

"Sorry? I, um, I don't know why. Darius must have his reasons."

Magelon's eyes narrow. "Yeah. He does." She studies me a while longer, then turns away. "Let's head back. Nothing else we can do here."

We jog back to the hole under the fence, but my mind is in turmoil. Even if Reece could amend records, would Marrick, being the person he is, feel obligated to give Joanna another chance? If so, how hard will I fight to take the position from her?

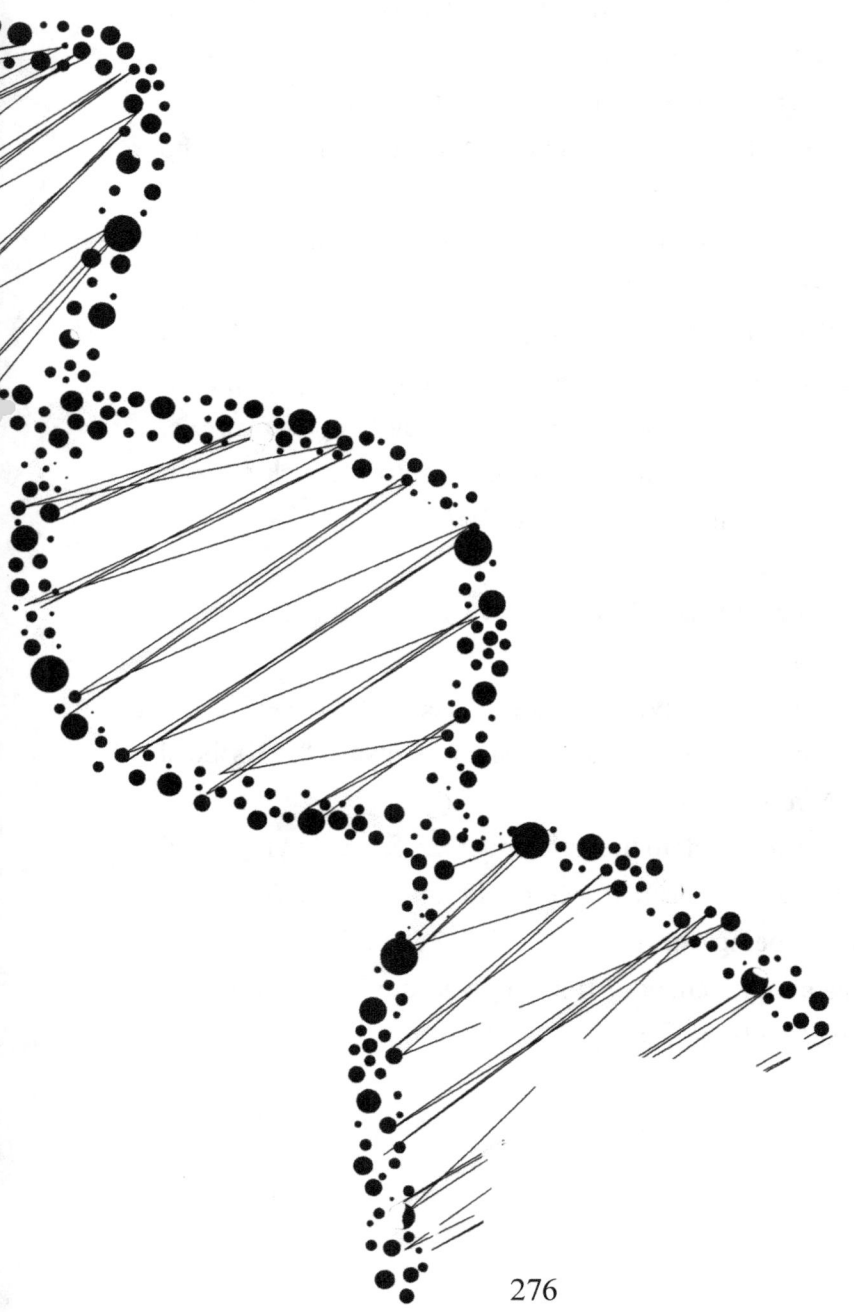

CHAPTER 24

P ROVING I'M WORTHY OF THIS team is like facing a graduation assessment, but with higher stakes. I want to stay with this team, more than anything, and not because Marrick captured my heart. They're everything I want in life. I'm going to fight for it.

Joanna, and not having graduated, aren't my only obstacles. Marrick needs to see I can work with every team member, in any capacity, without creating conflict like Joanna did. I want to earn my position, not have it handed to me because of our relationship.

Under normal conditions, I'd ace this assessment. But I have Joanna's memories, and they could prove fatal to my goal. Any of our interactions could cause me to exhibit Joanna's behavior, but I don't realize until after the damage is done.

I need to make sure I'm always me, so I practice on Reece when we return to the barn. Joanna liked him the least. We compare injuries, the burn on his leg against the stitches on my arm. He jokes about how I nearly shot him, which dampens my mood, but it lifts when he suggests I get a tattoo so Magelon and I can be ink buddies.

Nothing we talk about pulls Joanna into my mind, so my confidence grows when I spend time with Marrick next. I don't mention my conversation with Magelon. He holds my hand and traces his finger over the calluses on my knuckles while we talk about horse riding and rock climbing, and what it's like being the niece of a lieutenant. I reveal the truth, though it hurts. That it was hard growing up isolated from everyone. My only company was a security detail, and I had no friends.

I want Marrick to trust me, and that means letting him in. He makes it easy, no judgment, no sympathy, and I warm to him more. I turn the conversation to tactical operations and ask if what I learned at Red Bluff is the same as how he runs his team. That topic absorbs the rest of the morning and judging by Marrick's smile, I pass the biggest hurdle—professional versus personal.

Kelly and Darius arrive mid-afternoon, driving a metallic-blue, dual-cab style-side Chevrolet truck that would look like he drove it from the showroom floor if the panels weren't covered in dirt. When they pull up at the barn, Magelon grins from ear to ear.

"Hello, Betsy," she says.

There's that name again. "Betsy?"

Magelon nods at the personalized numberplate—BETSY11. "Kelly's latest purchase, his pride and joy. He left her with Rusty before we busted you out of Bio-Tech." She turns to Marrick, who stands behind us. "Things are definitely on the up."

Marrick nods, his brown eyes shining. He slips past us and goes to greet Kelly. Magelon and Reece follow. I stay away, content to watch their reunion. When Kelly gets out of the Chevy, Marrick slaps his shoulder, Magelon gives him a high-five. Reece gives Kelly a mock punch to his chest and is rewarded with a Kelly-style knockabout headlock and ruffled hair.

I turn my attention to BETSY. She's big and rugged, like Kelly. Now I've seen him in it, I can't imagine him driving anything else.

"What do you think of my wheels?" Kelly asks.

"Nice ride." I file away car talk for when I'm alone with Kelly.

Darius gets out from the passenger side. He casts his gaze over the barn, then approaches and clamps his hand on my shoulder. "How are you holding up?"

"Fine." I'm tempted to ask about Vera, but Darius is in trainer role. I don't want Marrick to see me as a cadet.

Excusing myself, I go to the back of the Chevy to help

unload the gear. Magelon inspects the contents in a black knapsack. Reece looks in a cardboard box.

"Did you get the sat-link and batteries?" he asks.

"Everything on your list." Kelly drags another box closer, and flips open the lid so Reece can see inside. It's filled with cables and computer equipment, unlike anything Reece used at the house.

"Perfect." Reece picks up the box, but I take it from him.

"I'll unload. You set up your laptop."

I carry the box past Darius and Marrick, who are deep in conversation. Marrick's running this op, but will Darius have the final decision, being Marrick's superior? That could be a problem when Darius finds out I'm going into Bio-Tech. He might order me to stay behind. I can't ignore him. A good team member follows orders.

We spend the rest of the afternoon organizing our gear. Reece sits at the hay bale table, typing on his laptop. Kelly reverses BETSY into the barn, parking it alongside the Jeep. Marrick and Darius sort through the gear Kelly purchased. Darius frowns when he sees three sets of black combat clothing, three vests, three pairs of boots. Magelon takes two bags and retreats to the corner of the barn. I join her to avoid a confrontation with Darius.

She sits cross-legged, dipping a short length of thin wire into a jar filled with red solution. At her feet is a handful of electronic chips, and a pile of flat plastic disks the size of a tennis ball that look like they snap into each other. I shouldn't be familiar with the components, but I can name them: Nichrome, the bridgewire—heating element. Pyrogen, the solution—pyrotechnic initiator. All that's missing is—

"Go easy with this stuff," Darius says, carrying over a small box. "It's all I could get." He gives me a pointed look—wants to ask about the clothes, I suspect—but he's called away by Reece.

Relieved to have dodged that bullet, I give Magelon my full attention. She slits open the box with her knife. Inside is a block of the same blue explosive she kept in Kelly's shed. She nods. "It'll be enough."

"What do we need blasters for?" I ask.

"To blow the mineshafts, so no one can follow us out. Won't know if it'll work until I see inside the mine. We'll check out the shafts tonight." She lays a pyrogen-coated bridgewire on a hessian bag spread out on the ground, then picks up another length of wire and repeats the process.

"Where did you learn how to make blasters?" We didn't learn this at Red Bluff.

"My dad. He's a pyrotechnics technician. Remote-detonating blasters aren't much different from setting off fireworks. A sensor chip attached to an electric match, attached to an explosive component. Heat, burn, bang." She grins.

"How do you ignite the e-match?" E-match? Is that

what it's called?

"Three ways. Radiofrequency or infra-red. I'll use radio, as that's what Reece has. I need a direct line for infra-red and it might not be possible in the mine."

"What's the third?"

She picks up a plastic disk and taps the center with the tip of her knife. "If the remote detonation fails, a direct hit with a bullet will create enough friction to heat the bridgewire, ignite the e-match and blow the explosive. Just make sure you're not in the detonation range when it goes boom."

Kelly appears beside me. "Those babies go off. Put them outside when you finish. Don't need to blow up another shed." Giving me a wink, he holds open the bag he carries and thrusts it at me. "Courtesy of Rusty. Help yourself."

I'm glad his cheery mood has returned and grateful for his forgiveness. Again, he's making sure we eat. The bag holds red and green apples and a handful of oranges. Fresh fruit after eating burgers makes my mouth water. Choosing a red apple, I bite into it, but spit it out; the red skin is bitter and not to my liking. I don't know why I chose it when my preference is green apples.

Kelly holds the bag open for Magelon, but she only gives the contents a cursory glance. "A waste bringing red ones. You know none of us eat those."

"Joanna does, " Kelly says. "She'll need something

to eat when we get her out."

I lose my appetite. If I unconsciously picked Joanna's favorite apple, what other Joanna behavior have I displayed? It must be how I knew the blaster components. Joanna would have seen Magelon make them. Joanna would also know how this team preps for an assignment. What if my memories crossed with Joanna's and I've been behaving accordingly? There's not a lot of difference between what Marrick does and what Red Bluff teaches. Am I securing my place with this team, or Joanna's?

Uneasy, I wander over to Marrick, throwing the red apple into the field as I pass the door. He's crouched on the ground, weapons spread around him. Three gun belts, their pouches empty, lie on the straw. Kneeling next to him, I pick up a belt to load the pouches, but hesitate. Am I reading the play, or doing what Joanna did?

"Everything all right?" Marrick asks.

"Fine." I force a smile.

Marrick picks a belt and slides a magazine into a pouch. But then he stops, the belt hanging over his hand. "About going into Bio-Tech. I want you to stay behind."

I stare at him, confused. "Why?"

"It's not that I don't think you're capable. It's just…" He sighs and fiddles with the belt. "I need to know you'll be here when I get back."

Is that it? He's worried I'll get hurt? I've put professional before personal. Why can't he? My first instinct is to refuse. Of course I'm going in. But I hesitate. Is that my response? Or Joanna's?

Magelon said Joanna always pushed to call the shots. If I say no, would that be like Joanna pushing to get her way? Marrick's giving a subtle order, and how I respond will either secure my team position or end it; it's the difference between working solo and being a team player.

I should follow his order and help from here. But returning to Bio-Tech is as much my suggestion as his. And his reason isn't professional, it's personal. Irritated, I pick up a magazine and jam it into a pouch. "I'm going with you. You'll have to cuff me to the Jeep to make me stay behind."

He grimaces. "Sarah—"

"You don't know the inside layout of Bio-Tech. I do, and what I don't, I'll remember. You also don't know what Flannigan is capable of, or who else he has in there. So, I'm coming. Because I need you to return safe."

Our eyes lock.

Marrick looks away first. "Okay. But you'll have to get past Darius."

I'm not worried about Darius. I've figured out his weak spot. But when Marrick resumes packing his belt, dismissing me entirely, it occurs to me I might have repeated what Joanna did to Marrick on the day she got shot.

CHAPTER 25

M ARRICK IS ALOOF FOR THE rest of the afternoon. I've caused a rift, but I don't know how to fix it, or even if I should. I might have given Joanna-type responses—though I hope to god I didn't—but Marrick should have separated personal from professional.

But did I do the same by saying I needed him to return safe?

I mull over our exchange while helping Kelly prepare food. He chats about his Chevy, how much he paid, and about the modifications Rusty made to the suspension. I half-listen.

If it wasn't for my rising predatory feeling, I'd consider telling Marrick I'll stay behind. But I meant what

I said. Flannigan can't be trusted. We also can't discount the black-eyed man. He might be in the third cell.

Thinking about him makes me edgy. Hunt it down and kill it? Am I the hunter, or the hunted? Fight or flight. Either option torments me. Protecting this team overrides both. I can't do that from here.

The day draws to a close and Marrick's coolness toward me doesn't abate. When he, Kelly, and Magelon set out to inspect the mines, I'm not invited.

Magelon pulls me aside as they leave. "What the hell's going on? It's arctic between you two."

"He wants me to stay behind," I say, keeping my voice low. "I said no. But I'm not sure if it was me or Joanna talking."

"Shit. Joanna's not even here, and she can still get to him." Scowling, she hitches her knapsack higher on her shoulder and strides from the barn.

I'm glad she understands how much Joanna's memories influence me, but don't know how she'll help. Joanna's Marrick's demon, but she's also mine. Annoyed at how we're both affected by her, I drag a hay bale to the table and sit next to Reece, wondering if I've given any other Joanna responses during the day.

Unable to tell, I rub my neck, hating Joanna for what she did to me, hating her for what she did to Marrick. Darius doesn't help my mood. He sits on the other side of Reece, frowning at me while watching a satellite image of

Bio-Tech on Reece's laptop screen. Any second, I swear, he'll ask about the third set of black clothes.

Reece zooms in, bringing up an image of soldiers patrolling the perimeter fence.

"Is that real-time imagery?" I ask.

"Yep. I hacked into Sat-Map, a geographical satellite imaging application used by mining companies. Have to be careful, though. If I'm caught using it to spy on a military facility, it's sayonara for me."

The depth of his hacking ability is impressive, albeit dangerous. But the three vehicles parked behind the building raises questions. "Has Flannigan increased security?"

"We won't know until we see the security changeover," Darius says.

"Do you know where they're from?"

"No. I don't recognize them."

"What about that soldier, Crohn? Did you find him?"

"I'll have a look now," Reece says.

He switches screens, logs into another portal, and types *Crohn* into the search bar. A list appears showing seven names of Crohn, each with different initials. Reece clicks on the first name and uploads a profile picture.

"Tell me when you recognize him," he says to Darius.

"Nope," Darius says.

Reece tries the next name, then the next.

When the fourth profile uploads, Darius jabs his

finger at the screen. "That's him."

Reece reads from the screen. "Transferred to Dardanelle base eight months ago, after failing basics at Camp Merrill. What do you know about Dardanelle?"

"It's a warfare training base run by Colonel Jeffries," Darius says, leaning back and rubbing his jaw. "A nut case if I ever met one. Wouldn't put it past him to be involved with an unauthorized raid on Kelly's house. He's as loony as the misfits sent to him."

Reece runs a search on the Dardanelle base. Data appears on the screen.

"Jeffries runs a skill upgrade course for anyone who failed basic training," Reece says. "There's no reference to standby teams or active-duty personnel. But it has choppers."

"Are they missing one?" I ask.

Darius sits up straight. "I don't like it."

"Why?" I ask. "If the soldiers Flannigan uses lack basic skills, getting past them will be easy."

"Inexperienced soldiers are dangerous. They're unpredictable. Shoot from nerves, not from sense. It explains my rough treatment. That's Jeffries' style of training. Beat into submission and ask questions later."

"If we're going in through the back, we won't cross paths. It's who's inside we need to worry about."

"Security in those lower levels is minimal," Darius says. "That area's off-limits to all but Flannigan's medical staff, according to Vera. If Marrick sticks to that level, it will be a simple in and out. Start logging the security detail. I want changeover times, how many soldiers in each unit, and where they patrol. Log it over twenty-four hours so we can calculate an entry window." He glances at his watch. "Starting from now."

"On it," Reece says.

"Show me what to do and I'll help," I say, not wanting to leave anything to chance. "You'll need to sleep sometime."

"I'll take a shift, too," Darius says. "I'll bunk down now. Wake me in four hours."

He goes to the other side of the barn, shakes out a bedroll, then lies down and closes his eyes.

Clasping my hands behind my head, I lean back and stare through the hole in the roof. It's dark outside but it will be darker in the mine. How far has Marrick travelled? What if they can't get through? A collapsed mineshaft would end our attempt to infiltrate Bio-Tech. Would that be a good thing? Three vehicles could mean three teams. That's fifteen soldiers. Why so many?

I jerk my hands down and stare at the computer screen. "Have you checked the Team Tracker lately?"

"Yep," Reece says. "Still no unusual activity."

"What about pop-up checkpoints around my home or Rusty's house?"

"Nothing. We expected Flannigan to work under the

radar, so if he sent teams, I won't see them."

"Yet, going by the number of military vehicles parked at Bio-Tech, Flannigan tripled his security. Isn't that overkill? What if he knows we're coming?"

Reece frowns. "How would he"—his eyes widen— "...Joanna?"

"She knows Marrick wouldn't abandon a team member."

"But she doesn't know he thinks she's alive," Reece says.

"What if she does? When she drugged me in my barracks, I called her by name. She must know I'm with Marrick if she orchestrated the raid on the house. Think about it. Flannigan hasn't requested more search teams. He's boosted Bio-Tech's security. Joanna knows we're coming for her."

"What do we do?" Reece asks.

I can't believe I'm going to suggest this. It means I'll never know why Joanna wanted me, but I'm not letting this team go on an assignment destined to fail. "We have to abort."

Reece frowns. "We should run it by Marrick."

I wave at the screen. "Why? He doesn't know this. He's not the only one who knows when to make a call." I clamp my mouth shut, unable to believe I repeated the exact words Joanna said to Marrick at their ill-fated assignment.

"Now I know what Magelon meant," Reece says.

"You sounded just like Joanna."

I wipe my hand over my mouth, a Darius gesture and now I understand why he does it—out of frustration, anger, or general annoyance at saying something he shouldn't.

"Have I said anything else today that sounded like Joanna?"

"A couple of things," Reece says.

I stand and pace the barn. My knowledge of blaster construction, choosing the red apple, my argument with Marrick—I've been confusing myself with Joanna all day. No wonder Marrick's cold toward me. In his eyes, I'm Joanna.

I need distance. Go somewhere Joanna doesn't know. I need to get her out of my head.

"I'm going for a walk."

"What? Where?" Reece asks.

Ignoring him, I stride from the barn and hurry down the road as far as the dilapidated farmhouse. There, I sit on the road, clamp my hands around my head and think about the rock pools, the mountain, Kelly's Hut, all the places Joanna hasn't been. It helps. My thoughts drift back to Red Bluff, to my sharpshooting round, my training months with Darius, my life with my uncle. Familiar places. My life, not Joanna's.

The moon rises, dulling the stars that cast their sparkling blanket across the sky. Marrick might be back by now, but I'm afraid to return until I'm sure I'm me. I rub my neck, wishing I could remove the implant. It hasn't twinged since we've been here—unless I've grown used to it and I'm subconsciously disregarding it—but I'm certain it's responsible for drawing out Joanna's memories so often. I should accept Magelon's offer to cut it out of my head.

Someone walks along the road, following a circle of torchlight. Recognizing Marrick, I stand to meet him.

"I'm sorry," I say. "I didn't mean to stay away so long. I needed to clear my head."

"Reece told us what happened," he says. "I should've realized. It must be hard not to be affected by Joanna's memories when you're doing everything she did. I can't imagine what it's like. Or how to help."

"Are we good?" That's all I want to know.

He hugs me to him and kisses my forehead. "We're good. I shouldn't have reacted the way I did."

We hold each other in comfortable silence until another light shines along the road—Kelly coming to look for us.

"Let's go back," Marrick says, releasing me. "Reece filled us in. You think we should abort?"

"Did you get through the mine?"

"All the way. It's exactly as you described it."

The uncertainty about whether anything I recall is real dissipates, but it returns with another doubt. "I'm not sure if it was me who made the call to abort."

"You think Joanna's influence took over?"

"I don't know, but this is important, and we can't chance it. You should keep me out of it and let your team decide."

Marrick hugs me again. "Now I know you're you. Joanna would never have said that."

I rest my head on his chest. The steady beat of his heart is calming and gives me an idea.

I look up at him. "Can you do something for me?"

He frowns. "Anything."

"Punch me next time I behave like Joanna. Hard."

He smiles. "Sure."

We walk back to the barn, collecting Kelly on the way. I'll ask everyone else to punch me, too. If I take enough hits, they might knock Joanna out of me permanently. If it stops her from infiltrating my mind, the bruises will be worth it.

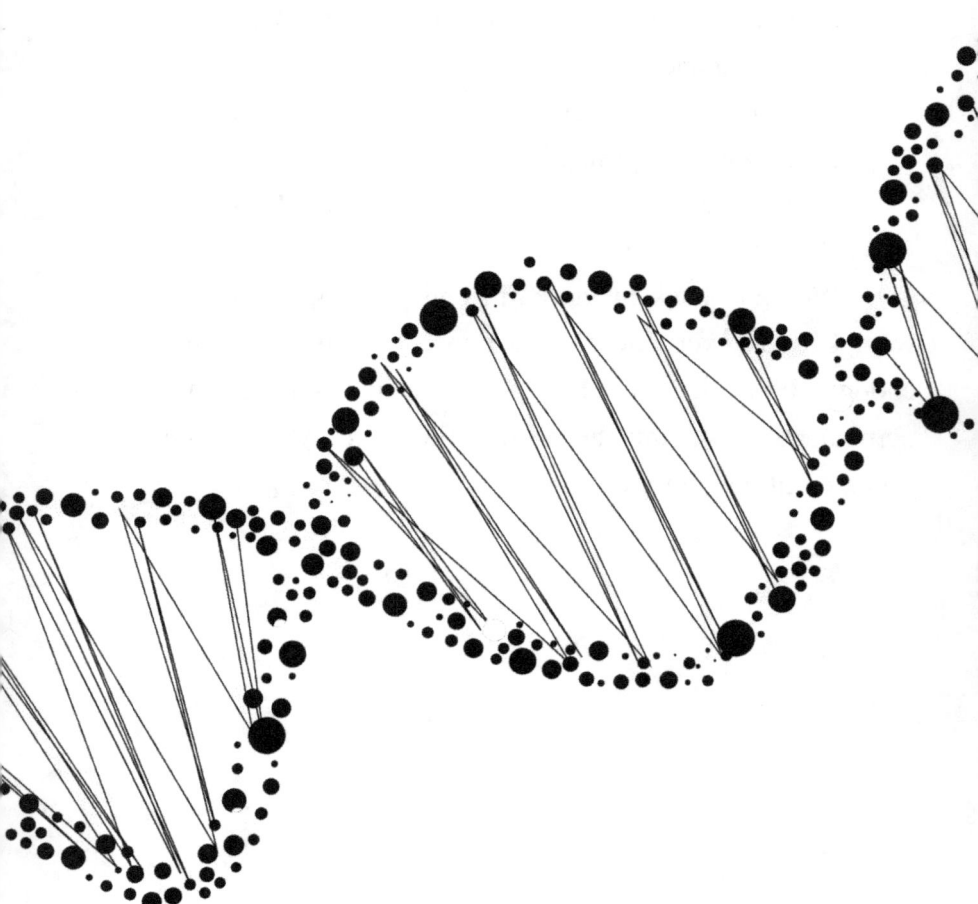

CHAPTER 26

MARRICK WANTS TO SEE THE twenty-four hours of security changeovers before we decide whether to abort. It's a good call, but it means another day of constantly checking I'm not behaving like Joanna. Thinking about the rock pools helps. So does Magelon, who stays within reach, flexing her fingers. Asking her to punch me isn't my smartest idea, even with her reassurance she's not aiming at me.

"How did they put up with Joanna for so long?" I ask Darius.

It's mid-morning and we're standing in the field outside the barn. Darius is another safe zone. Being with him takes me back to our training days at Red Bluff. The barren ground around us reminds me of their dry training fields. I'm confident, right now, I'm me.

"Marrick," Darius says, peeling the bark off a stick he found. "He gave Joanna more chances than she deserved. Probably why he took it so hard when it went to hell."

"Magelon said he wanted to quit."

"Yep. Would have, too, if not for his team. They refused to quit on him. It's that simple. I can't think of another team like them, the way they've bonded, except for Joanna. Thought I wouldn't see it again, but I'm wrong."

"You mean me."

"Yep."

I rally courage drawn from certainty. Once I take Darius down the next path, there's no turning back. "What if it could work?"

He stops peeling the stick. "Thought you didn't want this?"

"I want it." I let that sit for a minute as a softener for my next question. "How do you know Vera?"

He resumes picking at the bark. "Through your uncle."

"She helped my mother birth me. How did they know each other?"

"They worked together at Bio-Tech."

I scuff the ground with the toe of my boot. "Flannigan insinuated my mother did something she shouldn't have. I suspect she was genetically enhanced. Did she perform her experiment on herself?"

Darius sighs and tosses the stick into the field. "She did. But not for the reasons you might think. She wanted to know what happened to her brother, Jack. She thought if she had his memories, she'd learn the truth about why he murdered his team, then killed himself."

"Did she?"

"If she did, we'll never know."

I clasp my arms around myself. "She died because of the viral vector, didn't she?"

"Yeah." He rubs his brow.

"Would Vera know if my mother learned anything about Jack?"

"I've never asked her."

"Would I remember?"

He frowns and looks at me. "Why would you think that?"

"Isn't it why Flannigan wants me? To get my mother's memories? Since Joanna put the implant in my head, I've recalled things my mother did in vivid detail. If she had her brother's memories, wouldn't I have his memories, too? It would explain why I aced the Tactical Skills Program. Everything he knew, I know. Placed in a similar environment, I might jog a memory explaining his crime."

Darius's mouth pulls tight. "No. You're having enough trouble with Joanna's memories without dredging up Jack Arquet. Forget about the past and focus on your future."

I stare across the field toward Bio-Tech. The only way I can have a future is to know the past. Why Jack committed murder/suicide might be the key to not behaving the same way. Or will tapping into Jack, like how I've tapped into Joanna, cause me to be like him?

If that's possible, I can't think about him. Ever. If it was Jack who wanted to snap Flannigan's neck when I pinned him against the wall, I could behave like him again in a similar situation, without realizing I'm not me.

Darius clamps his hand on my shoulder. "Let's see where Reece is at."

We walk back to the shed, but I stop at the door. "Darius?"

"Yeah?"

"Why did my mother do this to me?"

He sighs. "There were worse decisions she could have made."

Like killing me? Destroying all evidence. I look away to hide my tears. It wouldn't have been an option if she hadn't subjected her child to her experiment. Why did she do it? So I'd recall her brother's memories because she couldn't?

All warmth toward my mother vanishes. Darius is right. I should leave the past behind. Look to the future. Burning down this barn might be the first step to doing that.

***

"TELL US WHAT YOU'VE got," Marrick says to Reece when we're all gathered.

"Shift rotation is every six hours," Reece says. "Three units, five soldiers in each, two patrolling here, and here." He points at two places along the perimeter fence. "The third unit stays inside the complex. They're focusing on the fire access trail, plus the road into Bio-Tech. Not once in the last twenty-four hours has any unit monitored out the back near the cave entrance."

"They must think we'll use the tracks again," Magelon says.

Marrick nods. "Joanna knows I have access to maps."

"It's one or the other," Kelly says, stroking his beard, staring at the screen. "Otherwise, they'd monitor that hole."

"Doubt they know about it," Reece says. "Even the satellite image doesn't pick it up."

"Because it's a rabbit hole." Magelon looks at Marrick. "Joanna must know we're coming. Sure you want to do this?"

"If she agreed to help Flannigan," he says, "she'll know everything about his drug trial, and who's involved with the vote."

"We haven't considered this avenue," Reece says. "I've been researching it. If you get Joanna out, we could arrest Flannigan for forcible abduction and medical malpractice and shut him down through military legal processes."

"Won't work," Darius says. "Military legal rabbit holes run deep. Flannigan's backers could fund a legal fight lasting for years. Best-case scenario? Flannigan goes to jail for a long time. Worst case? They label Sarah and Joanna a biosecurity risk and keep them quarantined indefinitely."

"Why a biosecurity risk?" Marrick asks, his gaze flashing between me and Darius.

The vector mutated. My mother's words rip through my mind. "Because of the viral vector used in the transduction process," I whisper.

Magelon tenses and crosses her arms. "If Flannigan performed the experiment on Joanna, will she die like the other test subjects?"

"We won't know until we see what condition she's in," Darius says. "Prepare for that."

"Prepare for what?" she snaps. "She's physically incapacitated?" She looks at Marrick, her eyes blazing. "What if she can't run through the mine? We'll be sitting ducks if she slows us down." She turns back to Darius. "What about Sarah? Will she die?"

I answer. "I don't think so. It's why Flannigan wants me."

Her eyes widen. "You're not sure?"

"Calm down," Kelly says, holding up his hands. "Let's lay this out. Reece, where are we at?"

I wish I hadn't said anything. Marrick's eyes darken, too. Worrying about me is a distraction he doesn't need. In one day, he found me, lost me, found me again. He can't bust into Bio-Tech thinking he could lose me a second time.

"Okay," Reece says, expelling a heavy breath that catches everyone's attention. "Your entry/exit point is uncompromised, but there's no cover between the generator plant and the building. We know security numbers but also need to factor in Flannigan's security guards, numbers unknown, and any medical staff on duty. We're assuming Joanna's in one of those cells, but she might not be if she's there by choice. We have Flannigan's swipe card, but he might have changed the codes."

"Blasters don't need codes," Magelon says, uncrossing her arms. "If I had more, we could level the entire complex."

"Not a bad idea," Kelly says, tugging at his beard.

"What else?" Marrick asks.

"Magelon's blasters will give you safe passage back here, providing you're on the right side when they blow," Reece says. "If you're not, you'll be stuck inside the mine with a bunch of angry soldiers and no way out."

"So our chances are good," Magelon says.

Reece grimaces. "Best-case scenario, you're in and out with no one realizing. Worse case, Joanna refuses to leave, alerts security, and you're all dead."

Magelon glances at Marrick. Kelly crosses his arms and rolls his shoulders back. Reece looks at Magelon, then stares at the screen.

"What do you think?" Marrick asks me. "Go, or abort?"

"Isn't this a team decision?"

"It is. We're split."

I have to give it to them for their silent communication. I suspect Marrick's in. Reece is definitely out. Kelly would back Marrick. But Magelon would prefer Joanna stay dead. How do I decide? Will I answer, or Joanna?

Unsure, I turn to Marrick, hoping he can read what I'm thinking.

"What does your heart say?" he asks.

It turns out he can. And he clues me in to how I'll know who answers. Joanna might have claimed my mind, but she hasn't touched my heart. I imagine sitting by the rock pools. In my safe place, I remember why I joined the military. I'm not sure if it's the answer anyone wants, but it's the answer I need to give.

"Our job is to save lives, even if it means risking ours. Whatever grievances we have with Joanna, we need to put them aside because she might need saving, too. I still don't know who or what I am, but if I'm immune to the vector, I might have something Joanna needs. So, I vote we go."

The energy in the barn ignites, lifting everyone's mood. Darius smiles like he knew all along I'd unite this team. Magelon and Kelly nod in agreement. Marrick gives me a smile that sets my heart on fire. Reece bounces on his hay bale and turns back to his laptop.

"We forgot one thing. Sarah busting into Bio-Tech is the last thing Flannigan will expect. After the way she took down that team at Kelly's house, Flannigan's security won't know what hit them."

He pauses, mouth open, realizing his mistake in revealing I'm an active participant.

Darius's face turns bright red. Then his tirade rocks the barn.

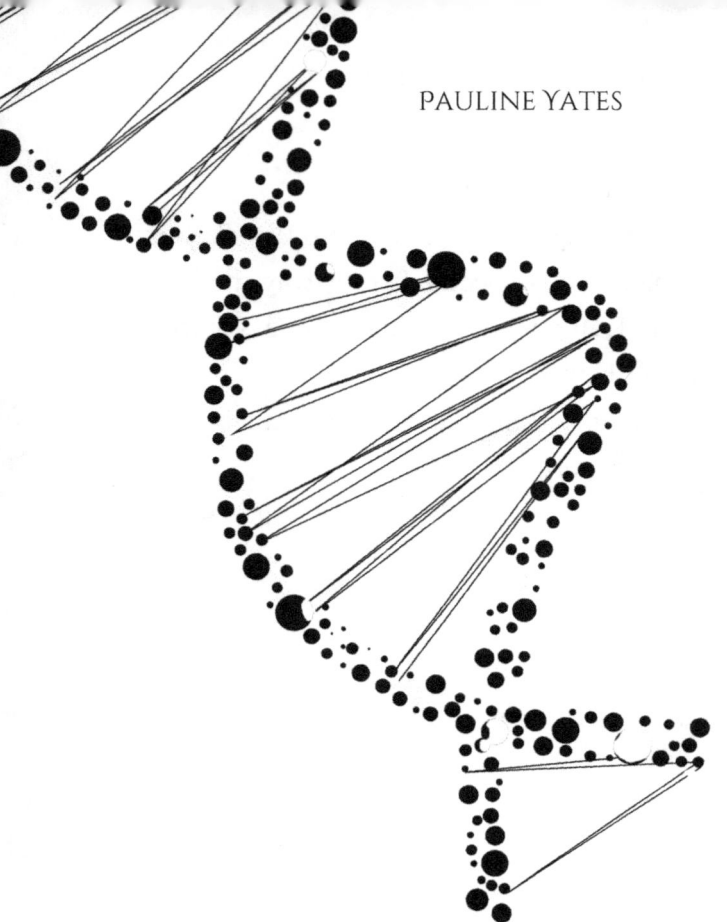

PAULINE YATES

CHAPTER 27

"OVER MY DEAD BODY!"

Magelon imitates Darius as we run toward the second mine entrance, our torch lights bright beneath the midnight sky.

"I thought his heart stopped when he realized you were coming. And the look on your face when you said, 'I've never refused an order from you, Darius. Don't make me start now.' No one stands up to him like that. What did you mean by 'you give me what I want, and you'll get what you want'?"

Running beside us, Marrick smiles. He knows what I meant. After my comment to Darius, Marrick's eyes lit up and his whole demeanor changed—confident, fierce, a step away from getting what *he* wants. But I don't want to raise his hopes higher by telling Magelon I'll join their team if we can make it happen. I'm struggling with memories of Joanna pushing Marrick to let her lead. I have to block them out. Marrick's in charge, and our success relies on following his orders.

"Quiet now," Marrick says.

We're at the entrance to the mine. I shine my torch at the door. The timber beams that held it shut are on the ground. Marrick pulls the door open and steps inside. I follow, Magelon behind me. The air in the tunnel is dead. If any fresh air entered when Marrick, Kelly, and Magelon ran through here earlier, the mine has sucked it into its bowels.

"Check radio communication," Marrick says.

I press my finger to my earpiece, making sure it's secure, then tuck the transmitter cord beneath the collar of my shirt. Being electronic, the earpiece could boost the implant's signal, but Reece assured me our radio communication isn't as strong as a cell phone, and I'd have to be holding a wireless signal detector for it to register. But fiddling with the earpiece causes a rise in adrenaline and my mother's words flit through my mind—

The spike in adrenaline may be triggered by the vector's natural defensive mechanism.

That might be the predatory sense I experience. I can't let the vector take over. I can't behave like Jack.

"We're at the entrance," Marrick says, his voice clear

in my ear. "Magelon?"

"Yep," she says, giving him the thumbs up.

"Sarah?" His voice helps me focus.

"Loud and clear."

"All good here," Reece says through my earpiece.

"Okay," Marrick says. "We're going in. Magelon, go first. Show Sarah where the blaster is."

Adjusting my gun belt so it's comfortable around my waist, I shine my torch at the ground and follow Magelon through the mine. The SIG Kelly got me sits snug in my hip holster, and I packed every available pouch with extra magazines. Magelon has the radio remote to detonate the blasters. We also have a second light on our safety vests. The fluorescent blue light isn't as bright as the torchlight, but it will lessen our chances of being seen.

The mine swallows us as we run along the shaft: Magelon, me, Marrick. Dressed in black, we blend into the darkness, but my torchlight throws Magelon's shadow up the wall, and it looks like another person runs with us. The ceiling is cut rock, the old timber supports sagging beneath the weight of the mountain. I thought the tunnel would be cold, but it's stifling hot. The dead air sticks in my throat. Sweat beads on my forehead and trickles down my face.

Deeper in, the air grows heavier. I shallow my breathing to avoid filling my lungs with the dust disturbed by Magelon's footsteps. Guided by my torchlight, I stay one step behind her, Marrick close behind me. The tunnel walls look like the memory tunnel, our torch lights the yellow orbs. A gap in the wall draws me toward it, another shaft leading to who knows where. The darkness sucks the yellow from my torch beam, creating a ghostly olive-green orb. I jerk my light away. Whatever memory this mine holds, it's not for me.

The tunnel turns ninety degrees to the right. A hollow appears in the wall to my left, a narrow tunnel, but the roof isn't as high as the main shaft. The black depth yawns at me, trying to suck me in. My mother's memory of the mine creeps into my thoughts. So do her emotions—a suffocating dread that makes me tremble. I think of the rock pools to chase my mother's memory away, but it lingers.

"You okay?" Marrick asks.

"I'm okay." I slowed without realizing; the gap between me and Magelon is wider. I run to catch up, a spike of adrenaline pumping through my muscles—dangerous if it triggers the vector, but it feels good. More at ease, I peer along the mineshaft. This section is narrow, the walls and roof reinforced with multiple timber planks. How much mountain is over our heads?

Magelon stops and shines her torch on the roof, illuminating one of the plastic flat disks.

"First blaster. There's enough explosive here to collapse this entire section. If we have to blow it, this shaft will be impassable, so make sure you're on the right side. You'll know where it is from this." She waves us forward, leading us out of the timbered section, and stops at a trench in the ground. "This is your marker. The blaster is fifty running strides back."

I commit the distance to memory, then follow Magelon over the trench. I gag at a sickly sweet stench. Something small and black flutters in my light. Startled, I shine my torch around. We're in a cave.

Jagged rocks rise to a high narrow ceiling. On the other side of the cavity, the tunnel continues, timber beams marking its entrance. More black residents dart around my head. I duck, raising my hand to shield my face. Bats.

"Cool, aren't they?" Magelon whispers, shining her torch at a black mass of wriggling bodies clinging to the cave's ceiling. Her light makes the bats chitter, their screechy voices echoing through the tunnels. Another bat swoops. Magelon ducks.

"How did they get in?" I ask. There must be thousands of them hanging from the rock.

"There'd be dozens of entry points in this cave system," Marrick says, shining his light at the ground. "Best not to disturb them. Let's keep moving. I'll lead from here."

I follow him across the cave, relieved to leave the stench behind. When we enter the next section of tunnel, Marrick slows, stepping around fallen rocks and broken pieces of timber. He picks up the pace when the shaft clears, his long, smooth strides making no sound. The air grows heavier, hotter. Sweat trickles down my neck. The tunnel runs straight for another long stretch, then turns left, then right. At each change of direction, timber beams support the roof. Most are in good condition, but some sag to the point of breaking. It wouldn't take much of a blast to make them collapse.

Marrick stops at a cutting in the wall and shines his torch at another blaster attached to a timber beam.

"This is the shaft that connects to the first tunnel. If all goes to plan, we'll take this exit out. It's shorter. Once we're through, Magelon will remote detonate the blasters, sealing both entrances to the mine. Anyone who follows will have to return through Bio-Tech. By the time they get around the mountain to the barn, we'll be on the road and gone."

"Where to?" I must have missed this part of the plan while outside with Darius.

"Reece organized a temporary rendezvous point at a trailer park in Willow Springs," Marrick says. "We'll reassess from there."

I shine my torch down the tunnel. It's narrow, a slice through the rock. My circle of light replicates a golden orb and jogs a memory—my mother, squeezing through, her swollen belly scraping the walls. "Have you been through it?"

"Yes," Marrick says. "It's tight but clear."

Magelon grins. "Tight is an understatement. Hope

you're not claustrophobic."

"How much farther?" I ask, shoving my mother out of my head. Failing to erase her completely.

"Nearly there," Marrick says.

He continues through the shaft and stops in a cave three times larger than the previous one. Smooth rock, carved from an ancient water source, creates a stunning geographical museum. A second bat colony clings to the roof. My mother's memory tries to push back into my mind, but I quash it, wanting to see this natural cave system through my eyes, not hers.

"Is that our rabbit hole?" I nod at a rope hanging through a split in the wall.

"We tied the rope to the mesh fence at the top, but it's an easy climb," Marrick says. "The rope will help if we have to come down in a hurry."

My mother again, slipping, sliding, moving so fast it's amazing she didn't fall and break her neck. Her fear of being caught radiates through me, making my hands sweat.

Marrick rests his hand on my shoulder, and I jump. "Sure you're okay?"

When I don't respond, he turns me to face him. "If you want to abort, just give the word."

I shake my head. "It's not that. It's my mother. I'm reliving her running through this mine." I hesitate. "She was so scared."

"Are you scared?"

I'm terrified. I'm returning to a place of pain—the memory tunnel, the inescapable white room. Marrick would boost my confidence if I asked for his help, but I need the part of me that knows no fear, even though it scares me more. I can't continue without it. Something in Bio-Tech ignites every sense in my body.

I slide my SIG from my holster and press the barrel against my forehead. It's cold against my hot skin, but I welcome the shock. Closing my eyes, I take myself back to the start of my sharpshooting round, the last time I was fully in my zone. I experienced the vector's predatory sense then, and it helped me perform above and beyond my best. Beyond my best is also extremely dangerous for anyone in my target zone, but I know what to expect now. This is what I need—if I can control it.

"Give me the lead," I say, lowering my SIG. It's not a demand, not Joanna talking. It's where the vector likes it best.

"Sarah's got the lead," Marrick says. No emotion. No hesitancy. Somehow, facing my fear of the vector helps Marrick to face his demons—the last time he relinquished the lead ended in Joanna's 'death'.

Behind us, Magelon whispers, "Yes."

Then louder.

"Sarah's got the lead." She sounds proud.

CHAPTER 28

CONNECTING THE VIRAL VECTOR TO my predatory sense explains so much. The vector is a living organism. When it perceives a threat, it defends itself by drawing information from its host's memories to enhance their skills.

Everything I know, including information from my mother's, Jack's, and Joanna's memories, is ammunition. The vector arms me with increased adrenaline and specific details about what has worked before, and I respond instinctively. I don't have to think about what to do. The vector does that for me.

Where I should be careful is making make sure my reactions come from me, which will be hard as I've been confusing myself with Joanna. If I can't tell the difference between us, how will the vector?

I'd like more time to recognize how I respond in a situation without being influenced by others, but we can't stop Flannigan without Joanna. We have to get her out now.

Reece's voice crackles in my ear. "Shift change in… but watch…"

Shift change; watch something; that's all I hear. Everything else is static. I glance at Marrick, who shakes his head, not understanding Reece either. He waits. What we do next is my call.

I cross to the rabbit hole. A washout in the cave, it leads to the surface about fifteen meters above me. I climb halfway up, then pause and listen for Flannigan's security patrols. Nothing. Just fresh night air streaming through the hole, cold on my hot face.

I switch off my torch and turn on my vest light. Marrick and Magelon do the same. Three fluorescent-blue circles shine on the ground. The end of the rope lies like a coiled snake at my feet. Using my hands to talk, I motion them forward, gripping my SIG in one hand, holding rocks to help climb with the other. The hole appears above me. I squeeze through easily, but stop, hearing a vehicle.

I hold out my hand, alerting Marrick and Magelon, who climb behind me. We hunker in the hole as tires crunch over gravel. When the engine fades, I peek out like a rabbit on alert for a fox. Seeing nothing, I scramble through and crouch in the tall grass.

Marrick and Magelon climb out and huddle on either side of me. I scan the surroundings. Reece said to watch for something, but I can't see any soldiers. The vehicle we heard could have been the shift change, or the new unit patrolling the perimeter fence nearer to our position. Though not in sight, I must assume they're close.

I point to my eyes, then to the fence, to let Magelon know to watch that direction. Then look toward the service door, our entry into Bio-Tech. I pat my pocket and swipe my hand. Marrick holds up Flannigan's keycard. Nodding, I creep forward, finger hard on my SIG's trigger.

The power generator plant is between us and the service door. Long grass grows up against the mesh enclosure, providing cover should the vehicle return. Staying close to the fence, I scoot toward Bio-Tech, Marrick and Magelon close behind, crouching again when the fence ends. A gravel road runs between the fence and the building. I point at the road, then at my feet, indicating to be cautious about making noise when we run. I imagine Jack doing the same thing in a similar situation.

I'd rather it be Jack than Joanna. She's reckless and makes mistakes, overly eager to prove her merit. Jack was an acclaimed leader, like Marrick. If I channel him, I'll be safe, to a point.

Signaling with a flick of my head, I run toward the building. Marrick and Magelon flank me. We're fast, silent, me checking one way, Magelon covering the other. Marrick runs ahead to the door and swipes the card over the lock. I hold my breath and pray the codes haven't been changed.

The indicator light turns green, and the lock releases. Marrick eases the door open. I roll around him, SIG outstretched, checking everywhere for movement, sound, or Flannigan's staff. Nothing comes at me. The door closes, and I release the breath I hold. We're in, unseen. What lies ahead is unknown.

We're in the maintenance room, but it's different from what I remembered. I should have expected that. My mother was here seventeen years ago. The floor layout is the same, but the fit-out's changed. Lights shine from a switchboard to my left. A fuse box is mounted to the wall on my right. Next to the fuse box is an air-conditioning unit. The walls are cluttered with boxes, brooms, cleaning equipment. Pipes run up the wall from gas bottles. An odd hum echoes around us.

Marrick steps beside me, asking for our next move. Tilting my SIG, I motion him to a door on the other side of the maintenance room. Magelon slides past me, covering Marrick. He grasps the doorknob, cracks open the door, then pulls it wide. Magelon rolls around him, gun outstretched. I follow her in, Marrick behind me. We're in the gymnasium, but it's been upgraded.

The room is still full of gym equipment, but it has an added raised platform on the other side. Protected by panels of safety glass, the platform holds a row of chairs, fourteen at a quick count. That must be where the officials will sit to watch Flannigan's drug trial.

"Spread out." My voice is tight. Those chairs remind me what's at stake. Fourteen votes will decide the fate of our military. My uncle will sit in one chair. Who will sit in the others?

Marrick and Magelon move across the room. I go to a computer near a treadmill. A green standby light blinks on the monitor. Hovering my hand above the keyboard, I recall inputting data. I jerk my hand away. Who did I imagine? My mother or Joanna?

I look around the room. There's another computer next to the bench press. The center of the room is covered in thick, square exercise mats. Interesting. Who will Flannigan's test subject fight to show off their combative skills?

Is that why Joanna wanted me? Not to be the test subject, but the sparring partner. I try to think if she said anything else, something I've forgotten, but all I do is refresh the memory of being restrained on the table while she punched the implant into my head.

Visions of the bright light, the sting of the needle, the heat travelling up my arm, make me bristle with fury. How dare Joanna abduct me and force a medical procedure without my consent. Who does she think she is?

Enraged, I hurry to the stairs, finger hard on the SIG's trigger. Marrick and Magelon catch up to me at the door.

Marrick gives me a questioning look—he must see the sparks spitting from my eyes—but I ignore him. The cells are on the other side. Joanna will, hopefully, be in one of them.

So could the black-eyed man.

Gripping my SIG, I grasp the knob and ease the door open. Marrick and Magelon roll around me, their guns outstretched. The corridor is empty. Dim lights cast our shadows up the walls. My predatory sense builds and I keep close to the wall, on the hunt. The last time I was here, I was afraid. I'm not now.

Marrick walks to the first cell and peers through the glass insert. He's outside *Procedure Room 1*, where I was held. Does he see the stainless-steel table, the broken restraint? I'm hesitant to join him, but my gun hand is steady—I'm in my zone and it would take more than the sight of the white room to shatter my confidence.

Marrick moves to the next cell, *OBR6*. Magelon stays on his left, aiming her Beretta along the corridor. I bring up the rear, conscious of building tension within me. The next door along is *OBR5*. I don't need to look through the glass insert to know Joanna is in there. Every cell in my body screams it.

Marrick goes to the door and looks in. He confirms with a nod of his head. "Cover me."

Holding my gun outstretched, I step behind him. He swipes the lock, and the door slides open.

Inside, Joanna sits on a bunk. She wears ordinary clothes, a light blue T-shirt, a pair of track pants, but they hang off her wasted body. Her skin is pale, like it hasn't seen the sun for six months. Dull eyes; her natural aqua has a hazy film. She looks at Marrick, then shifts her gaze to me. Her mouth curls into an expectant smile.

I choke on my breath. Everything I've been thinking is wrong. I'm not the hunter. I'm the prey.

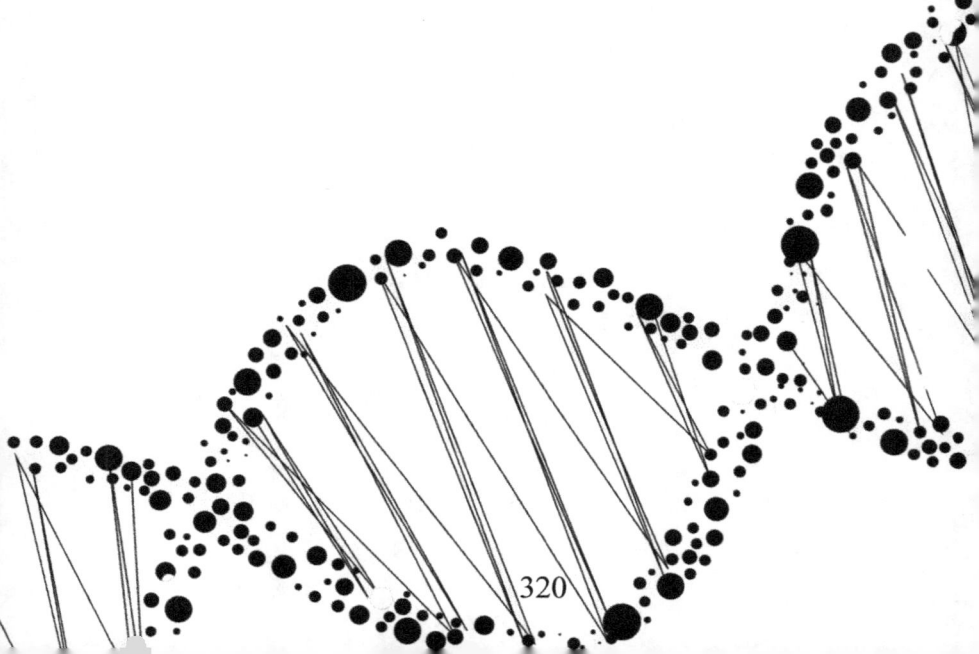

CHAPTER 29

T HE VECTOR PART OF ME takes over. Joanna is a threat, and I act instinctively. My finger is hard on the trigger, a millisecond from shooting her, but I jerk my SIG up when Marrick, oblivious to my intention, walks across my line of fire. Eye contact with Joanna broken, I roll away from the door and lean against the wall, breathing hard.

She expected us, as I thought. She knew Marrick would come for her, and knew I'd be with him. But something about her incites a rage so fierce I can barely hold my position. The vector part of me reacts to something. Does Joanna have the vector, too? She must if she underwent Flannigan's gene doping experiment.

If the vectors can recognize themselves in another

person, that must be why I've been compelled to return. That presents a problem I hadn't anticipated. How will we get Joanna out if I want to kill her?

Frowning at my erratic behavior, Magelon peeks through the door. Through my earpiece, Marrick reassures Joanna. I fume. She'll play on his emotions to get what she wants. Raising my SIG again, I step back to the door. Joanna stands with Marrick. Tears—they're fake—trickle down her cheeks. I'm tempted to shoot, but a thud against a door farther along the corridor draws my attention.

The black-eyed man.

"What the hell is that?" Magelon asks.

I aim at door that says *OBR3*—the third cell. "Everybody get out."

Another thud. The glass insert shatters. Then pummeling, like the man inside tries to break down the door.

"Go!" I shout.

The pounding against the door echoes up the stairwell at the end of the corridor. Will they hear it on the upper level?

An alarm triggers.

"We've got company," I say, shifting my aim to the stairs.

Marrick appears at my side.

"Help her," he says to Magelon. "We'll cover you."

Magelon darts into Joanna's cell. "Come on, come

on," sounds through my earpiece.

Joanna must resist because it should only take Magelon a second to return with her to the corridor. Fighting the urge to shoot Joanna so dragging her out is unnecessary, I focus on the stairs. The upper door opens. The sound of running feet travels down the corridor. A woman wearing a white laboratory coat steps into view.

Marrick shoots the wall in front of her, stopping her descent. I'm glad he thought to fire a warning shot. The woman could have been Vera. She scrambles back up the stairs, giving us a chance to get out.

Joanna holds us up. She refuses to leave, saying, "No, no, no," over and over like a broken record, and I wonder about the state of her mind. Or is she faking, like her tears, and doesn't care if her team is killed? She didn't care when she sent soldiers to Kelly's house.

The door at the top of the stairs bangs open. The pounding against the cell door stops. I keep my eyes on the stairwell. A security guard appears, gun outstretched. Marrick and I fire at the same time. A return shot strikes the wall next to us. Marrick's next bullet strikes the guard's shoulder. He topples down the stairs, landing on the floor face down and groaning.

"Help me," the black-eyed man says through the broken insert. "Please, help me."

Marrick steps forward, but I grab his arm. "Do *not* open that door."

"Help me, help me, help me." The man begs but I detect a wheedling, conniving edge in his voice. He doesn't need help. He wants to be let out.

Magelon drags Joanna from the cell. Hearing the man, they pause, but Joanna breaks Magelon's grip and runs toward the gymnasium. Magelon gives chase and catches Joanna at the exit door, but Joanna's expression is real fear. What does she know about the black-eyed man that would make her run?

I jerk my attention back to the stairwell. Multiple footsteps descend. My heart pounds. "Get out. Now."

"Keep going," Marrick calls to Magelon. "We'll hold them up."

"Move," Magelon says to Joanna.

The door opens and they're gone.

Marrick touches my arm and backs toward the door. I stay with him, but keep my eyes locked on the stairs. Soldiers descend, rifles at ready, one of the three security units on duty. I count two, three, four, five soldiers, then we're through the door. Marrick slams it closed.

Turning together, we jump down the stairs. Ahead of us, Magelon shoves Joanna into the maintenance room. Marrick and I run through the gymnasium. Behind us, the door opens and shots and shouts ring through the room.

Marrick dodges left. I dodge right. We turn simultaneously and fire. Three soldiers dive onto the viewing platform and use the safety glass as cover. Back in the corridor, someone yells. Multiple shots fire. Then an ominous silence makes the hair on my arms stand on end.

Did the black-eyed man persuade a soldier to let him out? One of the soldiers that dived for cover runs back into the corridor. The other two continue their assault on us. Bullets whizz over our heads as we run to the maintenance room—poor shots, typical of the soldiers Jeffries takes into his base. Reaching the door, I swing around, covering Marrick as he slams it closed. In the brief silence, hope lifts we'll get out of here alive.

"Where are you?" Magelon asks through my earpiece. "The fence line units are on the move."

"Keep going," Marrick says. "Don't wait for us."

He glances at me, his eyes saying we're not out of this yet. I run with him through the maintenance room, both of us exchanging magazines.

We reach the exit door, and Marrick pulls it open. He faces a rifle.

Marrick shoots first.

The soldier spirals backward, arms flailing. Four more soldiers push into the room. Shouts fire as fast as the bullets, but these soldiers don't work in unison. In the chaos, confusion reigns.

Unlike Marrick and me. Back-to-back we work in sync. We shoot, kick, punch our opponents until none are left standing.

Two soldiers from the first unit burst in from the

gymnasium. I fire: two shots, two dead. Another commotion sends a chill up my spine. I whip around to find soldiers from the third unit pouring into the room.

With five rifles trained on us, escape is impossible. If either Marrick or I shoot, we'll be gunned down before we can take all of them out. Marrick must know that too, because though he hasn't lowered his pistol, he hasn't fired, either. I'm not going down without a fight, so how do we get out of this?

Marrick shifts his weight onto his left foot. The movement is so slight, I wouldn't have noticed had Kelly not shown me how to predict the direction of a punch by my opponent's stance. Then, with lightning speed, Marrick shoulder charges the closest soldier and knocks him off balance. The soldier shoots, but the bullet hits the ceiling. Wrestling, they crash to the ground.

The diversion works. The other four soldiers shift their attention to Marrick, giving me a chance to act. Gripping my SIG, I shoot. One, two, three. Dead. Dead. Dead. The fifth soldier stands in the doorway, but instead of returning fire, he bolts outside. I leap forward, giving chase, but a harsh gasp stops my heart.

The crash-tackled soldier has Marrick in a choke hold, using a baton to cut off Marrick's breathing. Marrick struggles to break the soldier's grip, but he can't draw a breath and his eyes flutter closed.

"No!"

I shoot. One clean shot through the soldier's left temple, missing Marrick's cheek by the barest of a millimeter. The soldier slumps. So does Marrick.

Running to him, I rip away the baton and turn my cheek to Marrick's mouth, feeling for his breath.

"Breathe," I whisper. "Please breathe."

No breath warms my face. I press my ear to his chest. His heart pounds, but his lungs don't lift. I tilt his jaw up to open his airways, cup my mouth to his, and blow. His lungs expand, contract, then lift on their own. I rest my hand on his chest to check he keeps breathing, but glass smashing in the gymnasium followed by manic laughter sends me into flight mode—the black-eyed man is on the loose.

Hooking my hands beneath Marrick's armpits, I drag him outside, keeping an eye out for the soldier who bolted, who's nowhere. Hoisting Marrick onto my shoulders, I carry him across the road. As strong as I am, Marrick is heavier than Reece and unconscious, he's dead weight.

"Magelon," I say through my earpiece. "I need help."

"Take her, take…" Magelon responds but static interferes.

"Come on…" Kelly's voice booms against my eardrum. He must be guiding Joanna out so Magelon can return to help us. I hope that's what's happening.

"On…way…"

Magelon's coming back, but my flight response intensifies, pumping adrenaline through my body. I break into a jerky run, cradling Marrick, who bounces on my shoulders, while I keep an eye on the exit door in case the black-eyed man follows us out.

When I reach the rabbit hole, Marrick stirs. I lower him to the ground. He coughs and sinks to his knees, disorientated. I hold him upright, but my skin prickles all over, filling me with dread.

The black-eyed man walks outside, kicking the dead soldiers as he steps over them. He's dressed in white clothes, too. He picks up a dropped rifle, studies it, then tosses it aside and scans the surroundings. I clamp my hand over Marrick's mouth. If he coughs, we're dead.

The man walks onto the road and looks in both directions. My heart pounds so loudly I'm sure he can hear it. Beneath my hand, Marrick's breaths grow hot, and his throat constricts. He clears his throat, the forced exhale short but loud.

The man snaps his attention to the sound and stares in our direction. Dressed in black under a midnight sky, we blend into the darkness, but our position is known. Removing my hand from Marrick's mouth, I shove him into the hole. He bumps into Magelon, who pokes out her head.

"Help him." I turn and aim my SIG at the man.

He hasn't moved, still stares in our direction. I don't shoot. Not yet. We're far enough away he might be unsure what he heard. I also don't want to alert that other soldier by firing off a shot, although he could return with backup that will distract the black-eyed man, giving us a chance to get away.

The rope on the ground next to me pulls tight and vibrates—Marrick must be using it to climb down. I remain crouched, SIG trained on the man. He hasn't moved an inch. Is he assessing the threat, as I did? Flight or fight?

He jumps into a run, arms pumping like pistons, bulging muscles shimmering in the moonlight. He's genetically enhanced, but there's an abnormality about him, an experiment gone wrong, or right if he depicts Flannigan's idea of enhancement. One thing is certain: despite my enhancements, I can't fight him and live.

I unload the magazine's remaining bullets on him. He dodges with insane speed and uses the mesh fence for cover. Two bullets find their mark—one hits his thigh, the other his shoulder. His clothes bleed red, but he doesn't flinch, like his muscles are armor.

If bullets won't slow him, my best hope is to outrun him. Speed is my ultimate enhancement. But I need a new plan. As fast as they are, Marrick and Magelon won't escape this man, especially with Marrick injured. An idea forms. It will save them. I'm not sure about me.

Jumping into the hole, I grab the rope and shimmy down. Below me, Magelon's blue vest light shines in my eyes.

"Keep going," I yell. "Get to the connecting tunnel.

When you're through, blow it."

"Not without you." The desperation in her voice tears through my earpiece.

"Do it. I'll get out the other tunnel. Trust me."

"Shit." Her light turns away.

Behind me, the man slides into the hole. The narrow section slows him up, giving us a chance to get ahead. Rocks and soil fall onto me as he kicks his way through.

Reaching the bottom, I sprint across the cave. Ahead of me, Marrick and Magelon reach the connecting tunnel. Kelly's in my ear again, saying something about the Jeep, and Joanna, and waiting for us, and Reece's shrill voice breaks through in sporadic bursts, but I ignore everyone.

"Come on," Marrick shouts, his voice hoarse from his crushed throat.

I wave my empty SIG. "Go, go, go."

Magelon pulls Marrick into the connecting tunnel. I've time to make it through but can't risk the man catching up before Magelon blows the blaster. He can't escape the mine. He'll unleash hell on all of us.

I run past the tunnel, then turn and click a fresh magazine into my SIG. The man climbs over a rock and jumps onto the cave floor.

I shoot.

He drops to the ground, using a large rock for cover. My bullets hit the wall behind him. At the speed he moves, all I'm doing is wasting ammunition. That could be his intention.

He stands up as though taunting me to shoot again. I keep my SIG outstretched but hold my fire. I'm struck by the weirdest sensation, like I'm not me.

We stare at each other, sizing each other up. I take one step back. He takes one step forward. I step to the side. He steps to the side. I step toward him. He holds his ground. Now I understand. It's not me against the man. It's vector against vector. This is a battle for supremacy on a cellular level—a fight to the death.

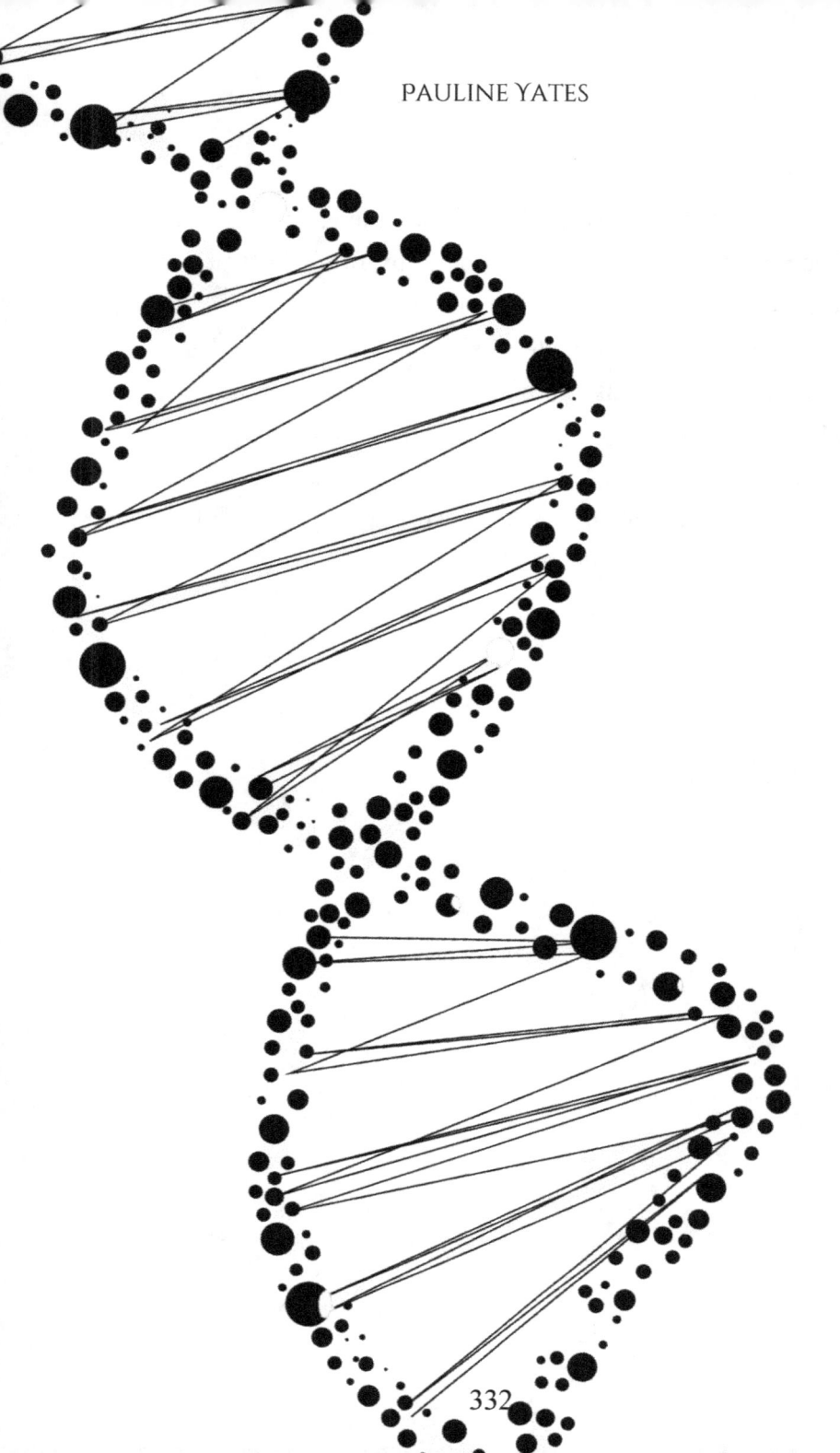

CHAPTER 30

I KEEP MY EYES LOCKED on the man and whisper into my radio.

"When you're clear, blow the first blaster. Give me a count. I'll tell you when I'm past the second."

Radio crackle breaks up Marrick's reply. They must still be in the tunnel. I hope my standoff with the man gives them time to clear the blaster range. I also hope Magelon follows my order to blow it. It's the only way we'll trap the man in the mine.

Magelon's voice breaks through the static. "On my cou...three...one..."

I turn and run.

The blaster explodes. Rock, timber, and dust spew through the mine shaft. The force of the blast knocks me against the wall, but I roll around and aim my SIG back along the tunnel. My vest light turns the dust blue, a hovering cloud that chokes up my throat. I can't see the man.

Magelon talks to me, Marrick too, though his voice is as bad as the static, both checking I'm okay. I don't respond.

Where is the man?

Where is he?

A shadow looms out of the dust.

I rain bullets at him for all the good they do, then push off the wall and sprint.

Hard breathing chases me. Will nothing stop him?

The dust travels down the mineshaft, making it hard to see, but this section runs straight. Shooting again is pointless. Speed is my best weapon now. I hope I'm made fast enough.

My light shines on timber beams. My brain screams turn, turn, turn. I skid around the bend, then run again, fueled by a flood of adrenaline. I listen for the man but can't hear him above the yelling in my ear.

"Dammit, Wilson, respond. Sarah?"

It's Darius. I'm back in radio range. "On my way out."

My moment of relief is short-lived. Footsteps pound the ground behind me, closer than expected—

She's vulnerable.

Why think of Vera now? Because I'm separated from my team by a mountain of rock? This plan was my call, but I'm vulnerable without them. Apprehension rising, I skid around the next turn and sprint so hard my calf muscles threaten to tear out of my legs. I need to reach the blaster well ahead of the man, but where is it?

The next section of the tunnel is the same as the last. Long. Dark. The roof reinforced with timber. But then the smooth cut of the walls changes to piles of rubble. I've reached the collapsed section.

Next, the cave, bats swooping in panic from the blast.

Then the trench. Jumping over it, I count my running strides. When I reach fifty—

The man slams into my back, an unstoppable machine hitting me like a Mack truck.

Flung forward, I twist as I fall, landing on my side.

The man follows me down and rakes his hands over my body, ripping out my earpiece and knocking the SIG from my hand.

I punch his arms, his face, anything I can hit, but he drives his fist into my ribs. My safety vest offers no protection. Gasping, I draw my legs up to kick him off, but he grips my neck and lifts me from the ground. Held up like a specimen, my feet dangle near his knees.

"So, you're the little girl our good doctor is so excited about?" he says, running his eyes up and down my body. "Underdone, but"—he brings his face close to mine—

"undetectable."

My vest light illuminates his grotesque face—this is my worst nightmare staring me in the eye. But I'm happy to be underdone and not have his abnormal muscles. As I am, I pass for a normal soldier, and my enhancements aren't seen until I use them—a genetically engineered solider, hidden in plain sight. But that won't help me now. I need smarts, not strength, to beat this man.

I drive my knee into his groin. He barely flinches, but his fingers around my throat loosen. Squirming free, I drop to the ground and scramble backward while searching for a rock, a lump of timber, anything I can use as a weapon— my gun is lost in the darkness. But this section of the tunnel is clear. The only weapon I've got is me.

"Flannigan failed you. Look what he turned you into," I say, hoping to distract him while I regain my momentum. Running isn't an option. He's already proven he's faster than me. My vector's switched to fight mode, anyway, and the adrenaline pumping through me incites murderous intent.

"Failed?" The man's mouth curls into a cruel smile, so the killer feeling must be mutual. "I am the future of the military."

He lunges at me, but I don't dodge. The vector's in control now and it's more than a component in a gene doping experiment. It's insidious. Lethal. It's using my body to exact its goal—dominance over the vector inside the man.

I jab at his face with pointed fingers. As strong as he is, he still has weak points. Eyes. Nose. Throat. He swats at my stabbing punches like I'm an annoying fly, his irritation evident in his blazing eyes. The speed of my attack surprises me; I've never moved this fast. But as quick as I am, I may as well be punching a pillow for all the damage I do.

The man backs up and circles around me, giving me a breather. He's not giving up, and nor am I. Jack pops to mind. If he foresaw this future—team members turning on each other until there's only one left—this might be why he killed his team. And then killed himself out of guilt, because who could live with that?

I block a glancing blow and duck out of the man's reach, but my mind churns. If I'm right about Jack, my team has nothing to fear from me. But they'll fear each other if Flannigan's experiment is given the green light, and they're forced to enhance their bodies to meet military performance expectations. I can't let that happen. They'll kill each other or die trying.

Like one of us will die now.

The man's fist comes at me like he's swinging a sledgehammer. I grab it mid-flight and twist his arm. He yanks free but kicks me in the stomach with a force that slams me against the wall. My head hits the rock with a smack, causing stars to burst across my vision. They clear just as quick and I prepare for another assault, but the man staggers, the first sign of weakness. Then he bends forward, breathing hard.

I didn't hurt him. It's something else, something internal. The earlier bullets I pumped into him might be behind his reaction—he's peppered with hits and his clothes are more red than white More likely his faith in Flannigan is misguided, and he's succumbing to the vector's negative health effects. Darius said no one left Bio-Tech alive. This man might be fighting his vector to the death, not me.

However long he has left to live won't help me. He rushes at me again, still curled over, and hits me like a battering ram. Slammed off my feet, I hit the ground hard, but manage to roll and protect myself with fists and feet. But the man stands over me, his mouth twisted into a sick grin. He's toying with me before the final death-stroke.

I climb unsteadily to my feet. I don't know how after being treated like a punching bag. The man sneers. Games are over. He raises his fist and punches at my head.

I block him like Kelly showed me how—anticipating the direction from his body stance— although the hit nearly breaks my wrist. He comes at me again, but my vest light glints off a slender metal barrel on the ground behind him— my SIG.

Ducking under his next punch, I scoop up a handful of dirt and throw it at his face. He jerks and swipes his hand over his eyes, and I use the precious seconds of distraction to dive for my gun. Grabbing the handle, I roll onto my back and aim at the man, who looms over me. He kicks my arm up as I pull the trigger. The bullets miss his head by millimeters—but one hits a round disk on the ceiling above us.

A direct hit from a bullet.

The bullet hits the blaster dead center. The force of the explosion throws the man at me, while shattered rock and timber beams crash on top of us.

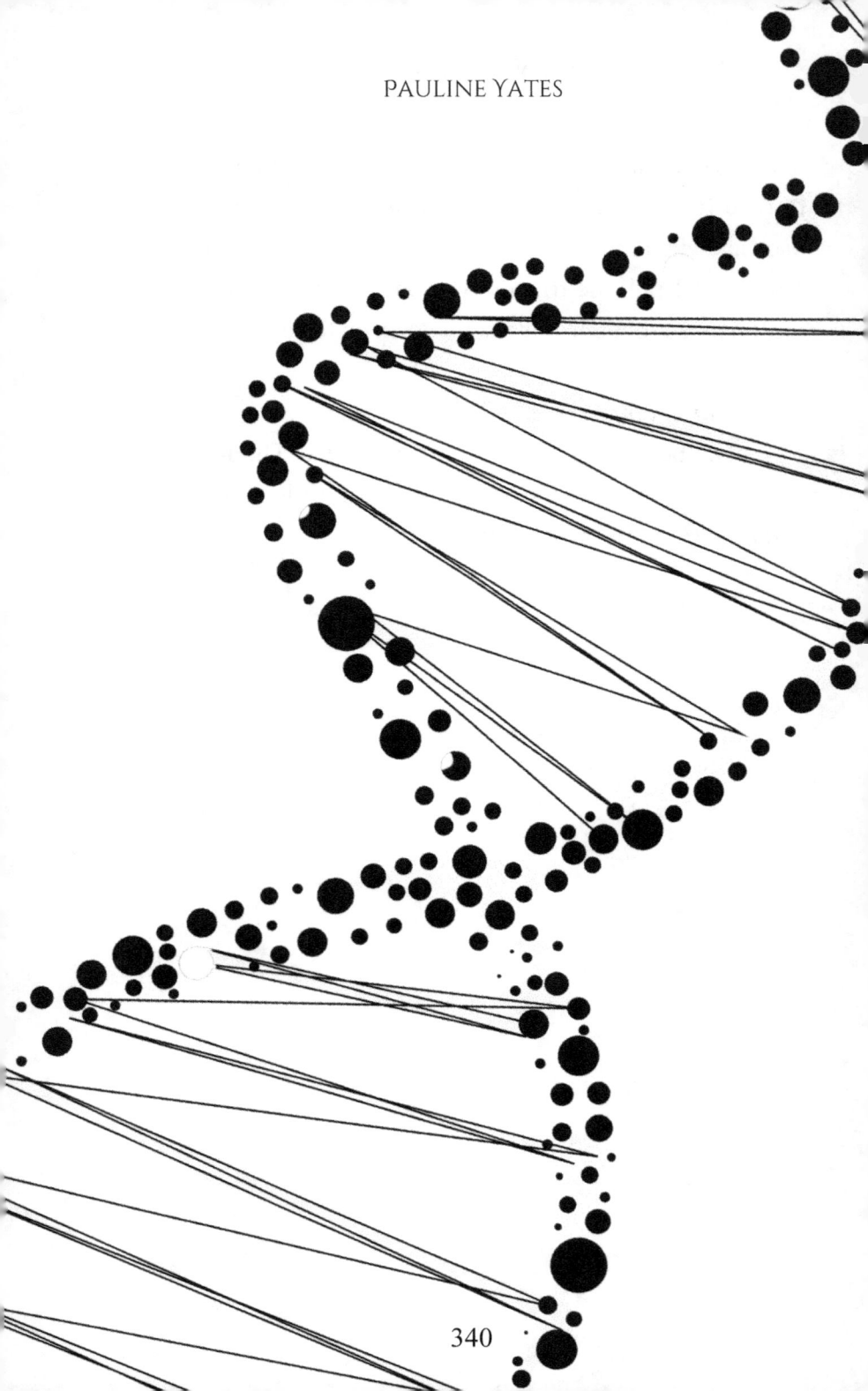

CHAPTER 31

MINERS HAMMER INSIDE MY HEAD, chipping at my skull. They whisper in my ear, want me to stay and haunt the tunnels. Their calls grow louder, demanding my attention—

The hammer splits open my mind and I jolt awake. It's not miners. It's me, trying to breathe through crushed ribs.

Dirt fills my mouth, my nose, my eyes. I roll my head to the side. My cheek slides across a clammy mouth. The man lies on top of me, dead. The whites of his eyes mock his last words.

Horrified, I squirm backward to free my chest. I gasp but suck in dust, then cough, shooting daggers through my lungs. It hurts so badly tears muddy my eyes.

Are my ribs broken? From the weight of the man, his punches, from the destroyed mineshaft? I rest my head back and wrestle with the pain. I don't want to die here, too.

A minute passes. Or is it an hour? The throbbing pain in my chest eases. I lift my head, carefully, because there's two of everything. Incredibly, my vest light still works. It exposes the cause of the man's death. A splintered timber beam tore out the side of his neck. Blood pools on the ground, thick, coagulated. All his? Or is some of it mine?

Wriggling my hips in a see-saw motion, I slide backward and gain another inch. My light shines on timber beams lying across the man's back. They fell in a crisscross pattern and form a new roof, a new tunnel, one that holds up the shattered rock. We're not buried. We're cocooned. I have to get out.

I drag clear of the man; his body slumps, dirt pouring off him, but the beams don't shift. I feel through the space around my head, where the light can't reach. Touching a spike, I roll my thumb over a point of a nail. Reaching higher, I feel another piece of timber. It moves, trickling dirt down my arm.

I sweep behind my head, feeling for obstructions. Finding none, I draw my arms back to my sides. I'm in a gap. If I can't squeeze through, this will be my coffin.

Pressing against the ground, I lever my body back. My ribs pinch and the hammering in my head increases. The nail I felt earlier snags my belt. I tug gently, but the beam above my waist slips, spilling rubble onto my legs. I stop, hold my breath and pray the structure doesn't collapse.

When nothing else moves, I slide my hand across my stomach, unclasp the belt, then push myself backward. The belt slides off my waist, but the timber drops, landing between my legs. The nail slashes my inner thigh.

Jerking my leg sideways, I suck in the searing pain with a sharp intake of breath, then jam my hands against the ground and heave myself out. The space between the beams above my head increases. I move like a snail, but my vest light shines on the roof of the original tunnel. My nose wrinkles at the sickly sweet stench of bats.

A wave of horror rolls over me. I'm on the wrong side of the blast zone. With both mineshafts sealed, the only way out is through Bio-Tech.

Don't panic, don't panic.

I arrest my spiraling thoughts. There'll be another way out. I need to assess my injuries first.

Crawling to the wall, I sit propped against the rock. Everything hurts, even to think. I'm covered in tacky blood. Most of it's from the man, but the blood on my leg is fresh, and it's mine. Hands shaking, I part the tear in my fatigues. Blood runs from a gash on my inner thigh the length of my hand.

If I don't bandage my leg, I'll bleed to death, too.

I pat along my body, checking for tears in my clothes

I might be able to rip. Nothing. Just blood-soaked fabric that stretches between my fingers. The vest has straps, but I can't break them. I could use my boot laces to make a tourniquet, though. My socks, a pressure bandage.

Drawing up my knees, I fumble with the laces and tug them out of eyelets. They're soaked with sticky blood—does the man have any left inside him? Jamming the toe of one boot against the heel of the other, I pry them off, then peel off my socks. I press them against the gash, securing them with the laces in a crisscross pattern so they don't slip.

Stretching out my leg, I appraise my effort. It's a crude bandage, but effective. I put my boots back on, then tighten the straps on my vest to support my ribs.

I use the wall to help stand, but the hammering in my head tries to knock me down. Swaying, I lean against the cut rock and concentrate on my breathing so I don't pass out. More stable, I shine my light on the rubble around me.

Magelon did a good job with her blaster. There's no way through this section of the tunnel. Retrieving the man's corpse, if it's found, would also be impossible. He's encased in timber and rock and moving anything could cause further collapse.

Determined not to share this plot with him, I wobble toward the cave. There'll be another way out. Another tunnel. Miners would have planned for a cave-in.

I count as I limp, my short steps tripling the fifty running strides to the trench. It appears in front of me, a dark slash in the ground. The smell of bat droppings mixed with the dust in the air tickles my throat and I cough, spearing more pain through my lungs. Bats flap around, startled by the blast. They swoop at my light. Fending them off with one hand, clutching my aching ribs with the other, I search the cave.

No long narrow gaps, no hollows. The bats got in. They must be able to get out. I shine my light at the mass of wriggling bodies above my head. Most bats fly in frenzied circles, darting from wall to wall. Others fly toward the trench and disappear into the darkness. Lowering my light, I aim it along the trench. There's a hole at the end. An exit?

The half-meter step into the trench slams my brain against my skull. I shuffle to the hole and shine my light inside. Bats whiz around me and zoom through the hole. It's wide enough for me to crawl through, but will it narrow farther in? I could get stuck.

It's either try, go back through Bio-Tech, or find a different tunnel. I doubt any others will lead out. Magelon set her blaster to seal the mine and Reece would have told us about another exit. Deciding to chance it, I lower to my knees and crawl into the hole, keeping my face down to avoid the bats.

The rock is cut smooth, machine drilled, but in the enclosed space, the bat stench is overwhelming. Short, shallow breaths help, but they increase my dizziness. I push forward, staying straight so I don't aggravate my ribs. I tire too quick for my liking—my knees drag across the ground. I hope I'm not climbing into my grave.

A whiff of fresh air tickles my nose. I double my effort. A steep slope tests my weakening strength. Jamming the toes of my boots into crevices in the rock, I inch upward, pausing every other inch to catch my breath. More bats climb over me, tangling in my hair and scratching my scalp. Face down, I pull, push, and slide forward, finally landing on flat ground when the tunnel changes direction.

I shine my light through the tunnel. A dark circle at the end absorbs the fluorescence. Air whistles past me, and my mouth catches the breeze. Rising to my knees, I crawl on.

When I reach the dark circle, it expands, revealing stars. Fresh night air cools my cheeks. I cling to the edge and look down. I'm above the gully that runs beneath the fence we climbed under. I can't see the second mine entrance, it's farther around. No vehicles are in sight.

Does my team think I'm dead? I assume they'd have heard the explosion. If they had, Magelon would know I shot the blaster, and they'd come to the mine entrance, expecting me to run out. When I didn't, did they enter the mine searching for me? Found the cave-in and assumed the worst?

I look to the east. A crack of light splits the horizon. Is it the same day, or the following morning?

No, only hours have passed, or the man would have been as stiff as the timber beams. But where's my team? Were they forced to leave because Flannigan found the hole we escaped through, and soldiers swarmed this area searching for us? Whatever happened, I need to keep moving and get as far away from this area as possible. Marrick planned to relocate to Willow Springs, so that's where I'm heading.

Switching off my vest light to conceal my position, I swing my legs over the edge and climb down the steep rock face. There are plenty of rocks to hold, but my feet slip on loose dirt multiple times. Lowering onto my stomach, I slide more than climb. When I reach the bottom, I collapse, exhausted. But I can't stop. I'm too exposed. I'll make it to the fence if I go slowly.

I push off the ground, but my legs are heavy and it's like walking through wet cement. I stop frequently because of the pain in my ribs, shortness of breath, and dizzy bouts that make my head spin. I listen for vehicles, but all I hear is silence.

By the time my fingers grasp onto the mesh, dawn has fled, and the rising sun promises a hot day. I rally my strength for the climb up to the hole under the bottom rail. It's a six-meter sharp incline, and the chiseled sides offer no footholds. Holding onto the mesh, I sidestep in a crab-like fashion, then grab the stump's exposed roots and pull myself under the rail. The effort saps my energy and, unable to continue, I lie on the ground, eyes closed, taking shallow, wheezy breaths. At least here, hidden by the scrub, Flannigan won't see me—

I snap alert. Reece won't see me, either. What if he's scanning the area using his satellite imagery? He wouldn't have seen me in the dark because I turned off my vest light. He will now it's daylight.

"Move, Wilson," I whisper.

Rising to my knees, I crawl through the scrub and stagger to my feet. I'm woozy, but able to hold the fence to stay upright. Dragging my feet, I creep along the fence line and imagine Reece shouting he's found me. Is it real? Or wistful hope?

My vision blurs. The fence becomes two fences. The dirt road I jogged along with Magelon wobbles and shifts. Afraid of passing out, I grip the mesh and pause. If I make it to the barn, I could rest on the straw, close my eyes, forget about bats and black eyes and hammers in my head. A sob gets stuck in my throat. I hurt. Badly.

The mesh rattles. I've slipped down. The wire cuts into my fingers where I grip. Pulling myself upright, I take another step. Something wet and heavy hangs off my ankle. I look down. My crude bandage fell down my leg. Fresh blood seeps through my fatigues. Sinking to the ground, I fumble with the laces, unravel the soggy mess, press the socks against my wound again and retie the laces. The gash looks worse in the daylight, but at least the blood isn't spurting out.

Bandage secured, I lean back against the fence.

I'm the future of the military.

I'd laugh at the man's declaration if I could. We might be stronger and faster, but we're not machines, and not indestructible. We're living, breathing, flesh and bone that can be ripped open by splintered timber, or crushed by falling rocks.

I wish I knew the man's name. He was a soldier before Flannigan changed him into a monster. Did Flannigan call him anything? Or was he a number, a strand of DNA, a host for a vector? I squeeze back tears. Will the vector die if I die? It must. Why else would it fight so hard to survive?

The sun burns the back of my head, making my headache worse. I touch my temple where it aches. It's swollen. What hit me? A piece of timber, a rock, the man's head? I glance at my leg. Can't tell the socks from my fatigues, they're both covered in blood. Ants run up my leg, but I've no energy to brush them off.

I haven't given up on Reece, but I should get to the barn. If I die before I'm found, I want to be in the place I was born. At least, I'll have made it to some resemblance of home.

Using the mesh as a crutch, I pull myself up and hobble along the fence. Like when I carried Reece over the mountain, the compulsion to keep moving intensifies with every painful step. It might be the vector generating more adrenaline, so I don't stop. If I'm right, the control it has over my body is disturbing. But if it helps me reach the barn, I welcome it.

My shadow grows longer. The dirt road shimmers in the heat. It's step after slow, agonising step, but eventually the barn appears in the distance. There's no movement, no sign of vehicles; the barn is as abandoned as when we first arrived. Good. I'd rather be alone when I close my eyes forever.

The sound of an engine shocks away my malaise. Is it my team? Or Flannigan?

I stop in the open, exposed. My hand automatically drops to my waist, but I'm unarmed. I can't reach the barn. I can barely shuffle. Clenching my fists, I stand my ground. The engine grows louder. A vehicle chased by a cloud of dust appears around the barn. I collapse with relief.

BETSY.

CHAPTER 32

I'M WITH MARRICK AT THE rock pools. How odd we're in a place we both love yet have never visited together. Water spills over the rocks but makes no sound. The forest is silent, like it's holding its breath. Marrick talks to me, his face strained, but I can't hear him. I can't feel his hand in mine either, though our fingers are entwined. I let him go and raise my hand to touch his face to see if he's real, but I'm sucked into a black tunnel, moving faster and faster, until I can't see anything but a dark circle splattered with stars—

"Can you hear me, Sarah?"

I open my eyes. Vera? Why is she with me?

Confused, I sit up, but she pushes me down and brings her mouth close to my ear. "You don't know me. I don't know you."

Her harsh whisper curdles my blood.

I look past her. We're alone, but a door is open. Is someone outside listening?

"Keep still," Vera says, her voice returning to normal. "You've got a lot of healing to do."

No, I've got a lot of questions needing answers.

"Where am I? Where's Marrick?" I keep my voice low in case they're the wrong questions. My throat feels like sandpaper.

"He's here. And you're safe." She presses her hand against my forehead. Frowns. "You suffered a concussion. And lost a lot of blood. Your friends were beside themselves. They didn't think you'd make it."

Friends? I hadn't considered that word to describe them. "Are they here? Can I see them?"

"Of course," Vera says. "Lie back now. Your ribs have taken quite a battering." She tsks, loudly. "You were fortunate I came along when I did. The ambulance wouldn't have reached you in time. It's a pity no one caught the number plate of the car that hit you. Understandable, being so dark."

A hit-and-run? That must be the cover for my injuries. Giving in to her firm hand, I sink into the pillow, head spinning. Did Darius contact Vera? They could hardly take me to a hospital. Imagine the questions.

I prod my ribs. The pain's gone. "Are they broken?"

"Unsure without x-rays," Vera says, taking my wrist and checking my pulse. "I'm treating them as though they are, but suspect they're only bruised. Considering the circumstances, you were lucky not to sustain worse injuries." She pats a wide bandage wrapped around my leg.

"Is Darius here? Did he stitch the gash?"

"Yes. You've given everybody quite a scare. I don't imagine they expected a journey to a simple training exercise to end like this."

Someone shuffles away from the door, a step, click, step, click. Vera visibly relaxes. I don't. She's feeding me snippets of a cover story, for who I dread to guess. But I need other answers—about my mother, about me. And what day it is.

I wear a short-sleeved, button-up shirt that reaches below my hips. Dried blood coats my fingers, and my skin feels tight, like the dust from the mine soaked up all moisture. I prop up on my elbows, not liking being bedridden.

"Slowly," Vera says. "I'll tell your friends you're awake."

"Please, I need to know—"

"I know. But first things first."

She leaves the room, closing the door softly behind her. I look around. I'm in what could be a guest room in a fancy estate. Pastel drapes cover the window. A painting of waves crashing onto bright sand hangs on the wall. A lamp on a set of oak drawers near the door fills the room with soft light. Plush blue carpet. A white-tiled en suite. The room contrasts with Vera's ordinary gray clothing. I doubt it's her house. She doesn't strike me as materialistic.

The door opens and Magelon enters, followed by Reece.

Magelon stands at the end of the bed, and glares at me.

"Trust you?" she says, her voice low, like Vera's. "You almost gave me a heart attack. We thought you were dead."

Reece sits on the edge of the mattress. "You're all right, aren't you, Sarah?"

Does he believe I'll come to no harm because of my genetic enhancements? I look at bluish-purple bruises on my arms where I blocked the man's punches. "I don't think I fared too well."

"Are you kidding?" Kelly says from the doorway. He glances over his shoulder, then closes the door. "Wish I'd seen it." He jabs the air as he walks to the bed. "Got a good picture, though. Doc had you doped up. You should've heard some of the stuff you were saying. Bats and vector's and—"

Magelon frowns. "Quiet down, will you."

My stomach churns. I remember everything up to when I collapsed in front of BETSY. It's a blur after that. I have a vague recollection of clinging to Marrick while he shouted at Kelly to drive faster. But nothing else. I shiver, wondering if I touched death. "Must have been a bad car accident."

Kelly grimaces. "Yeah. But you're alive. That's all that matters." He leans across the bed and rests his hand above the lump on my forehead. "Gotcha good, that did."

The door opens and Marrick strides into the room. My breath catches in my throat. Where the baton pressed against his throat is a long purple mark. How close did I come to losing him?

"Come on, guys." Magelon grabs Reece's arm and pulls him off the bed, then steers him and Kelly from the room, closing the door after them.

Marrick kneels beside the bed so we're face to face. His eyes swim with emotions I can't decipher. He leans forward and crushes his mouth to mine in a kiss so ferocious it takes my breath away. Then he rests his forehead against mine.

"What's that for?" I ask, dizzy from his kiss.

"That's for saving my life." He kisses me again, his lips soft, whispering forever promises; a kiss I would die a thousand times over to feel. Close to fainting, I pull away. "And that one?"

He strokes my cheek. "That's because I love you."

I clutch his shirt and hold him to me, never wanting to let go. He brushes my hair from my face and leans back, giving me a full view of the bruise on his neck.

Reaching up, I touch his throat. "I'm sorry. I should've been quicker."

He frowns. "Sorry? No one escapes an ambush like that. We should both be dead. We're not because of you."

"I should've been quicker through the mine, then. That man was a speed machine. But there's something else—"

He needs to know how the vector works and why it's not me he should fear, but each other if soldiers are forced to undergo Flannigan's gene doping experiment, but I'm interrupted by Darius entering the room, his face redder than hell.

He stops at the foot of my bed and glares at me. "I've seen corpses in better shape."

Is he exaggerating? With Darius, it's hard to tell. But if anyone will tell it to me straight, it's him. "That bad?"

"It took twenty stitches to sew up your leg. You have suspected cracked ribs. A shiner on your head. You're covered in bruises that put Magelon's tattoos to shame. The back of your neck's scratched like you've been through a paper shredder." He glances at the door, then lowers his voice. "I don't know how you walked out of that mine, let alone made it as far as the barn. By the time Marrick and Kelly got you here, you were nearly dead."

"I don't feel *that* bad," I say.

"I'm surprised you feel anything with the amount of pain relief Vera's given you. Give it a day or so. You'll feel your bruises when she cuts your dosage."

"How long have I been out?"

"Two days," Marrick says quietly. "Vera kept you sedated." Taking my hand, he entwines his fingers through mine, his expression darkening.

I squeeze his fingers to reassure him I'm okay. "Anything else I should know?"

Darius rubs his mouth. "For the moment, no. Just don't mention—"

"Yeah, I get it." I wish he'd close the door so we could talk openly. There are things I need to know. Like my next question. "Where's Joanna?"

"She's with us in the guest cottage," Marrick says. "She's resting."

"Am I allowed to ask where we are?" I try to whisper, but it comes out a growl.

"We're at Jim's private residence," Darius says. "Vera is his live-in nurse."

"Who's Jim?" I ask.

This time, Darius closes the door but returns with a grim expression. "Jim's a board member in the military's biosecurity division. He's semi-retired, works from home...and is one of the officials on the voting panel."

I sit up straight, nearly smacking my head against Marrick's. "He holds voting power? He'll know Flannigan and might know me. What were you thinking bringing me here?"

"We didn't have a choice," Marrick says, gripping my hand tighter. "You lost consciousness and we thought…" He frowns, but I see it in his eyes, a haunting shadow; he thought I'd die.

"Vera was closer than a hospital," Darius says, taking over from Marrick. "Jim doesn't know who you are, or that we're involved in what happened at Bio-Tech."

Does Darius seriously think Jim won't suspect our involvement? A breach of Bio-Tech's security resulting in the death of multiple soldiers, plus the loss of Flannigan's test subjects won't go unnoticed. "Isn't he questioning why a C.S.R. team arrives on his doorstep needing life-saving medical assistance? Surely he doesn't believe a car hit me?

"We've given him a credible story. If we keep our mouths shut, we'll walk out of here, no questions asked," Darius says.

"And Joanna? Does Jim know her?"

"He didn't indicate he recognized her," Marrick says, glancing at Darius.

Their silent exchange bothers me. "Does Joanna know Jim? Have you questioned her?"

Marrick sighs. "Yeah. It was Joanna who told us about Jim's involvement. She's been quite forthcoming with information. According to her, Jim's financing Flannigan's operations. And because of his connection to the other officials, they'll hold the majority vote."

"How can the trial proceed if Flannigan has no test

subjects?" I ask.

"The trial is set for a week from today," Darius says. "Flannigan could still prepare another test subject."

I don't like his chances, not after the confusion I suffered. But we shouldn't underestimate Flannigan. "What else did Joanna say? Did she say why she wanted me?"

"She admits to helping Flannigan," Marrick says. "In her defense, she thought her career would be over if the truth got out about her bad call. Once she realized the dangers in Flannigan's research, she tried to jeopardize his operations. As for you, Flannigan needed a sparring partner. Joanna suggested he'd find a suitable candidate at Red Bluff and picked you because of your combative assessment results. She knew we'd watch the sharpshooting rounds and intended to alert us. But Flannigan sent his men with her, and she had to drug you to make it look legit. You know the rest.

Snippets of her explanation ring true, but this is Joanna we're dealing with. "How did she explain the raid on Kelly's house?"

"Flannigan found out Darius trained both of us, or so she said. When I showed up, he connected us to you. Joanna said she refused to divulge information about your possible whereabouts, so Flannigan gave her DNA to the man you killed in the mine, and he recalled information about Kelly's property from her memories. Warning us was impossible. Flannigan kept her locked in the cell."

"How did she explain the beefed up security when we busted her out?"

He shrugs. "It wasn't unusual with the trial so close."

Joanna lies. She expected us, but not in the way she made out. What game is she playing? "Do you believe her?"

Marrick picks at the cuff of his sleeve then sighs. "I don't want to, but a lot of what she says makes sense."

"Can I talk to her?" I'm glad I didn't tell Marrick about the dominant nature of the vector. Joanna carries it, too—I didn't mistake her aggression when we looked at each other. Does she know how the vectors react in close proximity?

"You should steer clear of her for the moment," Marrick says.

"Why?"

Marrick looks at Darius.

"What aren't you telling me?" I ask.

"Nothing you need to worry about," Darius says.

It is something. Determined to find out what, I push Marrick's hands away, kick off the blanket, and swing my legs to the floor. I stand before he can stop me, but sway, a rush of blood making my head spin.

Marrick grabs me before I fall.

"Take it easy. That's not a small bump on your head."

"Then tell me what's going on," I say, reluctantly

sinking onto the bed. I suck in my breath at a twinge in my ribs. I don't like being incapacitated. How can I protect myself if I can't stand without fainting?

"Get some rest," Marrick says, cupping his hand to my cheek, pleading with his eyes.

Vera returns, perfect timing. I don't want to rest. I want to find Magelon. She'll tell me what's going on.

Vera takes one look at me and hurries to the bed.

"I must insist you both leave. There'll be plenty of time to talk later."

"I'll be back soon, okay." Standing, Marrick kisses my forehead, then leaves with Darius.

Vera follows them to the door and closes it behind them. Returning to my bedside, she glowers. "You have to be smarter than this, especially when you're at your most vulnerable."

I am so sick of that label. "I wouldn't be vulnerable if I was told the truth."

Vera's lips pull tight, but her anger at my outburst doesn't reach her eyes.

"I'm sorry." I tug the blanket over my legs and settle against the pillow. "I just wish I wasn't lied to all the time."

"Any lies were told to protect you."

"They're not helping. Please, how did you know my mother? You were with her when she birthed me, weren't you?"

Vera sits on the edge of the bed. "Your mother was

Flannigan's research assistant, and I was hers. We became...close friends. And yes, I helped you both after she gave birth."

The warm, fuzzy feelings toward Vera for being my mother's midwife are chased away by my next question. "Did my mother experiment on herself to find out why her brother died?"

Vera frowns. "Yes. And if you've remembered that, her research worked better than she anticipated."

I tense. "What does that mean? Why did she subject me to a dangerous gene doping experiment? She's turned me into a genetically enhanced freak. Is it because she couldn't recall Jack's memories and thought I'd be able to?"

"Your mother didn't do anything to you. When she performed the procedure, she didn't know she was pregnant with you. She never forgave herself." Vera tilts her chin up as though revealing that is hard.

Anger toward my mother softens. "She died because of the viral vector, didn't she?"

"Yes."

"And Joanna? Will she die?"

"Eventually, yes. I wish I could tell you more, but my knowledge of Flannigan's current research is limited. I only took this nurse position to keep my door open at Bio-Tech in case Flannigan found you. Unfortunately, it was the right move. Otherwise, I'd have fled with your mother after she escaped. I doubt the prognosis for test subjects has changed, though. Joanna shows signs of immune dysfunction, a typical reaction to the vector. I'll do what I can for her, but the help she needs is beyond my capability."

"Flannigan said I'd suffer my mother's fate without his help. I suspect I'm immune to the vector, but am I wrong? Will I die, too?"

Vera scoffs. "That's Flannigan's attempt at coercion using scare tactics. The truth, I hope, is he has no idea what you are."

"That I'm proof my mother's research worked?"

Vera takes my hands in hers. "You're much more than proof, Sarah. You're...different."

My chest grows tight. Darius said the same thing. "Different? How?"

"Jack Arquet and his team were the first test subjects. The viral vector used in the transduction of DNA to enhance speed, strength, stamina was thought to be inactive, but it reacted to increased adrenaline production associated with the physical enhancements. That triggered the vector's defense mechanism which in turn produced more adrenaline, resulting in raised aggression in the test subjects. After Jack killed his team, then himself, your mother thought if she could recall Jack's memories, it would help her better understand how the vector affected Jack's behavior."

I recall the man staring at me across the cave,

assessing me for strengths and weaknesses. "The vector detects another vector in a host and will kill to dominate. That's what happened with the man in the mine. But I'm also recalling everyone's memories: Joanna's, Jack's, my mother's. I think like them. Behave like them. I suspect the vector is using memory to arm itself. Am I right?"

"You've certainly inherited your mother's brightness. But, yes. It was an unexpected discovery during the early research. I don't know why Joanna gave you her DNA so you'd recall her memories, but you already had access to your mother's, and because your mother used Jack's DNA on herself, you'll access his memories, too. Their DNA, plus your father's, were the building blocks for yours. But Sarah, you must understand why you're different." She glances at the door, then shifts closer to me. "When your mother experimented on herself," her voice is barely about a whisper, "the vector attached to the developing embryo and mutated. It changed from a single cell and developed into a whole new organism." She squeezes my hands. "The vector is part of your genetic makeup. You are it, as much as it is you. And because of the vector's memory recall abilities, any memory in given or inherited DNA is accessible to you."

A natural yet unnatural creation. Funny, I don't feel as bad about that as I did earlier. If anything, I'm relieved to finally know the truth. "Is that the research you and my mother destroyed?"

Vera frowns, so I explain. "I remembered you both talking about destroying evidence…my mother refused to destroy me."

"Yes, but if Flannigan learns what you are and how you were created, he'll direct all future research down a path that would have far-reaching consequences."

I recall my mother's fear when she ran through the mine. "Are you sure he doesn't suspect?"

"With Flannigan, it's hard to tell. He doesn't possess the forward-thinking like your mother, and he's impatient for results. His connections in the military provide him with the test subjects he requires, but not in the numbers he'd like. Every death is a setback he can't afford."

"Joanna told Marrick that Jim is financing Flannigan. Is that true?"

"Jim makes a sizeable contribution to Bio-Tech in return for his medicines. How much of that filters through to Flannigan, I don't know. Your uncle would know more about Jim's financial interests than me."

"My uncle?" My skin prickles at this news. "How does he know Jim?"

"They spent time together when on active-duty. I wouldn't call them friends, per say, rather theirs is a delicate connection. To keep you safe, your uncle used Jim to stayed privy to Flannigan's operations, but any correspondence with Jim is short, discreet, and only to gain information about Flannigan's progress. Do not, and this is crucial while you're here, do not let Jim know you're related."

"But we're not."

"No," Vera says, her eyes growing sad. "I wish things could have been different, and I could've…" She shakes her head. "It was for the best. Your safety came first."

A lump forms in my throat. How different would my life have been if Vera had raised me? Leaning forward, I hug her. "Thank you, for being there for me, anyway."

She tightens her arms around me, holds me for a lifetime. "You should rest. Does your head hurt?"

I lie back on the pillow. "No, but—" I raise my hand and rub behind my ear. "Joanna put something in my head. Reece said it's a medical implant. Do you know what it is?"

Vera's eyes flash with anger. "It's a neurotransmitter designed by Flannigan that runs off brain electricity and stimulates long-term memory recall—unnecessary as the vector already excels at that. All it does is create information overload which causes confusion. I didn't think he still used it. He has enough evidence to show it causes more harm than good."

"Joanna put it in me. When I woke up, I wasn't sure who I was. She also put me in the white room, dressed in white clothes. Why?"

"A test subject is the most vulnerable the first day after the procedure. Their memories, plus the memories in the transferred DNA, are equally accessible. If placed in familiar surroundings, the test subject's memories will dominate, forcing other memories to recess. The white room interferes with that. With no identifiable stimulus to trigger a particular memory set, it allows Flannigan time to manipulate the memories he wants the test subject to recall. I suspect it's a method of compliance. Flannigan sought to control his test subjects, especially after the Jack Arquet incident. It's not a wholly proven theory, but enough evidence suggests given the right stimulus, the test subject would become anyone Flannigan wanted them to be, so they'd work with him, not against him."

"That's why I needed to return to familiar surroundings?"

Vera nods. "If you recall more of someone else's memories because you are in their familiar surroundings, who will you begin to behave like?"

"Oh, god." Of course. Haven't I struggled with behaving like Joanna? I entered her familiar surroundings the moment I escaped Bio-Tech. "How do I fight that? What do I do?"

"Know who you are so you can tell the difference," Vera says. "That will help you reject on a cellular level what isn't you."

She's assuming I know how the human body works. That's my mother's area of expertise, not mine. I could tap into her memories, but then I'd risk behaving like her and could lose myself in the process, like when I behave like

Joanna. "Should I go home? Would that help?"

"Being in your home would reset your memories, and force other memories to recede. You'd still suffer flashbacks or experience déjà vu as the vector taps into information it needs, but on a conscious level, you'd know the difference." She touches the side of my head. "Because of the neurotransmitter, you may struggle to hold the reset. I can't say because no test subject has lived long enough to provide that information."

"Can I take it out?"

She shakes her head. "I wouldn't advise it. Any attempt to remove it could damage your memory functions permanently."

"I can't continue the way I am. I'm behaving like Joanna."

"All I can suggest is that you avoid anything familiar to her until you've reset your memories."

It means going home. I'd have to go alone. I can't be around this team where everything about them triggers Joanna's memories. But how can I leave, when they are my 'home'?

CHAPTER 33

I KEEP THE CONVERSATION WITH Vera to myself. I know what I need to do but can't bring myself to do it. There has to be another way to reset my memories. Everyone's already on alert for Joanna-like behavior. They'd tell me, or punch me, in Magelon's case.

The mere thought of Joanna repels me. Probably because the vector part of me wants to destroy hers, but also because I want her spot on the team. I'm not sure which part of me is more deadly.

I want to see her but am in no hurry. Joanna's weak. I am, too. I stay in my room and adhere to Vera's instructions to rest. She insists I'm safe but talks loudly about random topics like her favorite weather or places she'd like to travel to whenever Jim lingers outside the door. With his financial connection to Bio-Tech and his majority hold on the vote, this is the last place I'm safe.

I've yet to meet him. I hear his step, click, along the hallway. He might be trying to get me alone, but I'm never without company.

Marrick returns and stays with me for the rest of the night, sitting in an armchair he pulled next to my bed. I tell him about my uncle's connection to Jim, but nothing about my genetic composition. Marrick evokes natural, human emotions in me, and I don't want to lose that part of myself.

I also don't ask what he's being evasive about. He's exhausted. When he nods off, I leave him sleep.

Kelly arrives at dawn with orange juice, poached eggs, and toast with lashings of butter. He describes Jim's expansive property—ten acres with rolling green fields and manicured gardens, a lake below the guest house, and the shed full of prestigious vehicles, though Jim no longer drives.

"The latest model Buick and a black BMW. He's even got a Ducati Superbike." Kelly's eyes glint with longing. "Must have cost him a packet. That model bike has a top speed of two hundred and two miles per hour. Be like riding a rocket."

The vehicles and property confirm Jim's wealth but chatting with Kelly makes it harder to leave. When Reece pops in to see how I'm faring, his funny quip about how "you flattened the other guy" like it's the most ordinary thing in the world, makes me abandon the idea of going home altogether.

Reece doesn't stay. Darius needs him for something urgent. I raise an eyebrow, questioning Reece, but he looks away, his eyes growing sad.

That puts me more on edge about what's going on.

Magelon will tell me. I'm waiting for us to be alone before plying her with questions. Vera is showing Magelon how much pain relief to give me after we leave. Where we're going, I haven't been told. It could be what Reece is trying to organize. The carnage I've left in my wake doesn't give us many options.

"Finally." Magelon closes the door behind Vera as she leaves and hurries back to my bed. "Want to get up without your guardian angel telling you not to?"

"The sooner I'm up, the sooner we can leave, right?" I gaze at the door. Leaving Vera will be a hard parting.

"Yep. I won't mind seeing the back of Jim," Magelon says. "He's the creepiest man I've ever met."

I swing my legs over the edge of the bed. "I hear him outside the room sometimes."

"Yeah, he's keen to meet you," Magelon says. "Too keen. Oh, before I forget, your cover name is Sarah Kingsley. Congratulations, Darius is your dad." She rolls her eyes and grins.

"That will be easy to remember. He behaves like my father." Grimacing at yet another name to add to my list, I stand, holding the bed head in case I wobble. I'm fine, at first. Then I sway, dizzy. I bump against Magelon, who slips her arm around my waist and holds me upright.

"Glad you're not Kelly. I'd never hold him up. Think you can do this?"

I breathe in, out, in, and regain my balance. "I'm okay, I think." I lean off Magelon and stand on my own. The stitches in my leg pull, so I lift my heel to relieve the pressure. My ribs don't hurt, or the bump on my head. "How much pain relief is Vera giving me?"

"Surprised you're not floating," Magelon says.

"Is it necessary to give me so much?" I don't like being under the influence of drugs after suffering hallucinations.

"Are you kidding? You haven't seen yourself."

She helps me to the bathroom and stands me in front of a mirror. I stare at my reflection, shocked. My cheeks are covered in angry red scratches. The bruise on my forehead is purplish-black, as are five finger marks on my neck where the man held me. My hair is a matted mess.

"How can Marrick love me looking like this?" I mutter.

Magelon raises an eyebrow. "He said that, did he? About time."

I blush. "Yeah. He must have been delirious." I pick at my hair. "I might have to cut it."

"And ruin his favorite feature? Let me fix it. But

shower first." She screws up her nose. "You smell like bat poop."

A compliment about my hair? That's a first. But she's right about my body odor. Only my arms are clean.

Magelon helps me strip off, then stands me in the shower while she fetches fresh clothes. Muddy water swirls down the drain. With my clothes off, I see my injuries for the first time—a large bruise on the side of my chest which lines up with my sore ribs, and another bruise on my stomach. I can't see my back, but suspect I have plenty of bruising there, too. The stitches in my leg look like I've taken to myself with a serrated knife.

I can't scrub without aggravating my ribs, so I soak under the hot water until Magelon returns. She brings the clothes I wore before we went into the mine. Dry and dressed, with a fresh bandage covering my stitches, she sets about untangling my hair, using a hairbrush found in the bathroom vanity and her nimble fingers.

"Much better," she says, smoothing my hair down my back and admiring her effort.

I catch her eye in the mirror. "Since when do you worry about hairstyles?"

She shrugs. "Nothing wrong with looking good."

That's it. I'm done with the evasiveness.

"I know something's going on." I adopt a sweet voice to cover my annoyance. "Are you going to tell me, or will I have to barge out of this room and find out for myself?"

Magelon scowls. "If you weren't already covered in bruises, I'd punch you. Hard."

I look at her, surprised. Then alarmed. "Did I sound like Joanna?"

"Sound like? God, if I wasn't looking at you, I'd swear you were her."

This is not good. Joanna's as potent as ever. I grit my teeth. "Hit me, please. I can't believe I'm still doing this."

Magelon tosses the hairbrush onto the vanity. "It's not your fault. Joanna does that. Gets under your skin and stays there. It will be better when—" She looks away, but the mirror reflects her face. Tears well in her eyes.

"Okay," I say, facing her. "What's going on? Nobody's telling me anything. And you never cry."

She wipes her eyes. "You're going to want to sit for this. Just don't tell Darius I said anything."

She helps me back into bed and sits at my feet.

"Joanna's laying it on thick. She expects to resume her position on our team. When I told her she'd caused too much damage, she parroted Red Bluff's expectation that team members sort out their differences. She's playing on Marrick's emotions the hardest, reminding him of his leadership responsibilities both on the field and off." Magelon stands and paces around the bed. "She's being Miss Remorseful and Miss Rectify and constantly reminds us how she risked her life gathering evidence on Flannigan. Emotional blackmail, that's what it is. She's made everyone feel guilty, especially when she learned you were to be her replacement. Technically, she's still our team member, but unless she's granted permission to step aside, there's nothing we can do."

The hammering in my head returns. I feared this would happen. Damn Joanna if she beats me on a technicality. "I suppose it won't matter, anyway. I can't join your team if I haven't graduated." I don't mention I'm prepared to repeat training at another base. Why get her hopes up?

She gives me a searching look. "So, you want to?"

"Of course...if you want me, that is."

"Want you? You're the best thing that's ever happened to our team. Of course, we want you." She wipes her hands over her face, then clenches her fingers. "I don't know why Joanna thinks she can reclaim her position, anyway. She's skin and bone. It'll be months before she's ready to resume."

Because she's dying if what Vera says is true. Should I tell Magelon? Or would it add another layer of guilt they don't deserve? I press my fingers into my temple to try to stop the hammering. "What happens now? I mean, where are we going from here?" We? More like, they. I'm a fool to think I can stay with them.

"Kelly suggested Rusty's house. Darius wants to confer with your uncle, but he doesn't want to call from here." She sniggers. "As far as your uncle knows, you're still at Kelly's house. Can you imagine how he'll react when he finds out what we've been doing?"

I don't imagine. I know—house arrest for the remainder of my life.

"The problem is," Magelon continues, "we've no way of knowing what Flannigan will do next. He has no test subjects. If he's granted an extension, we're back to square one. Reece has been trying to hack into Jim's financial records to see if there's any conflict of interest regarding the vote. Until he finds something, our only option is to give everything we've learned to your uncle and hope he can use his influence to discredit Flannigan's research."

Why hasn't he already? He knew what happened to my mother and Jack Arquet. Talking to him is another reason I should go home. I don't know why I'm fighting it. Marrick has his team to sort out, and I have my memories to reset.

There's a tap on the door, and Marrick enters the room. He looks from me to Magelon and frowns. "What's going on?"

Magelon mouths "sorry" which is unnecessary because none of this is her fault. She slips past Marrick, closing the door behind her.

Knowing what I have to do, I get out of bed.

"What's wrong?" Marrick asks, when I stand in front of him.

There's no hiding what I learned. And no avoiding the inevitable. I press my hand against his chest.

"I wish I could give you what you want. I want it, too. But it's not going to work." A tear slips down my cheek. I'm not only talking about joining his team. I lean into him, desperate for his warmth, his security, his love. But I have to be realistic. What possible future could we have, me being what I am?

I press my lips to his, telling him with a kiss what I can't say out loud. Then I cup my hand to his cheek. "We can't let personal interfere with professional. Your team needs their leader. And I need to go home."

"No," Marrick says, shaking his head.

I rest my finger on his lips, stopping further protest. "I have to do this. Vera told me how to reset my memories. You know how much trouble I've had behaving like Joanna, or my mother, or Jack. It's imperative I make sure I'm me, so I can keep my mother's memories buried deep. I can't let Flannigan get access to her research. Too much is at stake for all of us to put what I want first."

Marrick grabs my hand and pulls it away from his mouth. "Then I'll wait. And while I'm waiting, I'll deal with the other things that need fixing."

He kisses my fingers, then strides from the room, slamming the door behind him.

I shouldn't underestimate Marrick's ability to fix things. Whether it's changing team rulings so I can take

Joanna's place, or forcing her to quit, hope lifts there's a chance for us. Either way, I'm equally determined to be ready for whatever happens.

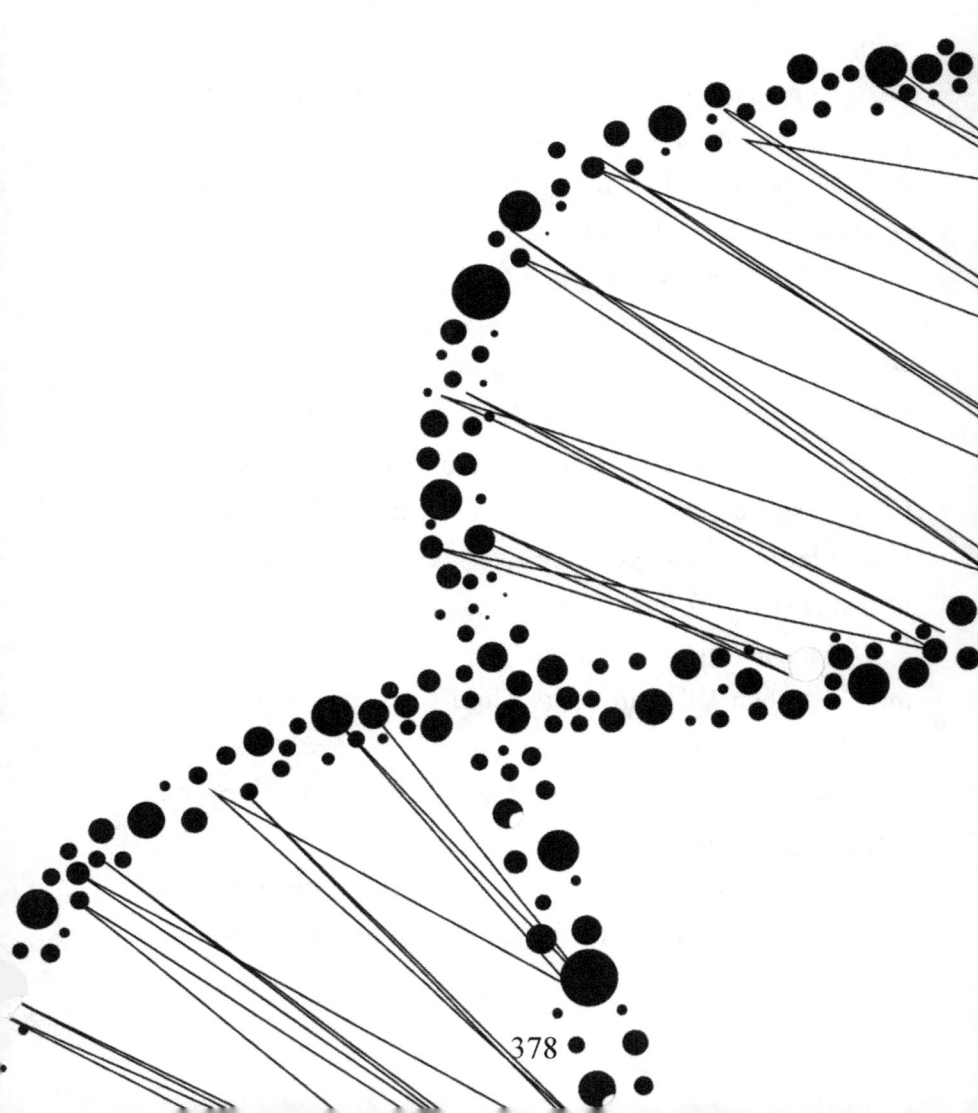

CHAPTER 34

I WANT DARIUS TO DRIVE me home. Time spent with him in the car is the first step to resetting my memories. We have six months of training I can revisit, familiar to me, not Joanna. Darius will also buffer my uncle's anger when he learns I left Marrick's guard.

Vera offers to fetch him but takes longer than expected. She might have struck trouble delivering my second message about refusing an escort to Anderson, which Marrick will insist upon. I can't have them following in Betsy. I'll know they're with me—that's a distraction I can't afford. My solution is to have Darius stay in contact with Reece via the com-links. Though escorted remotely, Reece will get us home safely.

A single rap at the door shatters the silence.

Expecting Darius, I hurry across the room and pull open the door.

It's not Darius. It's Jim. From narrow, piercing eyes, he looks right through me.

"Forgive me for the intrusion," he says, in a grating voice. "I had hoped to catch you before you left."

"Of course." I use my politest voice, though everything about him screams mistrust. "Would you like to come in?"

"I prefer the drawing-room, if you don't mind." He waves me down the hallway. "It's warmer there at this time of day. Better for my bones."

He leads the way, leaning heavily on his walking stick, his feet shuffling, step, click, step. Magelon's right in her appraisal. Jim's creepy. Liver-spotted skin covers his skeletal face. A thin moustache outlines straight, pale lips. Being in his presence causes the back of my neck to prickle; there's an unsettling aura about him—he's not as frail as he appears.

Needing a moment to gather my wits, I pause at a wedding photo hanging on the wall—a younger Jim and his wife. She hasn't been mentioned, so I assume she passed on.

Jim stops, too. "The only time I didn't wear a holster."

"You both look happy," I say, hoping it's a correct assumption.

"It was a beautiful spring day," Jim says, continuing into the drawing-room. He lowers into a black armchair and gives me a wistful smile. "A new beginning."

He doesn't invite me to sit, though there's a two-seater sofa on my left. I clasp my hands behind my back and remain standing. "Thank you for allowing us to stay. I hope we haven't been a nuisance."

"On the contrary, it's livened up my dreary days."

He smiles, I think. It's hard to tell because his skin pulls taut across his cheeks, enhancing his skeletal look.

"Introductions," he continues. "I'm Jim, but of course, you'd know that from Vera, my nurse. And you are Sarah…?"

"Kingsley."

The corner of his left eye twitches. He expected me to falter; he knows we're lying about my identity. I need to be careful, not knowing what I've walked into. At least talking to Jim is like talking to my uncle: I've had loads of practice maintaining an impassive expression. They're similar in age, both early sixties. That's where the resemblance stops. My uncle is as fit and healthy as Darius is at fifty. Jim's the opposite. His hands tremble, his skin is pale, sickly. I don't know what illness he suffers, but it doesn't extend to his eyes. They're soldier sharp.

"You've met my father, Darius, I presume?" I channel as much innocence into my tone as I can muster.

"Sergeant Kingsley, yes, we've been acquainted.

Shrewd of him to undertake pre-training with Red Bluff's top C.S.R. team before your induction into…" He gazes above my head and frowns, a pretense of forgetfulness. "Which program were you enrolling in again?"

"Whatever program my father thinks is appropriate." I'm treading in dangerous waters. I don't know what Darius told him. This line of conversation will trip me up. "Were you in the military, Jim?"

"I did my duty, if that's what you wish to call it." He leans back in the chair. "What I'd give to be young again. If you'll permit me to say, I'm envious of your speedy recovery. Up and about already? Impressive."

I raise my hand and prod the bruise on my forehead. "Vera's a wonderful nurse. Fortunately, she arrived when she did."

"Yes, the car accident. You gave your friends quite a scare."

There's that word again, punching me in the stomach so my breath catches in my throat. They aren't my friends. They're my life. And because of Joanna, I have to give them up.

"If you'll permit me to say, I don't think this team scares easily." The edges of my innocent composure crumble just thinking about them.

"Perhaps not," Jim says. "Still, I find it unusual they've taken time out of their busy schedule to help train you."

"Why is that unusual? If Red Bluff wants to produce the best, who better to learn from than the best?"

Jim leans back in his chair and clasps his hands. "In my day, the best soldiers were the ones who weren't distracted by, how would you say, external influences?"

This is unexpected. Does he know about my relationship with Marrick? It's not his business, but if he's anything like my uncle, I know what Jim implies. "I'm sure they can separate personal from professional."

"Perhaps," Jim says. "But in terms of maturity, they are a fledgling team, even if ranked at the top. Their level of bonding is far superior to any I've seen, but" —his fingers curl like claws around the end of the arm rests— "it's during these early years a member can become confused as to where his duty lies."

He refers to Marrick. I said the same, that his team needs their leader. But why does it matter to Jim? Because he's old school? "You think I'm a distraction."

Jim chuckles. "Your perception is flawless. You'll be an asset to the C.S.R. division."

But not this team, specifically. Jim obviously knows how tight-knit teams get, but it still doesn't explain why he cares?

"Don't listen to me," Jim says, with a dismissive wave. "The military has seen many changes since I polished a shine onto my boots. Of course, you should gain training wherever you can. The quicker the better, in my opinion. What's wrong with taking a shortcut here and there?"

Do I step through the door he holds open and take this chance to find out the depth of his involvement with Flannigan? It's too tempting not to. "Vera said you're in the biosecurity division. Is that a career pathway worth considering?"

Jim's expression hardens, giving me a glimpse of the soldier in him—a "take no prisoners" mentality.

"It's the enemy you can't see who's the most dangerous, Miss Kingsley. Such a thing could decimate the best-trained soldier. If we're to protect against that, it's crucial to understand what that threat is, its implications, and how to control it."

He knows who I am. The man in the mine called me undetectable. I decimated the teams sent to catch me at Kelly's house and Bio-Tech. The implications for the future have already occurred—I'm a new organism and the vector part of me will kill to survive. Controlling the vector's aggressive defensive response is up to me, but I still don't know how to do that. Neither does Flannigan, but with Jim's financial backing, the research will continue because Flannigan said I'm perfect. But uncontrolled is unpredictable, and even though that's an intrinsic part of warfare, our military can't risk another Jack Arquet incident.

"Perhaps some lines of research shouldn't be

followed," I say, not bothering with pretense anymore.

"The future of a strong military relies on exploring possibilities," Jim says.

The black-eyed man's proclamation about being the military's future fills my mind, but it's overridden by one of Jack's memories. I/Jack shake hands with a younger Jim, a younger Flannigan with them. This must be from before Jack underwent the genetic enhancement. The atmosphere in the memory buzzes with excitement. Would Jim express the same jubilance if he saw what evolved after twenty years of Flannigan's research? Or does he know about the black-eyed man and how many dead soldiers it took to create him?

Rising anger at the death of my real uncle heats my blood. "And what of the good soldiers lost in the process?"

Jim's face hardens. "There's no advancement without loss, Miss Kingsley. You'll do well to remember that."

I seethe. How much anger is mine, how much is Jack's, I don't care. "We're talking about soldiers' lives. Have you seen Joanna? She's dying because of Flannigan's research."

"And more soldiers will die without it." Jim is equally harsh. "Can you imagine the lives saved because soldiers are stronger, more resilient, and better trained because everything they need to know is already in here?" He jabs his finger against his head. "There have been setbacks, yes, but genetic manipulation of soldiers is the future of our military. If we don't embrace this now, we face annihilation by foreign armies who are already streets ahead of us in this type of research."

"You won't have an army if you continue to fund Flannigan." I could end this, cut Flannigan's line of finance with one snap of Jim's neck.

"Sarah!" Darius disrupts my murderous thoughts.

I grit my teeth. I don't care if I'm a step away from being Jack Arquet. I want vengeance for Flannigan's atrocities.

"Wait outside," Darius says.

This is not an order to refuse. Darius is fuming. With good cause. We'll be lucky if we make it down the road before Jim tells Flannigan I'm here—if he hasn't already.

Unless I shut Jim's mouth permanently. I step toward him.

Darius shoves me into the hallway. "Get outside. Now."

His rough handling jolts me back to my senses. If I don't regain control, I'll lose it like Jack. I can't let that happen. I can't lose myself in this.

I stride from the room.

"She has spirit, your daughter…" Jim's voice follows me out.

I take the first doorway and enter the kitchen. Crossing to an external door, I fling it open and rush outside.

And run into Joanna.

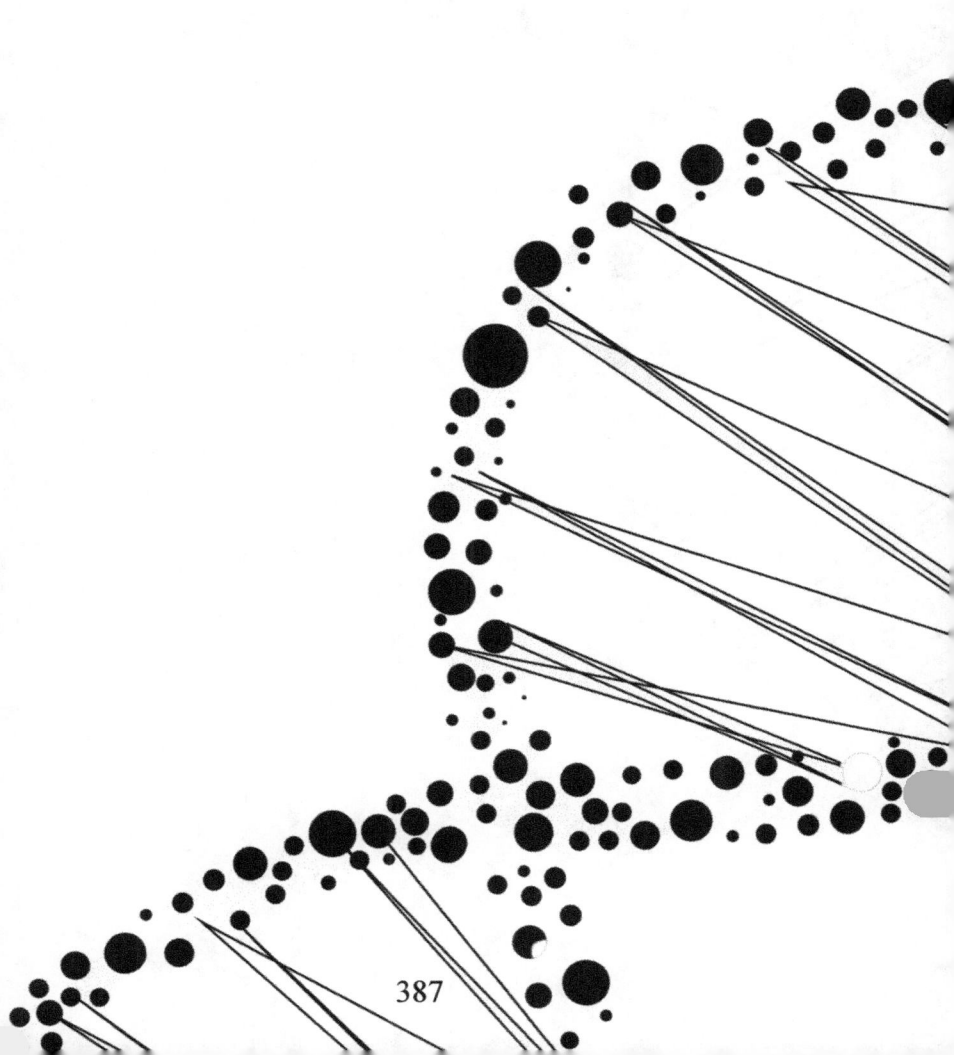

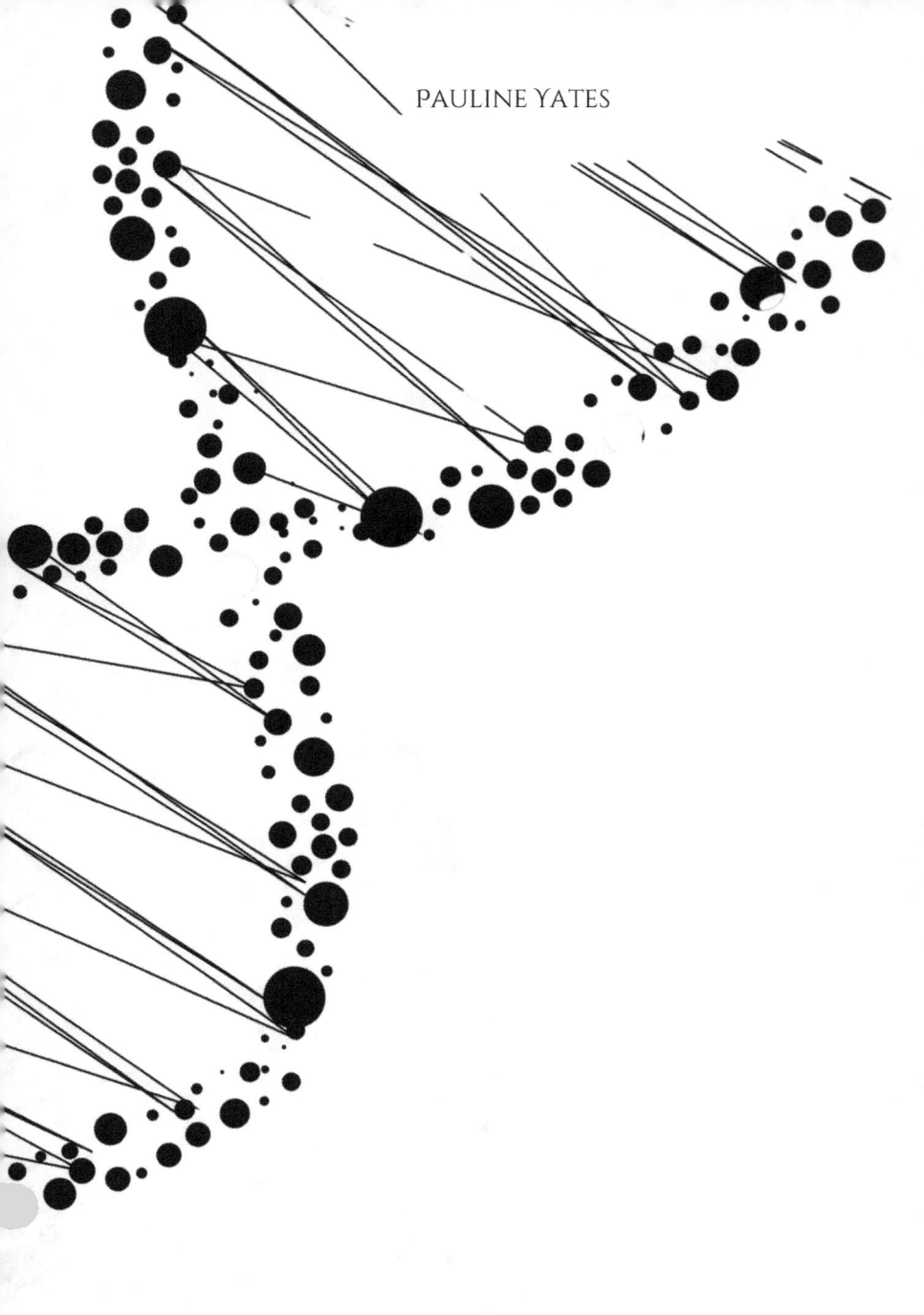

PAULINE YATES

CHAPTER 35

W E JUMP BACK FROM EACH other—Joanna to avoid my rush, me from surprise. In an eye-blink, my rage toward Jim redirects to Joanna. I circle her.

Joanna's eyes narrow. The need for dominance sparks between us but then she lowers her gaze and adopts a submissive stance—bowed head and slumped shoulders. She knows she can't beat me, not in her condition. I'll take it as a win.

"Why did you want me?" I inch closer but restrain myself. She can't answer if she's dead.

Joanna holds up her hands. "Please, I can explain." She glances at the kitchen door. If she expects Darius to emerge, it could be a while. A heated argument with Jim

389

drifts from the drawing-room. Good. Darius might finish what I started.

"You must have questions," Joanna continues, her voice low. "And I want to apologize. Had I known what you...are, I'd never have taken you to Bio-Tech."

She talks like I'm the plague, a freak of nature not to be touched. And her injured, fearful stance? Is it to lull me into a false sense of security? She does it well, I'll give her that, but her pitifully thin condition doesn't detract from who she is—Marrick's second-in-command on the best-rated team. She's also cunning, manipulative, and wants all the accolades for herself.

"Marrick said you were trying to stop Flannigan," I say.

"Once I realized the danger of his research, yes." She frowns. "I won't deny I wanted what he offered. Superior speed and strength. Who wouldn't want that? But I wasn't aware of the cost." She smoothes her hands over her vanishing waist. "It's a shocking price to pay."

If she's digging for sympathy, she won't get it from me. "You abducted me from Red Bluff and put a neurotransmitter in my head that screwed up my memories. You also said you'd prove Flannigan wrong. What did you mean?"

"Flannigan was adamant his test subject was unbeatable. But he refused to see the man's instability. When I learned you were already genetically enhanced, I thought you'd beat him easily. But that man, Sarah. You saw him. His speed and strength surpassed yours. I gave you my DNA, so you'd know everything I knew about him, and I used Flannigan's neurotransmitter to speed up access to my memories." Her eyes flutter closed. "So little time," she whispers.

She's either brilliant at playing her games, or I'm wrong about her. Is it possible she saw the error of her ways when with Flannigan? She's nothing like what I recalled from her memories. I could argue she's a different person. How can I take her team position when she's doing everything to make amends?

"I'm sorry about what happened to you." I truly wouldn't wish the effects of Flannigan's research on anyone.

"What happened is my fault entirely. I only hope…" She stares at the ground. "I don't blame my team for wanting to ditch me. I'm half the person I was. Look at me. My health's ruined. My strength's gone. I'm afraid…"

She's afraid she's going to die. But that's not why they don't want her. "From what I recall, you have a lot to make up for."

The corners of Joanna's mouth turn down. "I'm not proud of anything I did. Now I'm back, I want to make amends. And help shut down Flannigan. But mostly…" She frowns, as though struggling for the right words. Then she sighs. "Can I just say thank you? For helping Marrick get

391

me out of Bio-Tech. I don't know what would've become of me, otherwise."

"You don't need to thank me. We save people, remember?"

That draws a half smile. "The first time I met you, I said you needed to grow into your uniform."

I don't answer, because I never expected that day would be at the top of her list of recollections.

"You wear it well, Sarah," she continues. "I hope we meet again someday."

Wait a minute. This goodbye sounds permanent. "What are you doing now?"

"We're going to Kelly's brother's house," Joanna says. "Darius will take my information about Flannigan to your uncle, then we're taking a few weeks leave. We've had our problems, but it's incredible how being away from my team made me realize how much they mean to me."

I feel like I've swallowed a lead ball and it drops with a thud into my feet. Magelon mentioned Rusty's house, but I haven't spoken to anyone since I said goodbye to Marrick. "When are you leaving?"

"Right after you and Darius leave. Reece will still check the roads for you. He'll stay in contact with Darius, as you asked through Vera. They're packing, now." She looks over her shoulder toward a cottage beyond the manicured hedges. "They're not coming to see you off. Marrick said you needed to be away from them. It's probably for the best."

"What do you mean?" I didn't expect to see anyone before I left, but Joanna implies something else.

She wipes her hand over her brow, smoothing back her hair. "This is rather awkward. I know you and Marrick have become close. The thing is, we—Marrick and I—need some time alone, too."

Is she saying they're more than team members? I dismiss it, a ridiculous notion. But the day they ran through the forest slides into my mind—Marrick's warm smile, his appraisal of her effort. They were also alone.

No, no, no. What I'm thinking isn't possible. Marrick would have told me if they'd been in a relationship. Magelon would have.

Another thought freezes my heart. What if my feelings for Marrick came from Joanna? I behaved like her multiple times—felt her frustration; experienced her doubt about her abilities; her irritation at Reece when I snapped at him for being slow. Talked like her multiple times. Why wouldn't I express her love for Marrick, mistaking it for mine? Our relationship went from acquaintance to romance faster than taking a breath. Why? Because loving Marrick is Joanna's familiar.

How could I have been so stupid.

My love for Marrick isn't real. And though he said he loved me, it might not be me he loves. When Joanna died, grief torn him apart. Not because of team-leader responsibility. Because they were an item. No wonder Magelon fussed over my hair. Compared to Joanna, with her cover-model looks, I'm the ordinary girl-next-door. What's to love?

A gut-wrenching emptiness threatens to swallow me whole. "I'm sorry. I didn't realize."

"How could you?" Joanna says. "But please, don't be sorry. They mentioned how you behaved like me at times. I didn't know that would happen when I gave you my DNA. If anything good came out of this, you helped Marrick realize what he could never admit."

I ache all over with pain worse than any punch from the black-eyed man. Marrick's forever kiss wasn't for me. He's also making decisions based on a relationship that isn't real. I should have gone straight home to my uncle and never let Marrick into my life. He'll become what I fear most—another painful memory.

Blinking back tears, I run from the house. I can't wait for Darius. He's still arguing with Jim. Marrick might change his mind about saying goodbye, and we can't see each other again, ever. Not even via the com-link.

The Jeep is parked next to Betsy outside a shed near the driveway, but that's not the vehicle I need.

Pulling up one of the roller doors on the shed, I search through Jim's collection of vehicles: the dark-silver Bentley, the sleek black BMW. The vehicle I want stands in the end bay. Keys dangle from the ignition. A helmet sits on the seat. The Ducati Superbike, top speed 202 miles per hour—a rocket to rip me out of Marrick's life forever.

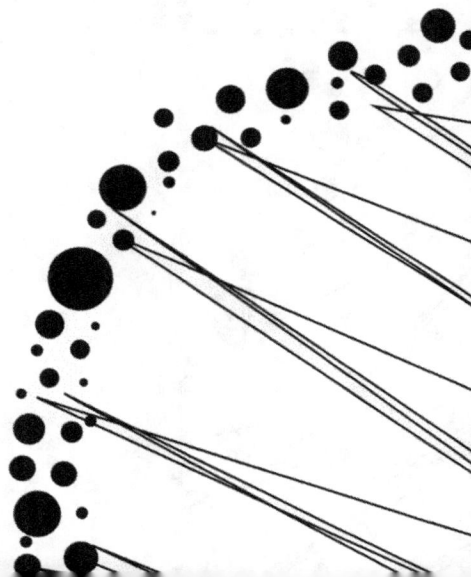

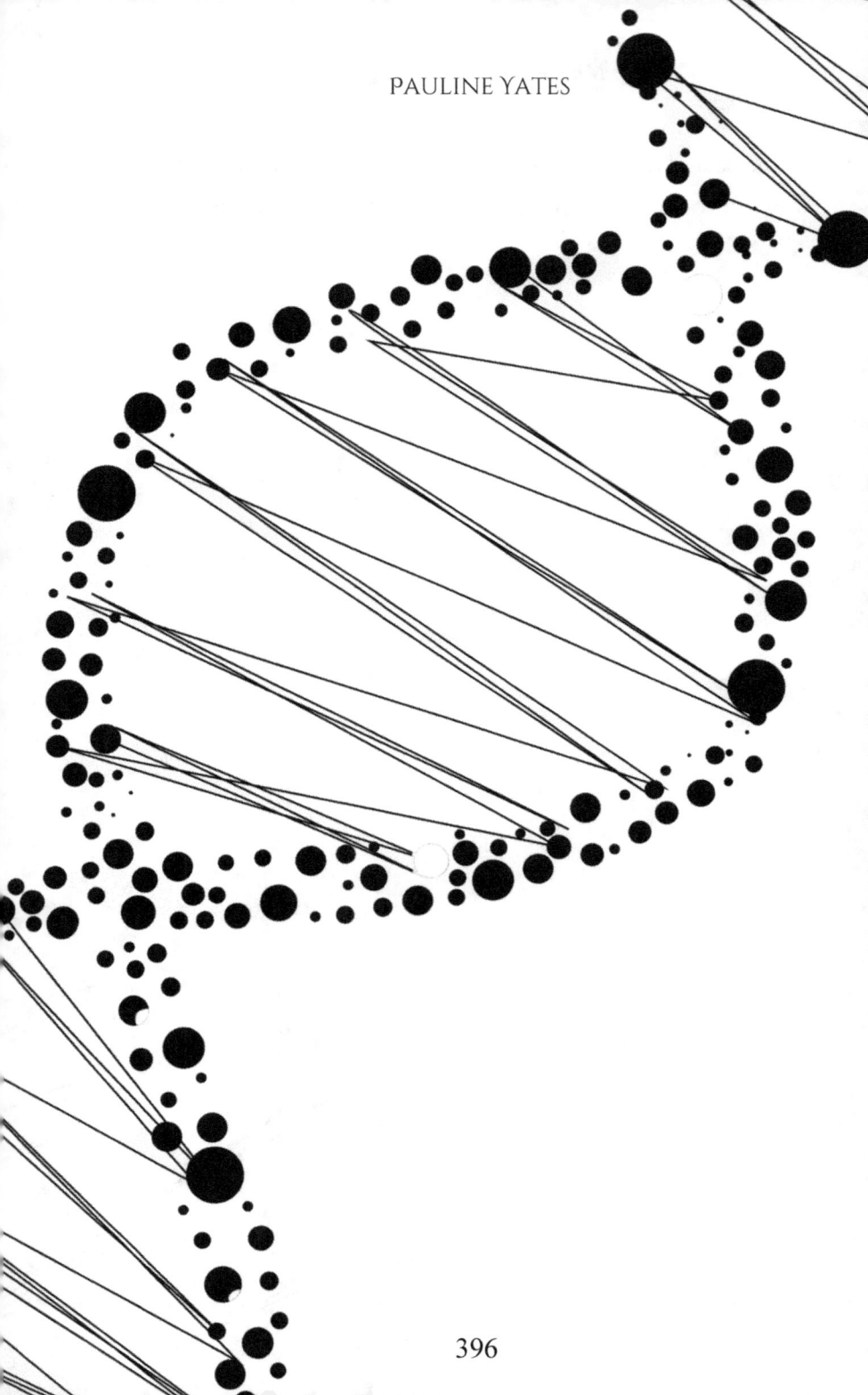

CHAPTER 36

DIZZY FROM PHYSICAL AND EMOTIONAL overexertion, it's a miracle I don't crash the bike. By sheer luck, I find the highway, but have to stop for gas and directions. I've got no money, so spin a story to the pump operator about escaping an abusive boyfriend. She looks at the bruise on my head, tells me to fill up, then slips me some cash from the register. She says I should call the cops.

I tell her he is a cop.

I complete the five-hour road trip in four, but not without racking up speeding fines from the highway patrol cameras. It was stupid to ride so fast. Jim will know which route I took when he receives the tickets in the mail.

I doubt it will matter. I'm home, and when my uncle

opens the door, I'll be back under his guard.

I hide the bike at the side of the house and collect my wits before facing him. He won't know I'm aware we're not related. I'm not sure how to confront him about it, or even if I should. Resetting my memories takes precedence over everything and I don't want to create friction that might interfere with that.

I sit the helmet on the bike's seat and study the house, absorbing the familiar unassuming split-level dwelling nestled at the end of a leafy cul-de-sac. The few neighbors are middle-aged or retired and keep to themselves. A lieutenant residing here gives no cause for concern. There's been no crime in this part of the neighborhood for as long as I can remember. The around-the-clock presence of plain-clothed security personnel when I lived here deterred that.

Light shines through a lower window—my uncle's office. He splits his time between here and his office at Red Bluff. He's home, but won't be expecting me—I'm with Marrick, he'll think. Unless Darius called. I imagine the Jeep roaring down the highway, a furious Darius at the wheel. He had no chance of catching up, not at the speed I rode. But if he sent a message ahead, why hasn't my uncle called in my usual security detail?

Unsure what to expect, I creep around the house to the front door. The motion sensor light flicks on, so I hurriedly arrange my hair to cover the bruises on my head and neck, straighten my jacket and smooth out my shirt.

And try to stand straight without flinching. The hours bent over the handlebars were murder on my ribs, and my leg stings where the bandage rubbed my stitches. I wish I'd thought to collect Vera's pain relief before I bolted. I'm going to need it.

I raise my hand to knock, but the door opens. My uncle stands in the foyer, as intimidating as ever. Six-foot-three with shoulders as broad as Kelly's, he's as tough and formidable as they come. Thick, bushy eyebrows make up for the lack of hair on his head and they perch over hawk-like eyes that miss nothing and record everything. He rarely dresses in anything but his military uniform, and tonight is no different. But it's late and though he's surprised to see me, the angry glint in his eye suggests he knew I wasn't where I should have been.

"By God, Sarah," he says, grabbing my arm and pulling me through the door. "Why aren't you with Daniels?"

I tug free and face him. "Did Darius call you?"

"No," he says, pushing the door closed and turning the lock. "Where is he?"

Telling him we were at Jim's house won't soften my homecoming. Besides, there's something I need to know first.

"Joanna's alive." How he responds will reveal if he already knew.

"Jo—what?"

"She's alive. Flannigan had her at Bio-Tech. We—" This could get tricky. My uncle's surprise confirms he didn't know Joanna was alive, but I forgot it would require further explanation. "She needed medical help. Darius took her to Vera. She was the closest."

My uncle straightens to his full height. "What was Kingsley thinking? You were the priority, not Johansson. Did he take you, too, because it would explain this?" He strides to his office, leaving me to worry about what *this* is. When he returns, he holds up a facsimile with a grainy image of me taken from the gas station.

"Every highway patrol from here to Reno is on alert for a biker using the roads like a racetrack. Your photo's also been picked up by the team I sent in a fake search for you. You were supposed to be with Daniels in a secure location. Do you have any idea the problem you've caused?"

"I've caused?" All intimidation from my uncle's fierce gaze vanishes. "I'm not the one taking injured soldiers from hospitals to use as test subjects in unregulated genetic experiments. Nor am I the one who lied about Joanna's death. And I'm not masquerading as an uncle raising his niece."

His mouth pulls tight, and he lowers the picture. "I see we need to have a discussion."

"We do."

"First, where's Daniels and his team?"

"On their way to Kelly's brother's house, the last I heard."

"Without you? Daniel's orders were to stay with you until further advised."

"It's not his fault. I wasn't safe and had to leave." And that's all he'll ever know.

"At least you had the sense to realize that. Why didn't Kingsley accompany you here?"

"I expect he's on his way. He was arguing with Jim when I left...Jim might know I've come here. He knows who I am."

My uncle's jaw locks tight. Keeping his eyes on me, he whips out a cell phone from his pocket, swipes and jabs the screen.

"This is John Wilson. Bring in your team. I want an immediate perimeter scout and secure at this location." He hits the screen again. "Issue a code four on that biker."

"How far away are they?" If I ever needed a gun, it's now. What if Flannigan's men get here first?

"They're close," my uncle snaps. "Do not step foot from this house until they've secured the premises, do you understand? You have no idea what's at stake if Flannigan catches you again."

A wave of mental exhaustion rolls over me, draining all penchant for arguing. "I know what's at stake, Uncle John. I know about my mother's research, Jack Arquet, and why you wanted me on Marrick's team. I also know Jim is financing Flannigan and that he and his associates will hold the majority vote if Flannigan's drug trial proceeds. What I don't know is how my mother knew you, and why you haven't shut down Flannigan."

My uncle stares at me, his expression giving nothing away. "Fair questions, but please, come and sit. You look exhausted."

If exhaustion is all he sees, I'm concealing my injuries well, but that doesn't mean I don't feel the angry throb in my leg, and the dull ache in my ribs. The stress of standing up to my uncle also brings back those miners hammering in my head, and it takes all my concentration not to pass out on the couch when we go to the living room to have our 'discussion'.

My uncle settles in an armchair opposite, hands clasped over his crossed knee. He frowns when I slump as I sit, but if he thinks showing concern for my welfare will sweeten my response to his answers, he's wrong.

"My mother?" I prompt.

He leans back in his chair like we're settling in for a nostalgic trip down memory lane.

"I met your mother at Red Bluff. She was a frequent visitor and liked to watch her brother train. We didn't meet again until the day she turned up on my doorstep. She feared for your safety and said she could no longer…keep you safe."

There's something in that pause he's not telling me,

but it's not the first time he's concealed information. There's no point asking. He'll tell me what I need to know, nothing more. I'll have to fill in the gaps on my own, as always.

"She told me Vera knew everything," my uncle continues, "and was willing to help. Vera secured a position with Jim who needed a live-in nurse. That gave her access to Bio-Tech without drawing attention so she could keep me informed about Flannigan's operations."

He sighs and twists his fingers together, so unlike him—he could be, for the first time in my life, telling the truth about everything.

"When your mother approached me for help—" he says, "I couldn't say no, not after what happened to her brother. I assume you know what happened?"

"Yes." My next question is hard. "Do you know what I am?"

He clamps his fingers together and gives me a hard look. "You're immune to the viral vector used in the genetic transfer of desirable traits. And that's all anyone will know."

He knows. And he's hiding the truth about my genetic makeup beneath a credible immunity lie should anybody suspect and raise questions.

"Does Darius know?" My voice comes out tighter than a twisted cable wire. How will I ever trust him again if he concealed the worst thing about me?

"He knows you're genetically enhanced, but that's all. Is Daniels aware?"

My relief that Darius didn't tell me because he didn't know is sideswiped by a twinge in my broken heart. "Marrick knows what Darius knows. Nothing more." And there never will be more, because I'll never see him again. I duck my head, feigning tiredness, so my uncle doesn't see the welling tears.

"Sarah, I've gone to great lengths to conceal the truth about your genetic makeup and will continue to do so. As will Vera. Our hope for you, your mother's hope—"

"Why didn't you tell me?" A tear escapes, but this one sprung from thirteen years of pent-up frustration. "What's the point of talking about hope when you kept me in the dark my whole life?"

He sighs and leans back in his chair, looking eighty, not sixty. "How do you explain to a five-year-old they're not one hundred percent human? As you grew older, there was nothing to suggest you were different from any other teenager, though you were exceptionally bright."

"Undetectable is the word, I believe."

"Yes, there's that. In other areas, you excelled in science. That would be your mother filtering through, I suspect. But you were drawn to a military career, understandable as you lived and breathed it, and it's in your blood. I wonder, often, about nature versus nurture, and whether I did the right thing taking you in, or whether Vera would've been better for the job. What we didn't know…" he grimaces, "well, there's still a lot we're yet to find out."

"Like whether I'm another Jack Arquet?"

"You're similar in many ways. He graduated top of his class, ended up leader of the top team. I'm not surprised you breezed through the Tactical Skills Program."

"But I didn't. Darius had me hide my skills." I tap my fingers on my knee, calmer now we've moved away from topics involving Marrick. "Why did Darius help conceal my abilities? What am I to him?"

"I thought you'd know that by now."

"He knows what happened to Jack and doesn't want to see genetic manipulation used in soldiers, is that it? That's why he trains us the way he does, to prove drug use isn't necessary."

"There's much to be admired about his methods," my uncle says. "But it comes at a cost."

The crux of the problem. "How much money has been wasted on Flannigan's research?"

"Unfortunately, there are some who aren't convinced Flannigan's research is a waste. After Arquet, the military's financial backing was cut, but an injection of private funds kept Flannigan afloat."

"Jim. He said Jack was the future of the military."

"A future that will be realized sooner than we expect. We're not the only country investing in genetic modification to enhance soldier performance. What

Flannigan offers is unique."

"Enhanced memory. But it's not an enhancement, is it? Rather, manipulation by the vector for its arsenal."

"An interesting discovery, though the credit should go to your mother."

"Credit?" I stare at him in disbelief. "There's nothing credit-worthy about any of this. Have you ever had your memory messed with and don't know who you are? Or behaved like someone you're not while so consumed by rage you've no control over your actions? That's what happened to Jack, and it's what I fight to control. There's no future in this line of research, only decimation of our armed forces. Please, you have the connections to stop Flannigan. More soldiers will die if you don't."

My uncle frowns. "Despite my position, my voice won't be heard above the many clamoring for advancement in soldier performance."

"You didn't see what Flannigan created. The soldier he planned to use as the test subject was barely human. I shot him. Multiple times. He didn't flinch."

My uncle's eyes harden. "When did this happen?"

Every time I answer, I bury myself further. I remain silent, but my uncle leans forward again.

"Tell me everything," he says.

So I do. I need to. Telling it out loud might help me process everything that's happened. Escaping Bio-Tech with Darius, my struggle with different memories, suspecting Joanna was alive, the raid on Kelly's house after Marrick returned to Bio-Tech. Our decision to go back in and find Joanna. The fight with the black-eyed man. Everything, from the moment Joanna drugged me at my barracks, to when I fled Jim's house on the bike. But not my relationship with Marrick, or how close I came to death.

"You participated in Johansson's rescue?" my uncle says. "What the devil was Daniels thinking?"

"It was my call, not his. We got Joanna out, but that man, the test subject, convinced Flannigan's security soldiers to let him out of his cell. He was like an armored truck with its accelerator pressed to the metal. But his vector controlled him, in the same way I'm controlled by the vector part of me. The vector's nature is to dominate, and it will kill to achieve that." I pause to let that sink in before delivering my final blow. "That's why Jack killed his team. If we go down this path, that's what the future of our military will look like."

I wipe my hand over my head, emotionally shaken after reliving everything up to this point. One thing I know for certain—Jack sacrificed his life and those of his team to stop that future. He's not a murderer. He's a hero.

"Where's Flannigan's test subject, now?" my uncle asks.

"Dead. Buried in the mine." I cringe. I didn't mention that.

"What mine?"

"The same mine my mother escaped through. It's how we got into Bio-Tech. I remembered the way."

My uncle stares at me for a long time. He might suspect it was me who needed medical help. Why else go to Vera? Whatever he thinks, he hides it behind a closed expression.

He unclasps his hands and sits up straight. "Where's Johansson now?"

"With Marrick." In his arms, probably. I stare at the floor. "I talked to her before I left Jim's. She said she'd give everything she knows about Flannigan to Darius, to give to you."

"And her state of health?"

"She's dying." I study his reaction. His expression remains impassive. "Joanna put a neurotransmitter in my head." I touch the back of my neck. "Vera said it's a device Flannigan made to electronically enhance long-term memory recall, his attempt to do what the vector does. But used together, it works too well...I remembered being born."

My uncle's eyes flick to my head and his expression grows the darkest I've ever seen it. He says nothing, once again, a closed book, but the fury in his eyes builds.

"First things first," he says, standing. "I'll bring in Johansson. And Daniels and his team. Despite his questionable decision-making, I want you back under his guard."

"That's not possible, not while Joanna's with them. They need time to reconnect."

"Time is something we don't have," my uncle says. "There's also no point when Joanna has no interest in being with them."

"You knew she wasn't happy?"

"I denied her initial transfer application. In hindsight, I should have allowed it. It takes time for a team to bond, but it was never going to happen with Johansson."

"I didn't get the impression she wants to leave."

"She will if I grant her the leadership position she wanted. If she's physically capable, that is."

I squirm on my seat. "Uncle John, I know you wanted me on Marrick's team to hide my enhancements, but it's not going to work. Having Joanna's memories complicates things."

"Then find a way to un-complicate them." He sighs. "Sarah, I'm thinking of your future. I'm not going to be around forever."

"Then find me another team." My reply snaps out of my mouth, not unintentionally.

"There are none anywhere near as good as Daniels. I also won't risk more people finding out what you are."

"Why not erase my records and pretend I don't exist? Our military has proven adequate in that department."

"It won't come to that."

"Won't it? I'm out of options. I've been so long

AWOL my sentence will run longer than your time in the military. I can't graduate without completing a training program, either. Besides, after finding out…" Shaking my head, I omit the truth about Marrick's questionable love for me. "I'd rather stay here, even if it means living with minders again."

"*AWOL* and graduating we can get around. As for staying here…it must be awkward for you knowing we're not blood-related, even though I've only had your best interests at heart."

Awkward, yes, especially after being lied to all my life. But right now? I need security and sleep. And time to reset. Everything else can wait.

"I'll stay, if you don't mind." Standing, I end discussion because nothing my uncle says will convince me otherwise. "When you hear from Darius, could you tell him I'm okay?"

"Of course. And Sarah?"

"Yes?"

"You don't have to call me uncle if you don't want to. But for appearance's sake—"

"It's okay. It'd be weird calling you anything else."

My uncle shares a rare smile. "It would be equally weird hearing something else."

His phone beeps.

"I need to take this," he says. "Get some rest. You'll find your room as you left it." He strides to his office, closing the door behind him.

I'm used to being alone in the house while my uncle goes about his work, but the silence torments me. I long for Kelly's laugh, for Magelon's fierce outbursts, for Reece's quips, for Marrick's reassuring presence. But to reset my memories, I need to forget about them. If only I could step into the white room and wake up remembering nothing.

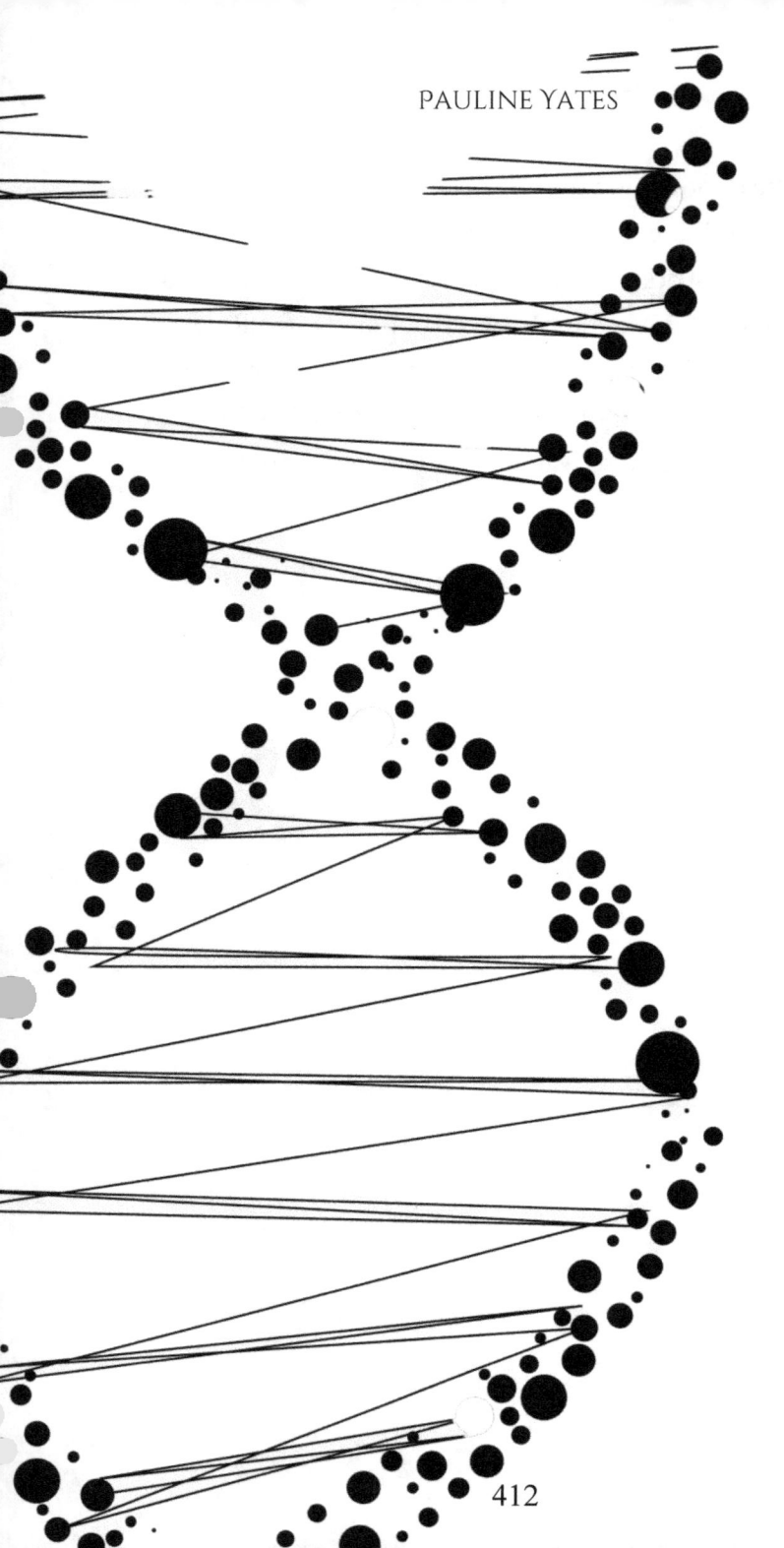

PAULINE YATES

CHAPTER 37

I LIE ON THE MOST comfortable bed I've had in months but have the worst night's sleep. Without Vera's pain relief, every bruise tortures me. My headache gets so bad yellow spots dance in front of my eyes. I clutch my head, wishing I'd pass out.

I must have because when I next open my eyes, sunlight streams through the window. My headache is gone, but I'm soaked in sweat—physically and emotionally drained, I didn't change into lighter clothes to sleep in. Eager to freshen up, I swing my legs over the side of the bed but sit before standing, not wanting to aggravate my ribs. They still hurt. So does my leg and every other bruise on my body. But my mind is the clearest it's been since escaping Flannigan.

Those yellow spots. They remind me of golden orbs in the memory tunnel. Did my memories reset? Could it work that fast? Why not? I entered familiar territory the moment I rode into Anderson. Being back under my uncle's thumb is the most familiar of all.

I look around my room. It's one of two bedrooms on the upper level of the house. The other bedroom is used for storage—my uncle sleeps downstairs on the main level in a room next to his office. Sleeping alone on the top floor scared me at first, but I like the en suite and the view of the street, though only now do I remember how many times I sat at the window watching for my mother's return.

The room is as I left it. Military training manuals sit stacked on the desk near the window. The bookshelf against the opposite wall is crammed with novels and exercise books filled with years of study notes. Textbooks—calculus, biology, chemistry—fill the bottom shelf. There's nothing personal in this room, no trinkets or photos, no posters on the wall. Nothing to show the fun in my life because there was no fun, just study and reading and plotting how to leave.

Standing, I go to the built-in wardrobe and slide open the door. My clothes hang on the rack; my shoes sit on the floor. The top shelf is crammed with bags of clothes I grew out of. Smaller shelves hold shorts, T-shirts, underwear, and socks, all folded.

I pick up a pair of leggings and run my hand over the

fabric. They don't jog a warm connection. Did I expect that? If anything, I feel detached, like these clothes belong to someone else.

Closing the door, I lean against it and gaze around the room. I know what's wrong: part of me is missing. I breathe in until my ribs protest, then blow out until my lungs are empty. That's how I feel. Empty.

Going to my desk, I drag my finger over the spines of the manuals I'd memorized before leaving for Red Bluff. I pull one out and flick through the pages, but don't see the words. The team is my missing piece. Without them, I'm not whole. With them, I belong somewhere, the only thing I want. And now that's gone.

I slam the manual closed, needing to focus on something else, something closer to home. Why not find my father?

My uncle said military runs in my blood. He wouldn't have said that if he didn't refer to my father. Being with Marrick's team showed me what it's like to have a family, and I want that more than ever. If I can't have the family I want, why not the family I lost?

I pull out fresh clothes: the leggings so they don't rub my stitches, a tank top, and a jacket. I shower and change, reusing the bandage over my stitches until I can get into the medical kit downstairs. Standing in front of the bathroom mirror, I arrange my hair to hide the bruise on my forehead and the finger marks on my neck. In casual clothes with my hair around my shoulders, I look nothing like a genetically enhanced soldier. I'm the ordinary girl-next-door again. Except for my eyes. Like Jim's, they're soldier sharp, forever a reminder of who I am.

Back at the wardrobe, I choose a pair of sneakers with worn tread and frayed laces—my favorite to wear around the house. Then I go in search of my uncle.

He exits his office as I descend the stairs. He stops, taking in my appearance. Who does he see? A biological entity, or his 'niece'?

"I trust you slept well." He's overly polite this morning; awkward.

"Yes, thank you." Yuck. So am I. "Do you have a minute?" He rarely does.

"Of course." A lie.

"Was my father in the military?" I don't ask if he knows my father. I don't want to put him off by what could be construed as an accusatory question.

"Yes," he says. "However, I'm afraid that's all I'm at liberty to share, though I'm surprised he hasn't revealed himself by now."

"Darius said he didn't want to interfere with my training," I say, my mood dropping six levels.

"I doubt it's the reason, but that's for him to explain."

"Have you heard from him? Darius, that is."

"A late text. He's been delayed." His cell phone beeps. Pulling it out of his pocket, he stares at the screen.

"I'm sorry, Sarah, I have to take this." He returns to his office, slamming the door shut.

It's the usual interruption. Frustrated, I lean on the end of the balustrade, wondering what delayed Darius. My thoughts drift to Marrick. If they left when Joanna said they would, they'd be at Rusty's house by now. How's Magelon coping with Joanna back? Is Joanna being nice to Reece, or do her normal derisive comments slip in? I hope not. She wouldn't be with them without his expertise. And Kelly? Is he cooking her breakfast, insisting she eat? Is Marrick holding her in his arms?

I stomp down the last step. I can't think about them. They're holes in my heart that will never heal, but it's time to move on. Searching for my father will keep me busy. He's in the military—that's confirmed. But where? At Red Bluff? He might be if Darius knows him.

Further along the hallway, the office door opens, and my uncle strides out, pulling on his jacket.

"I'm needed at base," he says.

"Is everything all right?"

"Yes, yes, the usual drama. I've recalled your usual security to replace the team outside; they're required elsewhere. Stay inside until they arrive. I'll be back as soon as I can."

He hurries through the house to the front door, giving me no chance to question him further. This is usual, too, my uncle rushing to work, leaving me home alone. It'll work in my favor, though. My uncle keeps a logbook of all current and former Red Bluff personnel in his office. I might recognize my father's name if I saw it.

I listen for my uncle's car pulling out of the garage. He keeps his bottle-green Jaguar in as pristine a condition as Jim's cars. Funny how they both have a penchant for prestigious vehicles, though that could be a generational thing. Hearing the Jaguar drive away, I go to front door, crack it open, and peek outside.

A soldier jogs along the driveway, his back to me. He holds a radio to his ear, and the rifle slung over his shoulder bumps against his waist. Two more soldiers stand on the road. A Jeep pulls up. They all get inside and drive off. I hope the neighbors don't gossip. My usual security is far more discreet, plain clothes and concealed handguns. What will they think, finding me at home again?

Closing the door—and locking it to keep my uncle happy— I hurry back to his office. After six months of living with Red Bluff's noise—soldiers shouting, gunfire, jeeps roaring past my barracks—the silent house puts me on edge. I glance around as I pass the kitchen and the living room, taking in the furnishings. This house is the only home I've known, but time away made me a stranger.

I pause at a picture hanging on the wall, my first attempt at drawing flowers. I've never given the picture more than a passing glance because my uncle didn't want to hang it, but my tutor insisted, saying a six-year-old child likes to have their efforts appreciated in the home. Looking at it through wiser eyes, I step closer and study the precise way I drew a serrated edge on the leaves, and how the stems bend as if swaying in a breeze.

But it's the petals that draw my attention. The clusters of yellow circles look like the golden orbs in my memory tunnel. Perfect in symmetry, some are large, some small, just as they appear in my mind. The vector's a part of me, so did I subconsciously draw what it does to bring my awareness to its presence?

Suppressing a shiver, I continue to my uncle's office. It's dark inside, with the blinds drawn. Flicking on the light, I examine the room. My uncle's desk, an antique mahogany monster, takes up a third of the space. It's covered in stacks of paperwork, folders, a pen holder, his laptop and another desktop computer. Four drawers on either side make the desk's legs. The wall opposite is shelving, with folders, books, and files filling every available space. A metal filing cabinet stands in the corner behind the desk. Above it, a framed certificate honoring my uncle's service to the military conceals a wall safe. There are no other decorations. This room is all work. Like my uncle.

The logbook is at the end of the middle shelf, a black-spine ring folder, thick with documents. Pulling it out, I take it to the desk, sit in my uncle's chair and flick through plastic sheet holders containing printouts of names, cataloged by year and group.

The first few pages list current C.S.R. team members and have a general soldier listing in order of rank. Eight sheets in, I pause. Marrick Daniels (RB), Joanna Johansson (RB), Magelon Caruso (LP Transfer), Kelly Olsen (RB), Reece Matthews (LP Transfer)—C.S.R. RB2510. My chest tightens. Flattening my hand on the page, I breathe them in, though I shouldn't, then turn the page and continue my search.

How far back should I go? To Darius's active-duty days? I flip through a whole section of pages, looking for his name, and find him in a list of twenty names from thirty-three years ago. Kingsley, Darius, 378RB Unit 5. They didn't have C.S.R. teams in his day. They came later, starting with Jack Arquet.

Running my finger down the list, I recognize many names as current Red Bluff instructors: Miller, combative instruction, Singleton, driver training, Hayes, Red Bluff's chief weapons instructor. Darius never mentioned they were in the same unit.

I tap my finger on the page. Darius knows my father, but keeps his mouth shut. He said my father didn't want to interfere with my training.

He's to never know.

An early childhood memory of my mother talking to Vera sneaks into my mind. My mother never told my father about me. That's forgivable, but how did he learn he had a daughter?

She looks exactly like her mother.

Anyone who knew my mother would recognize her in my face. That doesn't matter now because I know who my father is.

I clench my fists to stop my hands from shaking. How could Darius not tell me? He had ample opportunities and could have spared me the heartache of thinking I had no family.

I slam my fist against the page. What do I do now?

Nothing. That's what I'll do. My father had his chance to tell me. The fact he didn't reveals the truth—he'd prefer I didn't exist.

I flick the pages back into place. A page at the back slides out. Opening to that section, I release the ring and pop the page into place. The date catches my eye—forty-two years ago, around the time my uncle did his active duty.

Running my fingers down the long list of names, I search for John Wilson. I don't know why. Perhaps to check if he's real. The names are divided into groups of fifteen, each group allocated a reference number. His name's at the bottom of the page, John Wilson, 67A9RB-3. At least this confirms his identity. Beneath is another name I recognize. Jim Cartwright, 67A9RB-3.

Is it the same Jim? I don't know his last name. He's the same age as my uncle, and Vera said they were in the same unit. Pondering that, I flip the pages forward and search for Jack Arquet. He's there, with his team members—Scotty Towers, Rex Brueller, Clinton Houseman, Mitch De'veers—C.S.R. RB0001, the first of Red Bluff's C.S.R. teams.

I've seen enough. I close the folder and return it to the shelf. My uncle's connection to Jim plays on my mind.

My gaze drifts around the room and stops at the certificate on the wall. Going to it, I lift the frame off the wall and stare at the combination lock. What's inside the safe? My real birth certificate? Evidence of a deeper connection to Jim?

I'm fixated now. I don't know what I'm looking for, but something's here, I sense it, a knowing, drawn from snippets of information locked in my subconscious. Knowledge the vector draws out of me.

I don't know the combination to the safe. It could be anything, my uncle's birth date, his military number. I try both, to no avail, but suspect the combination is something related to the military. Back at the shelf, I pull down the folder and find my uncle's details. His group number? It's worth a shot.

I dial the knob, using the numbers from his group listing. There's a soft click, and the door swings open. Unable to believe my luck, I search the safe. In the pile of documents, I find my birth certificate. It lists my name as Sarah Wilson, my mother's name, Katherine Wilson, place of birth, Anderson—a cunning forgery designed to pass military scrutiny. There's no record of my father. My mood sinks at finding no conclusive proof of his identity. But I don't need that. The proof is in my memories.

Returning the certificate, I lift the corners of the other documents. House deeds. Insurance policies. Motor vehicle purchase records. Nothing of importance. At the bottom of the pile is a thick yellow envelope. Pulling it out, I slip my finger beneath the sticky tab and slide out the documents inside. A photo of a man jumps out at me.

His face—I know it. His eyes—hellish black. It's a headshot from his military file. His name: Jason Anderson. I know that, too. Nickname, Fox. He died a year ago from head injuries sustained in a vehicle roll-over. But he didn't die. Fox is the black-eyed man.

I overheard my uncle talking about his tragic loss a year before I started at Red Bluff. But I'm not holding his military file. This document has no header, no identifying information. Jason's details are scrawled beneath his photo. Below are dates, numbers, and letters that make no sense to me, words such as non-reactive, irregular heart rhythm, cardiac distress, rejection phase inconclusive—progress notes. The next line: terminal, underlined in red.

Did Jason know he's dying? Consumed by rage, he mightn't have. I pull out the next document. It's another headshot, different name, but has similar progress notes. Cause of death—stroke, underlined in red. A date catches my eye. This information is ten years old.

Kneeling on the floor, I pull out all the documents and

spread them around me. There must be forty, fifty files, spanning over the past twenty years. Some have no photos, just a name and scrawled notes. A common link is glaringly obvious—aneurism, myocardial infarction, stroke, multiple myeloma. All these people are dead.

A photo jumps at me from the pile—Joanna.

I tremble with anger. My uncle lied to me, again. He knew Flannigan had Joanna. When I told him she was alive, was he surprised because we found her, or because she wasn't dead? He says he can't shut down Flannigan, yet I'm staring at all the proof he needs. Even after everything we discussed, I still can't trust anything he says.

Leaving the documents on the floor so my uncle will know what I've discovered, I pace around the room. I can't think; fury ties my insides into knots. Will no one take Flannigan down? Stopping, I stare at the documents. Why not me?

I run from the office and jump the stairs two at a time to my room. An old pair of boots sits in the wardrobe, and a suitable heavy-drill jacket. Swapping clothes, I snatch a hairband out of a bathroom drawer and scoop my hair up into a ponytail. I'd like a gun, but Flannigan won't suspect my motive if I arrive unarmed. I don't need a gun anyway to shut him down permanently.

Hurrying back downstairs, I exit the house through the back door. The Ducati is still parked around the side of the house, the helmet on the seat. With no team around to stop me from leaving, escaping is easy. But as I sit astride the bike, Jim's black BMW pulls into the drive. The driver's side window rolls down. It's Joanna.

Heart pounding, I climb off the bike and hurry to the car. "What's wrong? Why are you here?"

"Oh, thank god you're here," she says, her eyes red— from crying? "I need your help. Jim called Flannigan. Magelon, Kelly, and Reece have been detained."

The cold of death grips me. "Where's Marrick?"

A tear leaks from Joanna's eye. "He's been taken to Bio-Tech. Flannigan plans to use him as the test subject."

The world falls away from my feet. Not Marrick. Oh, God, please no.

"There's still time to save him, but we have to leave now," Joanna says. "I'll get you inside. You're his only hope."

I run around the car, pull open the passenger door, and slide in. Is this why my uncle left in a hurry? Why didn't he tell me?

Because he never tells me anything.

Blind with fury, I slam the door closed. "Get me there."

I flinch at a sharp prick on my leg.

Joanna holds a syringe. "I'm sorry, Sarah. But I still need you."

I pull on the door latch. The door doesn't open. My hand grows numb and drops by my side. My eyelids grow heavy, and I sink into a familiar drug-induced fog.

Why does she need me?

Because I'm exactly who she wants…

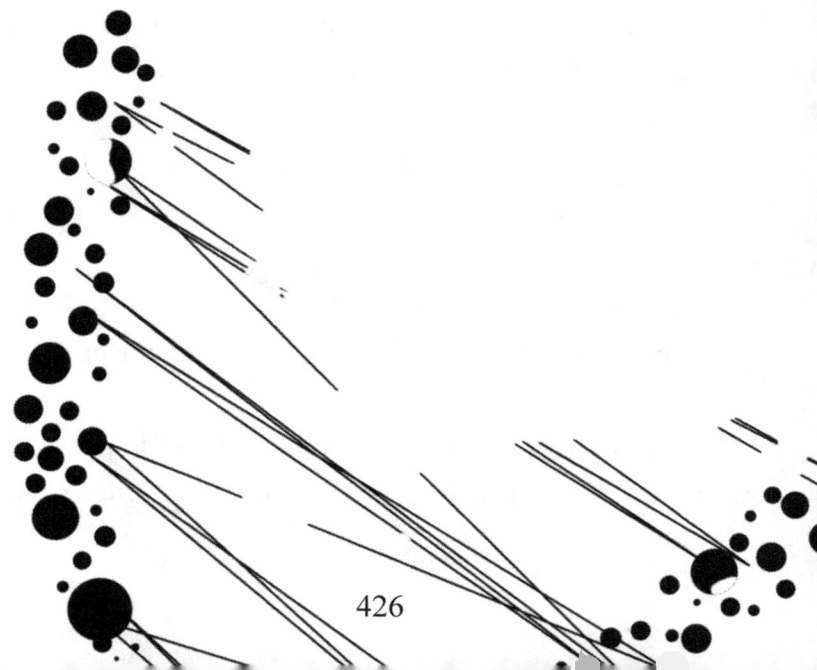

CHAPTER 38

SHADOWS MOVE THROUGH MY DRUG haze, indistinguishable shapes that flitter in and out of my consciousness. I add details from my memories. One shadow is tall and thin and moves with feminine grace—Joanna. The other is dark at the top, gray in the middle—Flannigan, in his laboratory coat. Soon, I'll see what I imagine. The drug Joanna gave me is wearing off.

The muffled ringing in my ears goes away first. Closing my eyes, I listen.

"Without my help, the trial will fail," Joanna says. "She's an expert at hiding her skills. How do you think she got through six months of training with nobody realizing what she is?"

"We can't guarantee it'll work, and I don't have time

to try," Flannigan says. "I'm expected to present my findings in three days. I won't be granted an extension."

"Did you not listen? She's already behaving like me, from what my team told me. With one more procedure, I'll control her. Don't deny me this. You promised I'd be the face of your research. I still can be, but she won't be compliant without me."

Compliance. The white room. Will she give me more of her DNA to turn me into an obedient test subject? How does she think she'll control me? One thing is certain. Joanna isn't trying to expose Flannigan. She's working with him.

Feeling returns to my limbs, pins and needles that fade when I flex my muscles. I try to raise my arm but am not surprised when I can't. I open my eyes. I'm in a chair this time, my arms secured by two sets of restraints, around my wrists and near my elbows. My ankles are lashed to the chair's legs. I rock from side to side. The chair doesn't move; perhaps it's bolted to the floor. Straining, I apply every ounce of strength I possess and jerk at the restraints. The Velcro on the elbow straps crackle but don't separate.

The noise alerts Joanna, who's with Flannigan at a computer on the bench along the wall. Seeing I'm awake, she crosses the room and stands in front of me.

I glare at her. "Where's Marrick?"

She smirks. "So precious, how the two of you think of each other first."

I twist my wrists, trying to loosen the restraints. "Where is he?"

"Hmm, let me see." She touches a manicured finger to her jaw. "At Rusty's, I expect. More importantly, away from you. I'd never have caught you, otherwise."

He's not here, thank God. But I am. I'm in one of the cells along the corridor, judging by the glass viewing pane in the door. Other than the bench, the computer, and the chair, there's nothing else in here.

Joanna walks to my side and brings her face close to my ear. "I know why Marrick likes you. You need protecting." She laughs.

I glare at her. "I don't need his protection."

"You do, from yourself." She moves around to stand in front of me again. "You're so trusting. Don't worry, I'll help with that."

If she refers to our conversation at Jim's, I've been played. To what depth, I'm afraid to guess.

"You're wondering," she says. "Am I gathering evidence against Doctor Flannigan or a willing participant in his research? I don't blame you for being confused, especially when you believed everything I said." She leans down so we're eye to eye. "All those terrible things I said weren't my fault. Abducting you, sending teams to Kelly's house, instructing Flannigan to triple his security? They were all me."

The ugliness in her heart spreads across her face.

How did I ever think she was beautiful? "Why? Why help Flannigan?"

"Because he's giving me what I want." She steps aside, putting me in full view of Flannigan.

He looks at my restraints and frowns. "Is she secure?"

"Of course," Joanna says. "I'd be dead, otherwise."

Immobilized, there's nothing I can do except soak in my hatred for them. And imagine their deaths.

Flannigan steps away from the computer and stands next to Joanna. "Tell me, Miss Arquet, could you identify the source of the memories you recalled? Were you aware some recollections weren't yours?"

I clamp my mouth shut. He'll get nothing from me.

"She won't talk," Joanna says, sounding pleased. "Unless you give her what she wants."

"Which is?" Flannigan asks.

"Answers." She smiles at me. "Ask him why you recalled my memories?"

I know why, so say nothing. My silence must aggravate Joanna because she steps to my side and clamps her hand on my shoulder.

"Ask him," she says, squeezing hard.

I grit my teeth. "No."

Her nails bite through my jacket. "Fine. I'll ask for you. Doctor, why am I recalling memories that aren't mine?" She steps back and stands in front of me again. "Why, Sarah," she continues, her voice now sickly sweet.

"Cellular memory is a fascinating subject. Tell me, have you experienced episodes of déjà vu? Imagined events that happened to someone else? You have? Oh, how did they affect you? Teach you skills? Provide crucial information?" She pauses. "Experience love?"

If I could get my hand free, I'd scratch her smile off her face for referring to my feelings for Marrick. However, at home and in my familiar surroundings, I didn't recall even one of Joanna's memories. Yet, my love for Marrick is as strong as ever.

The truth hits me hard. I love him. Me. Not Joanna. I admired Marrick before Joanna corrupted my mind, and my love for him grew from our interactions. The respect he showed me, how he treats his team members as equals. Whether his love for me is real, I won't know until I ask him. I won't get that opportunity if I don't get out of here.

"The theory behind Flannigan's research—" she speaks like a lecturer now, "is that cells store memories, both acquired and inherent. His research in this area is based on how we can retrieve those memories so information gained in the past can be accessed more readily—"

A sharp exhale escapes her lips. She squeezes her eyes shut and presses her hand to her chest. Her discomfort doesn't go unnoticed by Flannigan, but he does nothing to help.

Infuriated by his callousness, I strain against my

restraints.

"Help her. She's dying."

"Death, while unfortunate, is never a waste," Flannigan says. "Every test subject has provided volumes of data on how the body reacts to the viral vector."

"All your test subjects are dead," I say, thinking about the photos in my uncle's office.

"But not you, Miss Arquet," Flannigan says. "You're a curiosity, one your mother went to great lengths to conceal. You possess varying degrees of enhanced physical traits and express raised aggression, a typical characteristic of the viral vector we used, yet your blood work is normal and shows no evidence you carry the vector. Unusual."

Because the vector changed into a multi-cell organism and he's looking for the wrong thing. He mustn't discover that. "My abilities were inherited naturally, from my military father, and my uncle, Jack. Remember him?"

Joanna distracts me, pacing around the cell behind Flannigan, hand on her chest, sweat beading on her forehead. Her eyes glaze over, and she pants, the rise and fall of her chest erratic.

"If it were that, you wouldn't be here, Miss Arquet?" Flannigan says, ignoring Joanna. "No. The answer lies in your mother's research, the results she kept from me. It won't matter that you won't divulge the information. My assistant, Miss Johansson, is more than willing to help."

"My mother used to be his assistant," I say to Joanna.

"He didn't help her, and he won't help you. You'll die as she did."

Joanna smirks, her only response. Doesn't she care if she dies?

"She was foolish, your mother, but bright," Flannigan says. "Her attempt to understand the vector by performing the procedure on herself revealed a pathway I'd never considered."

I bang my back against the chair, seeing red. "How dare you patronize her. She was cleverer than you. You're nothing without her."

My insults bounce off him. He continues as though I hadn't spoken.

"To find you alive and in perfect health could only mean one of two things. The vector is either a natural part of your genetic makeup or it formed a symbiotic relationship with you during fetal development in the womb. Further tests will shed light on that hypothesis. Either way, it's the future generations I need to study. With what I can learn from you, I'm on the verge of creating a new generation of natural-born genetically enhanced soldiers."

My face turns cold. He's closer to realizing what I am than I thought. Visions of pregnant women held in these cells fill my mind, their bodies infused with the viral vector, their genetically mutated babies harvested. Did my mother foresee this? She escaped through the mine. She left me with my uncle, a lieutenant with access to high-level security. Everything she knows is stored in her memories, and, given the right stimulus, I'll recall it.

I won't share the information willingly, but if Joanna controls me as she claims will happen, she could access everything Flannigan needs.

"The neurotransmitter Joanna put in my head doesn't work," I say, desperate to cast doubt on any procedure they're planning. "It messed up my mind, nothing more."

"To the contrary, electrically stimulating the hippocampus, the central switching point for memories in the brain, proved successful, if what Miss Johansson told me about your interactions with people known to her are correct," Flannigan says. "Your escape, while untimely, placed you in an environment that provided the right stimulus to recall Miss Johansson's memories first. The addition of the neurotransmitter helped the vector recall the required information at a rate that surpassed my expectations. It's proven necessary, especially when a reduction in soldier training time is paramount."

Recovering from her episode, Joanna gives him a smug smile. "As I said it would."

Using the neurotransmitter must be what Joanna wanted to prove Flannigan wrong about. Vera said he'd stopped using it. For good reasons.

"It made me hallucinate. I didn't know who I was half the time. Joanna, please, don't do this. His research will destroy our military. Look what he did to that other man."

"We'll be nothing like him." Walking behind me, she gathers my hair in her hands and smoothes it down my back. "With one more procedure, my memories will dominate. Together, we'll be more than perfect."

I toss my head, hating her touching me. "What am I? The new test subject, with more of your DNA so I won't resist? Who's my sparring partner? You? In your condition, you won't last two seconds in the ring."

She chuckles. "Jeffries will provide our sparring partners, not that any of his soldiers are a match for us. Our skills combined are guaranteed to impress the officials, and we'll secure the votes required to get this line of research approved for use."

"And then what? You walk out of here a pin-up model for Flannigan's research? From the look of you, you'll be dead within a week."

"Oh, Sarah. Why would I keep this wreck of a body when I can have yours?"

I stiffen. Did I hear her right? I recall what she said, how I'm exactly who she wants. The blood drains from my face. She's not giving me her DNA to turn me into a compliant test subject. She wants to take over my body because her body is dying.

"You're crazy. That's not possible." But it is. Haven't I spoken and behaved like her without realizing it? Will I be aware of Joanna's control over my thoughts and actions, or cease to exist?

"Time is short," Joanna says. "We should begin."

"I'll prepare the serum." Flannigan strides from the cell, opening and closing the door with an impatient swipe of a keycard.

Joanna places her palms on my shoulders, touching me like I'm something to be cherished. But her fingers bite into my jacket, the vector in her keen to rip me apart. The feeling's mutual.

"I learned a lot about you while we were at Jim's. Not from what was said, but from how everyone"—her tone turns spiteful—"fell all over themselves to be around you. It must feel wonderful to be wanted."

"Your issues with them are your fault, not theirs." I wriggle my ankles, trying to loosen the straps, but they hold.

Joanna grabs my hair and pulls my head back, so I'm forced to look up at her.

"If you were denied opportunities to prove yourself, wouldn't you become frustrated? I was never good enough." Her eyes take on a faraway look. "I'll show them. I'll be better than anyone they've ever seen."

I tilt my head back further to relieve the tearing pressure on my scalp. "Why is that important to you? You were already better than everyone, and on the best team. What more do you want?"

"I'm not the best." She releases my hair and my head

snaps forward. "I was always Marrick's second, a hidden face in his team. If not for that stupid shooting incident, I'd be leading a team by now and the accolades would sing my name."

"We don't do our job for the accolades. And it wasn't a stupid incident. Your call got a kid killed."

"A call made from incorrect intel," she says, seething through her teeth. "In the hospital, when Flannigan offered me the chance to enhance my body, I jumped at it. Wouldn't you?"

I can't believe she won't own her mistake. "You got a death sentence, nothing more."

"I'd have been the force of an army," she snaps. "But of course"—she throws up her hands and laughs bitterly— "not even my body's good enough. The procedure didn't work, though we tried multiple times. My body rejected the transduction process and I'm left looking like this."

She spreads her arms. Only a day has passed since we were at Jim's and she looks thinner, paler. Her eyes are glassy and the vein in her neck throbs. Whatever time she has left, it's fast running out.

"The future Flannigan promised you is impossible," I say. "We both carry the vector. They'll make us fight to the death to dominate. You know I speak the truth. Think about what will happen if our military enhances soldiers using Flannigan's research. It'll be a bloodbath."

"Interesting, isn't it? This burning need to kill each

other." She closes her eyes and breathes in deep, like she sucks something from the air. "It's empowering." Opening her eyes, she fixes me with an icy glare. "I didn't know you were already genetically enhanced when I chose you. I just needed a body, and you were perfect—an orphan, highly skilled, and an uncle with connections. Flannigan couldn't believe his luck when I brought you here." She scowls. "He wouldn't let me touch you."

"If he wanted my mother's research, why didn't he give you or that other man my DNA to recall her memories?"

"He's paranoid about theft. Ironic, isn't it, when he's doing the same to your mother. He thinks if he gives your DNA to someone else, they could potentially steal your mother's work and end his career. No, no, no—" she walks around me, "he wants all of your mother's research safely contained in one body—yours."

"Isn't he worried about you running off with my mother's data?"

She laughs. "I've as much to gain from this as him. You could say we're...partners? I'll have the knowledge. He has the means to bring it to fruition. I've already proven my loyalty by bringing you back here. He thought you'd want to help, the fool. He knows better now. Once I control of your mind, I'll have access to everything you know. And I'll be untouchable. The viral vector is a weapon no one can see. It will arm me with tactical information taken from both our memories, and your enhancements will make me indestructible."

"You're wrong. You can die as easily as Flannigan's test subject."

"You didn't die," she says.

"Because I had backup," I shout. "Sure, I was alone when I fought that man, but if not for Magelon's blaster, I'd be dead, not him."

Joanna sneers. "You don't need anyone. You're an apex predator. With me in control, you'll only be better."

"Don't you understand? You won't be the only apex predator. Flannigan doesn't care about you. You'll be superseded at the same speed he ditched you for me. You'll be second again and there'll be nothing you can do about it."

That catches her attention. Her expression hardens. Then she smirks. "If he even thinks of crossing me, I'll sell *us* to the highest bidder. We'll make quite the valuable package once I gain access to your mother's research."

"Are you delusional? The second you walk out of Bio-Tech in *my* body, my uncle will insist I return to Marrick's team. They know you and will see you in me. The fact you're not with them now will raise suspicion, especially when they discover I'm not at home. I bet they're on their way here right now."

"Don't expect to be rescued this time." She pulls a com-link out of her pocket and holds it up. "Marrick thinks you're with Darius at your uncle's house. Your uncle thinks you left with Darius, who arrived *after* your uncle attended an urgent meeting at Red Bluff regarding the progress of Flannigan's trial. I'm with Vera, because the trip to Rusty's would have been detrimental to my health. As for Darius, he's no longer in the picture."

I slam against the restraints. "What did you do to him?"

She tsks. "So tetchy. You're worse than Marrick when it comes to Darius. Both of you treat him like some type of training god. His methods are outdated, and so is he."

Her plan for me is overshadowed by a horrific image of Darius dead. My mind turns to mush. What about Vera? Is Joanna aware of her connection to me?

A glimmer of hope rises. Vera's careful. She wouldn't have said anything about her role in my life, and outside of my uncle, I told no one. If she knows Joanna's here, she'll get word to Marrick, or my uncle, though I'm not sure if that's a good thing if he's known about Flannigan's research all along.

My hope for rescue is dashed by Flannigan striding back into the cell carrying a syringe. Even if it's discovered I'm here, no one will reach me in time.

"I'm ready to proceed, Miss Johansson," Flannigan says.

"Good. We're ready, too." She steps aside.

Flannigan approaches and jabs the needle into my arm.

I lock eyes with Joanna. "I will kill you."

"Yes, I expect you will. There can only be one of me." She reaches out and pats my cheek. "I'll make it quick."

My eyelids droop and blackness closes around me. Drugged and physically restrained, fighting my way free is impossible. But there's another way I can beat Joanna. Vera said I could reject what isn't mine. How I do that, I'm not sure, but if it comes down to a memory battle, I'll do everything in my power to help my vector win.

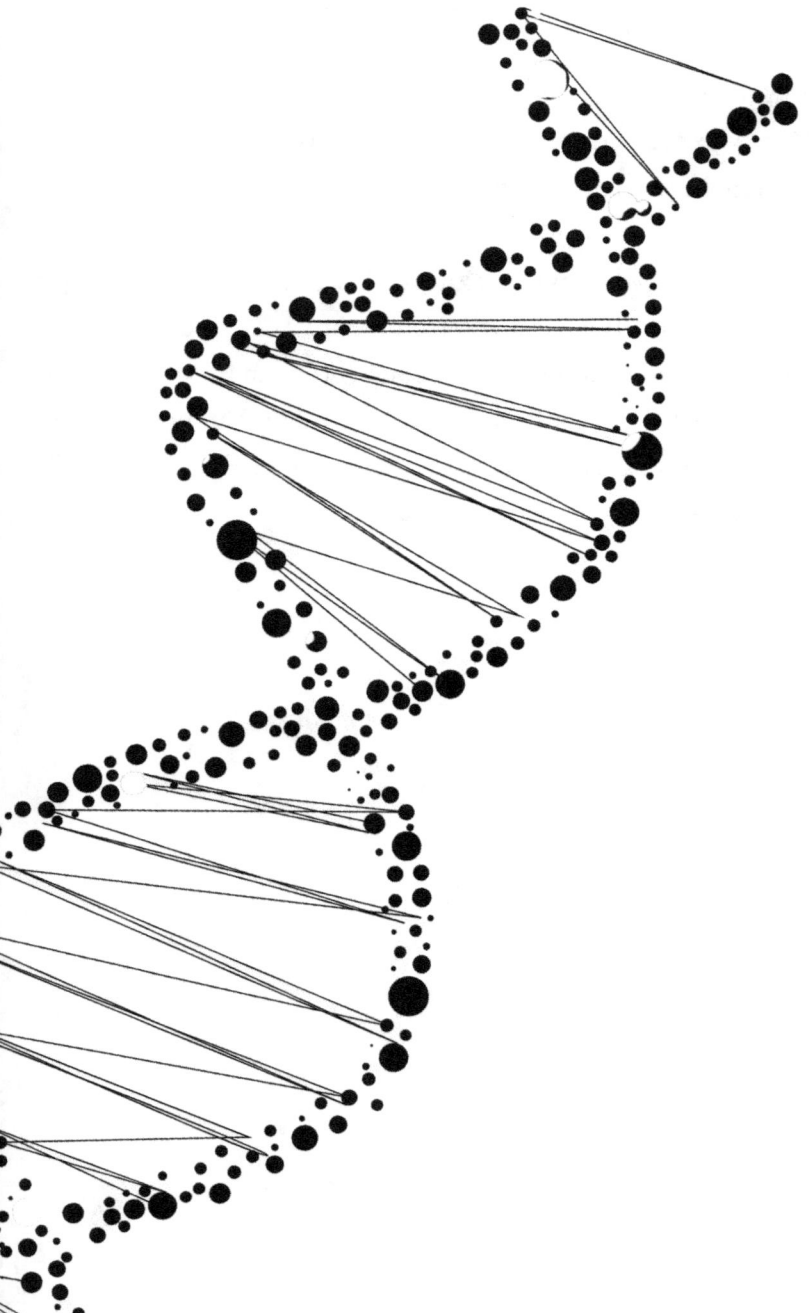

CHAPTER 39

I FALL THROUGH A DARK tunnel, with no beginning, no end. I reach out, touch the walls. They ripple beneath my fingers, fluid-like, but I feel nothing. The walls are an illusion, a drug-induced figment of my imagination. The memory tunnel. But the tunnel's not the same.

Golden orbs appear around me. The first one shows Joanna in the BMW, her eyes red from fake tears. The next shows documents scattered across the floor of my uncle's office. More orbs show a furious Darius, Jim's skeletal face, Marrick's fierce determination to fix things. My memories.

The golden orbs are surrounded by green orbs, and they hold memories, too—Joanna's.

My face appears in one, shocked after Joanna jabbed me with the syringe. The next shows me again, running from Jim's house. Other orbs depict Darius and Jim and Marrick, but the green orbs blend with the gold, and I can't separate them because we share too much in common: the people we know, the situations we've been in.

I'm not repelled by the green orbs like the last time, either. I know why.

In my search for the truth, I invited Joanna into my mind. I recalled her memories, spoke, and behaved like her. I unconsciously made her a part of me, and my vector can't tell the difference. Going home helped me to reset, but given another dose of Joanna's DNA, she's more potent than ever. How can the vector reject Joanna if it thinks she is me?

I have to find the difference between us, things that will leave no doubt she is Joanna, and I am me. But I'm running out of time. The green orbs absorb the gold orbs, and soon I won't be able to tell the difference. If I don't hurry, I'll cease to exist.

Panic creeps in, but I arrest it. If I find my memories and keep them in the forefront, I'll be okay. I search for gold orbs with Marrick, or Kelly, any of them will suffice, but all that does is draw out more of Joanna's orbs because she has history with them, too. I search for Darius, my uncle, Vera. Again, Joanna's orbs appear. Is there no one I know who Joanna doesn't? No situation I've been in without a connection to her?

The rock pools.

A gold orb appears, showing my view of the watercourse from the rock ledge I stood on. It gives me a moment's reprieve, for Joanna's never been there. But what good is one memory? I need more.

I look for images showing my training and the days spent with Darius. A gold orb blends with a green one—snippets of Joanna's training days mix with mine. I go back further, to my younger years living with my uncle. But much of that was spent alone and searching for my uncle draws out more green orbs showing Joanna's interactions with him at Red Bluff. The crossover of our memories is confusing; I don't know which are mine, which are hers.

I focus on a greenish-gold orb with an image of Marrick. His angry expression reminds me of how he looked the last time I saw him. The scene expands around him, but this isn't my memory: he stands outside the guest cottage, and I didn't go there. Then his voice echoes through my mind, holding me captive—

I know my duty, and it's no longer to you.

His fierce tone ripples the orb. He talks to Joanna, but it feels like he speaks to me. His rejection punches a hole in my heart. Or is it Joanna's heart? I'm not sure. I try to move back but can only go forward.

Desperate to break free of Joanna's memory, I push through Marrick's image. His fury isn't directed at me, but his rejection stabs my heart again. The green orb ripples around me, then I'm through and in the tunnel again. But the walls in this tunnel are a deep shade of green. Where am I?

I search for my gold orbs. They've vanished. Marrick's gone too. A green orb in front of me holds an image of Darius. He strides across Jim's kitchen, but something slams into his face. He falls, blood gushing from his nose.

Forgetting this is a memory, I jump forward to help him, but land beyond the orb and face Jim.

Lock him in the study. I'll alert Flannigan.

His raspy voice cuts through me. Joanna struck Darius, that much is clear. He's hurt, but alive. Furious, I push through the orb but face another orb in which I/Joanna hides the Jeep in the shed and locks the roller doors.

She moved fast after I left. Impressive, given her condition. Details unravel as I pass through more green orbs. Vera, hurrying through the house, her expression neutral though worry fills her eyes. Kelly nods at Joanna as they leave for Rusty's. Marrick has his head turned away, but Magelon glares at Joanna from the back seat. Reece keeps his eyes down, his brow screwed up in a frown. Did they suspect foul play? Magelon would have. But with the com-link in Joanna's possession, how would they know they're not communicating with Darius?

Continuing through the tunnel, I search the orbs for

more of Joanna's memories that will reveal the extent of her deception. I glimpse Marrick again. He's younger, his hair shorter, but his eyes have lost none of their intensity. I'm drawn to him, needing his strength to help me get through this tunnel. But what he says is unexpected.

I will fight by your side any day, but I can't be anything more than your team member.

Another punch to the heart, the hardest yet. But it's not my heart and not me being rejected. How could I have been so stupid? Marrick never loved Joanna. She played on my emotions to separate us because, while with him, I'm untouchable.

But this is an old memory. Marrick's feelings for her could have changed over time. I won't know until I ask him. And won't get that chance unless I escape Joanna's grip on my mind. I don't help by continuing to fall for her mind tricks. My uncle might be right about not mixing personal with professional. Marrick is my strength, but he's also my weakness. Trust Joanna to realize and use it to her advantage.

I push forward and travel deeper through the tunnel, searching for memories I'm not connected to. Something unfamiliar, so I can separate Joanna from me.

The next orb is a possibility. It holds a strange man with the coldest eyes I've ever seen. At a guess, he's the same age as Darius, but his words slice through me—

There are no points for second best, Joanna. You're

either leading a team, or you're a failure.

Who is this man? How can a second in the best team not be good enough? I'm struck by an urge to defend her, but I'm swept into another orb and the man appears again, younger this time, but with a similar cold expression. He holds a hand-drawn picture, then crumples it and tosses it in a rubbish bin.

Daddy, I drew that for you.

A child's voice, Joanna's, echoes through my mind. A plea to her father—

Go to your mother. I'm busy.

Like his older version, he shows no love for his daughter; another rejection she suffered.

His face fades and I continue through the tunnel. I have no idea where I am. Lost in my mind? Or blocked from my mind by Joanna? Either is possible. I haven't seen one golden orb among the green. The tunnel is narrower, colder, or their equivalent in this psychological arena. How deep into Joanna's memories have I traveled? I search for a way out, but the green walls close around me. Then the tunnel abruptly stops at a single orb.

There's no face, no scene, no splash of color. It pulses, though, like a throbbing heart. Reaching out, I touch it. It's fluid-like, the same as the tunnel walls. Dare I go through it? It could lead me out. It could also trap me in Joanna's mind, where I'll become a figment of her imagination or a forgotten memory. What choice do I have?

I can't stay here or go back. I drift into the orb.

It closes around me, and a different force pushes me forward, crushing my arms to my sides, squeezing me through another tunnel. Then, in a blink, a bright light replaces the green, and a familiar face glares at me. Joanna's father, younger still. The same cold eyes meet mine—

You promised me a son.

The first words Joanna heard.

They sting like a whiplash. I cry out, but a baby's wail echoes through my mind. I clasp my arms around myself. This is not me. This isn't me. That registers deep in *my* psyche, but it doesn't stop the crushing rejection. I curl into myself with one thought, Joanna's thought, now mine, and it became a notion she carried throughout her life: I'm not good enough.

Silence.

Is this non-existence? It can't be. I can still think. If I can think, I exist. If I exist, I can fight my way out of here.

Rationalize: I'm caught in Joanna's first memory, but what's holding me here? I'm not Joanna. How could I be? I'm good enough for her to want me. And for my mother not to kill me. Darius risked his life for me. Marrick wants me, as does his team. My life is full of lies and deceit, but I've never struck rejection. That's the difference between us. I'm not Joanna. I'm Sarah. I am good enough for me.

I slam my hands out. The orb shatters like I punched

through glass. Golden light streams through, raining over me like a sun-shower. Then in a starburst of bright light, the tunnel explodes, and I stare at a white wall.

I'm in the white room.

CHAPTER 40

M Y EXPERIENCE IN THE MEMORY tunnel lingers, but I'm not free yet. Flexi-cuffs cut into my wrists, securing my hands in front of me. They jog a memory: raise hands above head; roll shoulders forward; spread elbows; slam hands against stomach to break the locking mechanism, the weak point. Who knows how to do that? Of course—Jack.

I must be careful. By rejecting Joanna's memories, I've regained control over my mind, but with the neurotransmitter still in my head, it's too easy for my vector to recall anyone's memories, though, after this win, I'm confident of distinguishing between them. Returning to familiar surroundings will improve my control, but I won't get anywhere if I don't escape this room. I raise my hands, intent on breaking the flexi-cuffs so I'm ready when Joanna opens the door—

No. I should play this smart, or I'll end up back in the tunnel. If Joanna realizes I'm not her, she'll make Flannigan repeat the procedure until I am.

Lowering my hands, I scan my body for any physical changes after undergoing a second procedure. I don't appear any different. Beneath another set of horrid white clothes, my muscle tone is the same, not abnormal, like Jason's bulk. Will that come with more training, an extra enhanced ability to pack on twice the amount of muscle? I hope not. I like the way I am—undetectable.

Anger with Flannigan boils within me. Given free rein, he'd turn soldiers into monsters in his quest for perfection. No wonder Joanna agreed to help him—she craves perfection, too. Where are they? Watching me through a hidden camera? I glance around the room but can't see it.

My wrists grow numb beneath the cuffs. I flex my fingers to keep my blood flowing. I've no way of knowing how long I've been in here. I walk to where I think the door is and listen. Nothing. For all I know, I'm trying to hear through a wall.

They won't leave me in here forever. Joanna took steps to conceal my whereabouts, but my uncle will return home at some point. The documents I left spread on his office floor would raise the alarm, but he also has the fake message from Darius, saying we're together. My best hope is Vera, but I shouldn't rule out the chance something happened to her. I have to be realistic. Nobody may know I've been brought back to Bio-Tech. Escaping is up to me.

Could I pretend to be Joanna? She'll look for indications I'm her, not me, but I think I can bluff it. I know her as well as she does.

To test, I look up at the ceiling.

"Are you there, Doctor Flannigan?" I pronounce 'Doctor' like Joanna would and mimic her sugar-sweet voice—I'm fairly certain the way I sound would earn me a punch from Magelon. "Open the door." Not, "open the door, *please*." I'm polite. Not once did I see that attribute in Joanna.

The door beeps—they were watching. I'm glad I didn't break the cuffs. Keeping my expression impassive, I stand relaxed, hands clasped. When the door slides open, I tense, preparing to attack Flannigan the moment he comes into view. But it's not him. It's Marrick.

He aims his gun at me, then slowly raises his other hand, palm open in reassurance. Behind him, a soldier holds a handcuffed Flannigan by the elbows. Magelon stands on Marrick's right, lining me up with her Berretta. Two more soldiers stand on the other side of the room at the door, another three surround the table in the center of the room. All are dressed in riot gear. All grip rifles. I don't recognize any of them; they're not from Red Bluff.

A soldier I didn't notice steps around Magelon, shoving a handcuffed Joanna toward the door. She rakes her gaze over my body; what does she expect to see? She'd have heard me speak. Everyone would have.

"Sarah," Marrick says. "It's okay. It's over. You're safe."

Joanna laughs, drawing a frown from Magelon, who doesn't lower her gun.

"You're too late," Joanna says, jerking at the soldier holding her and pulling him to a stop. "This time, she's me."

Marrick's jaw clenches; he must believe her.

"Sarah, talk to me," he says urgently.

I want to. I want to tell him there's nothing to fear, that I beat Joanna and I'm okay. But Joanna's smug expression incites the need to finish her.

Dropping my Joanna impersonation, I fix my eyes on hers.

"I am, and always will be, Sarah." I inject the vector's venom into my words. "You weren't good enough for me."

I strike where it hurts her the most—the heart of her self-belief. Her eyes widen, then she bends over, gasping as though she draws her last breath. Could I have crushed her any better? Part of me, the human part, empathizes with her. The part that will kill to survive draws my attention to a shift in Joanna's stance. Turning on her right foot, she twists and grabs a handgun from the soldier's holster.

Caught off-guard, he grapples for the gun, but Joanna rams her shoulder against him, and swings the gun at me.

I'm already moving. Leaping forward, I crash against Magelon, who's in Joanna's line of fire. As we fall to the floor, two shots ring out, a millisecond apart. I roll onto my back and search the room. Marrick aims his gun at Joanna; her right hand bleeds from his precision shot and her gun lies at her feet.

Her bullet, the one meant for me, ripped a gaping hole in Flannigan's neck. Blood spurts from a severed artery and pools around his head. The soldier who held him clamps his hand over the wound, but he's wasting his time. Flannigan stares vacantly at the ceiling.

"No, no, no," Joanna screeches.

She drops to her knees and bends forward until her head touches the floor. Two soldiers grab her arms, but she's no threat now. Flannigan's research has died with him. And I will never tell.

Magelon jumps to her feet and helps me up. "Should know better to turn my back on her." Pulling a knife from her belt, she cuts my flexi-cuffs. "You okay?"

"Yeah." I rub my wrists. "How'd you find me?"

"How do you think? Reece sat glued to the Team Tracker. We suspected Joanna was up to something, but didn't know what. When the request for assistance from the team at your house came through, Reece traced it to an external source in Jim's department. He picked it as bogus in a second." She scowls at Joanna. "Anyway, he jumped onto Sat-Map. Caught you getting into Jim's car and pulled enough of Joanna's profile through the open window to confirm it was her. A call to Vera filled in the blanks."

"Is she all right? What about Darius?"

"They're okay. Come on. Let's get you out of here."

She grips my shoulder and turns me toward Marrick.

He's busy calling for medics, but he hands the radio to another soldier and hurries to me.

"Your uncle's on his way," Marrick says. "Bio-Tech's in lock down. Reece is organizing transport to take us back to Red Bluff. It's okay. It's over."

Is it over for us, too? I desperately want to fling myself into his arms, and Marrick's strained expression suggests he wants to do the same, but until I know who he loves, I can't. It wouldn't be fair to either of us and now is not the time to have that conversation.

Behind us, Joanna gives a scornful laugh. "You won't stay you. Not while the neurotransmitter is in your head. Every second you spend with Marrick will be spent fighting me. You will be me eventually."

"That implant won't be in her head long enough for her to even spit like you," Magelon says.

"Good luck finding a doctor skilled enough to take it out," Joanna says. "They'll risk damaging Sarah's memory permanently. She'll remember nothing. Not even who she is."

"Get her out of here," Marrick says, the harshest I've ever heard him speak.

The two soldiers drag Joanna away, but her parting words linger.

"She's right," I say quietly, hoping only Marrick and Magelon hear me. "I'll always be at risk of becoming her. Or Jack. Or my mother. I'm Sarah now, but if any of those other memories slip in, I could become any one of them without realizing."

"You may not realize, but we will," Magelon says. "Anyway, doctors can do amazing things these days."

"We'll get Reece onto it as soon as we get back to Red Bluff," Marrick says.

The thought of being under a doctor's microscope sends shivers up my spine. What if they find more than the neurotransmitter, like what I am? I rub the back of my neck, wishing for a way to remove the implant without—

It will kill another vector to dominate but will protect its host at all costs. Without a host, the vector can't survive.

I imagine my mother talking to Vera, her voice clear in my mind. Am I already succumbing to her memories because I'm inside Bio-Tech, her familiar territory? Or did I recall this particular memory for a reason?

I glance around the room, taking in everything. The vector arms itself using information in memories, so something my mother knows might give it what it needs. I scan the bench, the empty glass vials, and dispensed syringes. Nothing comes to mind. Nor from the table in the center of the room, the restraints, Flannigan's computer—

Flannigan? The end of a syringe sticks out of his pocket. He carries the Stinger on his belt. He armed himself despite Joanna's reassurance I posed no threat. After our last encounter, I don't blame him. The problem is, I'll always be a threat.

Flannigan and my mother had a vision: genetically engineered soldiers with enhanced memory recall. Jack tried to stop that deadly future, but was his death in vain? That future is now. I am the vector. I keep it alive. Unless I die, too.

What would killing myself achieve? DNA doesn't die. Neither do memories. Jack and my mother are proof of that. Flannigan's dead, but there'll be other Flannigan's and they could create another Jason, with eyes as black as the pits of hell. One drop of my blood, one cell from my body, could resurrect an apex predator like nothing we've ever seen. Who protects us if I destroy the only weapon that could defeat it—me?

I won't protect anyone if I don't protect myself.

Memories flood my mind, visions of Jason in the mine, smirking, thinking he's indestructible, blown off his feet when my bullet hit the blaster. The blast collapsed a real tunnel, but the memory tunnel in my mind should be shut down, too. It's held open by the neurotransmitter, and allows every memory, from anyone's DNA, to flow freely into the forefront of my mind, whether I want them to or not.

I eye the Stinger on Flannigan's belt. An idea formulates. Would it work? It's suicidal, but I'm not Jack, and I'm a hell of a shot. It must be an option because I'm compelled to go to Flannigan, crouch by his body, and take the Stinger from the holster.

"What are you doing?" Magelon asks.

Ignoring her, I raise the Stinger and press the metal prongs against the back of my head, tilting my elbow so my aim is in line with the implant.

Marrick's eyes widen. "Sarah, no!"

"Trust me." Because I am the vector, and I will not let myself die.

Marrick lunges toward me, but I'm too quick.

I pull the trigger.

PAULINE YATES

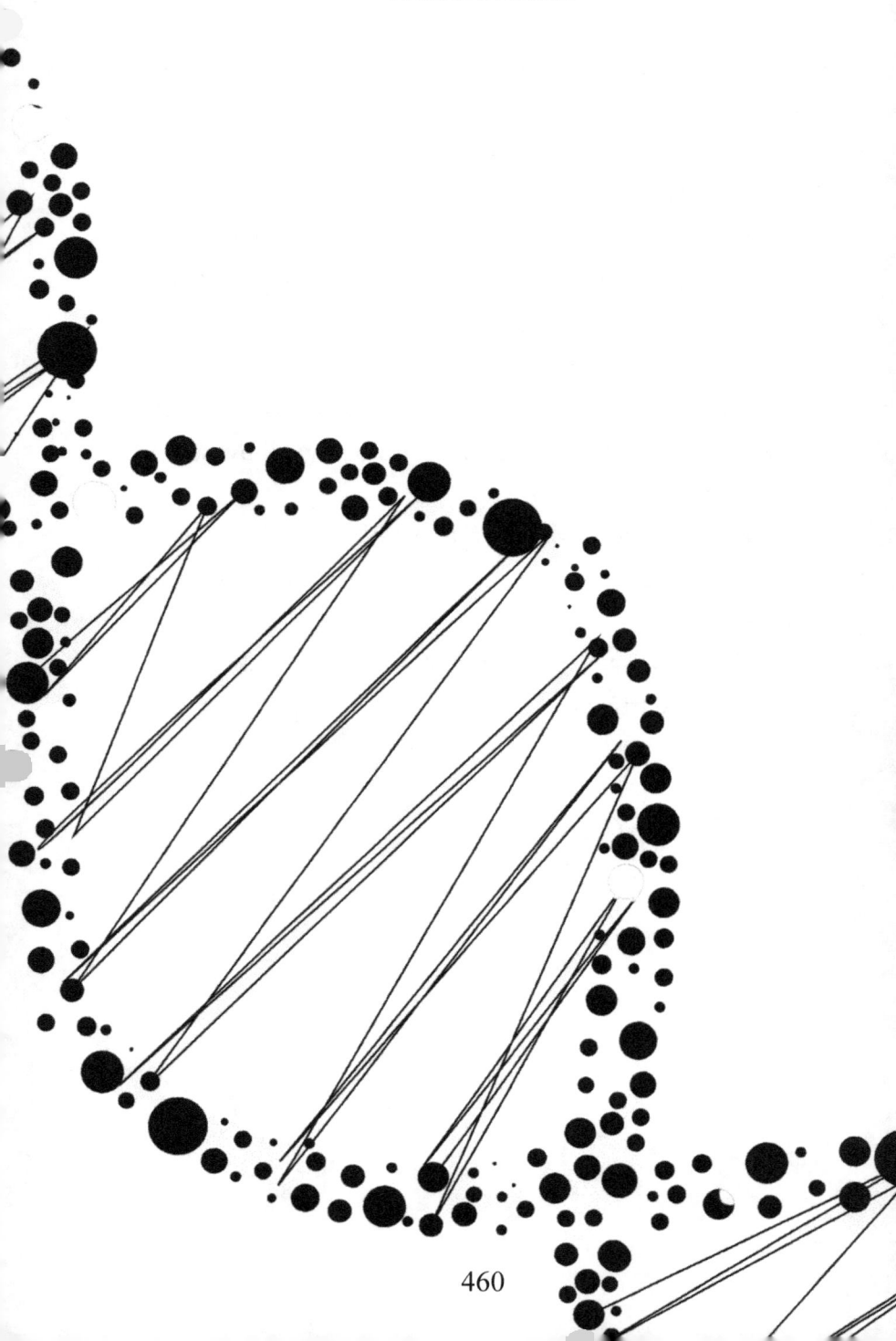

CHAPTER 41

MY HEAD HURTS—AN uncomfortable sting from a burn on my scalp. Raising my hand, I prod around the bandage covering a scorched area two inches in diameter. Considering the amount of electricity I shot into my brain, I'm lucky to be alive.

Not luck. A calculated maneuver using trust in my shooting ability, the vector's instinct to survive, and basic knowledge about what attracts electricity. We make a good team. But there's another I need.

My uncle—for familiarity, he'll always be my uncle—sits on a chair at the end of my bed. I've yet to ask him where I am, among other questions. I've been awake for hours but have been confined to this room; the only furnishings are the bed I lie on, the chair my uncle sits on, and a small table beneath the window.

The drawn blind blocks my view to the outside. The door to the room is closed, too. Neither stop sounds drifting in, though. Military activity: engines, orders, boots crunching over gravel, the occasional gunshot. I'm not at Red Bluff. The rooms in our med clinic are painted blue and white. This room is bland beige.

I glance at a clock above the door. Exactly twenty-three minutes have passed, and my uncle's still reading the doctor's report. Leaning forward, I adjust the pillow behind my back and sit up straighter.

My uncle lifts his gaze to mine.

"Don't over-exert yourself. The doctor said you can expect dizzy spells over the next few days. He also attended to the injuries you didn't tell me about." His gaze lowers to my leg.

I smooth my hand over my thigh. I'm still wearing the white clothes, and the new bandage covering the stitches shows through. My leg aches, and my ribs, but not enough to ask for pain relief. I suspect the low-level of adrenaline still pumping through me takes care of that. As for feeling dizzy, I don't. My mind's the clearest it's been since Joanna abducted me. But I'll play along. At least until I get answers to my other questions.

"What else does it say?" I ask, nodding at the report.

"Technically, you were dead. No pulse. No brain activity. The doctor can't explain it. He described your condition as a whole-body catatonic shock." He flips over a page. "He thinks the shrapnel in your head absorbed the electricity—"

"Shrapnel?"

"Taken during an explosives training incident. I had your medical files adjusted to hide the neurotransmitter. The less people who know about that, the better. As I was saying, the doctor believes the shrapnel protected your brain from receiving the full shock and left you with little more than a burn at the entry point. He calls it lucky. I call it incredibly foolish." His eyes meet mine. "What were you thinking?"

I shrug, not wanting to divulge anything more about the vector part of me, especially when I'm not sure whose side my uncle is on. "What happened to the neurotransmitter? Did the doctor remove it?"

"No. While capable, he isn't a brain surgeon. He took x-rays but deemed the metal fragments to pose no threat. When we get home, I'll arrange for a thorough examination."

I shake my head. "No more doctors. The implant's been fried. I can tell." No dull ache. No surfacing of memories belonging to Joanna, Jack, or my mother. If I think hard enough, and placed in the right environment, there's no reason why I wouldn't recall fleeting images— only the neurotransmitter's destroyed, not their DNA or their cellular memories. I'm in no hurry to test that. I haven't been *me* for what feels like a lifetime. I'm looking forward to getting reacquainted with myself.

"Is there anything else?" He'll know what I mean. You don't shock your brain and survive without questions being raised.

"No." My uncle lays the report on his lap. "The most crucial information remains concealed. For your continued safety, I must insist it stays that way."

I look at the door, wondering if it's locked. "What happens now? Will you take me back to Bio-Tech, or place me somewhere else?"

He leans back in his chair and crosses his legs. "The files in my office."

"Yes." I'm not afraid. I just want answers. "How are you involved with Bio-Tech? Are you a financial backer, like Jim?"

"I understand why you might think that but, no. Vera sent me those files, so I'd know what to expect had your health deteriorated. I had no idea how long you'd live after your mother left you with me. The information also alerted me to how Flannigan got his test subjects. He's a registered organ donor recipient. Details about any injury or death were sent straight to his inbox."

"But you had Joanna's file. Why did you express surprise when I said she's alive if you already knew?"

"I thought she'd be dead by now. And I told the team she died from complications during surgery because at the time, that's what I was led to believe."

Is he speaking the truth? I can't tell. He's an expert at concealing information. However, Joanna also excelled at delivering misinformation. My uncle would have been the first person she deceived when she agreed to go with Flannigan. "Vera sent you her file. Why not get her out then?"

He sighs. "Because her future was inevitable. She'll die, like all the other test subjects."

He'll never admit it, but I wonder if my uncle didn't act so the vacant position on Marrick's team remained free for me. "No one had to die. You had nineteen years of proof that could have shut Flannigan down."

"Proof that would have disappeared the moment I revealed it. You were my priority. Without you, Flannigan was destined to fail, again."

"He was close to figuring out what I am."

"Whatever he thought he knew is of no consequence now."

He sounds confident the truth about me died with Flannigan, but I'll never let my guard down in that area. We have no way of knowing how much he told Joanna, or what she'll do with that information if she does know.

"Will Joanna be charged with his murder?" I doubt I'll feel safer knowing she's locked up, but at least I'll know where she is.

"Her involvement in Flannigan's death will be

subject to investigation," my uncle says. "The usual process."

Which could take forever. "Where is she?"

"She's been admitted to a private palliative care unit, where she'll remain under guard until the investigation into Flannigan's activities is complete."

A knot tightens in my stomach. "Who's in charge of that? Jim? Or the nameless military personnel who supported Flannigan's research?"

His mouth twitches. I'm more informed than he realized. "Red Bluff's handling the investigation and I'll oversee it."

"Weren't you worried your influence would fall short?"

He frowns, probably because I'm challenging him on every detail for the first time in my life. "I've taken steps to expose Flannigan's activities in a way that can't be disputed."

And for every point I make, he has an answer, as usual. "Will I be questioned? Where am I, anyway?"

"Hawthorne Military Base. You're yet to be briefed by Matthews, so I'll insist you remain in this room until you are."

This news is a surprise. "Reece? Why's he briefing me?"

"I'd rather he explains. I don't want to confuse details...I underestimated Matthews. His suggestion, coupled with Joanna being alive, allowed me to take a course of action against Flannigan that should've occurred long before now."

What did Reece do? Something clever, knowing him. Did it involve his hacking abilities? I'm not game to ask. I'm not sure if my uncle knows about that area of Reece's expertise, but I'm not going to be the one to reveal it.

I glance at the window and redirect. "Why am I at Hawthorne and not Red Bluff?"

"Hawthorne was the closest base with a suitable doctor on duty." My uncle holds up the medical report. "Transporting you farther afield could have resulted in a different outcome, and I wasn't about to let that happen."

I pluck at my sleeve, not used to this new display of concern for my welfare. "Were the soldiers with Marrick from here, too?"

"Riverbank. They supplied the chopper and support teams after Daniels arrived at their base demanding assistance to conduct a raid on Bio-Tech. An overstep of his authority, but overlooked, given the circumstances."

It's easy to imagine Marrick storming Riverbank and rallying the support of teams and choppers. But…

"What did Marrick say to Riverbank to get them to agree to an unauthorized raid?"

My uncle grimaces. "It wasn't unauthorized this time. Matthews will explain." He glances at his watch and stands. "I'm needed elsewhere. Sergeant Kingsley will stay with you until you're ready to meet with Matthews."

I bolt upright. "Darius? He's here? Where? Is he all right? What about Vera? Where's she?"

"They're both fine. Kingsley's outside. Vera's gone to stay with an old friend pending the outcome of the investigation. Be rest assured, she is safe."

I sink back against my pillow, flooded with relief. "What about Jim?"

"I've strongly suggested if he wishes to retire in the comfort of his home, he makes amendments to his financial portfolio."

My cheeks grow hot. "He should be in prison for financing Flannigan. Someone should be made accountable for those soldiers' deaths."

"I agree. But if there's one thing I've learned in life, Sarah, it's better to keep the enemy where you can see them."

"What about the vote?"

"It won't proceed. Jim's issued a statement denouncing Flannigan's research, and the risks associated with genetic enhancement in general. He also recommended the military retain its hard stance against the use of performance enhancement drugs, in any form."

"How did you get him to agree to all that?"

My uncle smirks. "Gentle persuasion."

There's nothing gentle about my uncle, but Jim's not my only concern. "There's still a risk someone else will try what Flannigan did. What about Flannigan's research data, and the DNA he collected? What if that falls into the wrong hands?"

"No one will get hold of anything because Flannigan's data is in the process of being destroyed. I'm personally seeing to that." He checks his watch again. "I must go. Arrangements have been made to transport you all back to Red Bluff. Sergeant Kingsley will accompany you. And Sarah, I know you were indifferent to joining Daniels' team, but given the circumstances…"

I slump against the pillow. "Even if I wanted to, Joanna's still their team member."

"Not anymore. She agreed to step aside. The position is yours."

Just like that? Was she coerced, or compliant? Either way, other factors need to be considered. Like what the team wants. They won't have taken kindly to me shooting myself in the head. I also haven't graduated, and the *AWOL* charge hangs over me. But mostly, I don't know if Marrick loves me or Joanna.

"Uncle John, I understand why I need the extra protection. And you're right. There's no team better than Marrick's. But are you asking too much of them, protecting me? What future does that give them?"

"I don't get the impression protecting you will pose a problem. On that point, your status has changed. Be prepared for that."

He walks from the room without explaining, leaving me to imagine…what? I have no idea what he means. Why does he have to be so cryptic? He's as bad as—

Darius strides in, wearing a black bruise on the side of his face where Joanna struck him, and a strained expression—worry about me?

Getting out of bed, I meet him in the middle of the room. All our conversations refresh in my mind. Conflicted by a churning pot of emotions, I don't know whether to hug him or hate him. But he won't escape my questions this time.

"Why didn't you tell me you're my father?" I ask.

He stiffens, and I expect him to hide behind his usual impassive expression, but then his shoulders drop, and he sighs. "I've wanted to tell you for a long while."

Tears prick my eyes, but I don't bother wiping them away. "How long?"

"From when you started training." He shifts uncomfortably, sighs again. "I didn't know I had a daughter until you lined up with the other cadets looking every bit like your mother. I did the math. Your mother visited Red Bluff when Jack was there. We hit it off, dated a few times before she left to work with Flannigan. The distance wasn't a problem, but we were both busy, saw each other when we could." He shrugs. "She never told me."

How could she, being what I am. But shouldn't he know the vector does more than run through my blood?

He's my father. He's done everything in his power to protect me.

And had every chance to tell me.

I think about his excuses, about not wanting to interfere with my training. What if they weren't excuses? "Are you ashamed of me because I'm genetically enhanced? Is that why you didn't say anything? Because if you are, no one has to know we're related." I step back, putting distance between us, in case I'm right.

He stares at me, wide-eyed. "Ashamed? Never. None of this is your fault. Your mother"—he rubs his hand across his mouth—"we had an argument. She told me about Flannigan's research, and how she suspected the viral vector she used caused her brother to commit those atrocities. She blamed herself. Said she convinced him to participate in the trial because she believed it would help him do his job better. Before that, she didn't want to hear anything I said about how to naturally improve fitness levels. She said military expectations went beyond that. You haven't experienced it yet, run off your feet for thirty hours, no rest, expected to perform at your best around the clock. I never dreamed she'd experiment on herself using Jack's DNA, but after hearing about the memories you recalled, I understand why she did it. I wish—" He stops and shakes his head.

"What did you wish?" Do I want this answer? What if he wishes I didn't exist?

"I wish I made more of an attempt to track her down. I planned on making amends but couldn't find her. I figured she cut contact because she didn't want to see me. Had I known Flannigan held her captive, I'd have busted into that joint and got her out." He breathes in the past and blows it out in a long exhale. "After seeing you, I confronted your uncle. Got the truth out of him. He told me about his plan to place you with Marrick's team. I agreed. Why wouldn't I? I thought Joanna died, too. I intended to tell you about me, but I had no experience being a father. It was easier being your trainer. And I didn't want the truth to interfere with the plan."

The plan. It's always been about the plan. Not about what I want. Just slot me in and hide me among the best, without telling the best the truth about me. I'm trying not to be angry, but Darius is as bad as my uncle when it comes to concealing things.

"You must be pleased how things turned out," I say. "My uncle said Joanna's no longer their team member. The position's mine if I want it."

He scowls. "I'm not pleased about any of this. But after what's happened, why wouldn't you want it?"

"Because I haven't graduated, for one. I can't expect them to wait for me to repeat training. They also don't know everything about me. Neither do you." I turn away, angry with him, and with myself. How can I expect them to trust me when I conceal the biggest secret of all? What is any relationship without trust?

Darius places his hand on my shoulder. "I won't hold it against you if there are things you don't feel you can tell me. I deserve it, especially after not being honest with you. But don't lose this team. You need each other. For a lot of reasons."

I do. But on my terms. Not my uncle's. Not Darius's. "Where are they?"

"Outside. Reece is waiting to brief you. And don't worry about graduation. Reece has that covered."

I draw in a shaky breath, daring to hope that Reece found a way to wipe the sharpshooting calamity from my file. But that's not my main concern. I need to tell the team I'm not all human, even it means losing them.

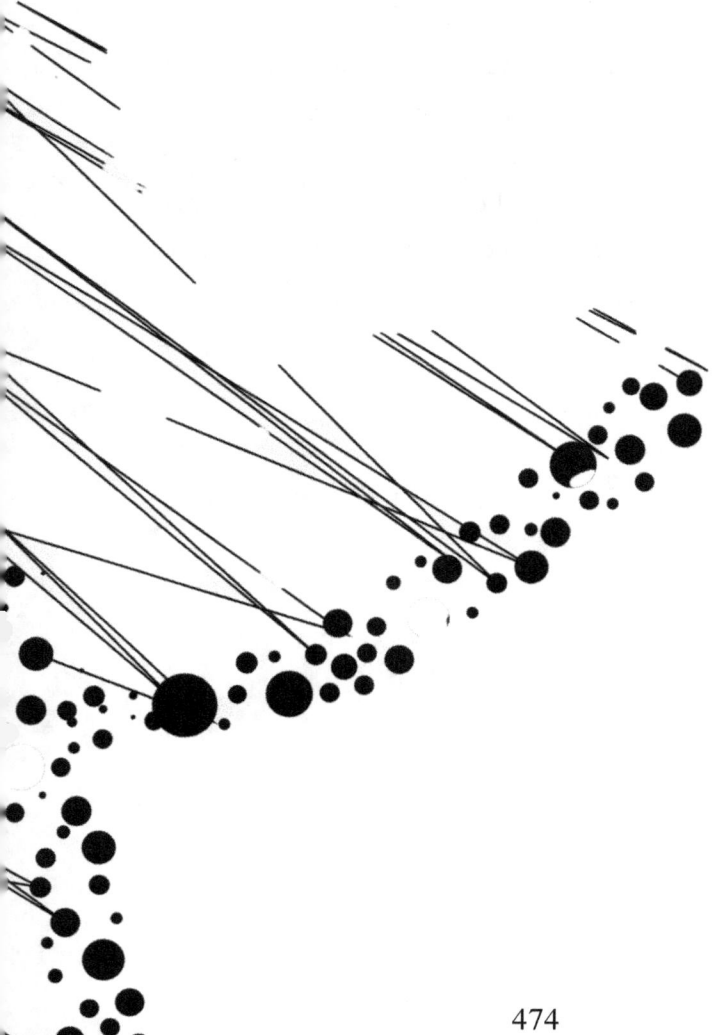

CHAPTER 42

DARIUS GOES TO FETCH REECE, leaving me to pace the room, an anxious mess. I pause at the window but resist looking out. My unknown status bothers me. The soldiers who arrived with Marrick saw me step out of the white room, and heard what Joanna said. She didn't mention genetic enhancements, though, only the neurotransmitter. My uncle covered it by saying it's shrapnel, but he can't stop gossip. Did Reece find a way to cover it?

A new noise echoes from the other side of the door: footsteps growing louder as they approach my room. I count one, two, three sets of boots—my heart bangs in cadence. The door flies open and Magelon rushes in.

"You gave me a heart attack," she says, crushing her

arms around me. "We thought you were dead. Seriously dead this time."

"Easy goes," Kelly says, pulling Magelon away and engulfing me in a bear hug. "You gotta stop taking one for the team, you hear me?" He raises his hand to ruffle my hair like he always does, but rests his hand next to the bandage instead, his eyes filling with worry.

"How can she breathe when you're smothering her like that?" Reece asks.

Kelly releases me and steps aside. Reece looks like hell—dark shadows beneath his eyes, tousled hair, crinkled clothes. Despite his obvious lack of sleep, he grins and looks extremely pleased with himself. "You're okay, aren't you, Sarah?"

I'm beginning to think he's right, that I won't ever come to harm. "What did you do? What's this about my status being changed?"

"You haven't been told?"

"No. My uncle didn't want to confuse details."

His grin widens. "It's brilliant, though the credit should go to Joanna. I used her lies to pull it off."

"Don't you go giving her anything," Magelon says.

"You know what I mean," Reece says. "Anyway, I've been trying to figure out how to excuse your sharpshooting round so you can graduate and give a credible reason to cover your *AWOL* status. I had an idea and ran it by your uncle, and he agreed."

"My uncle agreed with something he didn't think of? What did you do—bribe him?"

"Didn't need to. We uploaded a classified document stating how Joanna went to Bio-Tech undercover to gather evidence on a tip-off about Flannigan using illegal drugs on soldiers. That covers her faked death. Those documents you found on Flannigan's test subjects?"

"You know about those?"

"Yep. We turned those into evidence and said they were sent from Joanna. This is where you come in. When your uncle lost contact with Joanna, he feared for her safety. None of us could go in and find her because if her cover was blown, Flannigan would know us. You were instructed to purposely fail your last sharpshooting round so you could go undercover for us. You were sent to Bio-Tech as a trainee research technician, but you were looking for Joanna on the sly. When you found her locked in one of those cells, you alerted us, your backup team. You provided us with enough evidence to warrant a raid on Bio-Tech and arrest Flannigan on deprivation of liberty, crimes against the military, and a bunch of other stuff relating to the use of unregulated drugs. I know he's dead, but the charges will stick."

He makes it sound simple, but there must be holes. "What about the soldiers from Riverbank? They saw me come out of the white room and heard what Joanna said about the neurotransmitter. How are you explaining that?"

477

"No need to," Magelon says. "Everything's classified, not that *that* means anything. The only gossip circulating is about how Flannigan got away with it for so long. When it comes to our involvement, well, you know how everyone has stars in their eyes whenever Marrick's mentioned. Your uncle's version of events has been accepted, no questions asked."

"What about me? Aren't they questioning the use of a cadet for undercover work?"

"Nope," Reece says. "You were about to claim the top graduate title, so it's no surprise to anyone you assisted Red Bluff's top team in a covert operation. Not having graduated, Flannigan wouldn't know you, so it made sense for your uncle to send you into Bio-Tech. Flannigan can't expose you, being dead. Joanna's agreed to bear witness. And we have Jim's signature on every document, proving he was fully aware of the secret investigation."

"How did you get Jim to sign?" Did my uncle's gentle persuasion have something to do with that?

"Easy," Reece says. "I hacked into Jim's financial portfolio. He stood to make a fortune from Flannigan's research if it went ahead. Your uncle confronted him, mentioned conflict of interest, aiding and abetting the use of unregulated genetic material, and accused him of abusing his position on the biosecurity board for personal gain. Jim couldn't deny it, so he co-signed everything."

"Only to keep his boney butt out of prison," Magelon

says. "He's as chicken as Joanna. She agreed to everything, too. She'd have been charged with Flannigan's murder if she didn't."

"Yeah, that," Reece says. "Anyway, she's a hero, like Sarah. Not that Joanna deserves it. We couldn't pull it off otherwise. We needed her to be the main witness."

My jaw drops. "A hero? Are you serious? I'm not a hero."

He shrugs. "You are now. News has already spread."

"Just roll with it," Magelon says, grinning.

"You've also been awarded a special service's accreditation," Marrick says from the doorway.

Reece steps aside, putting me in full view of Marrick, who closes the door and crosses the room to stand in front of me. Everyone fades away. It's me and Marrick and a lot of explaining to do.

"The accreditation allows you to graduate from the Tactical Skills Program," Marrick says. "They didn't count the last target in your sharpshooting round, though. Your score remains a credible, but unremarkable, thirty-nine out of forty targets."

The unremarkable part is necessary, but who cares about an award? How furious is he with me for fleeing Jim's house alone and for firing a Stinger at my head? "I'm sorry. I shouldn't have let Joanna manipulate me. Or believed anything she said."

"You weren't the only one manipulated," Marrick

says.

Magelon huffs. "Some of us weren't."

Marrick grimaces. "Okay, she manipulated me, too. She's…"

"Convincing?" I offer.

"Yeah. I truly believed you and Darius had left. I had no reason to suspect otherwise. If Reece hadn't been keeping an eye on the Team Tracker, we'd have never known Joanna took you back to Bio-Tech. I only wish we'd been quicker—"

I raise my hand and press my fingers to his lips. I don't want to hear what he should or shouldn't have done. We were both played by Joanna; she's our shared adversary. What matters is he's here. We're all here.

He takes my hand in his and moves it away. "What you did was—"

"Incredibly foolish, I know." Easing from his grip, I place my palm against his chest. His heart pounds, like mine.

Marrick nods at the bandage on my head. "We saw the doctor's report. Did you know that would happen when you fired the Stinger?"

Does he think I intended to kill myself, like Jack? I'm happy to set that record straight. "I did." A small but necessary lie. It was more a calculated hope. "I'm not Jack Arquet, if that's what you're worried about."

He frowns. "I've never thought you were."

"But I was, at times. And Joanna." Looking at Marrick, touching him, being in his company, I've no doubt I love him. But does he love me?

Marrick's eyes bore into mine. "You're frowning."

I sigh. "I need to ask you something."

"Here we go," Magelon mutters. "Come on, guys. Give these two some privacy." She herds Kelly and Reece to the window. They turn their backs, but the room isn't that large. It won't matter. This team doesn't keep secrets from each other. Why start now?

"Joanna gave me her DNA," I say. "From that, I recalled her memories."

"I know that," Marrick says, his voice tight.

"What I didn't know was that I also experienced her emotions. In particular, her feelings for you."

"It's not you who loves me?" His voice stretches to a breaking point.

His anguish punches my heart. "I've never been more certain it's me who loves you, but when Joanna performed that second procedure on me, I saw other memories, of you and her—"

"I never loved Joanna," Marrick says.

"I know. But they were old memories." I pause, glimpsing Magelon shaking her head. She's angry, I can tell because Joanna's the topic and whenever she's mentioned, she has a way of ruining relationships. But this needs to be said. "Things can change over time. But some changes we don't realize until they're pointed out to us."

Marrick grips my shoulders. "What are you asking me?"

Something I wish I didn't have to. "You said you love me. But I behaved and spoke like Joanna multiple times without knowing. So I have to ask, is it Joanna you love? Did your feelings for her change over time, but you didn't see it?"

Silence falls over the room as though everyone holds their breath. It's a reasonable question, given Marrick's slide after Joanna's 'death'.

Marrick stares at me, seriously considering what I said. Then he sighs.

"You're right, I wasn't aware," he says. "But now you've pointed it out, I didn't think the way I treated Joanna would be construed as anything other than my responsibility to her as team leader. She wanted something I could never give her. I thought I'd made that clear. If I didn't, that's my error and I'll own it. But it doesn't change how I feel about you."

He looks me dead in the eye with his most intense gaze yet. "I didn't know it at the time, but that day we met in your uncle's office, you stole my heart. After watching you train, seeing you struggle through everything you've had to endure, being with you in circumstances I wouldn't wish upon anyone, you brought something unique and wonderful to my life and I wouldn't trade it for anything. I love you, Sarah. You. If it helps, it's time we reset our memories?"

Raising his hand, he tilts my chin and presses his lips to mine, burning a kiss into my memory that will stay with me forever. Could he make me love him anymore, how he understands the importance of solidifying *our* memories? When I pull back, reluctantly, but only because this kiss should be shared in private, his warm sunshine smile chases the darkness from his eyes and fills me with light. We're going to be okay. But only if I seal it with trust.

"There's something else I need to tell you. All of you." I step back so I can address everyone.

Magelon rolls her eyes. "This had better not be what I think it is."

"What?" I ask, curious.

"Another reason why you can't join our team."

"I'll let you decide that." I take a deep breath because this could change everything. "I need to keep this hidden. But I don't want to hide it from any of you." I take a deep breath and make sure I've got everyone's attention, then I spill it. "I'm not who you think I am."

"So far you've been Sarah Wilson, Sarah Arquet, and Sarah Kingsley." Magelon counts off her fingers. "Seriously, we don't care."

"Who are you?" Marrick asks, his voice soft.

I stare at his chest. "I don't just carry the viral vector. I am the vector. My mother experimented on herself, not knowing she was pregnant. The vector mutated into a multi-cell organism. It's a part of my genetic makeup. Vera explained it to me when we were at Jim's."

"No wonder Flannigan wanted you," Reece says, bouncing on his toes with excitement. "You're a walking laboratory. It must have happened early. During mitosis is my guess. I'll look it up. No wonder you're not dead."

Magelon punches his arm. "You're not helping."

"What?" he says, rubbing his arm and frowning. "Her mother's antibodies would have transferred through the placenta. It explains why she lived so long. It works both ways. Otherwise, she'd have miscarried."

My mother lived for five years, the longest of any test subjects, according to the documents in my uncle's office.

It became increasingly difficult for her to care for you.

My uncle's explanation drifts through my mind. Could my mother still be alive? Our vectors would have wanted to kill each other. Who was more in danger? Me from her? Or her from me?

Kelly pushes past Reece and clamps his hand on my shoulder. "Ignore this lot. The way I see it, you eat, you breathe, you fight, you love. Can't get more human than that." He looks me up and down, frowning at my white clothes. Pulling off his jacket, he slings it around my shoulders. "Better?"

"Much." It's more than a jacket he wraps around me.

But I can't ignore the problem I inherited. If my mother's immune to the vector because of something I gave her, it's even more crucial I'm never found. "What happens if another Flannigan finds me? We don't know if Jim will tell anyone else about me. I'll always need protecting. That's too much responsibility to put on you."

"Let them come," Magelon says, interlacing her fingers and cracking her knuckles.

Marrick slings his arm around me. "If you're trying to scare us away, it won't work. We want you with us. We won't take no for an answer."

I sigh. "But what if something happens—"

He silences me with another kiss, then pulls me close and holds me tight. "I don't care what you are," he whispers. "You'll always be Sarah to me."

I lean into him, soaking up his warmth, his love. Being with him, with this team, I'm more whole than I could ever imagine.

We're interrupted by the door banging open. Darius strides into the room. His eyebrow arches up when he sees us together, but if he thinks he has authority over my personal life because he's my father, he's wrong.

"Are you done?" he asks. "Our transport's waiting."

"She's stalling," Magelon says. "Where's the paperwork?"

"Got it here," Darius says, pulling a document from his back pocket. "Just needs a signature."

He gives the page to Marrick, who reads it, then hands it to me. "This will make it official."

It's a Red Bluff C.S.R. team member acquisition form. Everyone's name is listed under existing members. My uncle's signature is at the bottom, next to a red 'approved' stamp. The new member line is blank.

"Name and sign," Darius says, thrusting a pen at me.

"Go on," Magelon says. "Once you're with us, you're untouchable. It's the best protection you'll get."

"Okay, okay." I take the pen. What name do I write? Wilson, Arquet, Kingsley? It's a chance to start afresh. New name, new team, new life?

But some things can't change.

I sign it: Sarah Wilson. That name is how I identify myself. The neurotransmitter is gone, but it's crucial to maintain my familiar, so the vector draws out my memories first, which will keep the wrong memories buried.

Darius plucks the page from my hand. "I'll lodge it myself when I hand in my letter of resignation from the Tactical Skills Program."

"What?" I ask. "Why?"

"I've been re-assigned. Your uncle's doing. Though, I suggested it."

"Wouldn't have anything to do with us, would it?" Marrick asks.

"It's got everything to do with you," Darius says. "As of now, I'm your team supervisor. Lord knows you need someone to watch your backs. Let's move. And keep an eye on Sarah until we get out of here. It's a mob outside. Everyone wants to meet the new Red Bluff hero."

Kelly grins. "Is that our first official order, Sir?"

"No," Darius says. "It's a father's request to look out for his daughter."

He walks out the door, leaving a stunned silence behind him. All eyes turn to me. I swallow nervously. I have more explaining to do.

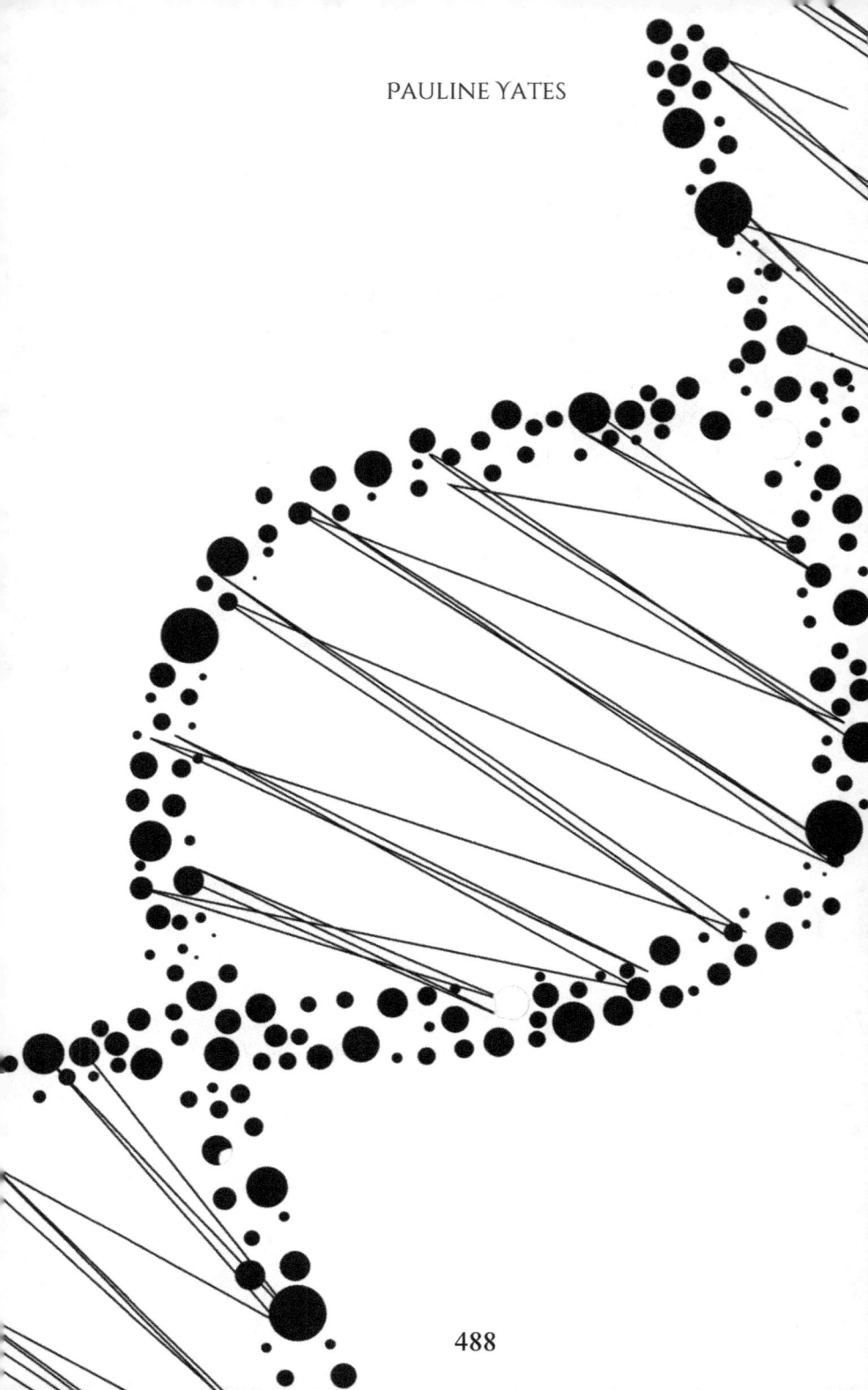

PAULINE YATES

ACKNOWLEDGEMENTS

Many thanks to the awesome team at Black Hare Press for loving my story as much as I do, and for their warm welcome into their tribe.

Special mention to Elena Hartwell Taylor, who believed in me when I wouldn't, and who helped uncover secrets about my characters that prevented me from moving forward. Thank you also to Savannah Gilbo for giving me the confidence to finish what I started; and to Andrea Barton for being the voice of reason when the doubt crept in, and for helping me reach "The End."

Big thanks to my sister, Donna, for her unwavering support throughout my writing career, her critical eye on the many stories I forced her to read, and for guarding the original version of this story with her life. My children—

my first audience: Jess, who answered more science-based questions than she ever did at university, and for gasping in all the right places; Chryselle, who made the ripple that propelled me to write this story, and for literally walking alongside my characters every step of the way; and Josh, who reminds me every day that action and adventure are fun. Thanks to my two Rins—L'Erin Ogle and Erin— for helping me keep things real. And finally, to my best friend Deb, who rode the highs and lows with me, and who knew before anyone the impact Sarah Wilson has on your life.

Last, because the best things are always at the end, to my husband, Marcus, for his belief in my dream, for his patience in my many moments of absence when I needed to write, and for being the best beta reader a writer could have, even if he doesn't realize it.

Pauline Yates

29th January, 2023
Queensland, Australia

PAULINE YATES

PAULINE YATES (she/her) is the Australian author of *Memories Don't Lie;* a fast-paced science fiction novel inspired by her love for dark and dangerous action and adventure. An Australian Shadows Awards finalist, her short-form horror, dark fiction, and poetry appear in publications including Black Hare Press, IFWG Publishing Australia, Redwood Press, Midnight Echo, PseudoPod, Aurealis, Tales To Terrify, Black Hart Publishing, Metaphorosis, plus others, and her AHWA winning short story, "The Best Medicine," was translated in the Mondi Incantati series produced by Riflessi di Lunare (RiLL), Italy. She's a member of the Australasian Horror Writers Association (AHWA), and the Horror Writers Association (HWA), and helps to judge the Australia Shadows Awards in various categories. On the social scene, she goes by @midnightmuser1 because she loves writing at midnight when her muse is the most volatile. She shares her writing space with her aged cat, who is determined to break the world's oldest feline record, and a dog who is terrified of the cat. She enjoys taking photos of the sunrise—if she wakes up in time—and loves to encourage native wildlife and birds into her garden. https://paulineyates.com/.

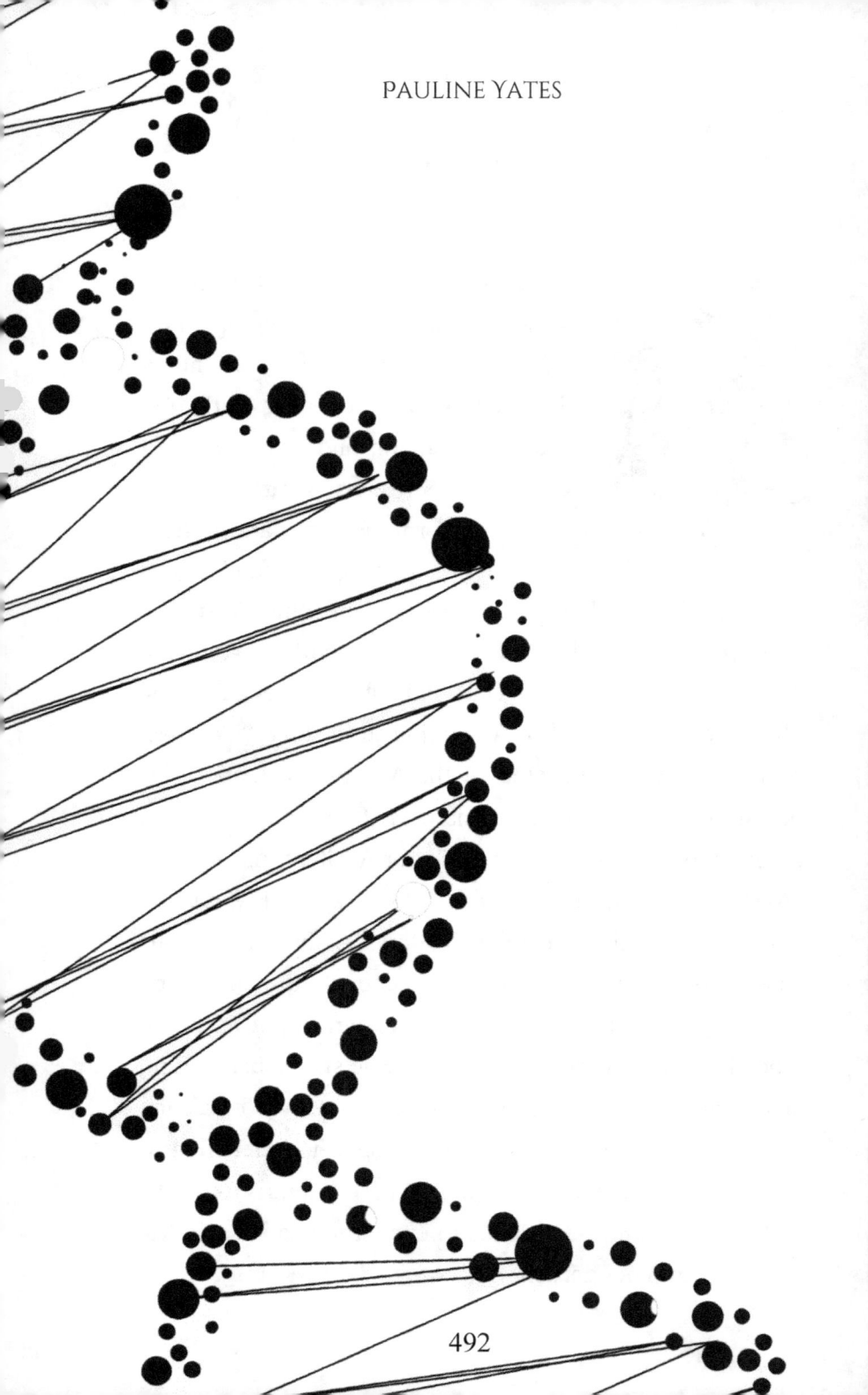

PAULINE YATES